THE SECRET

D0321565

Also by Peter Lovesey

ABRACADAVER
BERTIE AND THE CRIME OF PASSION
BERTIE AND THE SEVEN BODIES
BERTIE AND THE TIN MAN
THE BLACK CABINET
THE BLOODHOUNDS
BUTCHERS AND OTHER STORIES
CRIME OF MISS OYSTER BROWN
THE DETECTIVE WORE SILK
DIAMOND SOLITAIRE
DO NOT EXCEED THE STATE
THE FALSE INSPECTOR DEW
KEYSTONE
THE LAST DETECTIVE
A MAD HATTER'S HOLIDAY
ON THE EDGE
THE REAPER
ROUGH CIDER
THE SEDGEMOOR STRANGLER
THE SUMMONS
SWING, SWING TOGETHER
UPON A DARK NIGHT
THE VAULT
WAXWORK
WOBBLE TO DEATH

THE SECRET OF SPANDAU

Peter Lovesey

This edition published 2016
in Great Britain and in the USA by
SEVERN HOUSE PUBLISHERS LTD of
19 Cedar Road, Sutton, Surrey, England, SM2 5DA.
Originally published in Great Britain 1986 by
Michael Joseph under the pseudonym *Peter Lear.*

Copyright © 1992 by Peter Lovesey.

All rights reserved including the right of
reproduction in whole or in part in any form.
The moral right of the author has been asserted.

British Library Cataloguing in Publication Data
A CIP catalogue record for this title is available from the British Library.

ISBN-13: 978-0-7278-8612-5 (cased)
ISBN-13: 978-1-84751-709-8 (trade paper)
ISBN-13: 978-1-78010-770-7 (e-book)

This is a work of fiction. Names, characters, places and incidents
are either the product of the author's imagination or are used fictitiously.
Except where actual historical events and characters are being described
for the storyline of this novel, all situations in this publication are
fictitious and any resemblance to actual persons, living or dead,
business establishments, events or locales is purely coincidental.

St Helens Libraries	
3 8055 25002 2329	
Askews & Holts	23-Mar-2017
AF	£12.99

Foreword

The idea for this novel originated with Vere Viscount Rothermere and I wish to express my thanks to him for allowing me to use and develop it in my own way.

George Greenfield demonstrated once again that the role of a top literary agent is to inspire and enthuse his authors as well as promoting their careers. He made a number of creative and practical suggestions and introduced me to a tenacious man who spent many hours with Rudolf Hess and finally gained his confidence: Lieutenant-Colonel Eugene K. Bird, the former US director of Spandau Prison. I wish to set on record my gratitude to Gene Bird for guiding me around Berlin and so frankly and generously answering my numerous questions.

Any blemishes or errors in the writing are mine alone.

Peter Lovesey

THE SECRET
OF SPANDAU

1

The pilot stared.

Through the windscreen of his Messerschmitt, several thousand metres ahead, the North Sea ended in a dark shoreline.

England; the Northumberland coast, if his bearings were right. Above it, jutting through the mist and picked out in scarlet by the setting sun, a range of hills. But a *range*. He had expected one, the Cheviot, 816 metres high. He depended on this for his first sighting, the navigational key to his route inland. No doubt the Cheviot was one of those peaks, but which one?

Somewhere down there in the shadows were three destroyers, based between Holy Island and the coast. Any German pilot who strayed within range of their anti-aircraft guns would not be a pilot much longer. It was hardly a moment for indecision. Recalling a trick of Hitler's personal pilot, 'Father' Bauer, the pilot sniffed, snapped his fingers, chose one of the peaks and steered straight for it.

His luck was in. Seconds later, he sighted Farne Islands well to his right. He was safely south of Holy Island as he crossed the shoreline at an altitude of 2,000 metres. The time was 2212 hours.

Saturday night over England; 10 May 1941. Alone, the Deputy Führer of the Third Reich had piloted a Messerschmitt 110 from Augsburg, a journey of 800 miles, including a detour to confuse the enemy.

At home in Germany, they would say it was impossible, that he must have come down in the sea. They could not have known of the planning he had put into this secret flight. Eleven months of preparation: studying the maps; perfecting the technique of flying the Messerschmitt 110; having it modified for longer flights; arranging for special radio signals as an aid to navigation; checking the phases of the moon and the weather reports; and even ordering a military tailor in

Munich to make him the uniform of a hauptmann in the Luftwaffe. He wanted the British to be in no doubt that this was a German officer flying a Luftwaffe aircraft with the German black cross prominent on its wings and fuselage. He knew what they did to spies.

A stern test of courage lay ahead. He was to locate his target by moonlight, bale out and crash the plane. And he had never in his life made a parachute-jump.

Over the land hung that evening mist. He welcomed it. For the past hour, he had been in a clear sky, conspicuously open to attack. The Air Ministry in Berlin had promised a dense layer of cloud at 500 metres, but all he had seen so far were isolated patches that, from his position, had looked like pack-ice on the sea.

At full throttle, he dipped the plane towards the cover of the mist – barely in time, for in the void behind him had appeared the outline of a Spitfire. His plane carried no ammunition. A few minutes more, and the British fighter would have shot him out of the sky.

He dived clean through the mist from 2,000 metres and levelled out beneath it like a stunt pilot, perilously close to the ground. He had shaken off the Spitfire.

Down there below the mist, he could see several miles ahead. It was strange to have such clear light so late in the day, but the British were on double summer time, so it was only 9.15 p.m. at home, and he was also a lot farther north. Relishing the conditions, he hedge-hopped at speed, sometimes no more than five metres above ground, practically skimming the trees and farm buildings, actually waving to people in the lanes and cottage gardens. It was part exultation, part the satisfaction he felt each time he spotted a landmark he could identify. For on numerous sleepless nights, he had stared at the map he had pinned to his bedroom wall until it had become so imprinted on his brain that when he did sleep, he had dreamed of flying over British fields.

2220 hours. The Cheviot. The pilot gripped the joystick and raced up the face, judging it nicely. He was in his element: seven years before, he had won the air-race round the Zugspitze, Germany's highest mountain. He had been congratulated by Lindbergh, his personal hero – after the Führer of course.

Due west was another peak: Broad Law, in the centre of the Scottish Southern Uplands. By now, the moon was streaking the mountains with faint white light.

Then, at 2240 hours, his destination: Dungavel, home of the premier Duke of Scotland, the Duke of Hamilton, a large stone mansion with a cone-shaped hill nearby. It *had* to be Dungavel; but seized with the finality of that jump into the unknown, he decided to postpone it and make a second run, from the west.

He flew on to the coast, out to sea, where he jettisoned the auxiliary fuel tanks fitted to enable the Messerschmitt to make such a journey. Then he took his bearings, banked and came in over Troon. By 2250 hours, he had spotted the reservoir south of Dungavel. He climbed to 2,000 metres, the height for his jump, and switched off the engines.

One would not respond.

After a thousand miles of continuous flight, the plane had been pushed to its limit, and the red-hot cylinders were igniting the petrol vapour. The engine continued to turn. Calmly, he waited for it to cool, stutter and stop. Then he reached up and opened the canopy roof.

This was when inexperience let him down. He was pinned against his seat by the force of air. He could not possibly bale out. And the plane was rapidly losing height.

The brain can work fast on the edge of disaster. He had once heard a tip from a Luftwaffe pilot with experience of Messerschmitts: you had to turn the thing upside down and fall out. This had got quite a laugh in the officers' mess at Augsburg. He was about to find out if the tip had been serious.

Possibly he half-disbelieved it, because instead of pulling the joystick to the right, he tugged it towards him. The plane swung into a startling loop, the blood rushed from his head and he momentarily blacked out.

Near the top of the upward arc, he forced the steering column away from him. Instead of completing the loop, the Messerschmitt hung for a moment nose upwards in the sky. In the instant before it plunged earthwards, he recovered

3

consciousness. He thrust with his legs and felt a stab of pain as his leg struck some part of the fuselage. He fell clear and tugged at the ripcord on his parachute.

It opened.

2

At about 10.45 in the evening of Saturday 10 May 1941, David McLean, head ploughman of Floors Farm, near Eaglesham, south of Glasgow, heard the drone of an aeroplane overhead. McLean, a bachelor in his mid-forties, lived in a single-storey cottage facing the farmhouse. He was about to get into bed. His widowed mother and his sister Sophia slept in the other bedroom.

McLean was used to aircraft, because the RAF trained their pilots nearby; they had a flight-path that brought them from the airport at Irvine up to Renfrew and then down over Eaglesham to Dungavel, ten miles to the south. Dungavel Hill served as a landmark before they returned to Irvine. But tonight there was something unfamiliar in what he could hear, a different resonance in the engine-note. While he was listening, the sound altered, as if one of the engines had cut out. Then it stopped altogether.

A few seconds later, he heard a muted impact, perhaps a mile away. The earth under the house gave a perceptible tremor.

David McLean put out the light and pulled aside the blackout at the window. The full moon glowed pinkly through a light mist, and he could see over the garden, beyond the stone wall, to the fields and the dark hills. All looked as usual until a movement caught his eye, the shimmer of moonlight on something large and white drifting from the sky.

He knocked on the wall of his mother's room and called out that he had seen a parachute and was going outside to investigate. He pulled on his trousers, tucked the nightshirt inside and reached for his boots.

The parachutist was on the ground grappling with his harness when David McLean got to him. The billowing silk was tugging at the man, jerking him across the grass until he managed to disengage it.

'Who are you?' McLean called across to him. 'British or German?'

'I am a German officer. Hauptmann Horn, from Munich.'

From across the fields came a flash and a roar as the fuel ignited in the crashed aircraft. The German officer turned to watch.

'Was there anyone with you in the plane?'

'No, I am the only one.'

David McLean looked at the face picked out by the flames. This was not a young man, as the British pilots usually were. He had the stronger features of middle age, eyes set deep under thick dark brows, fine, wide mouth over a resolute jaw. He turned away from the blaze and attempted to stand, but his right leg would not support him. He toppled off balance and practically fell into McLean's arms.

'My leg . . . very painful.'

'You'd better come into the cottage. Are you armed? Do you have a gun?'

The parachutist shook his head, and lifted his free hand away from the side of his black leather flying-suit, inviting McLean to search him.

'All right. Can you walk if I help you?'

They hobbled as far as the gate, and rested there a moment. The German glanced back to where his parachute lay, still rippling and flapping. 'I would like to take that with me.'

To McLean, it was a reasonable request. The thing had saved the man's life. 'I'll get it if you promise not to go away.'

The German gave a faint smile. With one good leg, he could not have got far from the gatepost.

McLean gathered the parachute and came back with it bundled under his arm. Then he heard a voice from the farm buildings.

'What's going on out there? Who is that?' It was William Craig, who lived in the farmhouse.

'It's me – Davey,' McLean called back. 'A German has come down. Would you go and fetch a soldier from across the road, Mr Craig?'

'A German?' A pause; then, in the same even tone, 'Aye, I'll do that.'

By good fortune, several of the Royal Signals Regiment

6

were billeted at Eaglesham House, almost opposite the farm. Their work was secret, and they looked more like university men than soldiers, but they were certainly better equipped than a ploughman to deal with a prisoner of war.

The German was considerably taller than McLean. They made their way unsteadily up the path to the door of the cottage, where Mrs Annie McLean stood watching in dressing gown and slippers.

'Is it a Jerry?' she asked her son.

'Aye.'

'Och, what a life!'

'Aye.'

'Well, dinna stand out there. Bring him in and I'll make some tea.'

Inside the whitewashed living-room, David McLean dumped the parachute on the flagstone floor and helped the injured pilot into the single leather armchair. The man heaved a great appreciative sigh and eased his injured leg into a more comfortable position. He was wearing fur-lined suede leather flying-boots, easily the most elegant boots that McLean had ever seen.

'What did you say your name is?'

'Horn. Hauptmann Alfred Horn. I must see the Duke of Hamilton at Dungavel House. It is very important.'

'You want to see the Duke of Hamilton?'

'Would you take me to him?'

McLean grinned and prodded his own chest with his finger. '*Me*, take you up to Dungavel to see the Duke?'

'If you please.'

'Get away with you, man.'

But Hauptmann Horn was very persistent. He repeated the request. Apparently he believed there was nothing to stop the head ploughman of Floors Farm from rousing the premier Duke of Scotland from his sleep and introducing him to an enemy pilot.

Mrs McLean brought in the tea. Hauptmann Horn thanked her, and said he would prefer a glass of water. He unzipped the front of his flying-suit. Underneath, he was wearing the grey-blue worsted tunic of an officer in the Luftwaffe. He felt in an inside pocket and took out some photographs.

'My son. And my wife.'

David McLean glanced at them and handed them to his mother as she returned. 'His son and his wife.'

Hauptmann Horn took the water and drank it without taking a breath.

'Bonny,' said Mrs McLean as she handed back the snaps.

Someone tapped lightly on the door. McLean opened it and admitted two boyish soldiers in battledress. One of them, who wore steel-rimmed glasses, cleared his throat and said, 'We were told . . .' His words trailed away at the spectacle of the Luftwaffe pilot sprawled in the armchair with a glass mug in his hand.

McLean exchanged a glance with his mother. If this was the best the Army could send, he was not much impressed. He had scarcely admitted them and closed the door when there was more urgent knocking.

This time he opened the door to two of his neighbours who had been alerted to the emergency. Mr Williamson was the special constable. He wore a black steel helmet with the word POLICE painted on it in white lettering. His companion was Mr Clark, who was in the khaki helmet and uniform of the Home Guard. Clark was more than equal to the occasion. There was a whiff of Scotch whisky on the air. He said with authority, 'Hands up!'

Everyone looked at Clark and saw a large First World War revolver in his hand. They all half-raised their hands, even the soldiers, who then lowered them coyly.

'Is this the prisoner?' demanded Clark, gesturing dangerously with the gun.

'Aye.'

Turning to one of the soldiers, he said, 'We have a clear duty here. We must put him under close arrest.'

The soldiers looked uncomfortable.

'Is there anywhere suitable across the road?' asked Clark. They shook their heads.

The prisoner spoke up: 'Take me to Dungavel House.'

Clark raised the revolver higher. 'Nobody asked you.'

David McLean explained, 'He keeps asking for the Duke of Hamilton.'

Clark ignored that. 'If the regular Army has nowhere

suitable to confine the prisoner, we'll have him in the Home Guard hut at Busby.'

'I am a German officer.'

'On your feet!'

'He's injured his leg.'

'I don't propose to march him there. Mr Williamson is the owner of a motor car.'

Presently, the prisoner emerged from the McLeans' cottage supported by the soldiers, with Clark behind, pointing the revolver. Williamson opened the rear door of his small car. Before getting in, the prisoner turned towards McLean and his mother, thanked them, and dipped his head in a formal bow. Clark got into the back seat beside the prisoner and the car moved off into the night.

3

The Duke of Hamilton was not in residence at Dungavel on the night the German pilot parachuted into Scotland. He was some thirty miles away, at RAF Turnhouse, west of Edinburgh, where he served as commanding officer, with the rank of Wing Commander. Well known for his flying, the Duke had led the team that flew over the summit of Mount Everest in 1933.

He was in bed in his quarters when the telephone rang. He was overdue for a night's sleep, after long spells of duty leading flights of Hurricanes against German raiders over Scotland. But this was not a call to scramble. It was the sector controller asking him to come to the operations room.

There, he was told that the pilot of the Messerschmitt that had crashed at Eaglesham had asked to speak to him. It was mystifying. Earlier, the Duke had watched the tracking of the German plane. A fighter had been sent up from Turnhouse to intercept, but had lacked the speed to get on terms. A lively difference of opinion had developed between the RAF and the Royal Observer Corps as to the identity of the aircraft. Early sightings by ROC posts on the east coast had given it as a Messerschmitt 110, but no regular Me 110 was thought to have the fuel capacity to make the two-way trip, and the RAF had taken it to be a Dornier 215. Shortly after 2300 hours, the report of the crash had come in, followed by positive identification of a Messerschmitt 110: satisfaction for the ROC.

'He asked for me personally?'

'It seems he was trying to reach you, sir. He had a map strapped to his leg marked with a flight path terminating at Dungavel.'

'Do we know his name?'

'Horn, sir. Hauptmann Alfred Horn.'

'It means nothing to me. I suppose I'd better see the chap. Where is he being held?'

'They're taking him to Maryhill Barracks, sir. The Home Guard picked him up first and took him to a scout hut.'

'Maryhill. He'll have to wait until morning. See if you can raise the Interrogation Officer. I'd better arrange for us to see the man together.'

Before he returned to bed, the Duke did some checking. In 1936, as Marquis of Clydesdale and a Member of Parliament, he had visited Germany with a party of fellow MPs. The visit was officially to see the Berlin Olympic Games, but he was actually more interested, if possible, in getting a close look at the Luftwaffe. And it had been arranged. On 13 August, he had been introduced to Reichsmarschall Hermann Göring, who had obligingly laid on a tour of three German airfields. At Staaken, Döberitz and Lechfeld, the Duke had met a number of Luftwaffe officers, whose names he had kept for reference. This was the list he had now taken out to check. There was no Hauptmann Horn among the names.

Next morning at 10.00 a.m., the Duke, accompanied by Flight Lieutenant Benson, the RAF Interrogation Officer for South Scotland, arrived at Maryhill Barracks in Glasgow. First they were shown the personal effects taken from the prisoner: flying-suit, helmet and boots; Lufwaffe officer's tunic, trousers and forage cap; gold wristwatch; Leica camera; various medicines, vitamin preparations, glucose and sedatives; map-case and map; photographs of himself with a small boy and a woman; and two visiting cards, in the names of Professor Dr Karl Haushofer and Dr Albrecht Haushofer.

The Haushofers. So *they* were the connection.

The Duke's youngest brother, David, had introduced him to Albrecht Haushofer, the son, in 1936, during that visit to the Olympics. Albrecht, a bulky Bavarian, had impressed him as sapient, shrewd and possessed of independent views. Over dinner, he had shown a refreshing disrespect for certain of the Nazi leaders, mimicking von Ribbentrop and describing Goebbels as 'a poisonous little man who will give you dinner one night and sign your death warrant the next morning'. Surprisingly after that, Albrecht had confided that, in

11

addition to his duties as lecturer at the University of Berlin, he worked for the German Foreign Office. He favoured a policy of co-operation between Germany and Britain and he was a staunch worker for the preservation of peace. Moreover, he was a confidant of the Deputy Führer, Rudolph Hess.

In January 1937, the Duke, as Clydesdale, had taken the opportunity of a skiing trip to further the contact with Albrecht. This time he had travelled to Munich to meet Karl Haushofer, Albrecht's father, the professor of geopolitics whose theory of *lebensraum* – room to live – had been seized upon by Hitler as the moral and academic justification of his territorial invasions.

During 1937, Albrecht Haushofer had made two visits to Britain. In March, he had delivered a lecture to the Royal Institute of International Affairs, and afterwards had stayed in Clydesdale's London home. They had met again in June, when Albrecht was en route for America. In April 1938, Albrecht had visited Scotland and stayed at Dungavel. He was still talking of the need for an Anglo-German settlement, though with diminishing confidence. In July 1939, he had sent a long letter warning of the imminence of a war against Poland and in consequence a European War, and asking for a British initiative to forestall it. Clydesdale had shown it personally to Winston Churchill and the Foreign Secretary, Lord Halifax, and had then passed it to Lord Dunglass to put before the Prime Minister, Neville Chamberlain.

More than a year had passed – a year of war – before Albrecht had next penned a letter to his friend. It was a strange letter and the Duke had received it in curious circumstances. In the middle of March 1941, he had visited the Air Ministry in London, at the request of a Group Captain, who was 'anxious to have a chat about a certain matter'. The matter had turned out to be a photostat of a letter signed by 'A', who, evidently from the contents, was Albrecht. It was dated 23 September. A Mrs V. Roberts had sent it on from Lisbon. It had been intercepted by the Ministry of Information Censor on 2 November 1940, photocopied, and sent to MI5. It was almost six months old when it had finally reached the Duke in this photocopied form.

By Albrecht's standards, it was a short letter. He had

begun, as usual, with the salutation, 'My dear Douglo', and had gone on to offer condolences on the recent deaths of the Duke's father and brother-in-law. Then he had referred to the previous letter of July 1939, and the significance that the Duke and his 'friends in high places' might find in an invitation for him to meet with 'A' in neutral Lisbon. The reply was to be enclosed in two sealed envelopes and sent through another address in Lisbon.

British Intelligence had decided – after all those months – to ask the Duke to reopen contact with Albrecht Haushofer. He had been called for a second interview in April and asked to go to Portugal, to learn whatever Albrecht could tell him. This, the Duke had realised, amounted to working as a British agent. He had been told that it was the kind of mission for which one volunteered, rather than acting under orders.

After consideration, the Duke had written agreeing to carry out the mission, subject to two safeguards: he wanted the British Ambassador in Lisbon to be informed, as well as Sir Alexander Cadogan, of the Foreign Office. This had led to a distinct cooling in MI5's enthusiasm for the project, but it was still under discussion. In fact, the Duke had just written suggesting an alternative procedure for arranging the meeting with Albrecht. His letter, dated 10 May 1941, had not yet reached its destination when the mysterious Hauptmann Horn had parachuted into Britain.

'Shall we go in and see him?'

The prisoner was sitting up in bed, dark, morose and staring.

The duty officer announced the names of the visitors, and the prisoner's face lit up.

'I would like to speak to you in private,' he told the Duke. 'It is most important.'

The Duke turned to the other officers. 'Would you have any objection, gentlemen?'

Flight Lieutenant Benson and the Army officer agreed to withdraw, leaving the Duke alone with the prisoner.

The prisoner's eyes glittered triumphantly under the thick, black brows. He said, 'Yes, I can be sure you are the Duke of Hamilton. I saw you in Berlin in 1936, when we held the Olympic Games. You had lunch in my house. I do not know if you recognise me, but I am Rudolf Hess.'

4

A tall man with flame-coloured hair came out of the telex room of one of Britain's national Sunday newspaper offices, shoulders hunched and shaking his head, and passed into the labyrinth of the newsroom. He was Dick Garrick, the deputy sports editor.

'Bad news, Dick?'

Garrick stared across the copy paper and plastic cups and saw that the enquiry came from Cedric Fleming, the editor-in-chief. It was 10.35 on Saturday evening, and the top brass were gathered at the back bench, checking the first edition.

'We just lost our only world boxing title.'

'Already?' said Fleming. 'Didn't it go the distance?'

'Four rounds. Our boy was disqualified for low punching.'

Fleming screwed his fat face into an expression of shock. 'Deplorable. I presume he was innocent.'

'He was British.'

'Good point, Dick. The Marquess of Queensberry really ought to have put in a rule to safeguard our lads from over-zealous referees. Still, if it had to happen, rather the fourth round than the fourteenth, eh? It should make the late edition.'

'Mm.'

'It *was* Queensberry, wasn't it?'

'What?'

'Wrote those rules.'

Garrick shook his head. He moved closer, to make himself heard above the clatter of machines. 'It was a Welshman called Chambers. He got up a competition for amateur glove-fighters in 1867, and persuaded Queensberry to present some cups. They were known as the Queensberry Cups, and fighting was according to the Queensberry Rules.'

Garrick moved on to the sportsdesk and picked up a phone.

The night editor said, without looking up from the layout on the table, 'That's either a very bright young man or a nut.'

'Both,' said Fleming with approval. In his experience, the

14

ability to recall facts was the hallmark of a good journalist. He was not much impressed with the dictum that nothing is worth remembering that can be checked in a reference book.

He had poached Dick Garrick from the *Daily Telegraph* in 1978, when he had made a good impression subbing as a casual on Saturday nights. The lad had been assigned to the sportsdesk to fill a temporary gap, and stayed. Starting with no more than a mild interest in rowing, he had steeped himself in the lore of each major sport, and was now the paper's main authority on athletics, boxing, rugby football and water sports.

Towards 11.00 p.m. Fleming gave the nod to the front page, ambled across to the sportsdesk, and asked Vernon Padfield, the sports editor, to spare him a few minutes.

'It's about Garrick,' he said in the upholstered quiet of his office, as he poured a couple of scotches. 'How would you feel, dear boy, if I took him off sport for a bit?'

'Do you want a short answer? Shattered.'

'He's that good?'

'Dare I say indispensable?'

Fleming handed over the drink. His physical bulk and almost apologetic style of speech were deceptive. He was amiable to a point – the point of decision; at various times in his twelve-year tenure as editor, he had taken on the print unions, the NUJ chapel, the proprietor and the Press Council, and not merely defended his autonomy, but caused heavy casualties among the opposition. His capacity for survival was both legend and mystery.

He lowered himself gingerly into the bentwood armchair that had supported him through the whole of his journalistic career, starting with the *Ballroom Dancing Times*, a credit he coyly concealed from the compilers of *Who's Who*. 'Vernon, my boy, I'm going to come clean with you. Queensberry Rules, right? I need a ferret, a bloody good ferret.'

'You're onto something?'

'A sniff, just a sniff.'

'Soccer bribes?'

'Nothing to do with sport. Much bigger. Can't say more.'

'And you want Dick to do the digging?'

'Some of it. Others will be involved.'

15

'Would Red Goodbody be one of them?'

Fleming's eyebrows peaked in surprise. 'How do you know that?'

'He was tanking up in the Cock when I went over for a sandwich, announcing to the clientele that you summoned him back from Berlin to a house party. I thought you sent that guy to Germany to give us all a break.'

'I've got to use him for this.'

'Goodbody and Garrick? It's not up to me, I know, but are you sure the mix is right, Cedric? Dick is a first-rate journalist and he'll do your research as well as anyone I know, but he takes it seriously. He's not out of Goodbody's stable.'

'That's a relief. Two of them would be a pain.'

'He's TT, a non-smoker, doesn't play cards —'

'. . . lives on whole food and reads the Bible on the train to work. I get the drift, thanks, Vernon.'

Padfield said, 'Actually, he drives to work.'

'With his eye on the road at all times,' said Fleming. 'Who knows? Maybe rubbing shoulders with Red will improve the young man, if improvement is possible. Can you find a replacement?'

'For how long?'

Fleming lifted his hand and gestured vaguely.

Padfield stared into the whisky, rotating it slowly in the glass. 'I could say something extremely offensive.'

'Be my guest,' said Fleming, rising from his chair.

Padfield swallowed the rest of the drink. 'Forget it. Do you want to see Dick now? Shall I send him in?'

'I knew you would understand,' said Fleming as he opened the door.

5

On the afternoon of Sunday 11 May 1941, London was still fighting the fires resulting from the worst night of the Blitz. Over seven hundred densely-populated acres had been destroyed, causing more deaths and damage in one night than the Great Fire of 1666 had inflicted in several weeks. The House of Commons itself had been gutted by incendiary bombs. It was not a propitious time to call the Foreign Office and ask to speak to a member of the government.

One of Anthony Eden's staff had been persuaded to take the call. As he listened, he became increasingly dubious. The caller claimed to be the Duke of Hamilton. He asked for Sir Alexander Cadogan, the head of the Foreign Office. He said he had something of the highest importance to impart, but he was not prepared to discuss it over the telephone. He wanted Sir Alexander to drive to Northolt Airport and meet him there.

This was utterly impossible, the civil servant doggedly explained. If the matter were really important, he might be able to arrange an appointment at some time in the next two weeks. It was unrealistic to expect the head of the Foreign Office to motor out to Northolt to meet the Duke of Hamilton, or anyone else.

This last remark was overheard. John 'Jock' Colville, the Prime Minister's Private Secretary, had walked into the office.

'Who is it?'

The civil servant cupped his hand over the mouthpiece. 'I think he's a lunatic. He says he is the Duke of Hamilton, that something extraordinary has happened. He won't say what it's all about.'

Colville reached for the phone. Strangely, he had dreamed the previous night that Göring had flown from Germany with the bombers and parachuted into Britain. It was one of those dreams that linger in the mind.

17

'Colville speaking. Who is there?'

'Thank God! Listen, this is Hamilton. I'm trying to reach Alex Cadogan. Something has happened, something unbelievable.'

'What, exactly?'

'I can't say over a public line. It's just extraordinary . . . like . . . like something out of an E. Phillips Oppenheim novel.'

Colville hesitated. The dream surfaced again. 'Has somebody arrived?'

There was a pause.

The Duke answered, 'Yes.'

'Hold the line. I'm going to get instructions.'

Winston Churchill was at Ditchley Park in Oxfordshire, his secret headquarters for weekends when a full moon made Chequers vulnerable to bombing raids. It was a country house in a four-thousand-acre estate owned by his friend Ronald Tree. That weekend was the first anniversary of Churchill's appointment as Prime Minister, and thirty house guests had been invited. News kept coming in of the devastation in London, but Churchill was accustomed to adversity. He was jubilant that the RAF had shot down thirty-three Luftwaffe bombers. At his request, a film comedy, *The Marx Brothers Go West*, was to be screened after dinner.

Churchill was puzzled by the message from Colville. He knew the Duke of Hamilton as a friend and former colleague in the House, but he could think of nothing of 'urgent Cabinet importance' that the Duke would need to discuss with him. He sent Brendan Bracken, the Minister of Information, to the phone. Bracken came back with a more sensational version: the Duke had an 'amazing piece of information' to report, so sensitive that it could not be divulged over the phone.

Churchill decided to summon him to Ditchley. His own car was sent to meet the Duke at Kidlington airport.

Dinner was almost over when the Duke was admitted. Churchill stood to shake his hand. 'My dear Douglas, what a pleasure this is! Have you eaten?'

'Not yet, sir, but—'

'Then you must certainly join us.' Churchill beckoned a servant. 'A chair for his Grace, if you please.' Then, turning back to the Duke, 'You have whetted our appetites, too. Something certain to amaze us, we were told. What is this all about?'

'Sir, it is of a highly confidential nature.'

'Classifiable?'

'Indeed.'

Churchill took a deep breath. 'I see.'

Tactfully, the other guests started putting their napkins on the table.

Churchill said, 'I should like the Secretary of State for Air to remain.'

'Of course.'

In a moment, the Duke was alone with Churchill and Sir Archibald Sinclair. They waited for the doors of the dining room to be closed.

'Well, Douglas?'

'Sir, last night a German airman crashed his plane and baled out over Scotland. He was picked up and taken to Glasgow. He was wearing the uniform of a hauptmann in the Luftwaffe and he gave his name as Horn. He repeatedly asked to be allowed to speak to me. I was asked to interview him at Maryhill Barracks this morning, and I did. As soon as we were alone, he identified himself as Rudolf Hess.'

Nothing was said for several seconds. Churchill stared at the Duke of Hamilton in open disbelief, as if deciding whether this visibly exhausted man were suffering from hallucinations brought on by too much flying.

'Do you mean to tell me that the Deputy Führer of Germany is in our hands?'

'That is my conclusion, sir. The man I saw this morning bears a striking resemblance to Hess. He was carrying these photographs of himself and, I presume, his wife and child.'

Churchill put on his glasses and examined the photographs. He passed them to Sinclair. After another long pause, he pushed back his chair and said, 'Well, Hess or no Hess, I am going to see the Marx Brothers.'

19

6

Jane Calvert-Mead was in bed in her second-floor flat in Brook Green when the doorbell rang. She pulled the duvet around her ears and moaned. Caught again. A hangover: an occupational hazard for a newspaper diarist. But it should never have happened. If a peer of the realm so adored his daughter that he had hired Hever Castle to announce her engagement, wouldn't you think he would use genuine champagne in the bucks fizz?

One of the tenants downstairs could answer it.

Jane stretched and turned on to her stomach. Then there crept into her mind a recollection of something said earlier in the week when she was on her way down with the milk bottles. Both sets of people below were away for the weekend. Bugger. No one else was going to answer that bell.

It rang again. Bloody cheek, disturbing people on a Sunday morning. Probably boy scouts collecting jumble. How they ever grew up into passably attractive men, she couldn't imagine.

It was going like a fire alarm. Little fiends!

She couldn't stand it any longer. She hurled aside the duvet, wrapped her bathrobe around her shoulders, shuffled across the room, let up the blind, opened the window and looked out. The cold air made her sneeze.

The guy on the doorstep moved back towards the gate and stared up. He was like an advert in *Horse and Hound*: peaked cap, tweed suit with leather sections on the shoulders, dark green cravat and pale lemon shirt. She had no idea who he was. If he hadn't said, 'Miss Calvert-Mead?', she would have shut the window and gone back to bed.

'Yes.'

'Richard Garrick.'

'And?'

'I'm here to pick you up.'

'Is this a joke? Some sort of singing telegram?'

20

'Didn't you get the message? Cedric Fleming assured me he would tell you.'

'Cedric? God! You're . . .'

'Dick Garrick. Your lift to Henley.'

'What time is it, for God's sake?'

'Eleven-thirty. Well, nearer eleven-forty now.'

'But we're not expected for lunch, are we?'

'Exactly. I thought we'd eat on the way.'

'Hold on. I'd better come down and let you in.'

She came away from the window, pulled the bathrobe properly on, snatched up a hairbrush and tried to coax her short, blonde hair into something approaching the style that Serge had fashioned the previous Thursday. It was a lost cause without lacquer. She tossed down the brush, opened the curtains in the living room, carried a couple of unwashed plates into the kitchen, and went down the two flights of stairs to open the door.

He had the pale colouring that usually goes with red hair and is liable to break out into crimson blotches in moments of stress. He touched his cap and held out his hand. She extended hers, feeling ridiculous.

'I know you by sight, of course,' he said as they started up the stairs. 'Never had a chance to speak. It's all incredibly breathless on the sportsdesk.'

'So I gather.'

'I was told about this around midnight. I recorded a message on your answerphone this morning, but obviously . . .'

'Mm,' said Jane. 'I had this down as a morning off.'

'You *were* told to expect a lift?'

'Yes, Cedric promised someone would call. I assumed after lunch.' She pushed open the door of her flat. 'Give me twenty minutes. The kitchen's through there if you'd like to make some instant coffee.'

'Thanks. I don't drink coffee in any form.'

'Well, *I* wouldn't say no.'

He turned gratifyingly red. 'Of course.'

Her cup was waiting when, showered, dressed in a white lace blouse and black trouser suit, and as alert as she was capable of being within a half-hour of waking, she rejoined him. 'Any idea what this is about?'

21

'Only that it has nothing to do with sport.'

'Thank God for that,' said Jane. 'I spend half my working life knee-deep in mud and horse-droppings.'

She followed his rapid glance around the room, at the stuffed toys on their shelf, the fencing mask, the family snaps of her father, her two sisters and the dogs, the wooden plaque with the arms of Selwyn College, the skis, the print of Charles I on horseback, the Ecology Party poster, the bookshelves and the family tree, and she sensed that if she didn't think of something fast, Dick Garrick would start on his Sherlock Holmes routine.

She gulped a mouthful of the tepid coffee he'd presented her with, and said, 'I think we should do something about getting to Henley.'

7

A worried man arrived at the Berghof, Adolf Hitler's mountain villa at Obersalzberg, on the morning of Sunday 11 May 1941. He was Hauptmann Karlheinz Pintsch, the most trusted adjutant of Rudolf Hess, and he had travelled overnight from Augsburg in Hess's private railway carriage. On arrival at Berchtesgaden station at 7.00 a.m., he had phoned the Führer's adjutant, Albert Bormann, the brother of Martin Bormann, and requested an immediate appointment. Bormann was unimpressed. Everyone who came to the Berghof wanted priority and, as he frequently denied it to Reichsministers, he saw no reason to make an exception of a mere adjutant. He promised nothing except that a car would be sent to collect Pintsch from the station.

The approach to Hitler's private mountain was through a series of checkpoints in a forest thick with SS guards. A nine-mile perimeter fence enclosed other fences, barracks, garages, a hotel and the Berghof itself, an extension of Wagnerian proportions to the simple wooden house Hitler had built from the royalties of *Mein Kampf* in the 1920s.

Bormann was in the entrance hall when Pintsch arrived and reiterated the urgency of his request. Bormann told him that the Führer's schedule was already full. A day's appointments had been telescoped into three hours to make way for a reception for Admiral Darlan – the representative of the Vichy French, and the real power behind Marshal Pétain. Hitler was looking to the French for a stronger commitment to military collaboration, and he expected to get it that afternoon from Darlan.

The best Pintsch could extract from Bormann was a promise to try to fit him in at some point during the morning. Resignedly, he took his place in the crowded anteroom at the foot of the main staircase. Three hours later, he was still waiting. Among those who had arrived were Dr Fritz Todt, the Minister for Armaments, and Albert Speer, the Inspector

General of Buildings. Pintsch, 'pale and agitated' as Speer recalled him, asked each of them if he might be permitted to precede them to deliver the letter from Hess. While he was with Todt, a sudden commotion put a stop to conversation. People had sprung to attention and clicked their heels.

Hitler was coming downstairs. He wore a grey uniform without insignia, but the magisterial way he deported himself stamped him unmistakably as the Führer.

Pintsch took a step forward. 'My Führer – '

With a limp hand, Hitler waved him away. 'Wait your turn. Dr Todt is due to see me next.'

'My Führer, Dr Todt has graciously consented to my delivering this letter from the *Stellvertreter*.'

'A letter from Hess?' Hitler took it and strode through the anteroom to the salon.

Pintsch, after a moment's hesitation, followed. He stopped in the doorway, intimidated, as every visitor was, by the proportions and furnishings of the room. Sixty feet ahead was a picture window, reputedly the largest in the world, with a breathtaking view of Berchtesgaden and Salzburg. In front of it was a table made from a twenty-foot slab of red marble, quarried from the Untersberg across the valley. There were tapestries, paintings by Italian and German masters, a cabinet filled with priceless china, a sideboard practically as big as the table, and a bronze bust of Wagner mounted on an ornamental chest.

Hitler was standing at the window, facing the view. He had handed the letter to Air General Bodenschatz, Göring's adjutant, to open. Bodenschatz picked up a paper-knife, slit the envelope and took out the several sheets of writing paper.

Hitler took them and began to read:

My Führer, when you receive this letter, I shall be in England. You can imagine that the decision to take this step was not easy for me . . .

The muscles at the back of Hitler's neck tensed.

Pintsch felt his own muscles tauten.

. . . And if, my Führer, this project – which I admit has but very small chance of success – ends in failure and the fates decide against me, this can have no detrimental results

24

either for you or for Germany; it will always be possible for you to deny all responsibility. Simply say that I was crazy.

Hitler screamed: 'an inarticulate, almost animal outcry', as Speer heard it from the anteroom.

Bodenschatz exchanged a nervous glance with Pintsch.

Without turning, Hitler said, 'You had better tell me what has happened.'

'My Führer –' said Pintsch.

'Speak up!'

'The *Stellvertreter* took off from the airport at Augsburg yesterday at 1810 hours. He left me written orders. If he had not returned after four hours, I was to open them and read them. I was instructed to deliver the letter personally to you. I travelled overnight to get here.'

Hitler swung round and snapped at Bodenschatz, 'You hear that, Herr General? Hess has flown to Britain. What does the Luftwaffe have to say about that? Fetch Göring at once.'

'My Führer, he is at home in Nuremberg.'

'Get him here!'

'Yes, my Führer!' Bodenschatz snatched up a phone.

Hitler pressed a bell-push.

Albert Bormann, alerted by the scream, came instantly into the room.

'Where is Reichsminister von Ribbentrop?'

'He is about to go to lunch with Admiral Darlan, my Führer.'

'Get him out. I want to speak to him.' Hitler shouted across the room to Bodenschatz, 'Have you told Göring?'

'I am trying to reach him, my Führer.'

'Get Air General Udet as well. Get the whole of the Luftwaffe if necessary! I want to know what's been going on behind my back. And you, Hauptmann Pintsch . . .' Hitler softened his voice to a level that was more menacing than the shouting, '. . . you also will join us for lunch.'

Pintsch bowed, clicked his heels and withdrew. When he got outside, he found that the anteroom had been cleared and everyone sent upstairs. Then Martin Bormann, whom he knew well as Hess's deputy, appeared and took him to one side.

'What's happening?'

Pintsch explained.

'It's nothing to do with me,' said Bormann. 'Don't involve me, will you?'

Lunch at the Berghof was never notably conducive to the digestion. Members of the SS bodyguard in waiters' dress attended on the table. Hitler, a vegetarian teetotaller, frequently harangued his guests about their eating habits. But on this occasion, the food passed from plate to mouth uncommented upon, and practically unnoticed. Grouped around the table in addition to Hitler were his mistress, Eva Braun; Hess's deputy, Martin Bormann; Air General Bodenschatz; Air General Ernst Udet; the Press adviser, Otto Dietrich; one of von Ribbentrop's adjutants, Walther Hewel; Dr Todt; and the unenviable Pintsch.

Hess had put no constraint upon Pintsch about telling what he knew, so when Hitler asked for a full account, he was given it. Pintsch described the preparations: the work on the Messerschmitt; the practice flights; the daily weather reports; the arrangement with the Air Ministry to provide a radio beam; the three unsuccessful missions; and the detailed events leading up to the fateful take-off.

'This whole business stinks!' said Hitler. 'I trusted Hess. I took him for a man of honour. My God, I know him better than any of you. We were prisoners together in Landsberg Castle. I made him my *Stellvertreter*. He gave me a solemn promise not to do any flying. And now this!'

Pintsch cleared his throat.

'What is it?'

'As he explained it to me, my Führer, the promise he gave you was in September 1939.'

'So?'

'He said he pledged to do no flying for the period of one year, my Führer. He considered that after September 1940, he was free to fly again.'

Hitler sat back in his chair and rested his chin on his hand, making an effort to remember.

Martin Bormann, silent until this moment, quietly remarked, 'My Führer, last year, you put out an order for the duration of the war banning all Reichsministers from piloting their own planes.'

26

Hitler snapped his fingers. 'Correct! He defied my order. And others conspired with him. The Luftwaffe. Air General Udet, what do you know of this business?'

'Only this, my Führer: Herr Hess came to me last autumn and asked to do some flying from Tempelhof.'

'What was your answer?'

'I told him I would need to see a permit signed by yourself. He went away and I didn't hear from him again.'

'He went to Augsburg,' said Hitler, 'and he was provided with a Messerschmitt. We shall be looking into that. Well, Herr General, with due allowance for the conditions and the ability of Hess, what is your professional opinion of his chances?'

'Of reaching England, my Führer?'

'Scotland, Herr General. He was planning to visit the Duke of Hamilton. That is to say, near Glasgow.'

'Glasgow? That is out of the question, my Führer. Even if he was not shot down by the British, he must have come down in the sea. A flight of that distance in an Me 110 would test the best of our Luftwaffe pilots, with all the advantages of modern training and equipment. How would he land after dark? It's quixotic. I am afraid the *Stellvertreter* is dead.'

'That is the opinion of the Luftwaffe?'

'Anyone with a knowledge of flying would agree, my Führer.'

'We shall see if you are right,' said Hitler, as he took a last sip of mineral water. 'You and I may see this from different points of view, Herr General. You know flying: I know Rudolf Hess.' He turned to Eva Braun. She nodded to indicate that she was ready to leave.

Everyone rose and stood to attention.

Before leaving the room, Hitler spoke briefly to Martin Bormann, who followed him out.

The sense of relief was shortlived. Bormann returned with two officers.

'Hauptmann Pintsch, I have to advise you that you are under arrest.'

8

In its 10.00 p.m. news bulletin on Monday 11 May 1941, Munich Radio broadcast the following statement:

It is officially announced by the National Socialist Party that Party Member Rudolf Hess, who, because he has been suffering from a progressive illness for several years, had been strictly forbidden by the Führer to engage in any further flying activity, was able, contrary to this command, to come into possession of an aircraft again.

On Saturday 10 May at about 6.00 p.m., Rudolf Hess set out on a flight from Augsburg from which he has not so far returned. A letter he left behind unfortunately shows by its distractedness traces of a mental disorder, and it is feared that he was a victim of hallucinations.

The Führer ordered the immediate arrest of the adjutants of Party Member Hess, who alone had any knowledge of the flight, and did nothing either to prevent or report it, in contravention of the Führer's command, of which they were fully aware.

In the circumstances, it must be presumed that Party Member Hess either jumped out of his aircraft or has met with an accident.

At 11.23 p.m. the same evening, the following statement was issued by the Ministry of Information in Great Britain:

Rudolf Hess, the Deputy Führer of Germany and Party Leader of the National Socialist Party, has landed in Scotland in the following circumstances.

On the night of Saturday the 10th instant, a Messerschmitt 110 was reported by our patrols to have crossed the coast of Scotland and be flying in the direction of Glasgow.

Since an Me 110 would not have the fuel to return to Germany, this report was at first disbelieved.

However, later on, an Me 110 crashed near Glasgow, with its guns untouched. Shortly afterwards, a German officer who had baled out was found with his parachute in the neighbourhood suffering from a broken ankle.

He was taken to hospital in Glasgow, where he at first gave his name as Horn, but later on declared that he was Rudolf Hess. He brought with him various photographs of himself at different ages, apparently in order to establish his identity.

These photographs were deemed to be photographs of Hess by several people who knew him personally. Accordingly, an officer of the Foreign Office who was closely acquainted with Hess before the war has been sent up by aeroplane to see him in hospital.

Later that week, a second statement was issued by the German Government:

As far as it is possible to tell from papers left behind by Party Member Hess, it seems that he lived in a state of hallucination, as a result of which he felt he could bring about an understanding between England and Germany.

According to a report from London, it is established that Hess jumped from his aircraft near the town which he was trying to reach, and was found there, injured.

The National Socialist Party regrets that this idealist fell a victim of his hallucinations. This, however, will have no effect on the continuation of the war which has been forced upon Germany.

Dr Karl Haushofer, head of the Geopolitical Institute, Willi Messerschmitt, Frau Hess and others have been arrested.

9

Cedric Fleming's house was not, after all, in Henley on Thames, but in a hamlet two miles north of the town. It was approached through a wood, using a road so narrow and overhung that only the forewarned were likely to persist to the clearing where several stone cottages stood. A group of three in a terraced row had been converted into a single dwelling which demonstrably belonged to Fleming, because he was leaning out of a ground floor window feeding a small animal.

It ran off to the woods when Dick Garrick's Renault trundled into the rustic scene. 'It was a young deer!' said Jane delightedly. 'Cedric was feeding it, just like Snow-White.'

Garrick frowned, troubled by the comparison, as the paunchy figure of their editor-in-chief appeared at the door, wearing shorts and a string vest.

'Would you settle for St Francis?' murmured Jane, as Fleming came to meet them. 'That *was* a fawn, wasn't it?' she asked him.

'Full-grown deer,' said Fleming. 'Chinese muntjak. Pretty things, aren't they? Some escaped from the herd at Woburn a century or so ago and colonised the woods. We have mink as well. Exotic creatures in abundance, not to mention yours truly. Come in and have a beer. You must be parched.'

He led them through a hallway to a spacious kitchen, where modern appliances stood comfortably with a wooden dresser, cupboards and table of Edwardian vintage. Garrick put in a request for something non-alcoholic, so Jane had the lager that Fleming had taken from the fridge.

Fleming picked a cigar from a box on the dresser and went through the ritual of preparing it.

Garrick asked, 'Is anyone joining us?'

'Red Goodbody.'

Jane said warmly, 'Great! He wrote that terrific series a few months ago on the people who arrange escapes across the Berlin wall.'

'The *Fluchthelfer*,' put in Garrick in a murmur that was almost an apology for his habit of supplying salient information.

'Red had a couple of years as a general reporter, but I think it was before either of you joined the paper,' Cedric informed them. 'He isn't here yet.'

'Is he coming from Berlin?' asked Jane.

'He flew in yesterday and looked up some old friends in Fleet Street.'

'Does he have transport? We could have offered him a lift,' said Garrick.

'Knowing Red, I didn't suggest it,' said Fleming cryptically, adding, 'He won't have any difficulty getting here, but he may be late. With that in mind, I asked him to be here by three, although I don't expect to get down to business until four. Are your bags in the car? Let's get you settled in.'

They collected the luggage and re-entered the house from the opposite end.

'Slight imperfection in the design,' Fleming explained, as they went upstairs. 'It is possible, on a rainy day, to go from one end of the house to the other, but it means cutting through bedrooms, so we more usually keep to the original front doors. These are the guest-rooms, then, or three of them. Jane, which one would you like? All have shower-rooms attached.'

'The end one, then,' said Jane, mindful of rainy days.

'Right.' Fleming pushed open a door and showed her into an airy room with green and white blinds at the windows and white mohair rugs on a cork-tiled floor. The wall behind the bed was pine-clad and fitted with a shelf-unit containing paperbacks, wine-glasses and a mini-bar. He deposited her overnight case on the stool in front of the dressing-table. 'There's plenty of hot water, if you want to freshen up. We'll all meet at four in the living-room at the other end.'

'Should I bring my cloak and dagger?'

Fleming smiled and closed the door.

Jane went to the window and looked out. It was barely credible to Jane that she was in the country house of her editor-in-chief, recruited overnight for something big. She had always envied the newsmen sent at a moment's notice on assignments they could never predict. Her work as assistant on the diary never seemed like the real thing. Most of the stories were dreamed up by PR people wanting to push something. This one had the prickle of urgency about it – the summons to Henley, the reporter flown in from Berlin. And she – only heaven and Cedric Fleming knew why – was part of it.

She heard him go downstairs. One slight apprehension had been taken care of by the room arrangements: she was at the opposite end of the building from Cedric. Not that she had discerned even a glimmer of incipient lust in his small brown eyes, but she knew about executives and power and its supposed effect on subordinate women, and presumably so did he. She was the only woman to be invited. Having floated these sexist notions and seen them sink without trace, she felt annoyed with herself. It was no use demanding professional respect if you hadn't the confidence to recognize it when it was given.

She started to unpack. Towards four, she checked her face, freshened her lipstick, and came out of her room. She knocked on the third door along the passage. She was sure Dick Garrick had not been given the room next to hers, because she would have heard movements through the connecting door.

'Ready?' she asked, when he looked out.

'Certainly.' In response to Fleming's shorts, he had discarded his tweeds for cords and a shirt. 'How's your room?'

'Fine.'

'I wonder if Goodbody's arrived now.'

'Somehow I don't think so,' said Jane. 'I have a view of the road, and I haven't heard a car all afternoon.'

They came out of the house and entered it again by the door they had first gone through to the kitchen.

'This way,' Fleming's voice hailed them from a doorway on the left. 'Tea or coffee, Jane?'

They stepped into a low-beamed, red-carpeted room lined with books to halfway, and above them white plastered walls hung with cartoon prints by Gilray. One of the leaded windows was open, but the whiff of Fleming's last cigar lingered, asserting his occupancy. He stood at a trolley, coffee-jug poised. He had changed into a faded linen suit that might have been one of Sydney Greenstreet's cast-offs from *Casablanca*.

Jane took a black coffee and a salmon sandwich.

Fleming told them, 'I'm afraid Red Goodbody is late, later than I anticipated.'

'Nil desperandum,' Dick Garrick announced from across the room. He had spotted an old sports car, a white MG Midget, zoom into the clearing with two laughing girls in the front seats and a man in a leather jacket perched on the luggage behind them with a hand on each of their shoulders. They came to a screeching halt, sounded the horn, and all got out. One girl's hair stood up from her scalp and was streaked green and blue.

'Goodbody?' Dick enquired.

'Beyond any shadow of doubt,' muttered Fleming.

Jane joined them at the window. Red Goodbody turned to retrieve a well-filled carrier bag marked 'Berlin Tegel Duty Free' and an old wicker basket fastened with rope. His jacket was scuffed almost into suede and his cords that once might have been maroon had faded to coral pink. The type, Jane decided, who knows he's good-looking and deliberately cultivates a shabby appearance.

'Then who are the others?'

'If you'll excuse me, I mean to find out.'

In a moment, Fleming returned with the girls and Goodbody in tow. 'These young ladies were gracious enough to offer a lift to our colleague, Mr Goodbody.'

'We found him at Heston Services,' said one, almost too convulsed at the memory to get it out. 'He was sitting in the passenger-seat when we got back from the ladies. Cheeky sod. Gloria didn't half lay into him. Then he told us about this pub at Junction 3 that serves Fuller's.'

'The Queen's Head,' put in Gloria, as if everyone in the room was agog to know. 'We took ages finding it. We were looking on the wrong side of the motorway. If you ask me, he didn't know the pub at all. We were bound to find one called the Queen's Head eventually, weren't we.'

'Gloria, it *was* a Fuller's pub.'

'Now, about the little room,' the other girl prompted.

33

Fleming said darkly, 'Second on the right through there.'

'Ta-ta, boys and girls,' trilled Gloria, as they both set off in that direction.

'Well,' said Red, picking up a sandwich. 'Now, what are you waiting for, Cedric?'

10

Cedric Fleming did not respond to Red Goodbody's question, but crossed the room to the window and stood there, staring out. Even when the two girls emerged giggling from the house, climbed into the MG, started it up, revved it into a screeching turn and drove off the way they had come, he did not react. Goodbody, however, was in no way subdued by his host's introspection. He grabbed a handful of sandwiches and toured the room, making himself known to the others. Jane thought him brash and insensitive. He addressed her as 'love' in a manner she found patronising. His clothes were a disgrace and there was beer on his breath.

To compound her feelings about him, he smiled repeatedly, displaying a perfect set of shining teeth. And he had the most extraordinary pale blue eyes shading to green at the edges. She sensed in them the power to ambush a woman's emotions. He knew it, too, and she resented him the more. She noticed that when he spoke to the men, they were as reserved as she in their reactions. His brand of bonhomie was not making the impression he intended. She could not imagine him fitting into any group.

Yet she was bound to admit that some antidote was wanted for Dick Garrick's paralysing earnestness. Red Goodbody may have been a yob, but his arrival guaranteed that the house-party would not be dull.

When Cedric Fleming finally turned away from the window, he lowered his eyes as he started to speak, and the message, too, was faintly deferential in tone: 'I've not been very informative about why you are here, and I thank you for bearing with me. I don't mind telling you that I am more than a little apprehensive of your reactions. I want to invite you to work together on an assignment to unravel one of the last great mysteries of the war. You three have certain areas of expertise, but mainly I like what I've seen of your commitment, your energy, and . . .' (he looked deliberately at

35

each face in turn)'. . . yes, your temperaments. I picked you
as the most likely combination of talent to get to the truth of
this story. Let's begin.' He crossed the room to a TV set on
the bookshelf with a video-recorder beside it. He touched the
controls and a woman tennis-player appeared on the screen.

'If this is about gays in sport, forget it,' said Red. 'Sorry,
Cedric, but someone thought of it already.'

Cedric's way of dealing with Red was to ignore him. He
switched to the video channel, slid a cassette into the recorder
and touched a button on the remote control.

The BBC clock appeared on the screen. A voice-over announced the Nine O'Clock News with Sue Lawley. The
opening sequence gave way to a long shot of two men
emerging from a building carrying a sack. 'The end of the
siege in sight,' said the newsreader. 'Libyan diplomatic bags
on their way out.'

'The Libyan Embassy siege?' said Dick.

'This was months back,' said Red.

'Hold on,' said Cedric. The headline clips were replacing
each other fast on the screen. Libyan families at Heathrow,
moving out of Britain. A demonstration against the
Ayatollah. President Reagan in Peking.

Then a monochrome still of a strange, staring face, filling
the screen. 'A birthday in Berlin,' said the newsreader.
'Rudolf Hess, ninety today and still in prison.'

'Poor devil,' said Dick.

'Why do they always use that picture?' asked Jane.

'It's a great shot,' said Red. 'Once you see it, you never
forget it.'

Jane conceded that he was right. The look from that dark,
hollow-cheeked face pictured in the dock at Nuremberg
nearly forty years ago still had the power to disturb. Defiant
and fanatical, the eyes expected no mercy.

Cedric said, 'I'll move the tape on.' He pressed the search
button and the images speeded up. 'Just look at the pictures a
moment. I'll cut the sound.'

'Hess is our assignment?' asked Dick. 'What's new on
Hess?'

Cedric didn't answer. He set the tape to normal speed as
the picture of Hess came up again, projected behind the

newsreader. Then the screen was filled with a rooftop view of Berlin, dominated by the TV tower in the East.

'This is Wilhelmstrasse,' Red informed them, 'approaching Spandau Jail. You could get lucky and see me in a moment. I was there for the birthday.'

'Gate-crashing?' suggested Jane, as the blue front doors of the prison appeared, followed by close-ups of guards with dogs and a warning sign.

'I was interviewing his son, wasn't I?' said Red. 'That's him, going in to see the old man.'

'You mean him?' asked Dick, as a talking head appeared in shot.

'No, he's a former commandant.'

With nice timing, a caption confirmed Red's information.

A map of Europe came up, showing the flight path Hess had taken in 1941, followed by black and white footage of his wrecked plane and then a sequence at a Nazi rally. Some grainy film, obviously sneaked from a high vantage-point with a telephoto lens, came next: the solitary figure of Hess at exercise in the prison garden, wearing a grey, pillbox-type hat and a dark overcoat with the collar turned up, hands behind his back, moving at a measured pace until he found some small obstruction in his path and moved it with his foot. He had receding hair, but his face looked better-nourished than it had in the Nuremberg picture.

Cedric turned up the sound. . . . *developed an interest in space travel, but he stayed where he was. And his son blames the Western powers for that as much as anyone else.*

Wolf Rüdiger Hess, a man in his forties, was shown being interviewed outside the prison gates: *The Western powers are responsible because you can see American guards guarding my father today or during April, and British guards guarding him during May and French guards in June. So I think it's not true that the Russians are the only ones who get the blame.*

'A swipe at the Allies,' said Dick. 'Not like the Beeb to . . .' He gave way to the voice coming from the TV.

The British say that accusation is nonsense. They and the other Western powers have repeatedly asked the Russians to release Hess. The Russians refuse. To them he's a Nazi war criminal. He will stay here and die here.

'Which leaves us in no doubt who the real hard-liners are,' commented Dick.

Cedric stopped the video-tape. 'Red, you were there. Your story had a different slant, if I recall it right.'

There was a chuckle from the window-seat. 'I have to earn my living, don't I?'

'Don't duck this. It's important,' Cedric cautioned him. 'You quoted the son as saying that the Russians had shown greater flexibility during the time that Chancellor Schmidt was the German leader. They even gave signs of being willing to release Hess.'

'That's what Wolf Rüdiger Hess suggested,' Red confirmed. 'As a matter of fact, *The Times* picked up that quote as well, but I wouldn't get too excited about it. The guy has a vested interest in drawing attention to his father's cause. It's a crusade with him. He gave the media any number of angles. Maximum publicity. In his shoes, I'd do the same. Wouldn't you?'

'I'm sorry if I'm being naive,' Jane pitched in, speaking her thoughts aloud, 'but if the Russians were willing to release Rudolf Hess, why didn't it happen? Who objected?'

The question went unanswered. Cedric was in charge and he had clearly planned things in his own way. He removed the cassette from the video-recorder and slipped another into position. 'This TV documentary was transmitted quite a few years ago,' he said. 'It creaks a bit, and you'll have to make allowances for that, but it's still a useful account of what happened, and there are some crucial interviews with people no longer around to tell their stories.'

The opening sequence showed why Cedric had felt it necessary to apologise in advance for the programme. There was a filmed reconstruction of Hess's flight to Scotland in 1941. The close-ups of the actor in the cockpit immediately challenged credibility and the long shots of the Messerschmitt were unmistakably taken through studio smoke, using a model. The parachute-jump was a newsreel insert. There were smiles all round.

Then there was a cut to something more worthwhile: a

filmed interview with David McLean, the ploughman who had found Hess and taken him into his house until the Home Guard had arrived and driven him away. McLean came over as the eminently practical Scot, at a loss to understand why anyone was troubling him about so remote an event.

'Hess couldn't have picked a nicer man to drop in on,' commented Dick. 'Dead now, I guess?'

'Most of these people are, unfortunately,' answered Cedric.

Major Donald of the Royal Observer Corps followed, describing his interview the same night with the prisoner in the Home Guard hut at Busby. At that stage, he explained, nobody knew the identity of the captured pilot. The major had found him in a beautiful rig of light blue and looking slightly fed-up, sitting surrounded by police and Home Guards. At the sight of another service uniform, the man had got to his feet and bowed, but his leg was injured and he had soon been forced to resume his seat. He was refusing to speak any English, so Major Donald, who was a speaker of German, had asked him the questions the others had been trying to put.

The man had given his name as Hauptmann Alfred Horn and said that he had a secret message to deliver urgently to the Duke of Hamilton. When translated into English, this had created loud amusement among his captors. The prisoner, angered, had shown Major Donald his map, with Dungavel House marked with a red circle.

His face seemed familiar, the major went on, *so I asked him where he had come from, and he said near Munich. I remarked on the excellence of the Lowenbrau in the Munich Beer Cellar, and he looked as disapproving as a maiden aunt. He was a teetotaller, you see. Now I had heard of two Germans who were teetotallers. One was Hitler and the other was Hess. I asked him to sign his name against the Me 110 in my pack of aircraft identification cards, and he signed Alfred Horn. I said I was surprised that he had an Anglo-Saxon name instead of a good German one. He insisted that 'Alfred' was German, and I said, 'Ich Denke nicht' – the nearest I could get to 'Oh, yeah?' I told him, 'I will see that the Duke is informed of your request, and I will also tell the*

Duke that your true name is Rudolf Hess.' He jumped about fifteen inches.

In the event, the programme's narrator explained over a still picture of the Duke of Hamilton, the Major's theory wasn't conveyed to the Duke, who drove to Maryhill Barracks next morning, apparently unaware that the prisoner would identify himself as the Deputy Führer.

Dick cut in with a query: 'Isn't there an interview with the Duke?'

'Unfortunately, no,' responded Cedric, pressing the pause button on the remote control.

'He's dead now?'

'Yes.'

'Was he a friend of Hess?'

'No. They'd never met before Hess arrived.'

Dick frowned. 'That's certain?'

'Absolutely. The Duke brought a successful libel action against some people who made precisely that allegation in a pamphlet. Leading members of the British Communist Party. They were obliged to publish a statement in *The Times* unreservedly accepting the Duke's assurance that he had no sympathy with the Nazis or the German Government and that he had never met Hess, nor even received a letter from him.'

'There must have been some reason why Hess asked to see him,' ventured Jane.

'We're coming to that,' said Cedric in a tone that said they would have come to it sooner without the interruption. He started the video again.

The programme turned to Hess's life prior to the flight to Britain. His birth in Egypt in 1894, the son of a prosperous German wholesale merchant. Boarding-school in Germany and then business school in Switzerland, until the First World War. Distinguished service on the Western Front and in the Rumanian campaign. Towards the end of the war, the Imperial Flying Corps. A studio picture showed him in pilot's uniform, a young man of striking good looks, with the square facial structure and piercing eyes familiar in later shots, yet without the crazed stare of the Nuremberg picture.

Germany's defeat and the humiliating terms of Versailles

were documented with newsreel footage of the generals and politicians moving jerkily in and out of meetings. Hess, along with many of his generation, had enlisted in the *Freikorps*, a right-wing volunteer movement, and he was wounded fighting on the streets of Munich. In 1920, he joined a new extreme right-wing party who wore swastika armbands and were led by Adolf Hitler.

Predictably, Hitler was presented as one of the two major influences on Hess's political life. The other was a professor at Munich University, where Hess had enrolled in the same year. Karl Haushofer, a portly, moustached figure, had founded the new subject of Geopolitics.

More stills from the archives showed Hitler leading the Nazis in Munich in the twenties, attempting the unsuccessful Beer-Cellar *Putsch* of 1923 and serving his prison sentence in the relative comfort of Landsberg Castle, where there were tablecloths and freshly-cut flowers. Hess had managed to escape after the *Putsch* and hide in the Haushofer home for several weeks, but shrewdly decided to give himself up and join his leader in Landsberg. There, he had strengthened the friendship by acting as secretary and typist, actually typing much of *Mein Kampf* as Hitler dictated it.

At this point in the programme, an Oxford history don was brought on to show how Professor Haushofer's geopolitics, notably his theory of *Lebensraum*, had influenced Hitler and *Mein Kampf*.

Jane's attention shifted from the screen to her fellow-investigators. Dick sat forward in total concentration, mentally plugged in like a computer terminal. He wouldn't miss a fact. Unlike Red, who had just anticipated her glance by sliding his eyes in her direction, running them slowly over her legs and upwards, and grinning lewdly until she stared him out.

She returned to the programme, by now tracing Hess's blind loyalty to the man he called *Mein Führer*. Hess, too, acquired new titles, first as Hitler's adjutant, then, in 1933, his deputy, the *Stellvertreter*.

The Nazi rise to power was illustrated by familiar footage of the Nuremberg rallies, with Hess always on the rostrum first, to raise the mass to a crescendo of chanting, his arm rigidly extended in the Nazi salute, and exultation gleaming in his eyes as he announced the Führer.

Away from the public stage, Hess was shown taking increasing responsibilities in government: for schools, universities and religious societies. He was seen with Hitler and Frick signing the Nuremberg laws, which set in motion the persecution of the Jewish race and led to the 1938 pogrom and, ultimately, the death camps. He was shown at the head of the *Ausland* organizations that strengthened ties with the twenty million Germans living abroad and, under cover of *Ausland*, the Nazi Fifth Columns.

Then the war, and, surprisingly, no major role for Hess. In 1938, Hitler had nominated a second Deputy, Hermann Göring. Hess, it was Delphically announced, was still the Führer's Deputy in his absence, but Göring was the Deputy in Berlin. As Head of the *Luftwaffe*, Göring was involved in the conduct of the war, while Hess was on the sidelines, watching others – the Generals, von Ribbentrop, even Martin Bormann – exert more influence on events.

Hess, the commentary went on to suggest, began to look for a way of re-establishing himself.

Suddenly the screen went blank.

'They get into speculation after this,' Cedric explained, putting the remote control unit aside. 'Hess is shown making the flight to England in a crazy one-man bid to do a peace deal.'

'Crazy in the sense of insane?' said Jane.

'Disturbed, anyway. A very dubious proposition,' added Cedric.

'That's the version I always took as gospel,' admitted Dick.

'You're in the majority, then.'

Red was giving Cedric an interested look. 'You don't go along with the theory that he was out of his mind? Have you seen the film they took at the Nuremberg Trials?'

'It's used in the programme.'

'If ever a guy looked bananas, it was Hess.'

'Only that was 1946, five years after the time we're talking about,' Cedric pointed out. 'Let's not leap ahead. Do you know what happened after he was arrested in Scotland?'

'He spent the rest of the war in Britain as a prisoner, didn't he?' said Jane.

'Right. In 1945, he was flown to Nuremberg to join the other Nazis on trial.'

'When did he start the sentence in Spandau?'

'18 July 1947, together with six others.'

'. . . who all got out years ago,' Dick added.

'True. He's been alone in Spandau since 1966. The others either served their time, like Albert Speer, or were released on medical grounds. Of the three sentenced to life imprisonment, Admiral Raeder was released in 1955 and Walther Funk in 1957. Hess is still waiting.'

Jane was trying to keep her emotions out of this, but she couldn't suppress an outraged sigh. 'If there were medical grounds for the others, surely when a man gets to the age of ninety . . .'

'. . . his health ain't so bad,' murmured Red.

'Can't you contribute anything but cheap asides?' Jane rapped back without even looking his way. 'He ought to be released on humanitarian grounds. That old man has been a prisoner since before you and I were born. He was locked up in England when the worst of the Nazi atrocities took place. And let's not forget the reason why he flew here.'

'Which was?' Cedric asked her, like a schoolmaster drawing out facts.

Jane gave an exasperated sigh. 'To stop the bloody war. He was on a mission of peace, wasn't he?'

'That's not disputed by anyone now,' Cedric agreed. 'In Britain in 1941, it was kept secret for fear of undermining morale, which, of course, is a mortal sin in time of war. The Government couldn't deny that Hess had landed and was in their custody, because the story had broken in a Scottish daily, but they said nothing about the peace mission.'

'What did the Nazis say about it?' asked Dick, professional in his pursuit of the story.

'They waited twenty-four hours, and when there was no news from Britain they issued a statement that Hess had taken a plane and was missing, adding that he had become mentally unstable.'

'So the stories of his madness were Nazi propaganda?'

'Which Britain didn't choose to deny,' added Cedric.

Red suddenly asked, 'What did Fleet Street make of all this? It was one hell of a story.'

'It was also wartime,' Cedric explained. 'Everything was censored. The fact of his coming filled the headlines when it was official, and after that the story was spiked for as long as the war lasted. We've had to piece it together from what people have said and written since. Millions of words. Every second chap you meet has a Hess story.'

'So hasn't it all been said?' Jane suggested.

'Would I have brought you here from Washington if it had?' Cedric picked up an ashtray and pressed his cigar-butt into it. Then he placed it on the table and sat back with his hands locked under his chin in the pose he habitually adopted in crucial editorial meetings. 'Let's address ourselves to the crux of this matter: why is Rudolf Hess still a prisoner in Spandau forty-three years after his flight to Britain? The stock response in the West is to blame the Russians, but is it quite so simple as that? You heard Wolf Rüdiger Hess suggest otherwise.'

'OK, let's have it,' Dick turned to Red. 'You were there. What was your impression? Does Hess's son know something the rest of the world doesn't?'

Red shifted his position on the window-seat and took out a cigarette. He wasn't so comfortable, Jane observed, when questions were put directly to him. 'You mean has his old man told him something? Not a chance. Every meeting they have is monitored by all four commandants.'

'Someone else could have given him information,' Dick persisted. 'There are plenty of people who would like to see Hess given some mercy.'

'Plenty,' Red conceded. 'Human rights campaigners, churchmen, lawyers, people who actually participated in the Nuremberg Trials, All Party Committees of the House of Commons, successive German Chancellors – but what happens? *Niet.* The Russians won't agree. They have twenty million war dead to stiffen their resolve. Besides which, they like to keep their toehold in the West. The first thing they do when their tour of duty begins in Spandau is to erect their telecommunications antennae on the roof of the administration block. They even insisted on mounting a full guard – every watchtower – when Hess was out of the place, in hospital.'

Cedric had listened patiently to this exchange. Now he commented, 'All this is undeniable, but it doesn't tell us where the Western governments really stand on this issue. In 1970, the possibility was raised of saying to hell with the Russians, let's release Hess when it's our turn to guard him. The answer of Lord Chalfont, then Minister of State at the Foreign Office, was that the British Government wouldn't contemplate setting Hess at liberty without Russian consent because it would mean breaking solemn international obligations.'

'We break them when it suits us,' commented Red.

'If the will was there, we could release him tomorrow,' said Cedric. 'Does anyone really believe it would be the start of World War Three?'

There was silence as Cedric's remark sank in. He took another cigar from his pocket and lit it ostentatiously, taking stock of the effect of what he had said so far.

Dick Garrick cleared his throat. 'I'm not entirely clear about this, Cedric. Are you implying that the British have their own reason for wanting to keep Hess in Spandau?'

'Yes.' Cedric blew smoke at the ceiling.

'Presumably you have some evidence?'

Cedric nodded.

'But not enough to print?'

Cedric took time to watch the smoke disperse. 'I would prefer to have more.' He reached for one of the books on the table in front of him. 'This curious little volume is Exhibit One. *The Case of Rudolf Hess: A Problem in Diagnosis and Forensic Psychiatry.* It was published just after the war, in 1947. The editor was Brigadier J.R. Rees, the British Army's chief psychiatrist, and there were seven other contributors, all doctors and psychiatrists who attended Hess during his detention in Britain. The purpose of the book –' Cedric opened it and found the quote he wanted – 'is to show *to as wide a public as possible the considerable abnormality of a man whose influence on world history has been marked.*' He turned to another page. 'The Brigadier's conclusion is that: *Hess is a man of unstable mentality and has almost certainly been like that since adolescence. In technical language I should, on my present acquaintanceship, diagnose him as a psychopathic personality of the schizophrenic type.*'

Red gave a long, low whistle.

Cedric continued, 'The book gives numerous instances of Hess's strange behaviour, persistent fantasies that he was being drugged or poisoned, the frequent rejection of food, periodic loss of memory and two attempts at suicide.'

'Suicide? Genuine attempts?' asked Dick.

'What did he do?' asked Jane.

'The first incident was at Mytchett Place, near Aldershot, where he was held for a year. It happened within a month of his arrival in Britain. He called the doctor in the night, rushed him as he came in and threw himself over the banisters. He broke a leg. The second occasion was in 1945, at Maindiff Place, near Abergavenny, where he spent the rest of the war. He managed to obtain a bread-knife and stabbed himself in the chest, but it was not a deep wound. There must be doubts whether either was a genuine attempt at suicide.'

'So was he really off his head?' asked Red.

'That's the message in the book.' Cedric's flat response was like a gauntlet thrown down.

There was a pause before Dick said tentatively, 'But there's evidence to the contrary?'

Cedric nodded. 'From some pretty impressive sources. Winston Churchill was no psychiatrist, I admit, but as Prime Minister he was presumably getting reliable information. In a statement he prepared for the House of Commons – it was never read, but it's in the Public Record Office – he wrote – ' Cedric reached for a clipboard – '*He is reported to be perfectly sane and apart from the injury to his ankle in good health.* That was soon after Hess arrived, of course. Then four months later, in September 1941, Churchill asked Lord Beaverbrook to visit Hess at Mytchett Place and find out what he could.'

'Beaverbrook, the newspaper baron?' asked Jane.

'He was in the War Cabinet, and as close to Churchill as anyone,' Cedric threw out tersely, wanting to move on to other things. 'Let me tell you about Mytchett Place. It was an MI5 establishment, the headquarters of the Field Security Police. With MI5 in charge, Beaverbrook's visit was a bizarre occasion. They used assumed names for the benefit of the concealed shorthand-typist taking down the conversation.

46

Beaverbrook called himself Dr Livingstone and Hess was given the name Jonathan. Hess told his story and outlined his peace plan and Beaverbrook went back to report to Churchill. The PM asked, "Is he mad?" and the Beaver answered, "Certainly not. Hess talks quite sanely and rationally. He may have unusual ideas on health matters, but he is not mad."'

'So what was going on?' asked Dick.

'In Mytchett Place? Plenty.'

To ease them over another of Cedric's pregnant pauses, Red said, 'We're all ears.'

Cedric gave a rare smile. 'So were MI5. There were hidden microphones under the floor and in the chimney of Hess's quarters. In the thirteen months he was there, he underwent a series of interrogations and psychiatric examinations. He had to eat his meals in the company of German-speaking intelligence officers. He is reported to have shown symptoms of paranoia, but who wouldn't have? His complaints that his food was drugged may have seemed outrageous to fair-minded British folk in the 1940s, but knowing as much as we now know about the methods of the security services, can we be sure he was mistaken?' Cedric leaned forward in his chair. 'And can we say with any certainty that his lapses of memory were not induced?'

Jane had followed the trend of Cedric's argument with growing unease. She sensed that she was being led into making assumptions that were inimical to her deeply-held convictions. She dug in her heels. 'Induced? But why?'

'Because there may have been things our people wanted to wipe out of his memory.'

Jane frowned. 'Cedric, that's highly speculative.'

Cedric picked up the Rees book again and opened it at the front. 'Then I think you'll be interested in the statement at the front of the Brigadier's book. Apparently, Hess was asked to give his consent to publication, and he wrote a kind of foreword.'

'Hess did?'

'It's reproduced here in German, on prison notepaper from Nuremberg, with Hess's signature below it, and there's a translation.'

'He agreed to write a foreword to a book that claimed he was a psychopathic personality?' said Dick in amazement.

'Not only that, but he states that he welcomes its publication,' Cedric looked down to pick out the relevant words, '... *because one day it will be regarded as supplementary proof of the fact that in some hitherto unknown manner people can be put into a condition which resembles that which can be obtained through a hypnosis leaving its after-effects (post-hypnotic suggestion) – a condition in which the persons concerned do everything that is suggested to them, under the elimination of their own will, presumably without their being conscious of it.*'

'Brainwashing,' said Red.

Jane gave him a pitying look and said, 'You do have a flair for the melodramatic.'

He gave her a dazzling smile. 'That's why I'm in journalism, love.'

She turned to Dick. 'What do you say? Do you believe a word of this?'

He answered thoughtfully, 'Doesn't it come down to whether he was really mad or not? If he was, these suspicions of his are just a symptom of the condition. If he was sane, we ought to ask what MI5 were up to, and why.'

Jane asked Cedric, 'Is there any evidence whatsoever that they used drugs or hypnosis?'

He nodded. 'The book is categorical about one occasion. On 7 May 1944, at Maindiff, he was injected with the drug Evipan and interrogated in the post-narcotic stage for an hour and a quarter.'

There was a moment's puzzled silence.

'What about?' asked Dick.

'Details of the past.'

'Three years after he arrived in Britain?' said Jane in a high note of disbelief. 'Hadn't they got all the information he could give by that time?'

Red said, 'They wanted to find out how much he had forgotten.'

'Precisely.' A look of gratitude amounting almost to smugness spread over Cedric's features. 'This was 1944, when the D-Day landings were in prospect and Hitler's fortunes were fading. The end of the war was not impossible to contemplate. Some time in the future, Hess would be put on trial. In the spotlight of a show trial, what might he say about his reasons for flying to Britain?'

'What you're about to suggest is that the true reason would have embarrassed this country,' said Jane.

'I'm about to suggest we adjourn and prepare for dinner.' Cedric peered around the shadowy interior. 'My impression is that you need to think over what we've discussed so far. Shall we meet again for drinks in an hour?'

11

Red heaved his wicker case onto the bed and loosened the rope that held it together. He swung the lid open and looked inside, deciding what to wear for dinner. He hadn't brought a suit. There was a short-sleeved shirt with black and white stripes that he had acquired when the Harlem Globetrotters had come to Berlin, and the players were horsing around, throwing referee shirts to the crowd and inviting them on court to confuse the officials. Worn under his leather jacket, it usually got him into the less exclusive Berlin nightclubs, where he acquired his complimentary teeshirts. He was not much seen in the men's outfitters of the city.

He gave the shirt a sniff and a shake and dropped it on the bed. With that sartorial decision made, he stripped off his yellow teeshirt, socks, cords and pants and turned on the shower. It was the sort that you could adjust to a concentrated jet that massaged your back and shoulders. He stepped under it and sampled the pleasurable sensation. It didn't come up to the tiny fingers of a Vietnamese masseuse, but it was enought to cause a moment's reflection on the vagaries of a life that provided Cedric with showers like these in his guest bedrooms and himself with a lime-encrusted bath in a Berlin tenement.

After stepping out, he discovered the purpose of the sliding glass panel, which he had left open, seeing no cause for modesty. The bathroom floor was awash. More personally inconvenient, so were his clean socks and pants. He reached for a towel, rubbed himself dry and dropped it onto the floor with two others to minimise the possibility of damp ceilings downstairs. Then he padded into the bedroom to see if by some genius of foresight he had packed some spares. He had not.

He would borrow some. Cedric had mentioned that Dick Garrick was also in the end cottage. 'Ginge', as Red had privately named Dick, looked the sort who packed spares of

50

everything and would get positive satisfaction out of coming to the aid of a less organized fellow-guest. Some movements were apparent in the adjoining room, so Red rapped on the connecting door and said, 'Dick?'

There was no reply. Presumably, Ginge was in the shower and couldn't hear.

The key was on Red's side of the door, so he turned it, opened the door and put his head round. He was right that the shower was running, but he was not right about the occupant – unless Ginge had just stepped out of a pair of pink knickers in the middle of the floor.

Red called, 'Sorry, love. My mistake.' And closed the door and turned the key.

He lifted the cover off the bed, draped it around him and went along the passage to the door of the other guest room, which Ginge opened at once. He had a radio going, with some sports commentary in French. He had already showered and changed. He was very obliging, opening a drawer to let Red make his selection from a tidy stack of underclothes.

'I expect you didn't get much time to pack, having to fix your flight and everything,' he said companionably.

'Right on,' said Red as he dropped the bedspread and slipped on a pair of black jockey briefs and some grey socks. 'These'll do fine. I'll replace them as soon as I can.'

'Don't bother.'

'D'you smoke? I'll let you have some Duty-Free.'

'Actually I don't.'

'Wise man. What's your tipple? Beer?'

'Not really. I'm quite happy with mints.'

Red was not relating too successfully to Ginge.

Swinging the bedspread over his shoulder, he returned to his room.

He checked the bathroom and noted with satisfaction that the towels had soaked up most of the water. He retrieved the wet clothes, wrung them out and hung them over the shower framework. As he stepped back into the bedroom, a movement attracted his attention. The handle of the connecting door was being turned. He crept fast across the room and unlocked the door.

51

It opened slowly and a whiff of some musky perfume wafted in. Still dressed only in jockey briefs and socks, Red backed out of sight until Jane was inside, and then said, 'Looking for something special, darling, or just visiting?'

Jane had put on a dress of white wild silk. Her lipgloss was several shades deeper than it had been before. She let her eyes travel swiftly and clinically over Red's mainly naked physique. 'I didn't know you were in here. I thought I heard you speaking to Dick.'

'You did.'

'I wanted to check whether the door was locked,' she explained. 'You know how it is in a strange room.'

'Too true, love,' Red agreed.

Jane gave him a cool look and said, 'Sorry I didn't knock first.'

'No sweat, darling.'

She tensed a fraction. 'I don't care to be patronised, thank you.'

He grinned disarmingly. 'That's all right. I'm liberated. You can call me darling whenever you want.'

'All I want just now, Mr Goodbody . . .' she slid another disinterested glance over his torso '. . . if that *is* your name, is to have this key on my side of the door.' She took it out of the lock and held it in her open palm.

'Whatever you desire, miss,' said Red with a suggestion of servility in the voice, although his eyes belied it.

Jane put the key firmly into its new slot, stepped back into her room and closed the door.

Red weighed the conversation in his mind, and decided she was right: it was quits. He liked militant birds. They fought like hell and fucked like crazy.

12

One claim of Cedric's that nobody disputed that evening was that his housekeeper was a marvellous cook. The aroma of roast duck had penetrated to the room where drinks were taken and stimulated the guests' gastric juices long before the dish arrived on the dining room table. Cedric announced over the watercress soup that he would not be returning to the main business of the evening until the coffee was served, so the conversation flitted from the delights and drawbacks of life in the country to the danger of muggings in London and New York to the latest horror stories of press take-overs.

But the time arrived when the raspberry gateau was taken away, the coffee-jug deposited in the centre of the round dining-table, and the liqueurs served. Cedric reached for his cigar-box.

'Shall we return to Herr Hess?' he suggested. 'The Nuremberg Trials.'

'November, 1945, to October, 1946,' contributed Dick from his fund of facts, regardless of how smug he sounded.

Cedric went on, 'You may imagine the shock his appearance caused when he was flown in. After four years and a few months in British hands, his physique was emaciated. We've already talked about his skull-like face and staring eyes. In view of his alleged mental instability, the question arose whether he was fit to stand trial. The British were asked to supply a report, so three eminent authorities were appointed to the task. An interesting trio: our friend, Brigadier Rees; Lord Moran, Churchill's personal physician; and Dr George Riddoch, a consulting neurologist. They reported that Hess was technically a psychopathic personality, that he had a delusion of poisoning and other paranoid ideas.' Cedric pulled some notes from his pocket. 'We don't all have infallible memories,' he said with a sly smile at Dick, before starting to read: *At the moment he is not insane in the strict sense. His loss of memory will not entirely interfere*

with his comprehension of the proceedings, but it will inter-
fere with his ability to make his defence, and to understand
details of the past which arise in evidence.

'They wanted it both ways,' commented Red.

'Meaning precisely what?' Jane demanded, determined not
to let easy assumptions go unchallenged.

'It's obvious, love. He was sane enough to face the trial and
be hanged or locked away for life, but if he said anything out
of line, he was bonkers.'

She said without looking at him, 'That's simplistic in the
extreme.'

'Why do you think the Brigadier's book was written? Eight
doctors don't go into print to show that a patient is abnormal
without pressure from somewhere.'

'It was published in 1947 – after the Nuremberg Trials
were over.'

'Yes, but it wasn't *written* in 1947, was it? It was part of
the cover-up. You can bet there were typed copies circulating
in Nuremberg.'

Jane withdrew from the contest by turning to Cedric. 'Tell
us what actually happened at the trial.'

'Well, there's no doubt that Hess was the star turn, despite
the presence of figures like Göring and Ribbentrop. His
haggard, hollow-eyed look is the lasting image of
Nuremberg. In court, he ignored most of the proceedings,
switching off his earphones and preferring to read a book.
Sometimes he said, "I remember nothing." He had brought
with him from England twists of paper containing scraps of
food he alleged were used to poison him.'

'Paranoia,' murmured Jane.

'His counsel claimed repeatedly that he was unfit to plead,'
Cedric went on, referring to his notes. 'To quote, *He knows*
neither events which have happened in the past nor the
persons who were associated with him in the past. But the
report from the English doctors was upheld, and indeed
supported by the American and Soviet psychiatrists who
examined him.

'Then, sensationally, after weeks of legal argument, Hess
decided to make a statement. He told the court he had
feigned amnesia for tactical reasons, and he was fit to stand

trial. That night, he submitted to questions from the American psychiatrist, Major Kelley. This is important, so forgive me for referring to my notes again. Major Kelley writes: *He claimed that his memory now extended throughout his entire life, but on persistent questioning indicated that there were still a number of things on which he was not quite clear and for which his memory was still faulty.'*

'Like the real reason why he flew to Britain in 1941?' suggested Dick.

'That's pure speculation, and you know it,' said Jane, rounding on him as fiercely as she had on Red.

'Fine, have it your way,' Dick offered, with a shrug that left no doubt what he believed.

'After that piece of drama,' Cedric resumed, 'Hess took no interest in the trial for months, until the opportunity came to make a final statement to the court. He launched into a long, rambling speech, castigating his co-defendants for making shameless utterances about the Führer, and comparing the proceedings to the pre-war Soviet show trials, when defendants were induced to accuse themselves in an astonishing way. He finished with an unreserved tribute to Hitler as the greatest son his country had brought forth in its thousand-year history, and said, "I do not regret anything."'

'Hardly the way to the judges' hearts,' commented Dick.

'They found him guilty on two of the four counts,' Cedric said. 'Making preparations for war and, rather ironically, conspiring against the peace.'

'After the way he treated the court, he was fortunate to get away with a life sentence,' said Dick.

'Depends how you look at it,' Red remarked. 'Some people might think the Nazis who were strung up got a better deal than Hess.'

'What happened when he got to Spandau?' Jane asked. 'Did he remain unrepentant?'

'Oh, yes. Still is, as far as I know. He was the most difficult of the prisoners there. Disliked work and exercise. Often refused to eat or get out of bed. Frequently complained that he was ill. The inside story has been written by the fellow you saw briefly in the BBC news story, Eugene Bird, who was the US Commandant in Spandau.'

'*The Loneliest Man in the World*,' said Dick, on cue.

'Required reading?' asked Don.

'Obligatory.'

'And the rest of that stack in the other room?'

'Every one.'

'I need more coffee. It's going to be a long night.'

Jane leaned forward to prise more information from Cedric. 'So if Hess's memory was impaired, how can anyone know the truth about his mission? Did anyone else know what he was planning, or was it a spur of the moment thing?'

Dick said, 'Have you any idea of the logistics of flying from Augsburg to Scotland in a Messerschmitt?'

Cedric took a sip of cognac. 'Right. Let's face it, this was one of the most audacious schemes of the entire war. It isn't in the German temperament to trust to luck. According to Hess's defence lawyer at Nuremberg, the decision to fly to Britain was taken as early as June 1940, immediately after the fall of France.'

'Almost a year before it happened?' said Jane.

'Hess went to Willi Messerschmitt, found the most suitable aircraft and made over thirty flights from Augsburg. He had the Me 110 modified for solo flying, and had extra fuel tanks fitted. Meanwhile, secret moves were made to contact people in Britain.'

Cedric removed some documents from his pocket. 'These are translations in photostat form of letters and memoranda written by Hess and his closest friends in the autumn of 1940. They are on public record in the National Archives in Washington, where the German foreign policy papers are held. Remember Karl Haushofer, Hess's university professor? He's involved in this delicate process, and so, more actively, is his son, Albrecht, who was closer in age to Hess. He was an academic like his father – intelligent, well-travelled, critical of many aspects of the Nazi system and, above all, committed to achieving peace.

'Here's Albrecht reporting on a two-hour meeting with Hess on 8 September 1940: *I was immediately asked about the possibilities of making known to persons of importance in England Hitler's serious desire for peace. It was quite clear that the continuance of the war was suicidal for the white* race. *Even with complete success in Europe, Germany was not in a position to take over inheritance of the Empire. The Führer had not wanted to see the Empire destroyed and did not want it even today. Was there not somebody in England who was ready for peace?'*

'Hitler's serious desire for peace?' repeated Jane with heavy irony.

'Would you mind if I continued?' Cedric mildly admonished her. 'Albrecht comes up with a few names. He says, *I am of the opinion that those Englishmen who have property to lose . . . would be readiest to talk peace.* He mentions Sir Samuel Hoare, the British Ambassador in Madrid, and Lord Lothian, in Washington. Finally, . . . *the young Duke of Hamilton, who has access at all times to all important persons in London, even Churchill and the King.* Hess says he will consider the matter and send word in case Albrecht is to take steps. Interestingly, Albrecht records his strong impression that the conversation was conducted with the prior knowledge of the Führer.'

'But that doesn't necessarily mean Hitler knew about the plan to fly to Britain,' Jane pointed out. 'They were just discussing peace feelers.'

'True.'

'So Hess plumps for the Duke of Hamilton,' said Dick. 'Why Hamilton?'

It was Jane who supplied the answer. 'We just heard. The Germans thought the idea of peace would appeal to the property-owning class.'

'Which accounts for your invitation here,' Red slipped in. 'Our expert on the idle rich.'

Jane turned to Cedric. 'Is that really why you asked me?'

He drew on his cigar and answered with circumspection, 'It's not the only reason. But let's follow it through the way it happened, shall we? I ought to mention that Albrecht Haushofer was on familiar terms with the Duke. They'd met in Germany and in England on various occasions before the war. Albrecht had actually stayed at Dungavel House. Hess now asked Albrecht to make contact with the Duke. It was to be done discreetly, by letter, through a friend of the Haushofers, an elderly Englishwoman living in neutral

Lisbon. Hamilton was to be invited to Lisbon to talk to Albrecht.'

He paused. 'The plan misfired. The letter was intercepted by the British censor and passed to MI5. Hamilton wasn't given a sight of it for many months, in fact until March 1941.'

'They were vetting him,' put in Dick.

'Presumably. They suggested he made the trip to Lisbon with their blessing, to find out what it was all about, but he stalled. In effect, he was being recruited as an MI5 agent, and he asked for certain safeguards to be built into the arrangement. Besides, how would he explain his delay in answering the letter? It was still under discussion on 10 May, when Hess took off from Augsburg.'

Red was frowning as he asked, 'Are you telling us Hess had nothing back from the Duke and still went ahead with the mission? That doesn't strike me as good German organization.'

'It may surprise you, then, that this was Hess's fourth attempt to make the flight. He had been trying since December. Technical problems or bad weather caused him to turn back each time.'

'It doesn't square with all the preparation,' Red persisted. Would the Deputy Führer of Germany fly into enemy territory and throw himself on the mercy of some guy he'd never even met?'

'That's what happened,' murmured Jane.

There was an affirmative grunt from Cedric. 'Red's right. It's naive to suggest that Hess didn't have other information to act on. He had his own intelligence agency, the *Verbindungsstab*, sending back reports from Britain and other places. Anglo-German contacts were secretly maintained in several neutral countries besides Portugal. No, he wouldn't have come without some strong signal from a British source. The indications are that it was an acutely sensitive one.'

'We're back to the brainwashing,' said Red.

Cedric nodded. 'I think MI5 did their best to scrub it from his memory at Mytchett Place.'

'But you have a whisper who it was?'

58

Cedric eased his way around the question. 'Consider what happened after Hess parachuted down. He gave a false name and asked to see the Duke of Hamilton. When it was fixed, he insisted on speaking to the Duke without anyone else present. According to the report that Hamilton later wrote for Churchill, Hess claimed that his arrival was proof of his sincerity and Germany's desire for peace. He said Hitler was convinced that Germany would win the war, but he wanted to avoid unnecessary slaughter. Hess then asked the Duke to call together certain leading members of the Conservative Party to negotiate a peace, but the Duke told him there was only one party in Britain now, and that was the Coalition. Finally, Hess asked the Duke to contact the King, to secure a "parole" for him.'

'At what point did Winston Churchill come into it?' asked Dick. 'Presumably *he* wasn't on Hess's list of leading Conservatives.'

Red laughed. 'You've got to be kidding! The Nazis wanted Winnie out on his arse.'

'A fair summary,' Cedric agreed. 'Hess made it clear that Hitler would not negotiate with Churchill. He counted on the right wing of the Party forcing Churchill out of office when they were offered a peace settlement.'

'Where did things go wrong?' asked Dick.

'Right at the start,' answered Cedric. 'He was banking on the Duke of Hamilton's help.'

'He was on to a loser there?' suggested Red.

Cedric shrugged. 'It must have made sense from the German point of view. The Duke had been a Conservative Member of Parliament until just before the war and presumably knew the people in the Party who might favour a settlement.'

'You told us Albrecht Haushofer was friendly with the Duke,' Jane challenged him. 'He must have believed he would fall in with the plan. He must have had some grounds –'

Red cut in: 'It wouldn't have mattered if the Duke wore a brown shirt and jackboots. He was useless to Hess once MI5 had intercepted that letter.'

Jane was galled by the interruption, but she had to admit that Red had seized on the vital point. His thinking was sharper than hers, and probably anyone else's, and she was going to have to find a way of responding to him without rising to the bait every time. The mix of boorishness and dynamism, arrogant male chauvinism and sexual attractiveness was difficult for her to handle.

Cedric said evenly, 'Shall we keep to the known facts? After his meeting with Hess, the Duke drove to Turnhouse Airport, phoned the Foreign Office and asked for Sir Alexander Cadogan, the top civil servant there, to motor out to Northolt and meet him on a matter of the utmost urgency. He wasn't believed. The secretary who took the call believed it was a hoax. Then, by one of those curious quirks of history, Winston Churchill's Private Secretary, Jock Colville, walked into the room and overheard the conversation. In minutes, Churchill was informed, and Hamilton was flying south to report to him in person.'

'Mission aborted,' remarked Red.

A silence settled over the empty coffee cups. Don fiddled with the edge of his moustache. Jane studied her finger-nails. Dick stared, frowning, into space.

Red leaned confidentially towards Cedric. 'Are you going to tell them, or shall I?'

13

At one end of the sports-hall in Charlottenburg, West Berlin, two mixed-doubles pairs were playing table-tennis, and excited cries were coming from the benches at the side. Erich Ritter and Heidrun Kassner were practically unbeatable, but they still trained as if they were fighting for their places on the team. They had been at the table almost two hours with the club second pair, Frank and Renate, and the play was fast and intelligent. At this stage of the evening, they weren't scoring, but simply practising shots.

'Time to stop, I think,' Frank appealed to the others. He had a job as a drummer in a strip club, and liked to be away by 9.30.

'Not yet,' said Heidrun flatly. 'Erich's return of service is still rising too high.' She appealed to the benches. 'Yes?' She was popular with the club juniors, because she knew them all by name and took an interest in their progress, often sparing time to coach them. She'd come up from the juniors herself, made the first team as a singles player, and only changed to mixed doubles for the sake of the club, to strengthen one of its obvious weaknesses. The pairing of Erich with Renate had never been dependable. Naturally, there had been some red-eyed looks from Renate when Heidrun had displaced her, but it had been obvious that Erich deserved a better partner.

'No,' Renate declared, affirming it by laying her bat on the table. 'That's enough for me, too.'

Erich picked up his tracksuit top and turned to Heidrun, who was signalling her obstinacy in the way she was bouncing the ball on her bat. 'A coffee before I see you home?'

'What's the hurry?' asked Heidrun off-handedly. 'I fancy a swim. Renate, would you care for a swim?'

Renate gave her a long look. Everyone knew that Erich was hopelessly in love with Heidrun. He waited for her each evening outside the coffee-shop where she worked as a waitress. 'That's not a bad idea. Why don't you join us, Erich?'

But something had snapped. Erich reddened and said, 'No, thanks. I'm off.'

Frank offered him a lift, and the men left together.

There were times when Renate found Heidrun's treatment of Erich insufferable. When she had taken him over as her partner, it was all kisses and clasped hands and would you like to take me home, darling? Now that they were the regular first-team pair, she had switched off the sweet-talk, only resorting to it when Erich showed signs of losing interest in table-tennis.

As the two girls showered after their swim, Renate found herself doubting whether Heidrun had ever actually taken Erich to bed. She had no other lovers, but she was undeniably attractive – curvy, clear-skinned, big-breasted, all the things guys lusted over. Standing there now, massaging shampoo into her short, silver-streaked hair, Heidrun was clearly untroubled about Erich's leaving. Sport apparently gave her all the fulfilment she wanted. If those shapely thighs ever parted for Erich, she'd probably still be going on about his return of service.

'Something amusing you?' Heidrun suddenly demanded.

Renate reddened and turned away.

Heidrun shook her hair. 'Is this how you get your kicks – grinning at girls in showers?'

Insulted, Renate said, 'There's no need to be coarse. This is free Berlin. I'm allowed to smile if I wish.'

Heidrun stepped out of the shower and picked up her towel. 'It might not be a bad thing if people this side of the Wall were more serious.'

'They have reason to be serious on the other side,' Renate replied.

'Yes, but they beat the world at sport.'

14

Red's casual revelation that he was somehow in collusion with Cedric had made Jane coldly angry. Just when she was making efforts to modify her reactions to Red, she had to face the possibility that he was Cedric's sidekick. If he asked her to write the woman's angle on Hess, she'd bloody resign. It was so unjust. There she was, thinking she'd earned the right to be on an investigative team and lapping up the boss's praise, reciting her pieces like a good girl, when all the time she was way down the ladder. She was certain of one thing: she wasn't going to let any of them, least of all Red Goodbody, spin her around and make a fool of her. She'd find out what was trumps and then they could all watch out.

Cedric stood waiting for his guests to settle in the room where they had first met. 'I neglected to tell you at the beginning that Red has done some preliminary work,' he said without preamble. 'I should have mentioned it when we looked at the BBC news item on Hess's ninetieth birthday. Red was on the spot in Berlin, so I asked him to follow up the statements attributed to Hess's son.'

'Blaming the Western powers?' Dick prompted.

'Yes. And I also caught something on ITN. Their coverage of the birthday was briefer, but even more intriguing. They quoted Wolf Hess as saying that his father was being kept prisoner because he knew too much about British efforts to make peace with Germany in 1941.'

'*British* efforts?'

Cedric gave a nod. 'That's what they said. I obtained a transcript, just to be sure. This was a new angle so far as I was concerned, and I wanted to know more, so I asked Red to follow it up.' With a wave, Cedric invited a report from his Berlin correspondent, who had given up his window-seat to squat on the carpet with his back against the wall. Relieved to step out of the spotlight, Cedric picked up his cognac and sat down.

'You want to know what I got from Wolf Rüdiger?' Red asked without looking up. 'He says there were secret peace initiatives between Nazi Germany and Britain. Our people knew in advance that Hess was coming. Hess came over expecting to negotiate with the War Cabinet.'

'If that's true, it's dynamite,' said Dick. 'Britain *expected* Hess?'

Cedric must have been gratified. His team exhibited all the symptoms of shock, incredulity and craving for more information that sell a newspaper in millions. Dick fired a volley of questions at Red. Jane was pink with disbelief at this challenge to the legend of defiant Britain going it alone.

'Where did Wolf Hess get this information?' she pressed Red. 'From his father?'

'He's not saying.'

'Why?'

Red gave a shrug. 'Prison regulations. Hess still wants out, doesn't he? If you ask me, it comes from someone else. Hess isn't given a chance to talk about the war.'

'So who do you put your money on?' asked Dick.

'Maybe someone feeling angry about the way Hess has been treated.'

'But is the source reliable?'

'Wolf Rüdiger said he has proof.'

'Proof? Do you believe him?'

Red was non-committal. 'It's a new card to play, isn't it?'

'He won't say any more, off the record, I mean?'

Red shook his head.

'Cedric, it's bloody nonsense!' Jane said in a rush. 'Britain was in no mood for peace in 1941. It was all-out war, for God's sake! The country had come through Dunkirk and the Battle of Britain. Churchill said victory at all costs, victory in spite of all terror –'

'Don't quote Churchill at me, Jane. I was around at the time,' Cedric told her sharply, and then softened it by adding, 'even though I look so well-preserved. It wasn't all good old Winnie and knees-ups in the shelters, you know.'

Methodically, Cedric took his scalpel to the legend of a people united in the great war effort. He described the effects of months of night bombing by the Luftwaffe. He spoke of

64

the homeless, refugees and evacuees, of looting and tragedy in overcrowded shelters. He destroyed the myth of a dedicated workforce with the information that over a million working days were lost in industrial stoppages during 1941, and absenteeism doubled in the munitions factories.

Jane was restive. She was being manoeuvred into something alien to her thinking. 'All that may be true, Cedric, but the nation was solidly behind Churchill. There was no question of doing a deal with Hitler.'

Cedric shook his head. 'Churchill's credit wasn't so high as you make out, my dear. I can tell you from personal experience that those stirring speeches of his were greeted in at least one not untypical home with mild derision. You see, in 1941, he hadn't yet earned the right to undisputed leadership. He was rather a suspect politician.'

'People still wondered whether Chamberlain's way might have been better in the long run?' suggested Dick.

'I can tell you that many Conservatives still harboured resentment at the way Chamberlain had been ousted,' Cedric confirmed. 'What's more, we had a series of humiliating defeats abroad. In April of the year we're talking about, the British forces were swept out of Greece inside three weeks and out of Cyrenaica, by Rommel, in ten days. The Greek campaign was described as "another Winston lunacy" by Churchill's own military planners.'

'Hess certainly picked his moment to fly in,' said Dick.

'Too true. Three days before the Hess flight, Churchill faced a vote of confidence in the House of Commons, and took some flak from Lloyd George about the conduct of the war. The Commons backed Churchill handsomely, but the rift was there.'

'Not to mention the House of Lords,' added Dick.

Jane gave vent to an agitated sigh that said she was surrounded by bigots.

Cedric eyed her keenly, betraying concern. Clearly, he was uneasy at the prospect of one of his team out of sympathy with the others. If she was to be won round, it required a show of sensitivity from someone besides himself. Oddly, he decided that she might respond best to the least sensitive man in the room.

'Red,' he asked, 'do you think I'm wasting everybody's time?'

The answer from Red was not unhelpful. 'I'm still here, aren't I, Cedric?'

Jane pounced at once. 'But you're not convinced yet? You're not really convinced?' Her eyebrows peaked in anticipation.

Red grinned. 'I have my reputation to consider, don't I?'

Jane's posture relaxed a little. She glanced towards Red, then back to Cedric, and fingered a strand of her blonde hair.

'The plain truth is that none of us is totally convinced,' Cedric conceded. 'I've brought you together to investigate the story, to examine it, test it, probe for more evidence. To my knowledge, no other paper in the world has followed it up. OK, it's forty-three years on, but if there actually *was* a rebel group in this country doing deals with the Nazis, there must be people still alive who knew what was going on.'

'This is sensitive ground,' said Dick. 'A minefield.'

'But one hell of a story,' said Red.

Cedric hoisted himself upright and went round with the brandy.

'Would you care to give us a scenario?' Jane suggested to Red, with irony.

'I don't mind making a stab at it,' he offered. 'As I see it, the Nazis through 1940 and '41 are definitely looking for a deal with Britain. Hitler has conquered Western Europe and driven the British Army out of France, and now he has his sights set on Russia. Winston Churchill doesn't want to know about it, but he's new in the job and they reckon the British won't go along with all that stuff about blood, toil, tears and sweat. The Nazis get intelligence reports of some right-wing people who would like to ditch Churchill. Hess makes some soundings through his spies and gets encouraging noises back.'

'For which there's no evidence whatever,' put in Jane.

She stung Red into saying bitterly, 'For Christ's sake, you asked for a scenario, not a sworn statement.'

'Who were these people, then?'

'Big shots. We're not talking about a few eccentrics with Nazi leanings. These are establishment people. They have to be, else why weren't they exposed as traitors at the time? Why did MI5 erase them from Hess's memory?'

As no one responded, Red went on, 'So Hess devises this amazing plan to fly to Britain and make personal contact with these people behind Churchill's back. If they agree to ditch Churchill, Germany will offer them peace and guarantees about their property. That, or something like it, is the deal he offers the Duke of Hamilton on 11 May 1941. How am I doing, Cedric?'

'Carry on.'

'OK. Up to now, everything is shaping up, and then it all goes wrong. You see, Hess doesn't know that MI5 intercepted that letter to Hamilton. What can Hamilton do? He tries to get in touch with Sir somebody at the Foreign Office.'

'Sir Alexander Cadogan,' said Dick.

'Thanks. And by pure chance Churchill's private secretary comes in on the call. So it's curtains for Rudolf Hess. The whole plot is revealed to Churchill. A massive cover-up is ordered. Hess is handed over to the shrinks at Mytchett Place and soon forgets all about the people he came to meet. And just in case any of it comes back while he's at Nuremberg, Churchill's doctor and the Brigadier write that report saying his memory is unreliable.' Red stopped and folded his arms. 'Did I leave something out?'

Nobody was emboldened to answer. As he had promised, Red had made a stab, and it was a strong stab, rough, but close enough to the target to impress even Jane. As a journalist, she found the storyline, told in one piece, hard to resist.

So the silence was not a void. It was filled with thoughts of what needed to be done to test the truth of the story. Soon they would be talking assignments.

Dick gave Cedric a long look. 'But you still have something to tell us, haven't you?'

Their editor-in-chief declined to answer for a moment, self-indulgently holding back, mindful that his hold on the story had to be relinquished.

'There is something else, yes,' he admitted. 'Someone else. A possible contact.'

'Who is he?'

'That's the first problem. He wouldn't wish to be

identified. Used to work for MI5. Retired some time in the mid-seventies, so he's pretty old.'

'Is that the second problem?' asked Dick.

'No. The second problem is that he's a cantankerous old sod who may not tell you a thing if he doesn't like your face.'

'So it's a job for Jane,' said Red.

It was the nearest thing to a compliment she had heard from him and it infuriated her to realise that it pleased her. She didn't react.

Cedric shook his head. 'I think not. He has a chapter in his book on why women and homosexuals can't be trusted, and it gets up *my* nose.'

'He's in print, then?' said Dick.

Cedric winced in an exaggerated way. 'God, no! It'll never be published. It's the most turgid stuff imaginable. He offered us the first serial rights. Marched into my office one Monday morning with the manuscript. That's how I got to know him. It sounded promising. Ex-MI5 agent tells all.' He gave a hollow laugh. 'Bugger all. Not a single name worth mentioning. Everyone in it is coyly described as a personage, so you have a personage from the north, a personage of foreign origin, even an ecclesiastical personage. I asked him if he meant a personage from a parsonage, and he didn't see the joke, didn't see it at all. The shame of it is that he's prepared to *talk* pretty openly about personalities.'

'Hess?'

Cedric nodded at Dick. 'He claims to know the inside story.'

'Did you try to open him up?'

'It wasn't the moment,' answered Cedric. 'I was mainly concerned to explain why we couldn't publish his abysmal stuff.'

'Did he throw a fit?' asked Red.

'He expressed himself forcibly, and slammed the door as he left.'

'How do we follow that?'

Cedric held up his right hand and rubbed the thumb against the forefinger. 'He has an expensive lifestyle for a civil service pensioner.'

'So who gets the job?'

Cedric smiled. 'I'll tell you in the morning.'

15

Red entertained the house-party until after midnight with tales of the divided city. Not wishing to crack another bottle of brandy, Cedric had produced some six-packs of lager. By tacit consent, no more was said about Hess. Everyone needed a break to let Cedric's startling theories shake down, so Red talked vividly about the *Fluchthelfer*, the reckless characters who made a business of smuggling fugitives out of East Germany, sometimes for ideals, sometimes profit. The way he laughed off a suggestion that they were the Cold War heroes had the curious effect of revealing how closely he identified with them. Whilst not admitting to cross-border adventures of his own, he was vague about the way he had researched his highly original feature.

Jane was the first to leave the party, blaming the brandy for making her tired, and Dick moved off soon after, each of them taking one of the books about Hess which Cedric had thoughtfully distributed as bedtime reading. Eventually, Cedric left, muttering something about the bathroom. Red stretched out on the sofa for a last cigarette, and dozed.

When he stirred, it was 1.15 a.m. He stood up, picked up the book Cedric had left him, and on second thoughts put it down and picked up a lager instead, and made for the passage leading to the front door.

Outside, it was mild enough to let him take stock of the scene as he strolled towards the end cottage. He was amused to notice there were no lights at any of the windows; even Ginge was too tanked up to do the homework.

He let himself in, stripped and stepped into the shower, this time remembering to slide the door across. He was not too tired to enjoy the sensation of the cool jets striking his skin. He gave a thought to Jane, and the business earlier with the key of the connecting door. She amused him with her riding-school accent and Young Conservative opinions.

For all that, a bit of a feminist, he guessed. Not the sort who would muck out the stables for the riding-master.

Out of curiosity, when he was dry and ready for bed, he tried the handle of the connecting door. It was locked from the other side. Grinning, Red got into bed and was soon asleep.

Some hours later, he woke and it was light, that pale suggestion of dawn that he only ever expected to see when nature called him to the bathroom after a heavy night's drinking. Out in the woods, the rooks sounded like a peace demo. At least it wasn't in his head. With a sigh, he heaved himself out of bed.

While he was drinking to take the dryness off his throat, he was pretty sure he heard a click, followed by the creak of boards next door.

His thoughts were not at their most agile, but on the way back he decided to try the door again.

It opened. Jane was in bed on the other side of the room staring at him, apparently not in panic.

She said in her best county accent, 'Naked again, Mr Goodbody?'

Red answered truthfully, 'I sleep like this.'

Jane said, 'Snap,' and pulled aside the duvet.

16

Each time a statesman visits West Berlin and climbs the steps of the observation post at Potsdamer Platz to stare across the Wall and fifty metres of sand on the Eastern side, an image of the divided city is reinforced. Yet there is another strip of sand in Berlin that is rarely pictured, except in home movies and family albums. It has no barbed wire, mines, dog patrols, tank-traps, searchlights or watchtowers. It is the shoreline of the River Havel, some seven miles west of the city centre, running from north to south through broad areas of forest. In summer, Berliners flock there to bask and bathe along the east bank and beside the lakes.

Here, Heidrun Kassner had an appointment.

She took the 66 bus through the Grunewald Forest to Strandbad Wannsee, the largest and most developed of the Berlin beaches. As she stepped onto the promenade with its ice-cream vans and newspaper kiosks, a sense of guilt mingled with the curiosity she already felt. She was in forbidden territory. Days at the beach were prohibited to a serious sportswoman. All her time off work was scheduled for training and match practice. And she was not sure why it was necessary to come here.

She took off her trainers and jumped down to the beach among the sunbathers. The fine, dry sand was warm to the soles of her feet. In her blue teeshirt and white jeans, she was going to feel the heat if this went on for long. She made her way down to the water and rolled the jeans up to her calves. Then she took her bearings.

Wannsee is equipped with numerous wicker beach-chairs, each with a number painted on the side of the canopy. With a proper sense of order, they are ranged in rows along the beach. They are the most commodious public beach-chairs in Europe, two-seaters practically as big as beach-huts, with cushions, extending foot-rests and vast hoods with exotically-decorated linings.

Heidrun located the chair she had been told to find. It was occupied by a man in his fifties, silver-haired and in peacock blue shorts and white canvas sandals. He was leafing through a girlie magazine. He had two more on his lap. When Heidrun stopped by the chair, the man took off his sunglasses. She had met him before. His name was Kurt Valentin, and he was an East Berliner.

He remarked, 'You look hot, dressed up like that.'

'I can stand it.'

'Why don't you take off your shirt?'

'I don't wish to.'

'Look around you. Plenty of other women let the sun get to their breasts.'

She scuffed the sand with her foot. 'Is that why you chose to meet me here?'

He had grey eyes that took not a vestige of colour from the vivid sky. 'I heard about the unfortunate accident to your table-tennis partner.'

'Erich is a moron,' said Heidrun. 'You know how he broke his ankle? He got blind drunk the other night after training and fell down a hole in the road.'

'How long is he going to be out for?'

'At least six weeks.'

'And what do you propose to do about it?'

She gave Valentin a sharp glance. She could not understand the reason for his interest. He had never talked table-tennis to her before. 'I suppose I shall have to team up with the guy from the second pair. His partner won't like it, but what else can I do?'

'Who is he?'

'Frank Hennige.'

'Any good?'

'He slashes at anything that bounces high and his service is pitiful. Why do you want to know?'

'So losing Ritter is a serious blow?'

'You're not kidding,' said Heidrun irritably. She flopped down and made pits in the sand with her fists.

Valentin replaced his sunglasses and held out a bottle of Ambre Solaire. 'If you're worried about exposure, a light application of this will protect them.'

'I am not taking off my teeshirt.'

He moved smoothly back to the main topic. 'This sports club of yours. It apparently means a lot to you.'

'Of course,' answered Heidrun. 'I've put a lot into it.' A suspicion leapt into her mind. 'If you think you can tempt me across with better sports facilities, forget it. I may not be in sympathy with the system here, but it's my home, and I'm staying.'

Valentin raised an eyebrow. 'Have I ever suggested such a thing? You know that I have not.' He looked at his watch. 'Let's take a walk along the promenade. There's something I'd like you to see.'

He reached for her arm as he stood up, and continued to hold onto her. It was like being claimed by a sugar-daddy, and she resented it, but she didn't struggle. She knew he would say it was only to create an impression. If they had stayed much longer on the beach, he would have used the same ploy to get her to show her breasts to him. She would have done it, too, because actually she was afraid of him.

They climbed the steps and walked sedately along the promenade for a couple of minutes. She wondered if he was going to buy her a drink, but she doubted it. Their previous meetings had not been characterised by generosity. Probably he spent his expenses on the girlie magazines. The only bare breasts in East Berlin were in the Pergamon Museum.

'Do you hear anything familiar?' he asked her.

She listened through the shouts of the bathers and the children playing. 'It sounds like table-tennis.'

'Or ping-pong?' said Valentin, with a smile.

They presently saw three tables where play was in progress in the open air, just off the promenade. It was ping-pong stuff, for sure; small boys and giggling schoolgirls. A couple of guys were sitting on the edge of the promenade nearby, dangling their legs over the edge. They were speaking in English, with American accents. One of them had a good bat beside him.

'We're a little early,' said Valentin. 'We'll walk on for ten minutes and come back.'

'Why? I don't want a game here,' said Heidrun. 'I get plenty of practice.'

73

He tightened his grip on her arm and walked her past the tables.

A small crowd had collected around one of the tables when they returned, and the two Americans were playing. Heidrun was prepared for the fast, flashy stuff you expect from guys who fancy themselves as players, and one was dishing it up. He was the typical beach-bum who wanted everyone to know how brilliant he could be at any sport he cared to try – from surfing to throwing a frisbee – without, of course, really trying at all. He was barefoot, with tattered sawn-off jeans, copper medallion on a leather thong, long, sun-bleached hair fixed with a rubber band, and a cigarette in his free hand.

He was not the player he imagined himself to be. Certainly he was striking the ball hard and keeping it on the table, but only because the other player was setting it up for the smash.

'What do you think of him?' Valentin murmured in her ear.

'Not much.'

'And the other one?'

'I can't see him. Let's move to the other end.'

She instantly preferred what she saw. He was less flamboyant, meeting the ball with a variety of defensive shots, deliberately giving nothing back in aggression, though it was clear from the speed of his reactions that he could have switched to attack if he had wished. He was not even testing the beach-bum with artfully placed returns. He was using the play to practise dropping the ball across the net on a pre-selected spot. Naturally it flattered his opponent, but there was no question who was the player of class.

'He's better,' said Heidrun.

'How would he compare with Ritter?'

'I'd have to see him extended. The other one is rubbish.'

'Why don't you offer him a game?'

She turned to look at Valentin. 'Why should I? I don't know anything about him.'

'I can tell you a few things. His name is Cal Moody, and he doesn't belong to any table-tennis club.'

She continued to study Moody, trying to fathom why Valentin had been so eager for her to see him. From his short haircut, she guessed he was one of the US servicemen stationed in Berlin. It was light brown hair, with a slight wave. On his chest the hair formed small, tight curls. He had pale blue eyes without the dreamy look that often went with them.

Valentin said, 'He's probably better than the other Charlottenburg man.'

'Frank Hennige? Yes, very likely,' Heidrun responded. 'But he might not be any use at doubles.'

'Is Hennige?'

There was a fifteen-minute limit on each session. The Americans went through theirs without scoring a game. Heidrun joined in the applause when they left the table. Her throat was dry with nervousness or excitement. A pulse was beating in her neck. Suddenly she was aware that Valentin had released her arm. She looked around and could not see him in the crowd. The sense of liberation surged inside her. She stepped forward and asked Cal Moody, 'Have you had enough, or would you give me a game?'

He looked at his companion, who already had his arm around a girl. 'I guess if no one else wants to use the table . . .'

They didn't score. They simply knocked up, testing each other's play. His return of service was certainly better than Frank's, probably better than Erich's.

At the end, he said, 'You've got to be a Berlin league player, at the very least.'

She smiled, and told him about Sportclub Charlottenburg. She found they were walking towards the beach café where they sold ice-cream soda in tall glasses. He just sat down with her at one of the tables outside and ordered a couple.

She liked Cal. He was relaxed and he made her feel relaxed. After a bit, she asked casually, 'Have you ever played doubles?'

'Men's doubles, yeah, back in the States. I played in a club in Philadelphia, mainly singles, but there were times . . . you know?'

'Yes. I used to play singles, too.'

'And now doubles, huh?'

'Until my partner was injured.'

'Really? Too bad! What happened?'

'He broke his ankle. Cal, I suppose you wouldn't con-

75

sider . . . just for a short time, six weeks or so . . . filling in for my partner in league matches?'

He looked uncertain. 'Nice of you to ask me, Heidrun, but it's difficult. You see, my work times are a little irregular. I work shifts. It would depend when the games came up. We'd need some practice, too.'

'I'm at the sports hall every evening.'

'At Charlottenburg? I guess that isn't so far from me.' He rubbed his chin speculatively. 'About six weeks, you said?'

'Yes.'

'Maybe I could move my shifts around if they clashed. I could speak to the other guys.' He gave a wide grin. 'Yeah, why not? Let's give it a go.'

She put her hand over his as if to seal the agreement. 'Thank you, Cal.'

'Better leave the thanks until we win a game.'

'All right,' said Heidrun. 'When will you know about the shifts? Can I call you at work?'

He grinned again. 'No, that would be difficult. You see, I'm a prison officer in Spandau Jail.'

17

If anyone had breakfast that morning, it was not mentioned. Jane lingered in bed long after Red had gone, reflecting on what had happened. This was the first time she had treated a man as a stud, without a shred of emotional involvement. The few words that had passed between them had been to encourage each other. Rather to her surprise, she felt no adverse reaction after it was over. He had been good and she was satisfied, and no less independent for the experience.

Cedric appeared towards noon, enquired about hangovers and then suggested an *al fresco* salad lunch. 'I'd offer you a pub meal,' he informed his guests, 'but I want to outline the plan of action, and we can't run the risk of being overheard.'

So Dick and Red put up a trestle table on the sunny side of the clearing, and soon it was stacked with food from the fridge, a selection of meats, bread and salad, with two bottles of *vin rosé* and the last of the lager.

They were grouped around the table in an assortment of canvas chairs, with the exception of Cedric, who had wisely opted to entrust his weight to wicker. He leaned forward cautiously to say, 'I take it that you all still want to work on the story?'

Jane told Cedric, 'I think we're all with you.'

'You believe it now?'

Jane pointed to the wedge of Gruyère on the cheeseboard. 'I believe it's as full of holes as that.'

'Ah. But you're staying with it?'

'To find out the truth.'

Cedric nodded amiably. 'That's good enough for me. No prizes for guessing what I want you to research, Jane.'

'The far right of the Conservative Party in the first years of the war?'

'Spot on. There were people openly advocating a deal with Hitler. The Marquess of Tavistock was one. Lord Halifax pressed the case in the War Cabinet itself. Follow up the

77

names in the Haushofer correspondence – Sir Samuel Hoare and Lord Lothian.'

Jane frowned. 'When you say "follow up", do you mean compile dossiers, or what?'

Cedric shook his head. 'I'm not looking for a rehash of *Who's who*. Get me the stuff that has never appeared in print, Jane. Use your contacts on the Diary. Talk to the families. Get them to tell you what Grandad was up to in 1941.'

'Heavy on mileage,' Jane warned him.

'My dear, leave me to worry about the expense.'

Interested glances were exchanged around the table.

'Does that go for all of us?' Red tentatively enquired.

'Sorry to disappoint you, but I want you to work the patch you know: Berlin,' Cedric told him. 'Have another crack at Wolf Hess. Press him for chapter and verse.'

'I already have.'

'Try harder.'

'Anything else?'

Cedric gave Red a long look across the table. 'There is something, yes. What we are going to need is a line into Spandau Prison. If this story is to mean anything at all, we have to try it on the one man left alive who knows what happened.'

There was a moment's stunned silence.

Red began to laugh. 'You think we can speak to Hess?'

'*You* can,'

'For Christ's sake, Cedric, Spandau isn't an old people's home. I can't walk in there with a bunch of grapes and ask to see my Uncle Rudolf.'

Cedric made it plain that he was unamused and unimpressed. 'One way and another, some three hundred people are hired to run that place. If you can't find one of them willing to earn a few Deutschmarks on the side, you're not the intrepid journalist I took you for.'

'Yea, but how many of the three hundred ever get near to Hess?'

'Find out.'

Dick was eager to come in. 'Aren't we overlooking something? Hess lost his memory at Mytchett Place. There's no guarantee that it ever came back. He's probably senile by now.'

78

Cedric said firmly, 'My information is that he is not. Can't you people see that this will make our story the biggest thing since Watergate? The authentic voice of Hess from inside Spandau confirming that he was in league with half the British establishment. Imagine the sensation that will cause.'

'It's a *voice* now,' said Red, squaring up for the counter-offensive. 'You mean you want him on tape? You wouldn't like me to smuggle in a couple of TV cameras and Sir Robin Day while I'm at it?'

'All we want is his confirmation that our story is true,' Cedric responded. 'Have you read that book I gave you last night?'

'*The Loneliest Man in the World*? I haven't got around to it yet,' Red was forced to admit.

For the first time that weekend, Cedric barked out his annoyance. 'What the hell have you been doing with your time? Do you think I flew you over from Berlin for the pleasure of your small-talk? So far as I'm concerned, that book is the Michelin Guide to Spandau. Eugene Bird was the American commandant of the place. Everything you want is in there: prison routine, numbers of staff, a description of the layout, pictures of the cell-blocks, even an aerial photo. Plus, of course, the only interviews with Hess in nearly forty years.'

'Did the truth about the peace deal come out?' asked Dick.

'We wouldn't be sitting here if it had,' Red commented, quick to turn the fire on someone else.

'True.'

'Did Hess reveal *anything* of significance?' asked Jane.

Cedric pondered the question. 'His loyalty to Hitler has never wavered, even though he admits that his Führer would probably have stood him against a wall and shot him if he had flown back to Germany. He repeats *ad nauseam* that the flight was his own initiative.'

'Is it important?'

'It obviously is to Hess. He was shown photocopies of the Haushofer correspondence and he stressed that even his friends the Haushofers didn't know what he was planning.'

'What about his intentions when he got to Britain? Does he say much about that?' asked Dick, joining in the conspiracy to coax Cedric into a more genial frame of mind.

'The usual stuff about being an emissary of peace. He admits that it was a mistake to try to overthrow Churchill.'

'Nothing about the people he planned to contact?'

'No. He confirms that he had never met the Duke of Hamilton. There was no reply from Hamilton to the Haushofers' feelers. Time was running out for a peace deal, because the Germans knew America might line up with Britain any time.'

'Not to mention the fact that Hitler was about to attack Russia,' put in Jane.

Cedric's expression relaxed a little, as if somewhat reassured that his team was not entirely unreceptive. 'Operation Barbarossa. Yes. Quite a lot is made of this in the book. For a long time, Hess insists that he knew nothing about Hitler's invasion plan. Then, one evening in his cell when he has been reading through the manuscript of *The Loneliest Man*, he admits to Colonel Bird that he *did* know about Barbarossa. Later, he retracts the statement, but a day or two later, he wants it reinstated.'

'Are you sure he isn't gaga?' asked Jane.

Cedric shook his head. 'Colonel Bird describes him as a very intelligent man, well read, and with a most inquiring mind.'

Red cupped his beer-glass in his hands and stared into it. 'Leave it with me,' he said. 'I'll work on it.'

'Discreetly,' Cedric cautioned him. 'And that goes for all of you. Be aware of the sensitive ground we're about to disturb: over here, the security services and the establishment; over there, the most famous prisoner in the world, guarded by four nations. When Bird's book was in preparation, the CIA got to hear about it. His home was put under twenty-four hour surveillance, his phone was tapped, he was placed under house arrest, interrogated for hours, asked to resign his job as commandant and flown to Washington to appear before a board of the State Department.'

'Yet the book was published?' said Jane in surprise.

'Yes – with a signed statement from Colonel Bird that he was required to testify under oath.'

'Heavily censored?' asked Dick.

'Bird states that his original manuscript amounted to

160,000 words. Anyone can do the arithmetic. The book is at least 50,000 words short. It's still the only substantial account we have of life in Spandau.'

'So watch out for the men with bulges under their jackets,' said Red.

Dick looked up bleakly. 'I suppose that leaves me the cantankerous old sod from MI5?'

Cedric reached for another chicken portion. 'I'll set up a meeting. I have a hunch about him.'

'And after that?'

'The Public Record Office,' Cedric informed him with a reassuring beam. 'We need cast-iron evidence. Documentation first; then corroboration from people who took part in the events of 1940 and '41; and finally . . .' He leaned back in his chair and beamed at Red. '. . . a word or two from old man Hess.'

When lunch was over and the table cleared, Cedric invited Red for a stroll along one of the woodland tracks. It was not to admire the trees. He told Red candidly that he was worried sick. '. . . and if you want to know why, it's because of you. When I picked you for this job, I didn't have much choice. I needed a fluent speaker of German who knows Berlin, and that's you. You're a competent writer with a lively style. You're also foolhardy, impetuous and you shoot off your mouth too much.' Cedric paused, practically inviting a riposte from Red, but none came. 'I knew that, of course. I knew I was taking a blind running jump with you. I tried to tell myself that your cocksure manner is an asset that you might even use to charm your way into Spandau. I just hope the charm works better over there than it has on me. I'm handing you the greatest assignment of my editorial career. If you blow it, Goodbody, so help me, I'll see you never work on a newspaper again.'

18

Dick Garrick had not visited Brighton in years. The last time was in the early seventies with his parents. Then it had seemed to him a town in a time-warp, locked in the thirties with Woodbines and peep-shows, peppermint rock and characters from Graham Greene. It had its high-rise buildings and electronic games, but the pre-war atmosphere prevailed. So it was not inappropriate that Cedric's veteran secret service agent had selected as a rendezvous the beach in front of the Old Ship Hotel, approximately midway between the two piers. The period charm of the encounter was diminished only by Dick's dislike of early starts; he had to drive the fifty miles from London and be at the meeting-place by 7.00 a.m.

There were compensations. At that hour he was able to park the Renault at a meter along the seafront, almost opposite the hotel. And Brighton beach in the low-angled morning sun, with a minimum of people – a jogger and a few dog-exercisers – was a postcard scene of glittering shingle and flashing water. The only drawback was that the stretch of beach in front of the Old Ship appeared deserted.

Beside his car, Dick checked the time and found he had two minutes in hand. Possibly his contact was sitting at a window overlooking the beach and waiting for a positive move on Dick's part. There was nobody within sight along the promenade. He picked up his copy of yesterday's edition of the *Daily Mail* and sheepishly slipped the envelope Cedric had given him between the centre pages. This was pre-Greene in conception, he reflected, more out of Edgar Wallace or John Buchan. He was to carry the paper folded in his left hand, with the title prominent.

The watch showed 7.00 a.m. and no one had made a move. He had not driven fifty miles just for a sniff of the sea. There was nothing for it but to go down on the beach and stand where he could be seen.

He took the stone steps down and crunched across the

pebbles. Within a few paces, he realized what he had not appreciated from the road above: that there was a steep shelf, where the beach dropped by all of ten feet. Standing on the finer stones at the foot of the shelf was the grey-haired figure in the white Burberry and black trilby Dick had been told to expect. He was facing the sea, holding his copy of the *Daily Mail* behind his back.

Dick slithered clumsily down the slope, but the man ignored him until he was at his side. Mercifully, there was no secret form of words.

'I'm Dick Garrick. Cedric Fleming sent me.'

The man glanced at the paper in Dick's hand. He had sunglasses and a neatly-trimmed white beard. The thought crossed Dick's mind that perhaps, as secret agents in retirement got more remote from the trade, they compensated with this kind of role-playing.

'Garrick.' The man in the raincoat spoke the name thoughtfully and stared along the length of the beach, as if he were looking for a landing-craft. Apparently satisfied that Dick was not an enemy invader, he exchanged newspapers and thrust the one he had got from Dick into his raincoat pocket. 'So far as you are concerned, my name will be, em . . .' He stared around him again. '. . . Stones. Understood?'

'All right.'

'I thought it would not be long before the cormorant press descended on me. What morsels from my memoirs have whetted the appetite? I take it you have read my memoirs?'

After an uncomfortable pause, Dick answered, 'Not yet. Cedric Fleming isn't letting the manuscript out of his office as far as I know.'

'Sensible,' Stones decided. 'We'll walk along the water's edge.' He set off briskly down the incline, shouting over his shoulder, 'I'm happy to report that I'm in the pink of health, and I attribute it to walking by the sea. Brighton beach has a more invigorating air than anywhere else along the south coast. The locals tell you it's the ozone, but of course it isn't. Rotting seaweed is the secret.'

When they had stepped over several fly-infested heaps of Brighton's secret and reached the narrow fringe of damp sand, Stones said, 'One of those pocket tape-recorders wouldn't work too well down here by the waves.'

'I haven't brought one.'

'You're not making notes,' Stones pointed out accusingly. 'Why aren't you making notes?'

'I'm not looking for a statement. I simply want your version of certain things that happened in the war.'

Stones gave a snort. 'Your editor told me. Hess, isn't it? Not much story to him.'

'Did you have anything to do with him?'

Stones appeared unwilling to answer directly. 'He behaved like a madman, you know. Tried to kill himself barely a month after he arrived. He jumped over the stairs at Mytchett Place.'

'Why was that?'

'Stress, probably.'

'You said *behaved* like a madman.'

'Well, he was playing up, wasn't he? Cunning old fox.'

'To impress MI5?'

'I dare say.'

'There are suggestions that he was brainwashed,' Dick ventured. 'Is that possible?'

'Brainwashed?' The sunglasses flashed as Stones looked out to sea. 'I don't believe brainwashing had been thought of in 1941.'

Dick said doggedly, 'He was handed over to the psychiatrists as soon as the Foreign Office had extracted all the information it could.'

'Psychiatric care.'

'At Mytchett Place – the headquarters of the MI5 field security police?'

Stones gave a thin smile. 'Those whom the gods wish to destroy they first make mad.'

Dick was silent for a few paces. 'They said he was paranoid. Delusions of persecution.'

Stones made a sound of amused contempt. 'Delusions, my foot! Hess *was* persecuted by our people. I can tell you that for certain.'

Without appearing as eager for information as he felt, Dick asked. 'In what way?'

'I'll give you an illustration. You must understand that this was in time of war, mind. If he hadn't been wearing a service uniform when he landed, we would probably have shot him as a spy. When did Hess arrive?'

'On Saturday, May 10.'

'Well, about that time, a secret unit known as GS1 was set up near Woburn by Sefton Delmer.'

'The *Express* man?'

'Yes, a journalist – but with a first-class mind,' Stones added pointedly. 'GS1's contribution to the war effort was to produce black propaganda.'

'What did that consist of?'

'Basically, misleading information to confuse the enemy. The first assignment Delmer and his people were given was to produce an edition of the official Nazi newspaper, *Volkischer Beobachter*, to plant on Hess. They took a page from the actual issue of May 21, and grafted in a short paragraph of their own in similar type in the bottom right-hand corner.'

'For Hess to read? What did it say?'

'It was supposed to be a denial of certain rumours in the foreign press that Hess's wife and four-year-old son were being held by the Gestapo. It said the truth was that Frau Hess and her son were in a mental hospital in Thuringia.'

'Nasty.'

'That isn't all. They followed it up with this.' Stones took a newspaper cutting from an inside pocket, unfolded it and handed it to Dick.

'The *Telegraph*?'

'Another fake,' Stones explained. 'Just three copies were secretly printed for GS1.'

The piece was an account of statements allegedly made by Dr Paul Schmidt, Chief of the press section of the German Foreign Office, to John Cudahy, former US Ambassador to Belgium.

'Most of it's of no consequence,' Stones told Dick. 'Take a look at the paragraph marked with a pencil.'

Dick studied it. *Schmidt, like other intimates of Hitler's circle, had taken great trouble in the talks I had with him to impress upon me that Hess was mentally deranged. Rudolf Hess, he said, had long been suffering from an incurable disease which had now affected his brain. His small son Wolf Rüdiger had inherited his father's malady and was now undergoing treatment in a mental institution.*

'Totally without foundation, of course,' said Stones.

'Call it black propaganda – to me it sounds sick,' said Dick. 'When did we plant this on Hess?'

'The date of the issue is on the reverse.'

Dick turned the cutting over.

20 June 1941.

His voice was tight with outrage. 'Five days after his suicide attempt! What were they trying to do to the man?' After a moment, he said more evenly, 'May I keep this?'

'Certainly. It's only a photocopy.'

'I see the point of that quotation about the gods now. The treatment amounts to much the same as brainwashing.'

'Destroying his mental equilibrium?'

'And his memory of recent events,' Dick said in the hope that disclosures on his part would encourage Stones to open up even more. 'Highly sensitive matters.'

Stones commented drily, 'Which brings us round to your editor's theory about the right-wing conspiracy.'

'Cedric Fleming told you about that?' Dick asked in surprise.

'I *have* held an important position in the security service for many years, Mr Garrick.'

'Sorry.' But he still felt peeved, considering what a big deal Cedric had made about confidentiality.

'You want the facts?'

'Please.'

Briefly, conversation gave way to the slap of waves against massive wooden piles as the two men passed under the dilapidated structure of the old West Pier.

'You're in for a shattering disappointment, but here goes,' Stones told him. 'The pro-German people in Britain were very well known to us. The most extreme of them were detained in prison under the Emergency Regulations.'

'Fascists?'

'And others. One of the first was the Conservative MP for Peebles, Captain Ramsay. Parliamentary privilege didn't stop us locking him up. They were well known, you see. We had tabs on them all.'

'The nobility?'

'Everyone from the Duke of Windsor downwards. There was no secret about it. The noble lords didn't get interned, but they knew damned well that a conspiracy with Nazi Germany wasn't on.'

Dick stopped in his tracks and stared at Stones. 'Are you sure of that?'

'As sure as I can be.'

'In that case, what the hell was MI5 up to with Hess? He was a mental and physical wreck when you people finished with him.'

'He had to be sacrificed.'

'For what cause?'

'I never discovered. Very few of us did, if any.'

'Yet it *still* requires him to be locked up in Spandau Jail?'

'That is a fair assumption,' said Stones.

'They must be afraid of what he knows. Is it possible that something erased from his memory in 1941 could have resurfaced later? Is that why we haven't released him?'

Stones stopped and faced Dick. 'Mr Garrick, I am a superannuated secret servant, not a psychiatrist. I have told you everything I know about the unfortunate Herr Hess. I have sung for my supper. The song is ended. And now I think we should separate and make our way independently off the beach.'

19

The death of Siggy Beer, Germany's most venerable publisher, was widely mourned. St Peter's, Munich's oldest parish church, was crowded for the funeral. Academics, civic dignitaries and writers stood shoulder to shoulder in the pews with a surprising number of tearful, good-looking women who had mingled inconspicuously with the congregation as they arrived. The local press had reported that Siggy had died alone in his apartment after one of the famed parties at the Beer Verlag publishing house, but it fooled few of Siggy's female friends. It is more than likely that in the quiet moment at the end of the service, there were many silent prayers of thanks that the old publisher had not had his cardiac failure on a previous party night.

Siggy's son, Harald, was not available for comment. After the private service at the crematorium, he returned to the office, had one scotch and a sandwich at the chairman's desk, and spent the afternoon and evening examining files and assessing the current commitments of the firm.

He worked late. At around 9.00 p.m. he was alone in the building. His father had never been persuaded of the need for night security, so after the cleaners left at 8.00, the place was usually empty for twelve hours. The argument had always been that if you trusted people, they respected you for it; the presence of a man in uniform could have been a provocation.

As he replaced the cash-books in the safe, Harald noticed a heap of dog-eared documents on the lower shelf. He lifted them out and thumbed through them. It would take more time to sort them out properly, and he wanted to get away now. They looked like long-elapsed guarantees and service agreements for office equipment. But among them was a heavier item: a sealed package, about the size and shape of a script. It was sealed, literally, with red wax, stamped with a Beer signet that Harald had never seen before.

He examined the writing on the front. It was in his father's hand, written when there was still some snobbery about the use of fountain-pens. *Strictly Private and Confidential. To be opened only in the event of the decease of Herr Rudolf Hess, Prisoner in Spandau.* It was signed by Sigmund Beer in the presence of Janus Winkler, the firm's lawyer, on 26 April 1964.

Winkler had died some time in the seventies. Harald turned the package in his hands, fingering the edges. His father had never mentioned its existence to him. Once or twice in the past twenty years, he had made some remark about wanting to outlive the old man of Spandau. Another time, he had talked vaguely of some promise he had given about an unpublished work. Siggy was always going on about trust and promises that had to be honoured.

Harald put it back in the safe with the other things. He looked at his watch and reached for his jacket. Tomorrow he would start early. Better get some sleep.

He prepared to slam the door of the safe, hesitated, took out the sealed package, stuffed it into his briefcase, closed the safe and left the building.

20

On the following Saturday afternoon, Dick drove his Renault down the M23 through Surrey. Beside him, Jane studied the exit signs.

'We'll take the next one and work our way down towards Ashdown Forest,' she told him.

'The next one? Are you sure?'

She let him overtake a container truck, and then said, 'This is my trip, all right?'

'My petrol.'

'On expenses,' she reminded him.

Late on Friday, she had met him coming out of Cedric's office and remarked how dispirited he looked. He had told her it was the look of a man who had spent four practically fruitless days at the Public Record Office and just been ordered back there for another week. She had taken pity on him and invited him on her Saturday assignment.

But he was still grumbling about the PRO. 'I found two Foreign Office files on Hess, and it's obvious that everything interesting has been removed from them. You can see where the stuff has been taken out. There are two War Office files, and one of them has a hundred-year restriction on it.'

'Frustrating for you.'

He wasn't content with sympathy. 'I suppose you had a fascinating week, hobnobbing with the aristocracy?'

Jane stared out of the side window. 'There wasn't much of that, and what there was was unproductive, if you want to know.'

'But reassuring?'

'Reassuring? Why?'

'There don't appear to be any skeletons in the Conservative Party cupboard.'

Jane turned to face him. 'Don't push me, Dick.'

'I wasn't. I was about to update you on my meeting with the ex-MI5 man.' He related what he had learned on Brighton beach, pointing out that Stones had dismissed Cedric's theory of a right-wing plot. 'And I had to believe him. MI5 knew the people to watch. They'd declared them-selves in the pre-war years. Most of them belonged to pro-German or anti-Semitic organizations, like the Right Club. The worst of them were interned, and the rest either left the country or came under the closest scrutiny.'

'We might as well give up, then?'

'I didn't say that. I'm bloody sure there *was* a cover-up. You only have to look at the gaps in the files. I told Cedric we've got to go to sources that haven't been pruned and censored. Not books and files. People.'

'Which is why you came this afternoon?'

He nodded. 'Tell me about McTeviot.'

'Jacob? He's the only person I know who might have some-thing helpful to say. He's a retired diplomat, an old friend of my father. He was in the Ministry of Information in the war. He's over eighty now, and quite outspoken about the estab-lishment. Daddy says it's one of the mysteries of the twentieth century how Jacob ever got his knighthood.'

'I thought they came automatically to high-ranking civil servants.'

'Not if they campaign for the abolition of the House of Lords.'

'He's left-wing?'

Jane smiled. 'And slightly dotty.'

'A communist?'

'A sort of homespun example, the home being stately.'

'He sounds amusing. Is he discreet?'

'No!' laughed Jane. 'Not in the least. That's why I want to talk to him. Junction 10. This one.'

In another twenty minutes, they turned into the drive of Sir Jacob McTeviot's residence, to be waved down by a blue-uniformed official.

'Two? House and grounds, sir?' he asked Dick in an auto-matic way.

'Actually, we're personal friends of the owner.'

The man drew back a step and touched his cap. 'Very good, sir. There's no charge anyway. In fact, every visitor is given something: a copy of Sir Jacob's little red book.' He handed one through the window.

'Thanks.'

'If you feel like making a contribution to the upkeep, that's another thing,' the man went on, his fingers still curled over the top of the window. 'To save embarrassment, Sir Jacob suggests five pounds from his friends.'

Dick passed out a five-pound note and drove on without another word. Jane had to bite the insides of her cheeks to stop herself from laughing.

Judging from the rows of cars drawn up behind the house, Ashdown Towers was a popular venue for weekend drivers. It was a Gothic extravaganza of red brick, a peculiar structure dominated by turrets and gables and studded doors.

At the one marked 'This Way In', they were informed that Sir Jacob was not in the house. 'Step across the croquet lawn and the Alpine meadow,' the woman on the door advised them, 'and you should find him at Mao Junction.'

'At what?'

'A station on the miniature railway. Each one is named after a revolutionary hero.'

Half-way across the Alpine meadow, Jane spotted Sir Jacob McTeviot and waved. He was on the station platform ushering children into carriages. His faded blue jacket and peaked cap might have been an engine-driver's outfit, or the uniform of Mao Tse Tung. Tall and upright, with the extra inches on the waist that are acceptable in an old man, he busied himself with the task of seating the young passengers as graciously as if he were escorting the *corps diplomatique* to a Foreign Office reception.

Jane waited for him to blow his whistle, and then stepped across the track behind the departing train.

McTeviot held out his arms to her. 'Jane, my dear!'

Dick watched from the Alpine meadow. This was Jane's show, as she had stressed, and anyway she was likely to extract more confidences from the old man if she were not accompanied.

When the polite exchange of family news was complete, Jane told McTeviot she had no idea that she would find him so busy.

'Don't give it a thought,' he insisted.

'I'd be so grateful for a few minutes of your time.'

'On business? Something frightfully confidential for the

Diary?' said McTeviot with relish. 'State secrets, perhaps? I'm your man. Try pumping me and see what you get.'

'It's rather public here.'

McTeviot raised his finger like a preacher. 'There's nothing untoward in that, my dear. The people have a right to be informed.'

'They will be, at the proper time,' she solemnly assured him.

'There speaks the journalist. Very well, young lady, you shall have your exclusive.'

Minutes later, they were making an ascent in a hot-air balloon, red in colour, with *Power to the People* written on its side. For Jane, it was a maiden flight. If she felt tremors of nervousness at being borne skywards with an eighty-year-old eccentric at the controls, she tried not to betray them. She was pretty sure the old man led a charmed life, even if her own could not be guaranteed.

Conversation was impossible while the burner was working, so she viewed the grounds, seeing how fully Ashdown Towers had been equipped for visitors. Everything except a safari park was down there: funfair, boating lake, ponies, camels and llamas, go-cart racing, maze and a row of vintage cars and carriages.

Suddenly the burner was silent, and they were drifting through the void in stunning silence. McTeviot's misty blue eyes invited Jane to state her business.

She didn't hedge. 'You were at the Ministry of Information in 1941. What can you tell me about Rudolf Hess?'

The eyes glittered. 'That old fascist? How does he keep going? Are you preparing his obit, or something?'

'Something,' answered Jane, hoping he would leave it at that. 'What's the inside story?'

'On Hess?' Sir Jacob gave a wheeze and grabbed one of the main cables, jerking the balloon alarmingly. 'The inside story, as you put it, was a dog's breakfast. The entire cabinet were at each other's throats – Winston, Eden, Beaverbrook, Duff Cooper.'

'He was Minister of Information?'

'Dear old Duff, yes. My Minister. He had reason to be hopping mad. Hess landed on Saturday night, but nobody

told us. The first Duff knew about it was on Monday night –
and that was from the wireless, the blessed German wireless!
Winston finally phoned him at ten that night, forty-eight
hours after Hess arrived. It was a shambles from beginning to
end.'

'Why.'

He flapped his hand. 'The silly arses didn't know how to
handle it. Couldn't agree. The BBC were told to put out a
statement that Hess had been bumped off by the Gestapo,
and that went into the eleven o'clock news.'

'The Cabinet didn't want it known that he was in Britain?'

McTeviot sniffed. 'They didn't have a cat in hell's chance
of keeping it quiet. It was all in the papers on Tuesday
morning. Hess had a very good press. Clean-living family
man and all that. Winston was in a flap. He prepared a
statement for Parliament and showed it to Anthony Eden, the
Foreign Secretary. Eden disapposed and prepared an
alternative statement. The telephone wires were red-hot. The
argument raged into the small hours of Thursday. Duff
simply wanted some directive to clear up the speculation. He
went to see Churchill. Max Beaverbrook was already there.
The Beaver had a lot of sway with Winston, you know. He
persuaded Winston to leave it to him to handle the press.
They told Eden over the phone at half-past-one in the
morning, and he wasn't pleased.'

'Do you think they had something to cover up?'

McTeviot said, 'I know it,' and gave another blast on the
burner. 'Beaverbrook invited the press to lunch at Claridges
the same day and told them to go to town on Hess with as
much rumour and speculation as possible.'

'A smokescreen?'

'Any damn thing they liked. He came over to assassinate
Churchill, or to elope with Unity Mitford, or he was just
plain bonkers. It was supposed to confuse the Germans.'

'The Germans – or the British?' speculated Jane.

'I can tell you it didn't much impress the people closest to
events. There was bitterness about the way it was handled.'

'Did Duff Cooper know what was going on?'

McTeviot chuckled. 'The Minister of Information? Completely in the fog. He was a disillusioned man, and so was

Harold Nicolson, his Parliamentary Secretary. They tried their damnedest to get the truth. Duff banged the desk in Number Ten and Harold raised the matter over a private lunch with the Churchills. In a matter of weeks they were both sacked from the government.'

Jane's heart was pumping hard, and not because of the altitude. Her hunch had already paid off. She had learned more in these few minutes than she had all week. She felt intuitively that the old man had more to tell her if she could tease it out. 'Did you ever find out what created the panic?'

He shook his head. 'I'm afraid not, my dear. It was cataclysmic, I can tell you that. Winston was on hot bricks. I never knew him so jumpy.'

'Who else would have known?'

'Beaverbrook, for sure. He interviewed Hess, you know.'

'But that was later, in September,' Jane pointed out.

McTeviot gave her a sharp look. 'You *have* done your homework, young lady.'

'Other people interviewed Hess. The Duke of Hamilton, Ivone Kirkpatrick and Sir John Simon. Presumably they learned the real reason for the flight?'

'Presumably. Like Beaverbrook, they're all dead now.'

'If there was someone else I could talk to . . .'

'. . . you'd have to find your way into Spandau Prison,' said McTeviot, leaning over the side to wave to the children on the miniature train. 'He's the only one left who knows the truth, and maybe he's forgotten it by now.'

21

A small crowd had assembled near the entrance of Spandau Prison, but not too near. Notices in English and German attached to the steel fence at either side of the main gate read: 'WARNING. DANGER. Do not approach this fence. Guards have orders to shoot.'

There was a flurry of interest among the watchers as a bus with Soviet markings prepared to turn off the road. A few bold tourists focussed their cameras, oblivious of the signs stating that photography was forbidden.

The prison stands among trees on the Wilhelmstrasse, one of the main routes west from the city. It is located in the British sector, among military barracks. Like them, it is a red-brick building. When it went up, in 1876, it was a military fortress. Later, it was adapted as a civilian prison, with 132 single cells, five punishment cells and ten large cells capable of holding up to forty prisoners. During the war, the Nazis used it as what was euphemistically termed a clearing station for political prisoners. Berlin's Jews, Poles, dissidents and 'undesirables' were brought to Spandau to be interrogated and allocated to concentration camps. But some who arrived there were not sent elsewhere. The prison was equipped with an execution chamber containing a guillotine and a row of hooks, where eight condemned men at a time could be hanged by the method favoured by the Third Reich – slow death by strangulation.

In 1947, when the Allied Powers converted the prison to accommodate the seven Nazis, the execution chamber was converted into a medical room. The prisoners were housed in individual cells in the main cell-block in the centre of the prison complex. Outside the twenty-foot walls was erected a ten-foot steel fence topped with barbed wire. Between wall and fence was a six-foot electric fence with a 4,000-volt charge. Inside the wall, watchtowers were built, originally of wood, now of concrete. There are six in all, and they are constantly manned. The towers are equipped with spotlights capable of illuminating the entire area inside the prison and in the proximity of the wall outside.

The bus halted, and the Soviet Army Guards began to come

out, staring around them. It was Soviet policy that each detachment to Spandau should consist of men who had not performed the duty before. The official reason was that guard duty at Spandau was so demanding in difficult circumstances that no soldier should be required to repeat the excercise, but cynics from the West believed it was to minimise the opportunity for men to defect.

Once out, they formed three ranks, holding their machine guns across their chests. They wore red-banded peaked caps, tunics with high collars and the breeches and jackboots of the Soviet Army. At a few sharp orders from their NCO, they dressed from the left, turned right and marched briskly towards the castellated archway at the main gate. The coach drove off along Wilhelmstrasse. As the column approached the blue double doors, the right side opened and the men marched through. The door immediately closed behind them. The spectators waited for the changeover ceremony to take place inside. An empty bus arrived.

In ten minutes, the door opened again and out marched a triple column of French guards: two officers, eight NCOs and forty-four men, relieved after a month of guarding Spandau's solitary old Nazi. The same ritual had been enacted each month by American, British, French and Soviet forces ever since 1947. The French bus drove away and the crowd dispersed – all except one, who pushed his cycle across the street to the Melanchthon Church opposite, and continued to wait. On that side, the summer foliage obscured him from the watchtowers and the windows at the prison entrance.

He was Red Goodbody.

Since returning to Berlin the previous Tuesday, Red had been working on the problem of getting into contact with Hess. He had come out here each afternoon and stood by the church notice board, taking a demonstrative interest in the order of services whenever anyone passed. He knew every preacher for the next six weeks. Periodically, he walked his cycle across Melanchthon Platz, the intersection with Wilhelmstrasse, and sat on a bench in front of the five-storey apartment block there. Across the six lanes of traffic, he could see the battlemented profile of the prison directors' building.

Cedric Fleming's world scoop had seemed a thrilling prospect in the comfortable obscurity of a cottage in the heart of England. Against the reality of Spandau the best you could say about it was that it was improbable. But Red's persistence had at least told him a little about the prison routine. In another few minutes he expected to learn something more.

This sort of surveillance, or spying, or whatever it amounted to, was alien to Red's nature. He disliked lone assignments. All his best stories had come through face to face conversations, preferably over glasses of beer. It was not that he felt imperilled by keeping watch on Spandau; he was just a gregarious man who was not used to working this way.

He checked his watch. It was time to cross Melanchthon Platz again and stroll past the church where he would get a clear view between the trees of the prison gate. The timing was exact. A small door was built into the right-hand entrance gate. It opened and a figure in a blue and red tracksuit emerged and jogged towards Wilhelmstrasse, to turn left, in the direction of Spandau town. He was sandy-haired, average in height and probably around thirty years of age. Red had watched him set off on his run at precisely this time for the past three days. Today, he would be following him.

It was easy to be inconspicuous on the opposite side of a highway as wide as Wilhelmstrasse, and Red cycled at a leisurely pace along the pink track reserved for cyclists, allowing his man to stay ahead by at least fifty metres. Logically, he was going to be English or American. They were the jogging nations. The French preferred cycling and the Russians were not allowed to go out alone.

Presently, the jogger stopped at a crossing, preparing to come over to Red's side of the highway. Red squeezed the brakes, and took a consuming interest in the appearance of the apartment blocks to his right. Someone had written *Tommys Raus* on one of the walls.

He was soon on the move again. His quarry crossed the street and took a turn to the right. It led over a bridge across the Havel and linked with the busy Charlottenburger Chaussee. He continued running towards the city at an even, economical stride, passing the direction signs for the Olympic Stadium.

Shortly after the Palace of Charlottenburg came into view, the jogger turned right and set off down a smaller street. Several more minutes of steady running, and he entered a park where children were playing beside a modern, sculptured fountain. Further on was a car park, and beyond that a handsome, glass-roofed building that Red had not seen before: the new Charlottenburg sports hall. If the runner had plans for additional exercise, he was indeed a dedicated sportsman. Not the sort to open up over a few beers.

He went through the swing doors while Red was parking his bike. You don't throw your bike down in a heap in Berlin.

'That guy who just came in ahead of me – is he a track star?' he asked the girl at the ticket office.

'The one in the red and blue tracksuit? No. He plays table-tennis.'

'Table-tennis?' Red reflected on the six miles or more of pounding the pavements. 'It sure must have come a long way since ping-pong. Which part of the building is that?'

'The main hall. Straight ahead.'

'Is there a gallery for spectators?'

'The stairs at the end. Don't you want to play something yourself?'

'Darling, the only thing I play is my Barbra Streisand tape.'

The gallery was empty, except for a sleeping man stretched along three seats. There was a good view of the hall, where the table-tennis was concentrated at one end. All four tables were in play, but the red and blue tracksuit was not in sight. Red was unconcerned. He had already decided his man would need a shower. He glanced at the *Rauchen Verboten!* and at the sleeping man, and slid out his pack of Marlboros.

22

On the drive back to Hammersmith, Dick suggested supper at the Italian restaurant in King Street; afterwards, Dick drove to her flat in Brook Green, and Jane asked him in, stressing that the invitation was for coffee and coffee alone.

It was after eleven. Out of consideration to the other tenants, they crept upstairs in silence, without switching on lights.

'I'm in my usual chaos,' she said as she pushed open the door and grabbed a handful of underclothes that she had left on the radiator. 'Bathroom's through there if you want it. I'll stuff these in a drawer and put the kettle on. Find yourself a chair, won't you?' She went through to her bedroom.

She was not one of those people who claim to have extra-sensory powers, but, strangely, the moment she stepped into the bedroom she felt uneasy. Someone had been in there while she was out. Whether it was the trace of an unfamiliar odour or pure intuition on her part, she didn't know. It was a sensation she had never experienced before.

She stowed the undies away and changed into a white cashmere jumper, then sat at her dressing-table trying to ignore the feeling. She put on fresh lipstick and a dab of Miss Dior, raised a smile in the mirror and got up to attend to the coffee. Then she froze. She had proof that someone had been in there.

On the white table beside her bed were various things she liked to have handy: paper hankies, a couple of books, aspirins, a felt-tip pen, a notebook and a digital alarm clock with a narrow rectangular face. It was the clock that fixed her attention. The digits for hours and minutes glowed red and were separated by two pulsating points. After she had bought the clock, she had found that the reflection on the white surface of the table disturbed her sleep, so she always positioned it facing away from the pillow, at the forward edge. If she wanted to see the time in the night, she had only to wriggle down in the bed a few inches.

The clock had been moved. Someone had turned it towards the pillow.

'Dick!'

'Yes?'

'Would you come in here?'

She told him.

'You're certain? You couldn't have moved it yourself as you got up this morning?'

'I know I didn't.'

'You'd better check that nothing is missing. Your jewellery.'

Foolish, she thought, to leave it in such an obvious place as the dressing-table. She didn't possess much, some rings and necklaces and an antique silver brooch, but what she had was precious for all sorts of reasons.

She opened the left-hand drawer. Everything was in its usual place in the padded ebony box she had bought as a teenager in Paris.

'Nothing gone?'

'No.'

'What else do you have of value? Was there any cash lying around?'

'No. I had it with me.'

'Credit cards?'

'In my bag.'

'Passport?'

She went through to the living room and checked the filing cabinet. 'I think it must be missing . . . I'd better call the police.'

Dick was looking along the collection of letters, ornaments and photos on the mantelpiece. He picked out the passport and handed it to her. 'I don't think we should call them.'

'Why not? Somebody has definitely been here while I was out.'

'Your landlord? I expect he has a key.'

'I'll phone him.'

'It's late.'

'He won't mind. I need to know, Dick. I feel quite creepy.'

Dick shook his head. 'Better not use the phone in the flat.'

She stared at him.

He said, 'I'll ask the people downstairs if they heard anything. Just to be sure.'

While Dick was gone, she wanted to check things, but she couldn't. She knew what it meant to be paralysed with fear.

He came back quickly. 'You're right,' he told her. 'They heard movements about an hour ago. They assumed it was you.' He faced her and put his hands on her arms. 'Did you make any notes at Cedric's last weekend?'

She frowned, then understood the drift of his thinking. 'A few things. In the notebook beside my bed.' She shivered.

'And the interviews in the week. Did you tape them?'

'They weren't worth the trouble.' Jane ran her fingers distractedly through her hair. 'Dick, who do you think has been here?'

'Someone who got wind of what we're up to. Some crazy journalist from one of the tabloids wanting to find out more, I wouldn't be surprised. Or a freelance, or even one of our respectable rivals.'

'They'd break into my flat?' said Jane in disbelief.

'If they thought we were on to something really big. And we probably are, which is why we can't tell the police. Do you understand, Jane?'

She nodded.

'You're taking it well.'

'I shall probably scream in a moment.'

He put his arm around her shoulder. 'Would you like me to make that coffee? Then I think I should check whether my own place has been broken into. Want to come with me?'

'Please.'

'You might like to bring a few things with you and spend the night there.' Before she could respond, he added, 'I do have a spare bedroom.'

Jane thanked him. She couldn't face the night here, knowing that someone had come and gone with such ease, and not knowing why they had come or whether they might return. It wasn't like having the place ransacked by thieves. It was sinister. It made her flesh creep.

When they got to Dick's place, he checked it minutely and pronounced it exactly as he had left it. So Jane passed the night in the spare bed and lay awake for hours trying to decide whether to call Cedric in the morning and resign from the team.

102

23

Cedric had suggested Inner Temple Gardens as a good spot to meet, but at 12.30 there were so many people eating sandwiches there that he proposed a walk along the Embankment instead. 'Better than sitting on a park bench with the reek of hard-boiled eggs all around you,' he told Dick. 'I never eat lunch unless it's a business affair, but I have to admit to subversive signals from the inner man at about this time. A spot of exercise would be doubly mortifying to the flesh, and therefore beneficial. I hope you're not hungry, by the way.'

Dick shook his head. He had eaten a late breakfast and prolonged it with extra rounds of toast and coffee as he strove to convince Jane that she should stay on the team. Without really carrying the argument, he had persuaded her not to make an immediate decision. He had driven her back to Brook Green and entered the flat with her. Together, they had made a second check of her desk and filing cabinet. Nothing had apparently been removed. After a few minutes, she had thanked him and said she felt in control and there was no need for him to remain there.

He told Cedric about the break-in. 'Jane is understandably shaken,' he added. 'She's in two minds about going on with this. We can't let her drop out now, Cedric. She's been working flat out making contact with people out of the top drawer who might know something, and the results are starting to show.'

Cedric side-stepped the point about Jane altogether. 'The question is, who is on to us?'

Dick showed with a shrug that it wasn't his most immediate concern. 'One of the tabloids?'

Cedric pondered the possibility as they strolled past the black hull of the *Discovery*. 'I can't see it. All right, the word is probably out that we are launching a new investigation into the Hess affair, and they may know who is involved, but I can't see them breaking into a fellow-journalist's flat. Not the Fleet Street boys. It's not the same game as trespassing at Balmoral with a telephoto lens.'

'Who would you put your money on, then?'

'You say it was a tidy job?'

'Almost immaculate.'

Cedric nodded. 'Special Branch or MI5. Probably the latter.'

How would *they* know what we're doing?'

'Come on, Dick. Where were you all last week?'

'The Public Record Office. I didn't talk to a soul.'

'But you filled in applications for the Hess files.'

Dick clicked his tongue.

Cedric asked. 'Did you check to see if they bugged the flat?'

'It didn't cross my mind.'

'For Christ's sake, Dick! Make a point of it, will you? This isn't party games.' For a moment, the roar of a courier's motorcycle reverberated off the stonework of Waterloo Bridge. Cedric waited, then said. 'We're in trouble.'

Dick steered him in what he hoped was a more positive direction. 'Have you heard from Red?'

'Not a word,' answered Cedric morosely, 'but then I wouldn't expect to. He's not the type who calls the office for a chat. We'll walk as far as Hungerford Bridge. I'll pick up a taxi at Charing Cross.'

'There's something else?'

Cedric nodded. 'I asked our man in Washington to do some digging in the National Archives. He found a copy of the cable that Churchill sent President Roosevelt one week after Hess arrived in Britain. By then, Kirkpatrick from the Foreign Office had conducted three long interviews with Hess, and got the peace terms he was offering. Churchill makes no secret of the offer, but he tells Roosevelt frankly that Hitler refuses to negotiate with the existing British government.'

'Does he say who they expected to negotiate with?'

Cedric sniffed. 'Exactly as I told you last weekend. Members of a "peace movement" which would oust the Churchill government. Churchill brushes this aside as an example of the ineptitude of German intelligence. But Roosevelt wasn't convinced. Do you know the comment he's reported to have made to his staff? "I wonder what is really behind this story."'

They walked on for some way without speaking, past Cleopatra's Needle, towards the iron railway bridge. A passenger train trundled out to the suburbs.

'We found something else in the Washington Archives,' Cedric resumed in the same downbeat tone. 'A memo to Roosevelt from Sumner Welles, who was his Under-Secretary of State. On 22 June 1941, the British Ambassador, Lord Halifax, called on Welles. He was exercised about reports that were circualting in the States. It seems that Herbert Hoover, the former President, was openly saying that Hess had come with specific peace proposals and that leading members of the Conservative Party in England had called on Churchill with a demand that he give serious consideration to them. They were threatening to withdraw their support in the House.'

Dick whistled his reaction. 'It went as far as that, did it? Halifax denied it, of course.'

'In a curiously ambivalent fashion,' Cedric answered. 'He said that it was unnecessary for him to state that the reports were entirely untrue.'

'Foxy old devil!'

'And it never came to anything because, on the very day this conversation took place, Germany invaded Russia. Hitler had turned his attention eastwards, so the immediate threat of Britain being over-run was lifted. Churchill could tell the rebel Conservatives to take a running jump, and he probably did.'

Dick almost crowed his satisfaction. 'It's slotting into place, Cedric. What we've got is Churchill fighting for his political life in those six weeks after Hess arrived.'

Cedric was not so sanguine. 'It's no bloody use without names. Who were these rebel Conservatives? We're no nearer to identifying them.'

They had reached the Embankment underground station. They started up the stairs towards Villiers Street.

'Would you have a word with Jane?' Dick asked.

Cedric sighed heavily. 'Later.'

They reached the taxi-rank in the forecourt of Charing Cross Station. Once Cedric had climbed into a cab, Dick went down the steps of the underground. He took the District

Line to Hammersmith and spent an hour in the library there before going on to Jane's. At a shop in the Broadway, he bought a new lock for her door.

She had finished checking the flat. 'I'm more organized now than ever I was before,' she announced. 'I threw out heaps of useless bits of paper I'd accumulated. Clearing things out is a therapeutic exercise.' No more was said about resigning from the team. She certainly didn't look in a negative frame of mind. She had put colour on her eyes and she was wearing a green silk tee-shirt that turned every movement she made into a distraction. Dick gave her an approving glance, but each of them knew that their relationship was professional.

He told her about the meeting with Cedric, and they searched the apartment for hidden bugs and found none.

'So much for Cedric's theory,' said Dick. 'He's obsessed with this idea that MI5 are on to us.'

'I was thinking about it as I was going through the files,' said Jane. 'It could equally have been someone who heard that I was asking questions about the Hess affair and got worried.'

'You mean someone implicated with the Nazis?'

'Or their son, or grandson. Family honour still has to be defended at all costs.'

'Whoever it was, I'm changing the lock on your door.'

She smiled. 'Masterful. That leaves the feeble woman to make the coffee.'

Later, while she was watching him at work, he told her about his visit to the library. 'They have a copy of the diaries of Sir Alexander Cadogan.'

'The man the Duke of Hamilton wanted to meet after talking to Hess? Nice work, Dick. What did you discover?'

'If you remember, Hamilton called the Foreign Office and tried to set up a rendezvous. He wanted Cadogan to drive out to Northolt to meet him – which raises two questions. Why Cadogan? And why Northolt?'

Jane shook her head. 'Where exactly is Northolt?'

'About ten miles west of here. In a 1941 car, the Duke could have made it to the Foreign Office inside forty-five minutes, yet he wanted Cadogan to come to him.'

'For a private consultation?'

Dick nodded. 'Where they could set aside the usual FO formalities. Off the record.'

'That answers the first question,' said Jane. 'How about the second: why Cadogan?'

'Because he was a civil servant and not a member of the War Cabinet. He was in a privileged position, independent of the politicians.'

'There's no need to lecture me on politics,' she gently reminded him. 'Hamilton could have told Cadogan what Hess proposed without Churchill knowing a thing about it. Is that your point?'

'Yes.'

She drew up her shoulders and gave him a wry look. 'But as Hamilton wasn't able to get through to Cadogan, what are you driving at?'

He put down the screwdriver and turned to face her. 'Just this. Last week, I read Sir Anthony Eden's account of the Hess business. The way he tells it, Churchill's staff intercepted the call from Hamilton. *Intercepted*. The word is significant. This was a call to the Foreign Office, Jane, not a German spy tapping out a message to Berlin. The way I see it, Churchill was a fortunate man. If that call *hadn't* been intercepted, God knows what would have happened.'

'It would have been up to Cadogan, I suppose,' Jane commented evenly. 'What did you learn from his diaries, then?'

'He seems to have been the impeccable diplomat, scrupulously impartial in his dealings with politicians.'

'Do the diaries mention Hess?'

'Oh, yes. He says, on 12 May 1941, that in all the years he has kept the beastly diary, he has never been so hard pressed, and it was mainly due to Hess. On 14 May, he reports that Hess is the bane of his life.'

'Why?'

'Because the Cabinet is divided and Churchill is having tantrums and drawing up statements that nobody else will endorse.'

'That ties in with what Jacob told me. Is there any clue as to whether Cadogan would have given assistance to a right-wing coup?'

'On the Sunday when Hamilton was trying to set up the meeting at Northolt, Cadogan was weekending at his cottage in Sussex. The message *was* passed on, and a meeting was fixed for later that evening, but within half-an-hour Churchill was on the line to tell Cadogan he need not be troubled.'

'Fast work.'

The bleep of the phone cut through their conversation. Jane left her chair to cross the room.

'Careful what you say,' Dick cautioned her.

It was Cedric on the line, his voice terse and strained. 'Jane? Is Dick with you?'

'Yes. Do you want a word?'

'No. I just want both of you to get over here as soon as possible.'

'To your office?'

'Yes. And Jane . . .'

'Yes?'

'Don't speak a syllable to anyone.'

24

It was all down to the final game in the Berlin table-tennis league match between Grunewald and Charlottenburg. The singles had put Grunewald ahead by two, but strong attacking play by the Charlottenburg men's and women's doubles players had levelled the score, and now their new mixed doubles pair, Kassner and Moody, faced the Grunewald husband and wife, the Feuerbachs, who had a reputation for coolly picking up the vital points while their team-mates and supporters sweated.

The first game had been a whitewash: 21-7. Knowing that their opponents were playing together for the first time in a league match, the Feuerbachs had set out to confuse them with a combination of wide-angled play that stretched them to the crowd-barrier and net-skimming dropshots that had them clashing bats as they re-positioned. The tactics hadn't worked so well in the second game as Heidrun and Cal fought back more positively, and it went to deuce, and finally to Charlottenburg by 25-23.

Now, in the decider, it was 19-16 to Grunewald, with Cal's service to come. Heidrun waited to kill the returns, as watchful as a cat. The first, from Wolf Feuerbach, failed to climb over the net, and his wife Eva did no better with the second. Cal had switched from his usual quick forehand serve to a backhand that imparted vicious backspin, and neither of them had judged it right. Two good points to Charlottenburg. Heidrun smiled her encouragement. A disguised topspin on the next sent Wolf's return head-high, and Heidrun smashed it past Eva.

The scores were level at 19-19.

A woman in the seats behind the crowd barrier was shredding a Kleenex with her teeth.

Cal served a let. The second came back at a freakish angle from Eva and struck the edge of the table. Astonishingly, Heidrun reacted fast enough to retrieve it. Wolf produced a looping topspin drive which Cal returned. Eva tried a smothering shot and put the ball into the net.

20-19 to Charlottenburg.

The ball sat ready on Cal's uncupped palm. With a nod to Wolf Feuerbach, he tossed it extravagantly high and served with a strong sidespin bias. In controlling the spin, Wolf returned a bland shot down the centre and stepped the wrong way, blocking his wife. Heidrun gratefully tricked it out of Eva's reach – a satisfying *coup de grâce*. She grabbed Cal and embraced him heartily. The Charlottenburg people closed in for an orgy of congratulation.

From a bench at the edge of the gymnasium, Red Goodbody watched the rejoicing and planned some tactics of his own.

Twenty minutes later, when Cal Moody appeared in the refreshment bar and looked around for the other members of the team, Red drew him towards a table. He didn't go to the extreme of grabbing him by the lapels, but he used the authoritative manner that had served him on journalistic assignments before, speaking in rapid German. Cal was too bewildered to object.

'What did you want – a coffee? Black or white? Just sit there and I'll have it brought over. If you're wondering where your doubles partner is, she hasn't come down yet. We can keep a place for her. What's her name, by the way? I must have your names right.'

'Heidrun Kassner. Excuse me, what is this all about?'

'That's no German accent, I'm sure,' said Red in English. 'Are you over with the BAOR?'

'No, I'm from the States. Philadelphia. Cal Moody.'

'Red Goodbody. Never heard of me? Don't let it worry you, pal. My work is syndicated right across America, but I appear under various by-lines.'

'You're a journalist?'

'Right. Doing a story on the sports scene in Berlin. Isn't that your partner?' Red raised a hand to catch Heidrun's attention as she appeared at the door. 'He's over here, love.'

Heidrun hesitated, then spotted Cal and came over. Her hair was still damp from the shower, making dark streaks in the blonde. She looked radiantly pretty, in the sturdy mould of German sportswomen who swim twenty lengths a day and take their vegetables raw.

Red introduced himself. 'I was just explaining to Cal why I want to borrow a few minutes of your time,' he told her. 'I'm writing this piece about sports in Berlin. I shall probably need some pictures. You don't mind if I fix that later? Brilliant as my writing is, it helps to have a picture of a gorgeous girl above the text! But in your case, love,' he added quickly, seeing a frown develop, 'your sex appeal is immaterial. I want you for what you did on that table tonight. That was a stunning way to clinch the match. Heart-stopping. Let me order you a fruit juice or a yoghurt.'

'Are you sure you're a journalist?' Heidrun enquired with a penetrating stare.

Red was thankful that he had not strayed too far from the truth. 'Want to see my press card?' He took it out and waved it in front of them briefly. 'Who did you think I was? A spy from the other team?'

'Why should a foreign journalist take an interest in a table-tennis match of no importance outside Berlin?' Heidrun persisted.

Red tried his disarming smile and a string of sportswriters' clichés. 'That's where you're wrong, my darling. This *is* important. The public is sick to the back teeth with the monsters who earn millions out of professional sport: the drug-takers, the fixers and the freaks. Top-level sport is just a branch of showbiz now, a way for big business to turn a profit. What I want to tell the world is that there are still people like you who play sport in its true sense.'

Cal said supportively, 'Mr Goodbody's work is syndicated all over the States.'

Red modestly remarked, 'I expect to sell this story throughout Europe, too.'

'A story about table-tennis?' asked Heidrun, giving no sign that she even wanted to be convinced.

'Absolutely,' Red assured her. 'Only let's be clear about this. I want the personal angle. This will feature the two of you, the sort of people you are, the reason you play, the satisfaction you get from the game. I'm not interested in league positions and all that crap.'

Heidrun cut in, 'What do you mean: all that crap?'

'What I mean is that some guy reading his paper in Los Angeles doesn't give a toss about the piddling club you play for and how many points you get.'

'Charlottenburg is not a piddling club, whatever you mean by that, and I don't care about a man in Los Angeles, because I do give a toss,' said Heidrun, puffing up her chest. 'All the club members give a toss. And that is why we expect to win the league.'

'No question!' said Red with a slick change of tack. 'I can see what motivates you, my darling: the honour of playing for a great club.'

Heidrun said witheringly, 'It is not the custom in Germany to address a woman as darling when you meet her for the first time.'

'No offence, sweetheart,' said Red.

'I am not your sweetheart, either.'

Red winked at her. 'Cross your fingers. You never know your luck.' He switched to Cal. 'So you're American. What are you doing over here if you're not a soldier?'

Cal shifted in his chair and looked around him. 'I'm not sure if I should be talking about my job.'

'Secret, is it? CIA?' Red suggested blithely.

'Jesus, no.' Cal grinned at the idea.

'Don't worry. This is off the record. You can see I'm not writing down a thing.'

'Could I have a sight of anything you do decide to write about me?'

'No problem.'

'Okay, I work in Spandau Jail. I'm one of the US warders there.'

'Guarding Rudolf Hess? No wonder you need an outside interest. Is it true that he's crazy?'

'I'm not permitted to discuss Herr Hess.'

'Understood,' said Red. There would be opportunities later to prise the information out of Cal, and this was not the occasion to declare an interest. 'Tell me, do you two date each other, apart from table tennis fixtures?'

112

'Of course not,' Heidrun scornfully answered. 'We have more important things to do.'

'Jesus, yes,' said Cal, looking at his watch. 'I must be going. I'm on duty in twenty minutes. Maybe we can talk some other time, Red. You can find me at the sports centre most evenings.'

'Tomorrow?'

'You're on.' Cal mumbled his farewells and left in a hurry. Red studied Heidrun. He had to face it: she was not going to go away, not now and not tomorrow. She continued to sit at the table, sipping her fruit juice and looking at Red as if he owed her a better explanation. They were blue-green eyes with flecks of gold. She wore no make-up, yet she was not indifferent to her appearance, because she definitely plucked her eyebrows.

'Too bad Cal had to go,' said Red. 'I was hoping to interview the two of you together.'

'Then you should have made an arrangement,' Heidrun pointed out. 'He is a busy man. He works nights at Spandau to leave the evenings free for table-tennis.'

'Rather him than me.'

'It's only while the season lasts. In five weeks it will be over. He has only recently joined the club. My last partner had an accident. He broke his ankle.'

'Pity.'

'Not really,' Heidrun said matter-of-factly. 'Cal Moody is a better player.'

'Pity for the other guy.'

'The club is more important than any individual.'

Red commented, 'That's the totalitarian concept.'

'It doesn't make it any less true,' she retorted. 'All team sports proceed on that understanding.'

'And all dictators,' said Red.

She gave him another of her riveting stares. 'I don't believe you are a sports journalist at all, Mr Goodbody.'

He returned the stare. 'What's your theory about me, then?'

'I don't know who you are working for, but you are interested in Cal because of Rudolf Hess. You hope to find things out. It's transparently obvious that you know

113

practically nothing about sport, so what other reason can there be for your interest?'

Red's reply was so rapid that it sounded wholly convincing. 'I wanted to meet you, didn't I?'

With a blank expression, she asked, 'Whatever for?'

Equally solemnly, Red said, 'I'm crazy about you, darling.'

Heidrun's expression stayed blank, but it was suffused with a deeper shade of pink. Her voice was totally under control. 'You know nothing at all about me, except that I play table-tennis.'

'True, there's so much to catch up on,' said Red with a winning smile. 'Where would you like to go for a meal? I know a good French restaurant just a few minutes away, in Paulsborner Strasse. Very informal.'

'Do you seriously expect me to go out with you?'

'Do you believe me when I say I'm crazy about you?'

'Actually, no,' answered Heidrun.

'OK, call my bluff and have a *cordon bleu* at my expense,' suggested Red. Spotting a glimmer of indecision in her eyes, he added, 'While you eat, I'll tell you precisely why you're the most fantastic fraulein in Berlin.' He got up and reached for her sportsbag.

Heidrun asserted her independence with a shrug, and walked with him to the exit.

It went unsaid that Red was prepared to demonstrate his sincerity in Heidrun's bed. It was implicit in the offer.

Slightly over two hours later, buoyed up by Moselle and Armagnac, and jubilant at having carried conviction right through the meal, he followed her into her apartment, mentally reciting lines from Betjeman about adorable sports girls.

The place was better set up than he had expected from the outside of the block. Pine cladding and pale blue emulsion gave it the relaxing ambience of a sauna. There were Persian rugs scattered about the wood-block floor. Halogen lamps in white metal stands provided a soft, even light. The furniture was upholstered in white leather.

'The customers in Möhring's must be good tippers,' Red remarked.

'Like to see the rest?'

114

He was shown the kitchen first, ceramic-tiled and immaculate, with built-in gadgets, including a microwave.

'And the bathroom is upstairs.' She led him back into the living-room and up a wrought-iron spiral staircase. As a consequence he could not help noticing an extra swing to her hips as she mounted the stairs.

The bathroom was pastel pink. It looked more lived-in than the kitchen, with a range of bottles, aerosols, tins and glass pots along the shelf over the bath.

Red felt his wrist held in a tight grip. 'First we take a shower, hm?'

'Together?'

'Mixed doubles.'

She unzipped her tracksuit top, confirming what he had guessed across the table in the restaurant — that she was naked underneath. Facing him, she pushed the sides sufficiently apart to expose both breasts. She supported them with her hands, and lifted them a fraction for appreciation. They had deep pink aureoles the size of wine-coasters.

'Ladies' doubles,' said Red.

'A fine pair?'

'Top of the league.'

She slid back the glass shower-guard and turned the jets full on. 'I like to have it strong and hard.'

She turned towards him again and unfastened the top button of his shirt, then worked systematically downwards as far as his belt, unbuckled that, unzipped his fly and pressed her hand against him, arousing him with the warmth of her palm.

Red responded by easing the waistband of her tracksuit over her hips and tracing the curve of her buttocks, feeling the unexpected coolness on his hand. Her bottom clenched as she swayed forward, naked, and kissed him.

She tugged the rest of the clothes from his body and pulled him into the steaming shower.

'Christ, it's hot!' He reached out to adjust the taps.

'Come here and it won't touch you.' Heidrun grasped his penis like the handle of a table-tennis bat and tugged him towards her. She had her back to the tiled wall and her legs apart. The soles of her feet gripped the rubber shower-mat to prevent her from slipping. She guided him into her, shouting, 'Strong and hard!'

It was not a comfortable position. His knees were bent and his thighs ached. He had turned off the hot jet and now the cold cascaded onto his back with each thrust.

'Harder!' In her passion, Heidrun dug her fingernails deep into the flesh of his lower back.

His climax was slow in coming, and that seemed to suit her. They ended up in a heap on the floor of the shower, with cold water dowsing their fires.

'And now,' Heidrun told him brightly, 'I would like you to do it to me in the bedroom.'

25

In Spandau Prison, the weekly meeting of directors was in session. It took place in a section of the administration block dignified with the label of 'Conference Room'. In reality, the room was unimpressive. The walls were painted in institutional green and white that contained the minimum of simple furniture: a plain wooden table, chairs, a hat-stand and the small safe where the keys were kept. There was a large map of Europe on one wall and a calendar on another. There had been periods in the Cold War when this undistinguished room had been the only place in the world where East met West for discussions on an official footing.

Here, the four Colonels from Britain, France, the Soviet Union and the United States who shared the duty of commanding Spandau, had met regularly since 1947. Their discussions were, for the most part, humdrum, but the arguments over prison routine had been known to carry on from late morning to early the following day, prolonged by the need for everything to be explained in three languages.

This morning looked like being a quicker session. It was the Soviet director's turn as chairman; the office went to the nation whose troops were presently on guard. After just over an hour, they had reached the fifth item on the agenda: the current state of health of the prisoner. The usual report had been submitted by the Allied prison doctors, who also represented the four Powers and met regularly in the Conference Room.

Translations of the report were handed around the table. Hess, still known in official documents as Prisoner Number 7, was apparently in reasonable health for a man of his advanced years. His weight was 121 lbs, slightly less than at his previous medical, but this was considered normal with the onset of extreme old age. He still exercised by walking for an hour in the garden twice each day, and his heart and lungs were as sound as could be expected. His bladder problems were no worse.

Mentally, the report continued, Number 7 was alert and able to converse intelligently – for example about the latest space-shot, in which he had taken a lively interest. He was currently reading a NASA publication borrowed from the Berlin Public Library. However, it had not been possible to evaluate his memory because he still refused to discuss the past.

Following the medical report, the French director moved next business.

'It concerns a letter?' asked the chairman.

'*Oui.*' The French director explained through his pretty interpreter that in the previous week a letter had arrived for Hess from a German publisher, and he had thought it right to submit it to the meeting. It had been marked 'Private and Confidential', but every communication addressed to Hess had, of course, to be examined by the authorities.

'Jeez, not another offer for the old man's memoirs,' said the American. 'He could be a millionaire by now.'

'*Non.*' The French director explained that this was not the usual offer, but appeared to raise different matters that had not been discussed by the directors before.

'Is it in German?'

'The Colonel has obtained translations,' said the French interpreter.

'Nice work, sweetheart.'

They examined their copies silently.

The letter came from one Herr Harald Beer, Managing Director of Beer Verlag of Munich. It read as follows:

Dear Herr Hess,

We have not met, and I am not certain whether you met my father, Sigmund Beer, but I gather that in 1964 you signed an agreement with him for Beer Verlag to publish an original work entitled MEMOIRS 1894–1941 on condition that publication should not be initiated until after your death. I write to inform you now that my father died suddenly last month and I have succeeded to the chairmanship of Beer Verlag.

It was while sorting through my late father's effects that I came across the package containing the typescript of your MEMOIRS. My father, who was a man of absolute discretion, had not informed me of the contents of the package, so you may imagine my astonishment when I opened it this week.

I have now read the typescript, and I would like to congratulate you on your astonishing achievement. Without any question, the book is going to become one of the publishing events of the twentieth century.

Be assured that we at Beer Verlag are equal to the challenge of publishing a work of such historical and political importance, and also, as set out in the agreement, we shall negotiate the most favourable terms from publishers throughout the world.

There is one matter I would like to raise with you, and that is the proposed date of publication. It may be that, in more than twenty years since you signed the agreement, you have had second thoughts about your decision to delay publication until after your decease.

How would you feel about going ahead with publication this year? There may well be advantages in bringing your remarkable story to the attention of the public. I am not speaking merely of financial considerations, but I have in mind your present circumstances.

I would be grateful, Herr Hess, for your early consideration of this suggestion. If a meeting can be arranged, I will be more than happy to come to Spandau to discuss it further with you.

I look forward to hearing from you. Rest assured that we shall adhere to your instructions in these matters.

Yours sincerely,

Harald Beer
Managing Director

The Colonels stared at each other across the table. The Russian was ashen-faced. He muttered something to his interpreter, who got up and spoke quietly to the French interpreter and the shorthand-typist. The three of them left the room together.

The other directors exchanged significant looks. It was unprecedented for the chairman to adjourn a meeting without consultation.

'Gentlemen,' he said in English, 'I think we should discuss this letter among ourselves.'

'Off the record?' said the British director.

'Exactly. Clearly there has been a terrible breach of security.'

'Hold on, Colonel,' said the American in a pacifying tone. 'This letter is about something that happened twenty years ago. OK, the old man has outsmarted us, but he wouldn't be the first. Albert Speer was busy smuggling his diary out of here on scraps of paper for the whole of his goddamned sentence.'

'Hess may have learned the trick from Speer,' speculated the British director. 'Who did Speer use?'

'Any number of people,' said the American. 'Medical aides, warders, you name it.'

'My people are not going to like this,' the Soviet Colonel muttered. He was practically wringing his hands in despair.

'I guess not one of our governments is going to be over the moon about it,' commented the American.

'Can we stop it?' asked the Frenchman.

'You mean stop them publishing the book? No way. The publisher has the contract and a property worth millions of bucks. Plus the exclusive rights to sell it throughout the world. You think he's going to hand it back to the Allied Commission and say sorry?'

'It cannot be allowed,' said the Russian.

'Try and stop it,' said the American.

'The point is,' said the Russian Colonel, 'that this breach of prison regulations must be handled with the utmost secrecy. Of course it must be reported to the Commission and that will be my duty as chairman, but on no account must the public get to hear of it. That is why I asked the interpreters to leave.'

'Wasn't that a little late?' The British director turned to the Frenchman. 'Presumably your efficient young lady prepared these translations?'

The Frenchman nodded.

'You must caution her,' the Russian told him with such truculence that he might have been recommending a flogging. 'Until we receive instructions from our superiors, we must treat this as top secret.'

'How about Number 7? Will you let him see his letter?'

The Soviet director's clenched fists tightened until his knuckles were white. The others fully expected him to pound the table. 'That is unthinkable. He is in breach of prison regulations. I withdraw his letter-receiving privilege until further notice.' He scooped up his papers and thrust them into his case. 'I declare the meeting closed.' He marched out and slammed the door.

'I hope he makes it to the john. That is one shit-scared Soviet colonel,' commented the American director.

'Why?' asked the Frenchman. 'He was not here twenty years ago. None of us were.'

'Guillaume, when this gets out, as it will, the Russians are not going to like it. Why do you think they kept the old man locked up all these years? He knows things. They could never be sure if he'd got something on them, because he was so smart. He played the amnesia game for all it was worth and none of the damned shrinks could tell if he was bluffing. The Russians wouldn't take a chance on it, so they vetoed every move to release the old guy. It was cat and mouse all the way. Through the first twenty years or so he was convinced they meant to poison him. He used to switch plates with Speer. Only this mouse had a trick of his own. He wrote down the things he knew and got them to a publisher. Nothing will come out until after he dies, but he can die laughing. He's beaten the bastards.'

'Do you think we should show him the letter?'

'No point. He's too smart to be railroaded by some get-rich-quick publisher. He knew what he was doing in 1964 and the game hasn't changed. Rudolf Hess is coming out the winner.'

26

At Karlshorst, a suburb of East Berlin, a tall iron fence encloses a vast area that is guarded on the perimeter by East German police with dogs and at each entrance by Red Army sentries. Since the end of the war, it has been the principal administrative headquarters of the USSR in Germany. It is, in effect, a Soviet settlement. One group of buildings houses the Soviet High Command; another the Soviet Branch of the Allied Control Commission; and at the eastern end of the compound is a large hospital block that no longer ministers to the sick. It is heavily guarded, inside and out. It is the operations base of the KGB in Germany, second in size and importance only to Moscow Centre.

Here, this morning, the security was exceptional even by Soviet standards. The uniformed guard had been doubled, sniffer dogs had been brought in to check each room, and officers in plain clothes patrolled the corridors, challenging everyone. Nothing was being said officially to explain the increase in activity, but even in a KGB headquarters there is a grapevine. The word was that a top-level emergency meeting had been called. Two generals from the First Chief Directorate, the foreign intelligence service of the KGB, had been flown in from Moscow. Two generals from Moscow: nothing like it had been seen in Berlin since the swapping of the U-2 pilot, Gary Powers, for Colonel Rudolf Abel in 1962.

The meeting was taking place not in the regular conference room, but in a suite on the fourth floor normally occupied by General Raiko, Head of KGB, Karlshorst. Only Raiko and the two visiting generals were in session. No administrative staff were present and no record was kept, either on tape or in transcript. The entire third and fifth floors had been cleared for the duration of the meeting, and guards prevented anyone from using the elevator or the stairs.

Still within the KGB compound, but in the several detached houses that had once been the homes of affluent Berlin families, a number of smaller meetings were simultaneously in session. Up to fifteen KGB agents had been summoned to Karlshorst to make personal reports to their case officers. Their conversations were routinely taped.

In one of the houses, agent Kurt Valentin was reporting to the officer he knew as Julius. Julius was in his thirties, a slight, dark man with a relaxed manner. Like Valentin, he was wearing a suit tailored in the West. His concession to the system was a garish, vertical-striped pink and red tie, but it was fastened with a gold tiepin. He had apologised for the coffee several times.

Valentin's face was running with sweat. He had never been called to Karlshorst before. The meetings had taken place in various safe houses in the city.

'And is Moody proving a capable partner?' Julius was asking.

'As a player?' said Valentin tentatively.

'I understood that was the basis of the partnership.'

'Yes, indeed. They played their first match together recently and won.'

'Splendid!'

'He used to play for a club in Philadelphia.'

'You heard that from me, Kurt,' Julius pointed out.

Valentin took out a handkerchief and wiped his forehead. 'Of course. Sorry.'

'Don't be. So it's going well. How much longer do we have before the table-tennis league finishes?'

'About five weeks.'

'Not a long time.'

Valentin screwed up the handkerchief and returned it to his pocket. 'I was hoping that the relationship might have strengthened by then.'

'Into sex?'

'More like friendship. She says he doesn't seem interested.'

Julius frowned. 'We have no information that he is homosexual. Has she given him any encouragement? She's an attractive girl, isn't she?'

'I find her attractive, certainly.'

There was a slight smile from Julius. 'We know all about you, Kurt. What I am asking is why she is not attractive to Moody. We need a stronger tie than the fact that they once played table-tennis together.'

'I suppose she might be too domineering for some tastes.'

'Is there anyone else?'

'In Moody's life?'

'Fraulein Kassner's.'

'No one she has mentioned.'

'You might enquire. Perhaps she is not trying hard enough with Moody.'

'We don't want to make him suspicious.'

Julius shook his head. 'We won't. Most men are incapable of rational thought when they are offered sex. He may turn her down, but only because he doesn't fancy her, then at least we'll know where we stand. Talk to the girl about it, Kurt. She'll be much more likely to make him suspicious if she hangs on to him for no apparent reason.'

'All right.'

After a pause, Julius said as if he were asking a favour, 'Would you care to summarise what Fraulein Kassner has learned so far from Moody?'

Valentin tensed visibly. This was the crunch. 'It's early days,' he said in his defence. 'Moody isn't the loquacious sort. We know his hours of work. We know he has been a warden in Spandau since 1982. He's keen on fitness, jogs regularly, lives in old Spandau, within a mile of the prison.'

'We do have warders of our own in there,' said Valentin. 'We know all this, Kurt.'

'Yes.'

'Has Fraulein Kassner told us anything we would like to know, touching, perhaps, on Moody's contacts with Rudolf Hess?'

'She reports that he is sympathetic to Hess.'

'Better, Kurt. Go on.'

'Hess rarely confides in anyone. He is very self-contained, very taciturn.'

'I think we are beginning to scrape the barrel, aren't we, Kurt?'

Casting about for something to say, Valentin found himself remarking, 'He wouldn't have much conversation, would he, after more than forty years in prison?'

Julius said slowly, 'Was that meant to be clever at my expense?'

'No, not in the least,' said Valentin, flustered.

Julius stared out of the window as he said, 'I would like you to convey to Fraulein Kassner that Moody is more than just a ping-pong player, Kurt. If there is one man in Spandau with the glimmer of an understanding with Hess, we must monitor him. It may be Calvin Moody.'

'I understand.'

'Hess learned the hard way not to love the British. He wouldn't trust a Russian warder either. That leaves a Frenchman or an American.'

'Yes.'

'We wouldn't have brought you here for the coffee, Kurt. I won't hide it from you: there's a full-scale emergency on. Moscow Centre beating the drum. You and your ping-pong player may be more important to the security of the State than ever you realized. I won't promise you an Order of Lenin if you deliver, but I'll guarantee a knock on your door if you don't.'

Valentin had run out of responses. He simply lowered his head to signify assent.

Had he been privileged to sit in on the meeting of the three KGB generals, his worries would have increased. The First Chief Directorate as a matter of policy rarely authorises the liquidation of foreign nationals other than Soviet emigrés and spies. The KGB has scrupulously resisted any association with groups practising assassination to achieve political ends: the Baader-Meinhof Gang, the PLO or the IRA.

Yet by the end of the day the unanimous conclusion of the generals was that a 'wet affair' was inescapable. The highest interests of the State were under threat.

The order was given. The hit-man was briefed and issued with a weapon.

27

Dick and Jane crossed the floor of the newsroom to a chorus of good-natured abuse. There had been storm warnings all day from Cedric, and his blue-eyed boy and girl were slinking into the office as if they had been caught smoking in the toilets. All very entertaining if you weren't involved.

Inside, Cedric sat hunched over his desk in a posture of unmitigated gloom, the flab of his several chins overlapping his fists.

'Shut the door.'

When they were seated, he creased his features into something marginally more accommodating and said slowly, picking his words, 'I don't want you to take this personally, either of you. I've decided to blow the whistle on the investigation before someone else does.'

Jane exchanged a glance with Dick. 'Someone else? You mean whoever it was who broke into my flat?'

Cedric dipped his head. 'Or whoever gave the orders.'

'Dick told me you suspect the security services.'

'It was always a risk,' Cedric confirmed, trying to sound as if he had never been wholly in favour. 'We couldn't do this without making waves. I don't hold anyone responsible.'

'You're serious?' Jane said. 'You want us back in the newsroom?'

'Yes.' His small eyes studied her. 'My information is that you want to drop out anyway.'

She made a sharp intake of breath. 'Well, your information is wrong, Cedric. I have a personal stake in this now. My flat was broken into, and I'm angry. All right, I'll admit it shook me up at first, but that's turned to anger now. Why do these people think they have a right to invade my home? What have I turned up that is so fascinating to them? I don't want to pull out. I mean to get to the truth.'

Cedric shook his head. 'There isn't any point, Jane. They'd hit us with a D Notice before you could write the story.'

'A D Notice has no legal force. It's advisory.'

He sighed wearily. 'It's a warning that we'd be risking prosecution under the Official Secrets Act.'

'With a story about Rudolf Hess in 1941?'

Dick chimed in, '*The Sunday Times* ignored a D Notice when it exposed Kim Philby as a spy.'

'The case of Hess is in no way comparable,' Cedric insisted in a tight voice.

With a slight clearing of his throat, Dick challenged this assertion. 'For one thing, it concerns the reputation of MI5.'

'Mytchett Place?'

'Yes. I meant to tell you something I got in Brighton from that agent you asked me to visit. Did you know Sefton Delmer, the *Express* man?'

'Slightly,' Cedric grudgingly admitted.

'He was in charge of a secret service unit in the war. Black propaganda. His first assignment was to fabricate bogus news stories that were fed to Hess. Ugly stories, like the one that his wife and small son had been committed to mental institutions. Our people were doing that to Hess within a month of his arrival.'

'War is a dirty business.'

At that, Jane erupted. 'For Christ's sake, Cedric, don't fob us off with old B-movie clichés! You *know* there's a story, a bloody big story, that the people who run our country have tried to hush up for years. You know about the missing files on Hess, the stuff locked away until the next century. You know there's no reason why he should still be sitting in a cell in Spandau almost twenty years after all the others were released.'

'A life sentence means life to the Russians,' Cedric pointed out.

'Balls,' said Jane. 'You told us yourself that the only other lifers were released from Spandau in the fifties. Hess is still there.'

'They were sick men.'

'He's a very old man. If they were sent home to die, why not Hess? You know, and so do we, that something prevents it. Somebody is terrified of what might happen. What do they think – that the Deputy Führer is going to address Nazi rallies

127

at the age of ninety? And why are *we* about to be pulled off the investigation? Is it because someone on this paper is running scared as well?'

Cedric's face had been reddening since Jane started her harangue. He said in a stilted voice held in check with an obvious effort, 'Before we go any further, Jane, you can take back that remark you just made. The decision to shelve the story is mine. I am *not* running scared. I have made a professional judgement.'

There was moment's angry silence.

'I apologise,' said Jane flatly, 'but I can't accept that your judgement is right about this.'

Before Cedric drew breath, Dick spoke up, gamely drawing the fire. 'Why meet trouble half-way? No one has issued a D Notice yet. Won't you give us more time, Cedric? You hooked us on this story. We've slogged through the research. Don't you think – '

The phone in front of Cedric buzzed. 'This could be Red,' he said. 'I cabled instructing him to get in touch.'

It was an amplifying phone, so they heard the switchboard confirm that Mr Goodbody was on the line from Berlin, then Red saying, 'Cedric?'

Jane felt a surge of hope at the sound of that broad west country accent. If anyone could make an impact on Cedric, it was Red. Her own emotional outburst had misfired horribly, and she could already sense the resistance to Dick's more measured appeal.

'Decent of you to call,' Cedric responded with sarcasm into the box on his desk. 'You're still working for us then?'

'Round the clock, your excellency.'

'I'm glad.'

'You're going to be even more glad when I tell you this,' Red said with disarming confidence. 'I've got the line into Spandau. One of the warders. Doesn't say a lot, but he's a good lad. Just give me the questions whenever you and the others are ready, and I'll tell him what he has to do.'

'There's a hitch,' Cedric started to explain.

'No hitch,' responded Red. 'I'm ready to go.'

'A hitch on this side.'

'What?'

'A problem. Some, er, unsolicited interest.'

'Would you speak up? I'm in a bar.'

'God Almighty,' muttered Cedric. 'I can't explain now, but we're stymied. Can't go on.'

'Back to the drawing-board, you mean?' said Red with the disappointment clear in his voice. 'Jesus Christ, Cedric! That's all I need. I wasn't planning on a delay. I'm ready to go now.'

'That won't be possible,' Cedric told him firmly.

Red's voice now betrayed real concern. 'Easy, Cedric. This is a delicate situation for me. As a cover, I'm dating this warder's table-tennis partner, and she's a very demanding fraulein. She's match-fit. I'm short of training. I'm talking about another indoor sport. Get the picture?'

Cedric rolled his eyes upwards, then tactfully announced to Red, 'Dick and Jane are here with me.'

'Good. Give them my best and tell them I'm counting on them. I can't keep it up much longer. Dick'll know what I mean.'

Jane murmured, 'We all know what he means.'

'So˙let's agree to a deadline, shall we?' Red pressed. 'I'm serious, Cedric. I'm taking ginseng with every meal.'

'A deadline?' Cedric repeated with aversion.

Jane nudged Dick and they each nodded enthusiastically. Cedric glared back at them.

'You give me a deadline, and I'll give you a headline,' promised Red. 'Hess – The Truth.'

Cedric rubbed the side of his face. 'All right,' he said resignedly into the phone, 'Call me this time on Wednesday for further instructions.'

'Will do. Love to all.'

The line clicked.

'Thanks, Cedric,' said Jane.

'You've got Red to thank, not me. The chance of a line into Hess is too tempting for any editor to pass up.'

'So we have forty-eight hours,' said Dick.

28

A day with the lawyers. Harald Beer was enjoying it, too. Unlike his father, he was a businessman first, then a bookman. The first few days since he had taken over at Beer Verlag had been devoted to the accounts. Now it was contracts.

He had asked to see every contract in the building. They made a staggering sight in his office. They covered his desk and half the floor. Of course some of the older stuff had lapsed and could be thrown out immediately. He filled a tea-chest with half a century of his father's and his grandfather's mistakes and had them taken out before the lawyers arrived. There weren't even any autographs worth saving.

He sifted through the rest and set aside any that still yielded a profit, or might be worth renegotiating. There were some good things in the backlist: classics of German literature that would certainly ensure the survival of the firm and ought – with more discrimination – to have taken it to the top of the publishers' league. The future was not wholly bleak.

But there was still plenty of dead wood to hack out, and he had brought in the lawyers to help. They were painfully cautious. They had to be harried and bullied into finding clauses that gave Beer's a let-out, or at least the opportunity of paying off the unwanted authors. Harald rapidly developed a facility for locating the phrase . . .*shall discharge the publisher of any obligation* . . . and by the end of the morning he reckoned he had discharged obligations to the tune of six million Deutschmarks. It was salutary to discover how the costs of slim volumes of mediocre poetry and dull criticism mounted up.

So by the morning's end he felt elated. Beer Verlag was slimmer and in better shape. In future the policy would be to publish bigger books that appealed to a wider section of the public. The one he had foremost in mind was the Hess memoir. Without any doubt it was destined for the bestseller lists.

The lawyers had gone to lunch and Harald was sipping a scotch and still contemplating Hess when a call was put through to his office.

'Herr Beer?'

'Yes?' He answered warily. He had informed the switchboard that he was unavailable to incoming calls from authors or their agents. Any decisions about contracts or scripts would be communicated by post the following week. It was always possible, however, that one of the less experienced girls was doing the lunchtime stint on the switchboard.

'This is in regard to your recent letter to an old gentleman.' But it was not the voice of an old gentleman. The voice was firm and articulate, the accent local.

'Which gentleman is that?' Harald asked.

'This must be confidential, Herr Beer.'

'You may speak freely to me.'

'You are alone?'

'Yes. Who are you?'

'The letter you sent indicated that you are in possession of a book in typescript that your late father negotiated to publish.'

The Hess memoir. Harald reached for a pen. 'That is quite correct. Before we go on, may I have your name?'

'Pröhl. It is not important. I am just a go-between, speaking on behalf of the writer.'

Pröhl. It was familiar to Harald, but in what connection? He was certain it had come up since his father's death. Not in the contracts. Not in the accounts. Where?

'Are you still there, Herr Beer?'

'Yes.'

'I have been asked to thank you for the letter and the suggestion it contained.'

'Merely a thought in passing,' said Harald, trying to sound casual.

'For obvious reasons,' Pröhl went on, 'the author of the book is unable to respond in person.'

'I follow you, Herr Pröhl.'

'He asked me to inform you that his wishes in regard to the book remain unchanged.'

131

'Unchanged?' Harald's hand trembled. This was not what he had expected to hear. It was a blow he could hardly stomach. 'Are you quite certain of this?'

'Absolutely.'

'Has he considered the points I raised – the probable advantages that publicity would achieve?'

'He has given his answer, Herr Beer.'

Harald flicked his tongue around his lips. 'Surely he is open to further discussion.'

'I am sorry. He is inflexible. It's not surprising, is it? He has lived with inflexibility for the past forty years.'

'I am aware of that. I was suggesting a way of breaking the deadlock.'

'But it's not on. Goodbye, Herr Beer.'

'Wait!' Harald was desperate. The biggest opportunity of his life was slipping away from him. 'May I contact you again about this?'

'It won't be necessary.'

'But when he dies . . .'

'. . . his executors will contact you, I'm sure.'

'But I'd like to consult him about the illustrations,' said Harald on an inspiration. 'I know he is very particular about illustrations. He says something in the typescript about a picture several books have used that is supposed to be of himself and his sister as children. It's incorrect. We at Beer Verlag have high standards. We can't afford to make a mistake like that. I'd like to submit some agency pictures for him to approve.'

'I'll mention it,' said Pröhl.

'What is your number?' Harald asked. 'I'd like to be able to contact you about this.'

To his profound relief, Pröhl gave a local number before putting down the phone.

Harald was still shaking. He poured himself another scotch. There had to be a way of overcoming this. He couldn't submit to the will of that stubborn old Nazi in Spandau.

While his brain worked on the problem, he went to the safe, unlocked it and lifted out the packet, still in its wrapper with his father's handwriting on it. He removed the typescript and the contract. This was one contract he would not be showing the lawyers.

He leafed through the flimsy sheets of typing. To be brutal, Hess was a dull writer, but that would be no problem. There were professional editors upstairs who could whip the book into shape. Its selling power was Hess's unique knowledge of events in the years before his capture. Things that would change the history books, sensational things that he had kept silent about for all these years. He meant them to be revealed to the world only after he was dead. Why? Could his silence have been his guarantee of survival?

As Harald turned the pages, a name caught his attention, and it was the name he had tried to remember earlier. Pröhl. Hess had married Ilse Pröhl. So it was one of the family who had made the phone call.

Harald's mind worked faster. Who was likely to benefit from the huge advances that the memoirs were certain to attract? He took down a tax guide from his shelf and began to work on the figures. It was a question of comparing income accrued before death with the tax levied on an estate.

After twenty minutes, he picked up the phone and dialled the number Pröhl had given him.

'Herr Pröhl?'

'Speaking.'

'This is Harald Beer. I have been thinking over what you told me. I wonder whether a compromise is possible.'

'I don't see how,' said Pröhl.

'We could take another look at the contract. I'll be perfectly straight with you. We obtained the rights to this book in 1964 for two million Deutschmarks, which was a tidy sum then, but looks like a bargain now. Frankly, it will make much more money that that. The contract gives my firm the exclusive right to sub-license to other publishers throughout the world. It means that if we abide by the agreement, and no money changes hands until after the decease of the writer, there will be a very big pay-out to the estate for one or two years, and an extremely heavy tax-bill. I've been looking at the figures – '

'Before you go on, Herr Beer,' Pröhl put in, 'I'm not empowered to discuss money with you.'

'All right. But at least you can convey an offer from Beer's?'

'I suppose so.'

'Five million now into any bank account your client cares to name and another five million to his estate on publication. As well as increasing our offer fivefold, it will represent a tremendous saving in tax.'

'I see.' There was a pause. 'I won't promise, but if I were able to call you tonight . . .'

'I shall be here at my desk until nine this evening,' said Harald, smiling for the first time in an hour.

The afternoon session with the lawyers went particularly well. He could confidently commit the firm to a five million advance. He would, of course, dangle the bait and then make it conditional on publication within two years, irrespective of Hess's survival thereafter. Once the family had contemplated an immediate fortune, they would soon prevail on the old man to sign a new contract.

He tried to keep occupied as the evening closed in, but time still dragged. He had asked the switchboard to let all incoming calls come through to his office, which meant taking a few tedious enquiries from people who had tried to reach him in the day, but he cut them short with some excuse about a call from New York on another line.

By eight, he had the building to himself, and he was unable to concentrate on any kind of work. He sat by the phone, consuming claret left over from the last party. Across the room, his spade-bearded grandfather stared out of the portrait. Rolf Beer had been born only a few years earlier than Hess. He had once been Burgermeister. Very likely he had known the Hess family. There must have been some solid reason why Hess entrusted his memoirs to the house of Beer.

9.00 p.m. Nothing. Harald's nerves were on edge. He had promised himself not to phone Pröhl again. It would betray his eagerness. He was trying to cultivate the laid-back manner of the smooth negotiator.

A buzzer sounded.

He picked up the phone, but it was dead. For a moment he was disorientated, thrown by the unexpected. It was the intercom with the front door that had sounded.

He switched it on. 'Who's there, please?'

'Pröhl. We spoke earlier.' Clearly enough, it was Pröhl's voice.

Harald pressed the button that released the door. 'I wasn't expecting you in person, but please come in. It's the door at the end of the hallway.' He quickly stowed away the claret bottle and glass just as the knock came on his door. 'Come in, Herr Pröhl.'

The visitor was a good match for his voice: about thirty-five, a slight, compact figure, neat in his movements, elegantly dressed in a grey pinstripe and white shirt with a gold collar-fastening under the dove-grey tie. 'In the end I decided it would be more practical to come in person,' he explained to Harald as they shook hands. He clicked his heels in the old-fashioned way. 'These are highly confidential matters, and one hears such disquieting stories about telephone-tapping.'

'True,' said Harald, gesturing Pröhl into an armchair. This was encouraging, now that he had taken it in. The indications were that the family was ready to do business. 'Would you care for a drink?'

'I don't take it, thank you.'

'I must apologise for the state of the office,' Harald said, waving his hand towards the contracts stacked against the wall. 'There is so much paper-work when one takes over.'

Pröhl nodded. The courtesies done, he appeared to be waiting to do business.

'So you have passed on the offer I made?' said Harald, seating himself in the chair opposite Pröhl. 'How is Herr Hess?'

'I am here to verify one or two things, Herr Beer,' Pröhl said curtly.

'Whatever you wish.'

'First, your copy of the manuscript. It came into the possession of your firm some twenty years ago, is that correct?'

'In 1964,' said Harald. 'As a matter of fact, I noticed only today that Herr Hess signed the agreement on April 26.' He paused, but there was no reaction from Pröhl. 'His seventieth birthday.'

'Interesting. Tell me, how did it come into your possession?'

'My father's, actually. I was not aware that the book existed until I found it a few days ago in the safe over there.'

135

'I see.' Pröhl frowned slightly. 'You understand that we would like to confirm its authenticity.'

Harald assumed a slightly hurt expression. 'I can assure you that Beer Verlag deals only in authentic works, Herr Pröhl. You are not suggesting that the script in our possession is some sort of forgery?'

'I'm sure Beer Verlag is irreproachable. However, one has to be on one's guard. You remember the lamentable affair of the so-called Hitler Diaries? The perpetrators fooled some eminent military historians as well as hard-headed journalists.'

'There is a significant difference in this case,' Harald pointed out. 'Herr Hess is still alive to verify the work.'

Pröhl made a dissenting sound with his lips and shook his head. 'The authorities would not allow it. They are extremely agitated to learn of the existence of the book. Hess has been reprimanded by the directors and had his letter-writing privileges taken away. It is only thanks to a friendly warder that we are able to keep in communication.'

'That is distressing,' said Harald. 'I would not have wished to be the cause of any discomfort to Herr Hess.'

'It may be for the best,' said Pröhl dismissively. 'Tell me, do you have the original manuscript?'

'His handwritten version? No. Presumably it was passed out of the prison on scraps of paper, as the Speer Diaries were. What we have is the top copy of the typescript. Would you care to examine it?' Harald went to the safe and took out the package.

'But you have no idea who typed this?' said Pröhl as he took the script from its wrapper.

'None whatsoever. My father dealt with it. That's the agreement on top of the script. You can see that Herr Hess signed it.'

'Do you happen to know of the existence of any other copies?'

Harald shook his head. 'I haven't even made any spares for myself. It's a very hot property, as you will understand when you get a chance to read it.'

Pröhl looked up sharply, and his brown eyes locked with Harald's. 'What do you mean by that, Herr Beer?'

'Some of it is explosive stuff. I can understand why the authorities are disturbed, if they have any idea what Hess has written.'

'Such as . . .?'

'The British are in for shocks when this is published. And the Russians will go berserk.'

'The Russians? Why?'

'Because of what he reveals about the massacre of Polish soldiers in the war. You've heard about the Katyn Forest graves?'

Pröhl nodded. 'Hess knew something about that?'

'Yes, indeed,' Harald went on with relish. 'I dare say you know the salient facts. In 1943, the German Army found mass graves near Smolensk containing over four thousand corpses of Polish officers, each shot in the back of the head. They accused the Russians of the atrocity, because the area had been part of Soviet-occupied Poland. They said it took place in the spring of 1940. But the Russians made a counter-accusation, saying that the Germans had carried out the killings when they invaded the Smolensk area in July and August of 1941.'

'Herr Beer, this argument has been going on for forty years,' said Pröhl. 'The Germans deny responsibility and so do the Russians. The forensic evidence seems to point to the Russians, but so what? It was a tragic episode, but it's not an issue any more, except to the historians.'

Harald leaned forward challengingly. 'With respect, Herr Pröhl, you could not be more wrong. I know Poland. I have many friends there. Katyn is still an open wound. Each Polish government since the war has endorsed the Soviet version – that it was a Nazi atrocity – but, believe me, the mass of the people are not taken in.'

'They blame the Russians,' said Pröhl. 'So?'

'Four thousand bodies were buried at Katyn, but up to *fifteen* thousand Polish soldiers disappeared from the face of the earth in the early part of the war.'

'Numbers get exaggerated in stories of this sort,' Pröhl commented, continuing to turn the pages of the typescript in a preoccupied way.

'They were men taken prisoner by the Russians when they

occupied Eastern Poland in 1939,' Harald proceeded as if he hadn't heard. 'Over half of them were officers, the élite of the Polish Army. The Russians kept them in three large prisoner-of-war camps. They were permitted to write home until the middle of April 1940, when the letters suddenly stopped arriving. The camps were evacuated and the men transported in railway trucks to unknown destinations. The bodies at Katyn account for less than a third of the missing men.'

'What does this have to do with Hess?'

'Well, in 1940, he was head of the AO.'

'The *Auslandorganisation*?'

'Yes – which as you know was officially set up to strengthen links with Germans living in foreign countries, but was also set up as a cover for intelligence-gathering. If you study the chapter he has written on the events of 1940, you will see, Herr Pröhl, that he received reports from German agents that confirmed –'

Pröhl said mildly without looking up, 'Katyn?'

'Not only Katyn. Dergachi and Bologoye.' Harald noted with satisfaction the bemused expression on his visitor's face, before going on to explain, 'The two other sites where up to ten thousand more of the missing Polish soldiers were murdered and buried by the Soviet NKVD.'

Pröhl raised his head in surprise. 'These are places in Russia?'

'Dergachi is ten miles north of Kharkov. The men from Starobelsk Camp were taken there. Bologoye, where the Ostashkov prisoners were liquidated, is on the main route between Moscow and Leningrad.' Harald got up from his chair, too wound up to remain immobile any longer, and paced the room. 'God knows what will happen in Poland when the book is published. Those murdered men are coming back to haunt the Russians. With Solidarity barely suppressed, it's all that's needed to trigger an anti-Soviet uprising.'

A sniff from Pröhl indicated reservations. 'Even if it's true, it won't ever be proved. No one is going to be allowed to dig for evidence in Russia.'

'Don't you see?' Harald broke in excitedly. 'This book provides overwhelming evidence. Turn up the chapter Hess has written, Herr Pröhl, and look at the precise dates, the locations, even the identities of the NKVD units responsible and the names of the officers in charge. And the whole point is that Hess was in custody in England when the Germans invaded Russia, so there can be no question any longer that the Russians carried out these terrible events.'

Pröhl put down the typescript and said, 'Fascinating. But why didn't this come to light when it happened, and Hess got the information from his agents in Poland?'

Harald turned to face his visitor, using his hands to reinforce the point. 'This was 1940. Remember? We were friends of Russia then. We had signed the Non-Agression Pact.'

'So Hess kept the news to himself?'

'He told Hitler and Göring, but it went no further. And at the end of the war, Russia was one of the Allies in judgement over the Third Reich. It was not the time to tell the truth about the killings. Plenty of people knew about Katyn, but it was conveniently brushed aside at Nuremberg. The Germans were in the dock, not the Russians.'

Pröhl appeared to have grasped the point now. 'And Hess has lived with this secret since 1940?'

'Right! The Russians are still not certain how much he knows, but they simmer with suspicion. The Soviet judge at Nuremberg was ordered to demand the death penalty, but it was over-ruled by the other judges. Hess played the amnesia card at the trial to fox the Russians. He said nothing about the massacre in his evidence. Yet his first years at Spandau were dominated by the secret. He suspected that the Allies would poison him if they learned what he knew. He didn't even dare discuss his knowledge with the other prisoners.'

Pröhl still seemed reluctant to be totally convinced, almost as if it were a point of family honour that was at issue. 'If all this is true, I can't understand why he has waited so long to tell the world about it. Is he still in fear of being poisoned?'

'You must read the book!' Harald almost cried out in his enthusiasm. 'He is the most tenacious man I have ever come across. No, he isn't concerned about himself. He has old-fashioned ideas about honour and justice. He wants the facts to be known, so that the Third Reich will be absolved of any suspicion over Katyn and the missing thousands. If he is ever released—'

'He will never be released now,' said Pröhl. 'God knows, the family has tried to get him out.'

This was the very point that Harald had wanted Pröhl to make. He pounced on it. 'But there is a chance if we publish now. The effect will be sensational. Everyone will clamour to read the book. This won't simply be his family and a few people holding banners outside the gate of Spandau Prison. The attention of the world will be focussed on his cause. The pressure to release him will be irresistible.'

Pröhl nodded. It might have been in confirmation.

'Would you care to discuss my offer now?' Harald asked him civilly. As he spoke, he reached for the script. It was a gesture not without significance; the property had been licensed to him.

Pröhl's hand clamped down on the package first. 'Before we do,' he said, moving it away from Harald, 'there is something I must check, Herr Beer.' He got up and walked towards the door.

'Just a minute!' said Harald in alarm. 'Where are you going with the script?'

'Oh.' Pröhl turned, smiled and rested the script on a table between them. 'My mistake.' He continued to move towards the door.

'Is there anything wrong?' asked Harald.

Pröhl opened the door a fraction and looked out, as if checking for an eavesdropper. Harald meanwhile picked up the Hess memoir and held it possessively to his chest. Possibly Pröhl had heard something outside. The old building sometimes creaked as the temperature dropped in the evening.

Pröhl stepped outside the door.

Suddenly a second man had replaced him in the doorway. Harald stared in petrified amazement. The man was wearing a strange mask. He was holding a hand-gun, a clumsy-looking weapon with a long barrel. He was pointing it at Harald's face. He squeezed the trigger.

Harald Beer only had time to utter the words, 'What is it?' before he succumbed to the onset of vertigo and loss of breath. The respiratory centre of his brain was paralysed. He reeled, staggering into a pile of contracts and fell dying on them, permanently discharged of any more obligations.

The murder weapon was a seven-inch gas-gun fired by a KGB hit-man. Really it was just a sophisticated version of that simple toy, the water-pistol, except that the spray it fired was concentrated hydrogen cyanide.

The hit-man took a step backwards into the hall again and closed the door. Julius, the KGB agent known falsely to Harald as Pröhl, was waiting there.

'Done?'

'Done,' answered the hit-man.

'And now we must wait?'

'Five minutes. There is a mask for you in the case.'

They had brought in the briefcase containing their equipment when Harald had released the electronic lock on the front door to admit the visitor. The hit-man had come into the building with Julius and waited in the hall for his cue to kill. Had Harald greeted them in the hall, the hit-man would have been passed off as one of the Hess family.

While they waited for Harald to die and the fumes to disperse, Julius reviewed the encounter. He felt he had handled it reasonably well. In a few minutes he would take possession of the typescript and the contract. That was the good news.

The bad news was that Harald Beer had not been able to disclose anything about the present whereabouts of the original manuscript, the hundreds of scraps of paper that Hess must have managed to smuggle out of Spandau. Harald had not even known how his father had acquired the typed copy. At Karlshorst, they would not be overjoyed about that. This assignment was by no means completed.

The other piece of news – about the mass slaughter of the Poles – was best forgotten. For Julius, it was superfluous, but dangerous knowledge. It would not be prudent to mention it at Karlshorst. The KGB chiefs would read it for themselves in the memoir. And he would make a point of mentioning that he had made only a cursory inspection of the typescript.

The hit-man was looking at his watch. 'Ready? Better put on our masks.'

'One moment,' said Julius. He took a cigar from his pocket and struck a match to light it.

'You can't smoke that thing now,' the hit-man testily told him.

'I need it.' Julius inhaled to get the cigar well alight, then cleared his lungs with several deep draughts of air. Holding the cigar between two fingers, he drew the gas-mask over his head. Then he pushed open the door of Harald's office.

Harald's body lay sprawled among the contracts, the eyes fixed in a hideous stare, the teeth clenched and traces of froth at the edges of the mouth. The hit-man felt for the pulse at the side of the neck, then confirmed with a nod to Julius that the job had been successfully executed. There would be nothing to tell that the death was due to anything except a cardiac arrest.

Julius still had instructions to carry out. It was necessary to force each of the dead man's fingers away from the Hess memoir to obtain it. He checked that he had the correct script. Then he opened a filing cabinet and spent a few minutes searching for the office copy of the letter Harald had originally addressed to Hess.

When he had found it, he held the flimsy paper at arm's length and touched the lighted cigar to one corner until a small flame was kindled. He placed the burning paper next to a heap of contracts, which soon ignited. There was enough paper in the place to ensure that the fire would not go out. The desk was of wood, and the walls were panelled oak.

As a final touch, he pressed the cigar between the dead man's fingers.

The room was already filling with smoke as Julius and the hit-man left the building unseen and walked two blocks to where their car was parked.

29

'Forty-eight hours.'

'One thing's certain,' said Dick. 'I'm not spending a minute of it in the Public Record Office. Feel like a trip to Brighton?'

Jane frowned. 'The ex-MI5 man? I thought you'd got all you could from him.'

Dick steered the Renault out of Shoe Lane into the flow of traffic westward along Fleet Street. 'It's true he answered my questions about Hess, but he was incredibly jumpy. He broke off the meeting very abruptly.'

'You believe he could have said more?'

'I didn't press him as I should have done.'

Jane turned to face Dick as they stopped at a traffic signal. 'Are you sure you want me to come? I thought he didn't trust women.'

'Have you wondered why?'

'Tell me.'

'Women could be his weakness. Unfashionable in the spy world, but not unknown. One smouldering look from you, and he may open up.' Dick eased the car forward again.

'How are we going to find Stones? We don't have an address.'

'We'll stop off at my flat and make a couple of phone calls.'

The homeward movement west was already slowing the traffic, but once they were through Knightsbridge, they had a clearer drive on the Cromwell Road and reached Dick's flat in Shepherd's Bush soon after 4.00p.m.

Cedric was inquisitive when Dick got through to him at the office, but he could hardly refuse to provide Stones' number.

'What now?' said Jane. 'Will Directory Enquiries give us his address if we call them?'

Dick shook his head. 'We don't even know his real name, do we?' He tapped out Stones' number.

Jane stared at Dick in surprise. 'You're going to call him direct?'

Resonant with suspicion, the voice at the other end said, 'Yes?'

'This is the telephone engineer, sir,' said Dick breezily. 'Just checking that your fault has been corrected.'

'I didn't report a fault.'

'Didn't report it?' said Dick. 'Are you Mr Hatton of Trafalgar Street?'

'No, I'm not. I'm Salter-Smith of Regency Square.'

'My mistake,' said Dick as he wrote it down. 'Sorry to have troubled you, sir.'

They stopped for beer and sandwiches in Putney on their way out to the A23, but were soon back on the road. A steady drizzle smeared the windscreen without providing enough moisture for the wipers to work, except with the washer. They were in the thick of the rush-hour now, and each car had its slipstream of mud particles.

'I'm looking forward to this,' Jane announced. 'I've never met a real MI5 man. As far as I know, that is.'

'Don't expect too much of this one. He has no respect for the cormorant press, as he calls us.'

'What are we going to call him – Stones, or Salter-Smith?'

'Neither, if we can avoid it.'

'We'll get nothing out of him if we're not civil.'

It was around seven when the grey band of the South Downs was behind them and they cruised into Brighton in a stream of traffic. Their headlights picked out the floral displays along the edge of Preston Park, the sprinklers working on them, despite the rain. They kept straight on through the Grand Parade and the Old Steine to the lighted sea-front, and there turned right by the Palace Pier.

Jane had a town map open. 'Keep going for a bit. Regency Square faces the West Pier.'

They parked in the King's Road on the front, close to where Dick had stopped before.

To locate Salter-Smith, they had to make a tour of the elegant Georgian entrances, looking at the names against bell-pushes, a familiar exercise to them both. Salter-Smith's, when they found it, was not handwritten, nor even typed, but printed on a visiting-card. *Damian Salter-Smith CBE.*

'It sounds better than Stones,' said Jane.

'It doesn't suit him so well.'

Dick pressed a bell marked *Maggie, Davina and Ruth.*
Jane frowned at him. 'Why did you do that?'

'You never know your luck.'

She gave him a dig with her elbow, but not too hard, because it was the first real attempt at humour she had heard him make.

The footsteps on the other side of the door promised someone the size of a Sumo wrestler, and whether it was Maggie, or Davina, or Ruth who opened the door, or all three of them in one set of clothes, the promise was fulfilled. Her folded arms were like two small pigs asleep on the shelf of her stomach.

'Er, Miss Salter-Smith?' tried Dick in all solemnity.

She shook her head. 'Salter-Smith? Upstairs.' She gestured with her thumb without unfolding her arms.

Dick thanked her, guided Jane across the threshold – not easy in the circumstances – and stepped inside himself. The reason for the stratagem dawned on Jane as they started up the stairs: if Salter-Smith had come to the front door, they might not have got past it.

He had another of the visiting-cards neatly mounted in a gilt frame on his door. Dick knocked.

The door opened slightly. It was secured with a safety-chain.

'What the devil . . .' piped the ex-MI5 man.

'Sorry,' said Dick, at the same time sliding his foot inwards to prevent the door being slammed. 'Haven't brought a *Daily Mail* this time. Brought a young lady to see you instead.' He motioned to Jane to step into Salter-Smith's narrow strip of vision. 'Miss Jane Calvert-Mead. The Court and Diary correspondent on my paper, and very well connected.'

'I hear you're a writer,' Jane remarked in a piercing cocktail-party voice. 'Is the book published yet? It sounds a super subject. I simply adore books about the secret ser-'

'Not here!' Salter-Smith cut her off in alarm. 'You'd better come in.' He unfixed the chain.

He was wearing a faded blue overall that rather tarnished his MI5 image.

There was a sharp chemical smell in the apartment that

145

Jane recongnized as soon as she saw a squadron of model aircraft suspended from the ceiling in the hallway: modelling-cement. They were shown into a living-room where Salter-Smith had been at work. A balsa-wood castle was partly erected on a table covered with newspaper.

'Colditz, isn't it?' Dick observed, aided by the glossy photos pinned to the wall above the table. More aircraft waged a dogfight above their heads, and battleships were at anchor on the window-sills. A framed press picture of Stalin, Roosevelt and Churchill at one of their wartime conferences hung over what looked like a victory procession of hand-made soldiers on the mantelpiece.

'I thought I made it abundantly clear when we last met that I didn't want this kind of intrusion,' Salter-Smith barked accusingly at Dick, at the same time brushing wood-shavings off a chair for Jane. 'How do you like your sherry, my dear?'

With an amused glance in Jane's direction, Dick made a tactical retreat to an armchair the other side of Colditz. A video of *Reach for the Sky* was running on the television.

So the initative passed to Jane. She decided to lead the ace right away. 'I'd give anything to read your book,' she said. 'You chaps in the security services are the real heroes of our time, and you have to put up with so much ill-founded criticism from the media.'

'Can't defend ourselves because of the Official Secrets Act,' Salter-Smith said resignedly, basking in the flattery. He poured her a large amontillado, ignoring Dick. 'Hope it's all right. Never touch the stuff myself. Have to keep a clear head at all times.'

'Of course. It's no accident that your work is known as intelligence. Did you get a very good degree? I expect it's all in the book.'

'As much as I felt I could disclose in the national interest. I think it makes a damned good read. Do you read for a publisher, Miss Calvert-Mead?'

Jane hesitated, and then countered well. 'That's amazing! Hardly anyone ever gets my name right the first time. I suppose it's your training. Actually everyone calls me Jane. Do you have a photographic memory, Mr Salter-Smith?'

'Damian.'

All this was encouraging to Jane, but there was calculation in the way her new friend Damian watched her. They were definitely in a contest, sparring, looking for openings, and none were coming. She kept nudging him back to the topic of his book.

'It would be interesting to your readers to know how you trained your memory.'

'Perhaps you'd like to see a copy of the script,' he suggested. 'Do you have an hour to spare? I dare say you've been through one of those rapid reading courses.'

'What a wonderful suggestion, Damian.'

'Perhaps you can help me to find a decent publisher.'

'Well, I won't make any promises, but if I could take a copy back to London . . .'

He took hold of one of her hands and placed his palm over it affirmatively. 'You shall read it here. Garrick can watch the film and I'll carry on assembling Colditz.' He crossed the room to a writing-desk and fussed behind the flap. When he turned back towards Jane, he wasn't holding a manuscript, but a gun, a large black automatic. 'Garrick, come out and join the lady,' he ordered. 'I'm damned if I'm risking a bullet through my castle.'

Dick was as surprised as Jane. He moved around the table and stood beside her. 'Who do you think we are?' he said. 'We haven't come to do the place over.'

'Say precisely what you want from me.'

'At the point of a gun?'

'It's in good working order. I keep it ready for emergencies like this.'

Jane kept very still. This was bizarre and dangerous. You didn't take chances with a nervous old man holding an automatic, and she hoped Dick wouldn't try anything rash.

Wisely, he decided on the reasoned approach. 'What you know about us is the truth. Jane is on the team with me investigating the Hess story. When you and I met on the beach, I handled it badly. I wanted a second . . .' He hesitated. '. . . shot.'

Salter-Smith grinned. 'Fire away.' The grin was no comfort. He had a very unreliable look to him.

Dick talked on, trying to sound unalarming. 'I came away

with the impression that you felt Hess has been unjustly treated by our people.'

'So you still believe there's some great mystery?'

'We're both convinced of it.'

'And you think I can help solve it?'

'That's why we're here.'

'I never met Hess.'

There was an interval of silence. Dick appeared stunned by the admission.

Jane stepped in. 'But you were in the service,' she insisted. 'Is there anyone in MI5 who might be willing to help us?'

Salter-Smith shook his head. 'They're all gone. They were senior people, not youngsters, as I was then.' He broke off for a moment, his eyes losing their sharp focus as his mind wandered.

'There *is* someone?' Jane asked him eagerly.

He rubbed his chin with his free hand. 'No, I was reminded of something else. An incident in Bedfordshire . . .' He was distracted again. The gun was starting to dip towards the floor. Then his concentration returned. He eyed Jane and Dick in a calculating way. 'If I were able to recall the details, would you guarantee to answer a question truthfully?'

'Yes,' answered Jane at once.

'Of course!' Dick confirmed.

'Let's try it, then. From what your editor has told you, what chance does my book have of being published? A straight answer. No fudging.'

Dick took a deep breath and answered, 'No chance at all.'

Jane confirmed it with a nod.

'Thank you,' said Salter-Smith gravely. 'Very difficult to get an honest answer. Made a fool of myself.'

'No less than we did,' Dick commented.

'That's permissible in the young. Old men should be wiser, or shut up.' He placed the gun on the writing-desk.

Jane glanced towards Dick and then told Salter-Smith, 'I feel ashamed. It must be obvious that I haven't been very honest.'

He gave a bleak smile. 'That was obvious from the beginning, my dear. I bear no malice. Pretty young women don't often deceive me these days. I think I *will* have a drop of

148

sherry. Let's all imbibe, and then I'll keep my side of the bargain, for what it's worth.' When each of them had a glass, he picked up his own and said, 'First, a toast. To one very old man who has kept his dignity. I think you know who I mean.'

They drank.

He went on, 'This is the only thing I can recollect. In 1941, when Hess parachuted into Scotland, I was a very junior MI5 officer based in Bedfordshire, supposed to keep a lookout for Fifth Columnists in the civilian population. It was dreary, I can tell you. Until one night in June, five or six weeks after Hess arrived. I got a message telling me to report to Luton Hoo because two Germans in civvies had been detained by the Special Branch. Well, they were Germans all right, and pretty damn scared by the time I questioned them in the police cells. They'd parachuted in during an air-raid. Still had the harness-marks on their shoulders. They were wearing German-made suits with the labels ripped out. And they were carrying maps. They had Cockfosters marked – that was the RAF interrogation centre, you know – and also Dungavel.'

'The Duke of Hamilton's house?' said Jane in excitement.

'Yes. It was fairly obvious that they'd been sent to locate Hess, though whether to rescue him or murder him I never discovered. They were SS men, quite young and pathetically inept. They tried telling me they were part of a peace mission, and it didn't impress me much, but one of them did claim to have come to Britain three months previously. His story seemed fantastic to me. He said he'd been part of a German delegation that came in via Dublin to negotiate a peace. He'd actually remained in Dublin while the senior members of the party flew into Britain.'

Dick stared at Salter-Smith. 'Germans in Britain in 1941?'

'I know it sounds a tall story,' said Salter-Smith apologetically, 'and there may be nothing in it, but the fellow swore it was true. He told me how to verify it. Came up with the name of the British pilot who met the group in Dublin and flew them out.'

'Who was he?'

'A Warrant-Officer Perry. Out of interest, I checked. There was a pilot of that name based at Kidlington, in Oxfordshire. The next day, after these chaps had been taken over by pukka

MI5 interrogators, I tried phoning Perry. He wasn't available, but my call was intercepted, and within the hour I was carpeted and warned off by my boss. Whatever Perry had been engaged in, it was top secret. So I never met him. But I did hear indirectly that he had some bad luck later. Lost both legs in an air-raid. From time to time I've wondered about him, whether it was just a tall story from a frightened German, or not.'

'What happened to the two SS men?' asked Jane.

'They were interrogated by B Division of MI5 at Latchmere House in Surrey and executed.'

'Without trial?'

'Those were the rules of war, my dear.'

30

6.00 a.m. on Sunday morning. The temperature already rising. It had been a warm night in Berlin. Heidrun lay sleeping on her stomach, naked under the sheet, her face, puffy with heat and sex, cradled in one of her plump arms. She was breathing lightly and evenly, and Red was lying with his back to her, eyeing the china ashtray on the floor on his side of the bed. It contained three used stubs.

Another Sunday. He thought of London and the paper. The late edition on the vans. The satisfaction of studying the rival papers and picking holes in their stories. He could almost get nostalgic for subbing.

Our Berlin correspondent, Red Goodbody. In his Fleet Street days, fresh from cutting his journalistic teeth on *The Cornishman*, listening wide-eyed to the old hands telling stories in 'The Grapes', would he have seen himself, even in his wildest dreams, spending Sunday night on assignment in an energetic fraulein's bed? In the event, he was wondering how much longer it had to last. He was not averse to lustful women. His equipment still functioned as it should, even under heavy pressure. But that was how it was with Heidrun. Mechanical. *Now you can do it to me again, Red.*

Since he had got back from England, his thoughts kept returning to Jane, and that one short time in the early morning in Cedric's house. Jane's love-making was no less positive than Heidrun's, yet it managed to be cerebral as well as physical. She whispered and talked and coaxed as they made love, and it came over as a complex mix of associations: schoolgirlish curiosity, puritan guilt, assertive feminism and quaint social snobbery. The effect on Red was intensely stimulating. It had galvanized the act of intercourse. Each pass of his hand across her breast, each movement he made within her, had elicited intimate phrases, confidences, expressions of ecstasy. No one could really know Jane without making love to her.

151

He stretched and looked at his watch. Soon he would make an excuse to leave. He had only himself to blame for the present situation. He had let it develop. It had seemed the obvious thing to do when Heidrun had got suspicious. He had needed to get close to Cal, and Heidrun was Cal's minder. He hadn't reckoned on her appetite for sex, though. And he hadn't mastered the logistics of getting time alone with Cal, either. Heidrun was so domineering, and Cal so evasive. There was always a fresh shift coming up at Spandau. The previous evening, they had played a home match against Siemensstadt and won decisively, humbling the opposition in straight games. Red had watched it, counting on a euphoric celebration – if only over skimmed-milk and *apfelstrudel*. But Cal had packed his things into his sportsbag and left before the tables had been taken down. The victory rites had devolved on Red.

'What time is it?'
Christ, she was awake. 'Early.'
'Before seven?'
'Long before seven. Get some more sleep.'
'I'm awake now, and so are you.'
'Mm.' He tried to sound ready for sleep again.
A few seconds passed.
Then she said, 'I would like you to do it to me.'
'Mm.'
'Red?'
'Mm?'
'Do it to me, please.'
'Again?'
'It's another day now.'

Ten minutes later, another cigarette-butt joined the three in the ashtray.

When he woke next, it was 9.15. He got up and showered. He could hear Heidrun in the kitchen. Appetizing fumes of grilled bacon wafted upstairs. Red put on his things and went down the spiral staircase.

'Smells good.'
Heidrun was wearing shorts and an apron that barely covered her breasts. She said, 'Don't expect too much. I'm not used to cooking.'

'I'll have to go after this,' he told her while they were eating.

'Why? You can stay if you like.'

'I have to earn a living.'

'On Sunday?'

'It's a Sunday paper.'

'Idiot!'

'I'd still like to finish that interview with you and Cal. I scarcely know the guy.'

'He's difficult to know.'

'Do you think we could fix a session this afternoon?'

'With Cal? I can try. He should be off duty, unless the shift has changed again. Where would you like to see us?'

'How about the garden at Charlottenburg?'

The doorbell chimed suddenly.

'The Palace garden? Yes, it should be quiet there,' said Heidrun. 'Excuse me. I'd better see who that is.'

She tightened the neckstring on her apron and went out.

Red heard a man's voice in the hall. In the bedroom, there was a photo of a guy who had signed it *All my love, darling, Erich*. Was this the amorous Erich? Could be embarrassing. It wasn't a good morning for a punch-up.

Heidrun brought her visitor in and he definitely wasn't Erich. He was middle-aged and silver-haired, with tinted glasses and an expression suggesting he didn't care for the smell of bacon. Or something.

'Kurt Valentin: Red Goodbody,' Heidrun announced in a subdued voice. 'Kurt advises me about tax and things,' she explained to Red.

'I was about to leave,' said Red. 'I'll call you later about that meeting, love.'

She came to the door with him. 'He's a boring old man, I wish I could get rid of him.'

'I was leaving anyway,' repeated Red.

They kissed perfunctorily, and Heidrun closed the door and went back to Valentin.

He was still standing in her kitchen, grotesquely out of place in his pale linen suit, red cravat and matching pocket handkerchief. The fine line of his mouth was turned down at the ends in disapproval. The glasses flashed.

153

'Who was that?' he demanded.

'I told you. Red Goodbody.'

'I heard his name,' Valentin rasped. 'He was eating breakfast. You slept with him last night.'

She started to busy herself tidying the table. His manner scared her.

'Answer me!' said Valentin.

'What is the question?'

He reached out and knocked the plates from her hands, smashing them at her feet. 'Slut! Who is he?'

She backed away a step. 'Some fellow from England. A sports reporter. He's writing a piece about Cal and me.'

'So you let him screw you, eh? Where did you meet him?'

'In the sports-hall.'

'What paper does he work for?'

'A Sunday paper.' She hesitated, thinking back to the first meeting with Red. 'Well, he may be freelance,' she added, her voice betraying the sickening realisation that Red might have lied to her. 'His work is syndicated all over the world.'

'And he comes to Berlin to write about you playing table-tennis?' Valentin's voice was raised too high to project sarcasm. It was not far short of a scream.

'Yes.' Heidrun brought her hand protectively across her chest.

'And you believe him?'

She blurted out impulsively, 'My private life is my own. When some guy fancies me, I don't need to have him vetted by the KGB.'

He stepped towards her menacingly, and she backed away until she came up against a shelf unit. He came so close that she could feel his breath on her face. His hand darted towards her and she gasped and swayed. Instead of striking her as she expected, he grabbed a glass water-jug from the shelf.

He held it to her face, pressing the hard surface against her cheek. 'Who pays for this place?' he said between his teeth. 'Is this the kind of apartment where a common waitress lives? Who paid for this?' He swung the jug down against the edge of the working-surface, smashing it. The handle remained in his hand, with a jagged piece of glass attached to it. He brought it slowly towards Heidrun's face. 'Answer me, Fraulein Kassner. Who pays?'

154

She answered breathlessly, 'You do. Please don't hurt me.'

'Untie the apron.'

A shudder passed through her. She sobbed, 'No.' It was more in appeal than defiance.

He actually touched the edge of the glass to her cheek. 'Do it. Expose your breasts.'

She whispered, 'Please, Kurt. Please don't cut me.'

He said, 'I'm waiting.' He drew the glass far enough back from her face for her to obey the instruction, but still held it ready.

She reached for the loop of the apron-string behind her neck and drew it forward over her head. The top of the apron still covered her breasts. It was held in place by cold sweat.

As Valentin's free hand snaked towards the dangling string, Heidrun took the only chance she had. She jerked her knee upwards, into his genitals. Then she shoved him away with all her strength and dashed for the door. She raced for the spiral stairs and she started up them.

The structure of a spiral staircase is not designed for rapid ascent. Before Heidrun had got half-way up, Valentin had recovered enough to pursue her. She was wearing flipflops on her feet, and one of them hit the stairs at a difficult angle, causing her to slip one step. It broke the rhythm of her movement, and gave Valentin a chance. He reached through the iron-work, grabbed her by the shin and held on.

Heidrun turned as well as she could to face him. He was standing on the living room floor with both hands clamped round her ankle, but the curve of the stairs prevented him from reaching her without letting go.

For the moment he seemed content to hold on. Possibly the pain in his sexual parts had put a damper on his plans. He was breathing hard. He said ineffectually, 'Are you going to come down from there?'

Heidrun shook her head.

He tugged at her legs and it skinned her shin, but there was nothing else he could do without letting go. And then she would run into the bathroom and bolt the door.

Valentin apparently had taken stock of the situation, because he switched his approach. He told her in a voice held in control, even attempting to sound reasonable, 'I didn't intend to hurt you. I simply wanted to impress on you how reckless you have been. There's an emergency on, and you could find yourself called to account. Do you understand?'

'No, I don't.'

'The orders are coming direct from Moscow. It's the real thing, Heidrun. They wanted to know what progress you made with Calvin Moody, and I couldn't tell them much.'

'I see him several times a week,' said Heidrun.

'For table-tennis,' said Valentin with contempt. 'Is that more important to you than your work for us? You should be devoting all your energy and resource to Moody, and I find you feeding breakfast to this Englishman who obviously laid you last night. What am I going to tell them at Karlshorst?'

'What do they want?'

'Haven't I impressed it on you enough? They want to know about Hess, what he is doing, saying, writing, thinking. Moody is closer to him than any other warder. Something is going on, something big, and it concerns Hess. Get closer to Moody. Get into his bed if you can. Get him to talk. And do it soon.'

'I'll try.'

'You'll try, and you'll succeed,' Valentin told her in a voice heavy with intimidation. 'If you don't, and quickly, don't expect me to deal with you. It will be someone else. And it won't be the china and glass that gets smashed.'

He gave her ankle another wrench, released it and walked out, slamming the front door.

Heidrun sat on the stairs and sobbed uncontrollably.

31

Red turned up early at the meeting-place – the central fountain in the Palace garden, hoping to get some time alone with Cal Moody – but the hope was frustrated. Heidrun and Cal arrived together precisely on time at 3.30 p.m. wearing identical 'Olympischer Sportclub Charlottenburg' tracksuits. It looked as if the interview would be as formal as the setting.

This must have been stage-managed by Heidrun. From what she had said before, she had strong doubts of Red's ability to sustain a conversation on table-tennis, even after the crash course he had lately undergone as a spectator. The idea of testing him out probably appealed to her competitive streak. She certainly had a mean look this afternoon. She was like a boxer staring out the opposition before a fight.

Red didn't let it trouble him. He had too much on his mind already. This was his big opportunity. He had set it up, and he didn't mean to let it slip. There were vital things that he needed to know about the routine in Spandau, and Cal's part in them. In twenty-four hours, he might be ready for the dialogue with Hess.

The garden was laid out in the French eighteenth-century ornamental style, which meant that nothing in the main area was permitted to grow more than knee-high. The result was that the sun beat down fiercely on anyone lingering for long in the centre. Red had cooled off for short periods in the fine spray of the windward side of the fountain, but it was no place for a press interview, so he suggested a move to the shadow of one of the avenues that lined the sides of the garden.

'Does this kind of garden appeal to you?' he asked Cal sociably, without expecting his question to lead at once to the subject that interested him most.

Cal cast his blue eyes rapidly over the dedicated efforts of two centuries of gardeners and commented, 'Not much. If you gave me a choice, I'd be happier walking around the prison garden in Spandau. It's a little overgrown these days, but I like it.'

157

'Speer's garden?'

'That's what we call it. He was Hitler's architect, so while he was serving his time he devoted himself to making a place where the prisoners could walk. The directors encouraged it, naturally.'

'Because it was work for the prisoners?'

'Right. In its prime in the 1960s, that garden must have been one of the prettiest in the city. There are linden trees, pines, birches, lilacs, roses, hydrangeas, beds of irises. Some of us put in a few hours' work there now and then to keep it from turning into a wilderness.'

'I suppose Hess is too old to help?' Red prompted him. This start was as good as a flier. For once, Cal was talking freely about prison life.

Cal grinned. 'From what I hear, he was *always* too old to help. Maybe that's unfair, but I know he only ever worked there under protest. They used to find him asleep in the wheelbarrow.'

Red laughed. Heidrun managed a slight smile.

Cal, encouraged, went on, 'There's a nice story that happened long before my time, when all seven Nazis were in Spandau. Hess had been detailed to water the garden, and he refused. When he was reprimanded, he said, "Why should I do it? That's a job for the water department: Dönitz and Raeder. They are both Admirals, so I leave it to them." He has a nice sardonic line in humour.'

Red nudged the conversation on. 'How do you get on with him yourself?'

The nudge was too obvious for Cal. 'Hell,' he said, 'we don't want to talk about Hess all afternoon. Wouldn't you like to ask us about the table-tennis league?'

'Sure, but I'm also interested in you two as personalities,' Red told him, 'so your job comes into it.'

Stiffly, Cal announced, 'I'm not at liberty to say anything about my job.'

The flier had been a false start. 'Yes, you told us before,' Red carried on, 'and I wouldn't dream of getting you in schtuck with your bosses. I'll tell you what, Cal: I'll guarantee not to mention Hess in the profile I write about you two. I mean, we three are buddies. If you happen to mention Spandau in passing, I'm interested and so is Heidrun, but it's strictly between friends, isn't that right, Heidrun?'

Heidrun confirmed it with a nod and then, realizing that something more was wanted, added, 'What are friends for, if you can't trust them?'

Cal didn't appear to be entirely convinced, so Red slipped in a confidence-restorer: 'Getting back to table-tennis, how did you two first link up?'

'Shall I say?' Cal asked Heidrun.

'Go ahead.'

For the next fifteen minutes, Red endeavoured to give a passable imitation of a sports reporter winkling out the facts for a profile piece. It was by no means the first time in his journalistic career he had waded into a subject he knew nothing about. The trick was to get the experts talking. In this case, a question about choosing the right bat unexpectedly did the trick. Red had a vague idea that the pimpled rubber covering affected the speed and spin of the ball, but it emerged that there were over three hundred rubbers on the market. There were tacky rubbers capable of picking up a ball on the underside of a bat, and long-pimpled rubbers which buckled on contact with the ball and flicked it back with the spin reversed. All this was revealed as they strolled up the gravel path between two double rows of evenly spaced trees towards the lake, Cal and Heidrun talked non-stop, leaving Red to ponder how on earth he could get back to the topic of Hess.

It was a red squirrel that came to his aid, one of the many that waited for titbits along the walk. Heidrun stopped in mid-conversation and gave a cry of delight as the squirrel stopped a few yards ahead, sitting up on its hind legs to assess its chances. To their right, some people were feeding another squirrel, and Heidrun went over and asked them if they could spare a few nuts. In a moment, the squirrel was feeding from her hand.

Cal looked on benignly and came out with a remark that put Red in good humour, too. 'I wish we had them in the garden at Spandau,' he said. 'The old man would like squirrels. He's very attached to his birds. They know his

159

times. They gather in the trees about ten minutes before he's due to exercise. He'll be out in the garden this afternoon, feeding his birds.' He looked at his watch. 'Actually he went back inside at 3.30.'

'His exercise times are still as precise as that?' Red asked, hardly believing his luck.

'One hour twice a day if the weather is right. 10.30 in the morning and 2.30 in the afternoon.'

'But never longer?'

Cal grinned. 'Most times longer, but not this month.'

'Why not this month?' asked Heidrun, getting up, all the nuts gone.

'It's the Russian month. There's one watchtower with a view of the garden, and you can bet that if we give him five minutes too long when a Russian is up there, we get bawled out by the director next morning.'

'What does he do in the garden, apart from feeding the birds?' asked Red, as they moved on.

'He walks around the path. 215 steps. He used to make twenty-eight circuits, but he's cut it down now. He sits on the bench that Speer made and reads a book.'

'And if you're on duty, you stand and watch?'

'Right. While another warder searches his cell.'

Heidrun asked suddenly, 'What is that for? What do you expect to find?'

'Anything he's not supposed to have. Just now his letters have been stopped. He's normally allowed to write and receive one letter a week of not more than 1,300 words. We have to make sure a letter hasn't been smuggled in.'

'So he's in trouble,' said Red. 'What's he been doing – trying to climb over the wall?'

Cal gave a grin that said he had heard jokes like that a thousand times before. 'He can't even get up the iron stairs to his cell now. They had a small elevator installed for him. I don't actually know what his latest offence is. When the Russians are in charge, they can be very severe with him.'

'How does he take it?'

'He wasn't too happy when I saw him last night, but you never know with Hess. He's used to the Soviets. There was something else disturbing him. It was an item he read in the newspaper.'

160

'About himself?'

Cal shook his head. 'No, anything about himself or World War II is cut out before he sees the paper. This was a report about a fire in Munich the night before last. It gutted a nice old building there. He lived in Munich, you see. A man died in the fire, but Hess seemed more upset about the building. He has a different perspective than the rest of us. I guess all the people he knew are dead anyway.'

'What's one building, when so many were destroyed in the war?' commented Red.

'It must have had some importance for him,' said Heidrun, suddenly more animated than she had been all afternoon. 'Did you speak to him about it, Cal?'

'A little. He isn't one of the world's great talkers.'

'But maybe he confides in you sometimes?'

'I wouldn't say so.'

Heidrun was not so easily shrugged off. 'If you find something when you're searching his cell, do you report it?'

'That depends. If it's some small infringement, I might let him know that I found out. I don't see the point in hounding an old man who is no danger to anyone.'

'And let's face it, love,' added Red in a stagy aside to Heidrun, 'if Cal finds anything, it's probably been smuggled in to Hess by another warder. Cal isn't going to grass on his mates.'

'I think you are wrong,' Heidrun answered before there was any reaction from Cal. 'It's a matter of loyalties. Cal has a responsible job to do, and he does it well. He has a higher loyalty, and that is to the directors. So if it is necessary, yes, he – What did you call it? – grasses on the other warders.'

Red shook with amusement. 'Cal, if you're ever looking for someone to write you a reference, you know who to ask. *A first-class man. Won't hesitate to drop his mates in the shit.*'

Heidrun glared at him. 'I don't think that is very funny.' She tucked her arm under Cal's. 'He *is* a first-class man. He's good at his job and I am proud to know him.'

'He isn't a bad table-tennis player, either,' Red remarked, winking at Cal. 'Let's get back to the interview, shall we? I heard Cal's account of the way you two first met on the beach at Wannsee. Heidrun, would you like to tell me what you saw in Cal's play that impressed you?'

161

'Shall I tell him?' Still gripping his arm, Heidrun looked up and practically fluttered her eyes at Cal, in a show of togetherness that Red supposed was intended to make him jealous. Privately, it came as an immense relief, as good as a bugle-blast from the US Cavalry.

Heidrun gave what was, for her, a rhapsodic account of her first sight of Cal in play at the table. She made no mention of Kurt Valentin.

The talk stayed on table-tennis for an appreciable interval, Heidrun missing no opportunity to coax and flatter her way into Cal's affections. They sat for a time on one of the benches beside the lake, and she rested her hand firmly on Cal's thigh until he stood up, professing an interest in waterfowl. Soon after, he announced that he had better be getting back, if Red had got all he wanted.

'You're not on duty again?' asked Heidrun.

'No, but I have things to do, like visiting the launderette. Not very exciting things, but they have to be done today.'

'I have a washing-machine and drier,' Heidrun informed him. 'I don't mind washing your things.'

Cal smiled. 'Thanks, but I can manage.'

Red chipped in, 'Don't turn down a good offer, mate. I've got a stack of dirty washing at home. Let's all meet at Heidrun's place and make it a party.'

Heidrun gave him a withering look, and said, 'I'll issue my own invitations.'

But Cal was still looking for an exit-line. He said, 'I think I'll jog back now. Nice to see you guys.'

Heidrun reached out and gripped his arm. 'But we haven't even fixed a time to meet on Tuesday.'

'Tuesday?' repeated Cal uncertainly.

'The match against Moabit.'

'Is that Tuesday?'

'Yes. Is anything wrong?'

'I'm sorry. I won't be able to make Tuesday.'

Heidrun suddenly went pale. 'Why? I don't understand.'

Cal rubbed the side of his face. 'It's, em, the way things have turned out. There was a change of shifts. I've taken plenty of evenings off lately. One guy is off sick and another was promised Tuesday night, so I have no choice.'

162

'But you know it's the Moabit match,' Heidrun protested.
'Right. I meant to tell you before this. I'm really sorry.'
'Can't you get someone to change with you?'
'No chance.'
Heidrun's eyes had reddened at the lids. 'Please, Cal. I won't have a partner.'
'Honey, if I could have fixed it, I would. I'll make the next game for sure.'
Heidrun bit her lip. Cal backed away a couple of steps, nodded to Red, muttered some form of farewell, and jogged away through the trees.
'He promised to play all the games,' said Heidrun, dabbing a tissue to the corners of her eyes. 'He promised. What's gone wrong? I couldn't have been nicer to him. I tried, Red, I really tried.'
There was a note of desperation in her voice that Red couldn't understand. Frustration, yes. But desperation? And tears? It wasn't like Heidrun at all. She should have been kicking a tree or throwing stones at the swans.
He said, 'You're really in deep, aren't you?'
She gave him a penetrating look. 'Why do you say that?'
'I know you're upset about the table-tennis match, but it's more than that, isn't it? You made a pitch for Cal and it didn't come off.'
She started walking back in the direction of the Palace.
'OK, he didn't succumb to your charms,' Red persisted, increasingly interested in rooting out the truth. 'He's an idiot, but there it is. You win some, you lose some. Maybe he's a fag.'
Her cheeks were glistening with tears. 'Leave me alone.'
'You're scared of something.'
She didn't respond.
'Is it that guy who turned up at your apartment this morning? Valentin?'
She stopped and looked up at Red with her moist eyes as if she were making up her mind.
'What is it, love?' he asked.
She reached out and held both his hands. 'Take me back to your place now and let me stay.'

32

On the same afternoon that Red had his meeting with Cal and Heidrun at Charlottenburg, important things happened in England that transformed the Hess investigation.

The task of tracing the legless ex-pilot, Warrant-Officer Perry, was right up Dick Garrick's street. He had spent the morning putting out requests for information to as many organizations as he could reach on a Sunday. He had started with the RAF Association and the British Legion. An Air Commodore (retired) was given an urgent message at 9.45 on Banstead golf course and abandoned the fifteenth hole to drive to London and consult an Air Ministry list of disabled pensioners. He reported at 11.50 that Warrant-Officer Perry had received regular payments from the RAF Benevolent Fund until 1977. He had lived in Motspur Park, Surrey, and supplemented his pension by working at home, wrapping cutlery in plastic for a catering firm who supplied British Airways passenger flights. His wife had died that year, and he had notified the Trustees that his circumstances had altered, and he no longer needed assistance. He had moved from Motspur Park, and the RAF had lost touch with him.

A phone call to the house was unproductive. It had changed owners three times since the Perrys had left, and none of the neighbours could help. The catering firm, too, reported that they knew nothing of Warrant-Officer Perry's present whereabouts.

The trail went cold. At the back of Dick's mind was the stark possibility that Perry was dead by now. The RAF records showed that he would be eighty-three if he had lived this long.

'Where else can we try?' asked Jane, who had sat with him by the phone for the whole of the morning.

'Pensions and Social Security,' said Dick, 'but not until tomorrow when the offices are open again, and God knows how long it will take to trace him in their records. It might save us time tomorrow if we check the Death Registrations.'

'We've got to assume he's alive.'

'True.'

'Medical records? He must have had a doctor in Motspur Park. The doctor must have known him well. He would remember an amputee.'

Dick clicked his fingers. 'Better than that, the limb-fitting centre at Roehampton. He must have gone there for artificial legs. It's the only place this side of London. They must keep up-to-date records.'

He got on the phone again. A few minutes later, he lifted his thumb to Jane. 'Found him! He's alive and well and living on Richmond Hill at the Star and Garter home for disabled ex-servicemen.'

They were there within the hour, presenting themselves to a sister who told them how pleased she was that they had come. 'I can't remember when he last had a visitor, and he's such a darling. I wheeled him out onto the terrace.'

'How's his mental state?' asked Dick.

'I won't answer for it if you give him too much of that,' said the sister, eyeing the bottle of scotch in Dick's hand. 'In the normal course of events, he's very sharp for a man of his age. Would you like to come this way?'

Warrant-Officer Perry was in a wheelchair, looking down on the sinuous sweep of the Thames. He appeared so frail under his blanket that Jane hesitated to shake his hand, but he extended it, bony and heavily pigmented with liver spots, and gripped hers surprisingly hard. Under his straw hat, his eyes were misty brown behind glasses that magnified them strongly. Receding gums had given him the nutcracker look of old age, but he kept up appearances with an RAF tie.

Once the introductions were over, and the whisky stowed away under the blanket, Dick explained that he wanted to talk about the war.

'You can call me Frank if you like,' said the old man.

'Fine. This is Jane and I'm Dick,' he said, for the second time. 'As I said, I'm interested in what you did in the war.'

Frank said, 'I appreciate the hard stuff. Good of you to bring it.'

'I believe you were a pilot, Frank.'

'I'll keep it in my cupboard. It's not the others I don't trust. It's the nurses.'

Jane said quietly to Dick, 'Don't rush him. He'll tell us in his own time.'

'I was in the RAF,' said Frank. 'We're in a minority here. The place is full of the army. I did plenty of flying until I was bombed out in 1944 and lost my legs. Direct hit on my house in Raynes Park. One of them VIs. Buzzbombs, we called them. I was down the Anderson shelter in the garden, but we caught the blast, you see. The door blew in and the whole damn thing fell in on us. The wife got out with just a few scratches, but I was trapped. They had to take one of my legs while I was lying there. The other was no good either. I didn't know much about it.'

Having got his story over, Frank said, 'Got a cigarette?'

Jane produced one from her bag and helped him to light it. She said, 'What were you flying, Frank?'

'Ansons mostly. You wouldn't have heard of them. I don't mind betting you've heard of Spitfires and Hurricanes, though. I wasn't one of them glory boys in the Battle of Britain. I was ferrying people about in my old bus.'

'VIPs?'

'All sorts.'

'It was important work, though,' ventured Dick.

Frank Perry drew thoughtfully on the cigarette. 'Who sent you here? You must have had the dickens of a job to find me.'

'You wouldn't know his name,' Dick started to explain.

'D'you mind?' said Frank quite sharply. 'I may look old to you, but I haven't lost my faculties. I can remember plenty of people I knew in the war. Flight Sergeant Whittingham. He was a card.' It was the beginning of a rambling catalogue of RAF personnel, a roll-call of everyone still billeted in Frank Perry's memory. As it was plainly a point of self-esteem that he remembered so many, it was difficult to cut him off without offence. Probably he recited this list by the hour to anyone in the home who would listen, and probably no one would.

The question in Dick's mind was whether the old man's memory would recall anything it had not included in the recitative. He exchanged a look with Jane, and broke into the monologue: 'Did you ever make a flight to Dublin?'

166

Frank Perry carried on for a moment as if he had not heard, and then asked, 'Where?'

'Dublin. Did you fly on missions to Dublin?'

There was a long hesitation. 'Why do you ask me that?'

Dick sighed, and Jane took over. 'It could be important to us. We work on a newspaper.'

The old man chuckled. 'And you come to me for news? Young lady, the only news I ever get is who gets out on the terrace first in the morning. I gave up reading the papers when my eyes got bad.'

'People want to know what really happened in the war,' persisted Jane. 'We were told that you flew on several secret missions.'

'Who told you?'

'A former MI5 officer.'

'MI5 told you?'

'That's how we heard about you,' said Dick.

Warrant-Officer Perry stared down at the Thames Valley as if he had never seen it before. 'They told me to keep my mouth shut. Why do they send you to see me if I'm supposed to keep my mouth shut?'

Jane was about to speak, but Dick mouthed a negative and shook his head slightly. The crucial question had just been put. Its impact would be greater if it had an unrestricted drop.

Frank Perry made up his mind. 'I suppose it's not important any more. In my day, if you made a promise, you kept it, and I have until now. I'd almost forgotten about it. But if those secret service Johnnies have changed their minds, I suppose there's no harm in it any more. Yes, I'll tell you about my trips to Dublin. The first one was in 1940, before the Battle of Britain, but not long before.'

'July?' suggested Dick.

'About then. I was based at Uxbridge. One morning, the CO calls me into his office and leaves me there with two blokes in civvies. I didn't know it at the time, but they must have been secret service. They give me a lot of stuff about top security and then brief me for a flight to Dublin. I have to pick up a party of four civilians at the airport and fly them to Kidlington. That's Oxfordshire.'

167

'We know,' said Dick.

'They kept telling me it was top secret, dangerous talk costs lives and all that, and even my CO didn't know where I was going. I was a steady sort of bloke and I think they picked me out for this one. Anyway, I flew into Dublin and found myself being shunted out to the edge of the airfield, a mile away from the main buildings. There was one small hangar there, for private planes. I refuelled and had a cuppa, and I remember I had to pee against the hangar wall, begging your pardon, miss.'

Jane smiled. 'We've all had moments like that.'

'Yes, well, in no time at all a big black car drives out to the hangar, and four men get out. One is English, your civil servant type, very nobby, and the others are foreigners.'

'Germans,' said Dick.

'As I discovered,' Frank Perry confirmed. 'Well, the Englishman gets them aboard and tells me to take off. I ferry them over the Irish Sea and down to Kidlington using the flight path MI5 had given me. When we land, a staff-car comes out to the runway to meet them, and off they go. My orders are to make the return trip next morning, and that's what I done.'

'Just the once?' asked Dick.

'No, six times.'

'*Six*?'

'That's what I said. In the end it was getting as regular as a twenty-seven bus.'

'Can you remember any of the dates?'

'I can, as a matter of fact. The second trip was on my birthday 18 September 1940. There was another one about three weeks later, and then nothing until the middle of March. Then it got busy. One in April and one in May. Then it stopped.'

'This was May, 1941? Do you happen to remember the date of the final trip you made?'

'Yes, it was the first Friday in May. There was always a NAAFI dance at Uxbridge, and I had to miss it, more's the pity.'

Dick was making notes. He asked Frank Perry to confirm the dates again. July, 18 September, and October 1940; and mid-March, April, and 2 May 1941. 'I expect you wondered what it was all about,' Dick prompted him.

'Wasn't my business,' said Frank firmly. 'I'd been told to keep my nose out of it, and I did.'

'But you discovered they were Germans.'

'Well, it was obvious, really, from the way they talked. They was speaking English most of the time, but you can tell it's a Jerry from the way he says certain words, can't you?'

Dick nodded. 'Did you overhear them, or did you speak to them yourself?'

'I never spoke to them myself. But in the old bus, they had to shout to be heard above the engines.'

'We heard that one of them knew your name.'

Frank thought for a moment. He seemed to be tiring. 'Now you mention it, something happened on one of the later runs. I got to Dublin and refuelled at the hangar as usual, and when the motor-car arrived, the British bloke who always escorted them told me one of the Germans wanted to search the plane before we took off. I wasn't too pleased and I told him. I mean, what did they expect to find – a bleeding bomb? Well, these civil servants know how to smooth you down, don't they? He told me they had a security wallah with them. Gestapo, I suppose he was. Quite a young fellow. We had to play along with him. So he went through the plane with me, and of course he didn't find anything except my flying-jacket on the back of the pilot's seat. Blow me if he didn't pick it up and take my documents out of the pocket. "So you're Warrant-Officer Perry," he said. "Yes," I said. "Want to make anything of it?" He gave me a dirty look and handed back my papers and that was the last I saw of him. He must have stayed behind in Dublin, because he wasn't on the trip to England.'

Dick went on probing, as conscientious in his way as the Gestapo officer had been. 'Were the Germans you flew to England the same individuals each time?'

'I think two of them were,' answered Frank. 'There was always a third one in the party, but I can't recall that I ever recognized the same bloke on another trip.'

'Would you say they were probably diplomats?'

'I don't think they were servicemen, anyway.'

169

'And it was always the same routine in England? You flew to Kidlington and there was a staff car waiting?'

'Yes.' Frank took off his glasses and wiped them. 'I mean no. We didn't always fly into Kidlington. Once it was Brize Norton and another time it was Benson. And there's something else I wanted to tell you, if I can remember it.' He replaced the glasses and stared around the terrace. There were only two other residents outside, and they were well out of earshot, but he still leaned forward confidentially. 'The driver. I had a word with the driver of the car a couple of times, when we were getting the party aboard. He was in the Army. A Sergeant in Transport Command. One time I asked him where he took them, and he said it was usually some big house in the country, miles from anywhere.'

'The same one?'

'No. Different each time. But there was one thing the same. Whichever house he had to take them to, there was always this big saloon car standing in the drive. Being in Transport Command, he knew all about cars. It had no markings, no flag or anything, but he knew who those Germans had come to see. Who do you think? Only the blinking Prime Minister, Winston Churchill!'

Jane's mind reeled. Churchill, the greatest Englishman, the man who had exhorted the nation to defy the Third Reich in the darkest days of the war, had been secretly, regularly, receiving its envoys. *Churchill*, who had pledged that Britain would go on to the end, fighting in France, on the seas and oceans, the beaches, the landing grounds, the fields, the streets and the hills, defending her island, whatever the cost might be.

She was numb with the enormity of it. She was not a blind worshipper of Churchill. She had often rebelled against her parents' image of the man as a mix of the finest qualities of the British bulldog, St George and Jesus Christ. She would remind them of blots on his war record, like the fall of Singapore and the bombing of Dresden. Yet how could anyone begin to account for this massive inconsistency? She was so stunned that she totally failed to notice the silver-haired man in a dark blue suit who was waiting to intercept Dick and herself as they moved off the terrace and into the building.

She just heard his voice saying, 'May I have a private word

with you both?' She and Dick stopped together. She found herself looking into a pair of expressionless grey eyes above a thin, insipid smile.

Dick came down to earth first. 'What about?'

'If you would kindly step outside the building . . .' His voice was mild in tone, but so overloaded with reproach that he might have been apprehending shop-lifters.

'Who are you?' Dick asked.

'Not here, if you don't mind.'

Dick exchanged an uncomprehending glance with Jane and they allowed themselves to be led through the building to the main entrance. Three or four old soldiers were outside in wheelchairs, watching the traffic pass in and out of Richmond Park. The grey eyes flicked over them and then focussed in the opposite direction.

'Let's walk towards the Terrace Gardens.'

'If you've anything to say, you can say it here,' Dick obdurately told him.

Another glance at the war veterans. 'Very well. I think it right to inform you that the residents of this home are all ex-members of the armed forces, and come under the jurisdiction of the Official Secrets Act. They are not at liberty to disclose information to the press about sensitive matters.'

'Just who are you?' Dick angrily demanded.

'A member of the security services.'

'There's nothing illegal in what we're doing,' said Dick. 'It's supposed to be a free country.'

Jane added, 'We phoned the matron to arrange this visit.'

'I know you did, Miss Calvert-Mead,' said grey-eyes, pausing to let the fact that he knew her name sink in. 'But you omitted to advise the matron of the matters you wished to raise with Warrant-Officer Perry.'

'He was under no duress,' said Dick.

'He is an old man, Mr Garrick. Sometimes people take advantage of old men. As I mentioned, he is covered by the Official Secrets Act. Any information he may unwittingly have disclosed to you is also likely to be covered by the Act.'

'So what do you intend to do about it?' Dick snapped back. 'Prosecute? Haul the old man into court in his wheelchair? Is that the way this country treats its war veterans?'

'No, but we can prosecute journalists who take advantage of the same old man.'

'Is that a threat?' said Jane.

He ignored her. 'I doubt if this line of enquiry will reflect much credit on your newspaper, either. I believe you pride yourselves on being one of the more reliable organs of the press. Old men's memories are notoriously unreliable.'

Jane started to say, 'We wouldn't publish anything we hadn't confirmed,' but Dick gripped her arm, over-riding her words with some of his own.

'Leave it, Jane. We don't have to justify ourselves to someone who doesn't even tell us his name.' He steered her towards his car.

As they turned away, the security officer said to their backs, 'You'll be wasting your time if you go on with this.'

'What did he mean by that?' Jane asked Dick when they were fastening safety-belts.

'It sounded ominously like the threat of a D Notice.'

She took a long breath. 'They can't kill this story. It's got to be told.'

He started the Renault, and backed it slowly, watched by the security officer.

'What a wimp!' said Jane.

'Just a functionary, doing his job.'

'A bloody obnoxious job. If he goes back inside and scares that old man . . .'

'He won't,' said Dick. 'He's assigned to us. Watch him get into his car and follow. I reckon we alerted them by going to see Salter-Smith. The pressure is really on now.'

Jane watched in the wing-mirror, and saw Dick's prediction confirmed. Grey-eyes got into a blue Volvo and cruised into position behind them.

'Where are we going now?'

'To my place to check some facts,' answered Dick.

'We're going to need all the evidence we can get to win this one with Cedric.'

Jane saw the sense of that. Dick was right about the pressure. It was coming from every direction: the secret service, Cedric, and Red in Berlin. And now there was this incredible lead on Churchill: a vast new avenue of enquiry to explore.

Would it lead to Hess, or off into new territory? She kept thinking of Red, primed for action. On the phone to Cedric he had joked about some German girl making demands, but that was typical of Red. The message that had come over to Jane was a strong appeal for quick results. She sensed that he saw trouble looming, and in Berlin trouble came in ugly forms.

'I'm going to call Cedric as soon as we get there,' Dick announced. 'We've got to go out to Henley and see him tonight.'

Mindful of phone-tapping, Dick kept the call as uninformative as possible. Fortunately, Cedric caught on to the urgency of the request and agreed to see them at whatever time they could arrive. It was already 4.00 p.m.

Dick put two meat-pies in the microwave and brought out some Perrier water. At his suggestion, they spread a large sheet of paper on the floor and made a simple timetable: a vertical line down the centre: on the left, the dates Frank Perry had given for the German visits; on the right, the principal developments in the corresponding period of the war.

GERMAN MISSIONS	WAR EVENTS
1940	
	10 May — Churchill becomes PM. Hitler forces break through France
	24 May — German advance on Dunkirk halted on Hitler's orders
	2 June — Dunkirk evacuation complete
	22 June — Franco-German Armistice
	16 July — Hitler orders preparation for invasion of Britain

	19 July	Hitler offers Britain peace in Reichstag speech
(?) July – First mission		
	10 Aug	Battle of Britain begins
	17 Sept	Hitler postpones invasion of Britain indefinitely
18 Sept – Second mission		
(?)Oct – Third mission		
	14 Nov	Blitz begins
	(?) Dec	Hess's first attempt to fly to Britain

———————————— 1941 ————————————

	(?) Jan	Hess's second attempt
(?) March – Fourth mission		
	6 Apr	Germany invades Greece and Yugoslavia
	10 Apr	German advance in Libya
	21 Apr	Allies withdraw from Greece
(?) Apr – Fifth mission		
2 May – Sixth mission		
	10 May	Hess arrives in Scotland
	16 May	Blitz ends
	22 June	Germany invades Russia

Before it was all on paper, Jane could see a pattern emerging, a pattern dominated by Hitler's curious love-hate attitude towards Britain. He had not planned to go to war with Britain. He had counted on a bloodless agreement on terms that would recognize Germany's power over mainland Europe.

174

When Churchill had succeeded Chamberlain as Prime Minister, there were fighting words from the new leader about blood, toil, tears and sweat, but Hitler, of all people, understood rhetoric. His tanks had rolled through France and the Low Countries, providing their own eloquent testimony to German invincibility. They could have annihilated the British Expeditionary Force, but Hitler astounded his Panzer commanders by arriving in person at battle headquarters and ordering them to halt. The miracle of Dunkirk, the evacuation of over 300,000 British troops, was by grace of the Führer. Why? Was it a magnanimous gesture to the new Prime Minister? When the last troops had been lifted off the beaches, Churchill thundered his response: 'We shall never surrender.'

Hitler was unconvinced. He had completed the defeat of France. He had signed an armistice allowing the Pétain government jurisdiction over two-fifths of the country: another display of magnanimity.

He still had no desire to invade Britain. He was counting on a compromise peace. But in July he made preparations, and massed his forces on the Channel coasts.

This was the pattern: a show of strength followed by an offer of peace. As Operation Sealion ostentatiously got ready, Hitler stood up in the Reichstag and issued a 'final appeal' to Britain's 'reason and common sense'.

And at about this time, in July 1940, according to Frank Perry, a party of Germans had been secretly flown into Britain for a meeting with Churchill. Numerous peace feelers had been put out through neutral countries, but this was in another class. If it were true, it was sensational: Churchill actually talking to Germany.

'What do you think?' Dick asked, when he had finished.

Jane didn't conceal her excitement. 'You can almost see Hitler's mind at work. He makes a concession, and then sends his people over to get a reaction from Churchill. The Reichstag speech, then the cancellation of the invasion, then two deputations to Churchill in three weeks. It looks as if he really believed he could pull off a peace deal.'

'Let's not forget that the Luftwaffe were given a drubbing in the Battle of Britain.'

'Exactly!' said Jane. 'What better incentive for Hitler to stop the conflict?'

Dick nodded. 'Hitler's motives are clear from the start, but that's not the story, is it? The story is Churchill. What was *he* up to, talking to the Nazis while he was hurling defiance at them in Parliament?'

Jane had asked herself the question a dozen times and found no answer. Everything she knew about Churchill rebutted it. For all his faults, he had never made any secret of his implacable opposition to Hitler and the Nazis. 'You ask: "What is our aim?" I can answer in one word: "Victory!" Victory at all costs, victory in spite of all terror, victory however long and hard the road may be: for without victory there is no survival.'

She made an effort to be analytical. 'Either he was seriously considering Hitler's overtures, or he was boxing clever, trying to win time.' As she said it, she found the latter idea so engaging that it showed in her voice.

'. . . and that's the more appealing explanation?' Dick suggested in a voice that showed he disagreed.

'History supports it,' Jane answered stoutly. 'There wasn't a deal and the Allies defeated Hitler.'

'Six sets of talks was boxing very clever indeed,' said Dick with heavy irony. 'The Germans must have felt they were getting close to a deal.' He casually threw in another shaft. 'And where does Hess fit in?'

'Hess?' Jane had almost forgotten him. 'He acted independently. He has always said he came without Hitler's knowledge.'

Dick raised one sceptical eyebrow. 'Yet he was regarded as totally loyal to his Führer, the most reliable of all the Nazi leaders. So far as I know, he has never to this day repudiated Hitler.'

'Hitler repudiated *him*. He was in a screaming fury when he heard what had happened.' She hesitated, staring at Dick. 'What are you suggesting – that Hitler was play-acting?'

'No. He was angry, all right – in despair that Hess had failed.' Dick leaned towards her in a more conciliatory way. 'Like you, Jane, I've read everything I can find on Hess. I simply can't accept that he flew to Britain without Hitler's prior knowledge. He was with Hitler from the beginning, in prison with him, helping him to write *Mein Kampf*. I think he was sent by Hitler to clinch a deal with Britain. It was to be the culmination of all the secret missions, the ultimate proof of Hitler's good faith.'

'Are you saying that Hitler thought Churchill was ready to come to terms?'

'Listen, we heard this afternoon that they'd been talking secretly on and off for ten months. Churchill must have given the Germans enough encouragement to keep coming, but there were no tangible results for Hitler. Time was running out, and he was getting impatient with Churchill, but he had the ace of trumps to play.'

'What was that?'

'Barbarossa. The invasion of Russia. In their political thinking, Hitler and Churchill had many differences, but they shared one dominating principle: a pathological hatred of Bolshevism. They both believed that Russia wanted world domination. So why not sink their differences and smash the Soviet menace together?'

'Hitler and Churchill on the same side?' Jane shook her head at the suggestion.

'You've got to see it in terms of Britain's desperate position in 1941,' Dick urged. 'We were alone in Europe. Churchill hadn't persuaded America to join in the fighting. Things had gone badly in the Middle East and the Balkans. Our cities were being blitzed. Parliament itself was a heap of rubble. The pressure to cut our losses must have been overwhelming.'

Jane said, 'Yes, but Britain wasn't in the business of invading other nations. Our people wouldn't have consented to that.'

'Some of them would. Remember that Hess tried to get in touch with the diehards – the extreme right wing of the Conservative Party – and in those days some of them were very extreme indeed.'

'That doesn't square with what you were saying just now,' Jane pointed out. 'Why didn't he go straight to Churchill?'

'Because basically Hess was sent to raise a posse. As Hitler saw it, Churchill had dithered for too long, listening to the secret delegations, maybe even talking terms, but refusing to come to a deal. The German plan was to win support from the diehards, put pressure on Churchill, and give him an ultimatum: join us, or face a revolt from your own supporters.'

Jane was intrigued, if not entirely convinced. 'But the plan fell through because Churchill got to hear of it prematurely?'

'No,' said Dick, surprising her. 'That wouldn't account for what happened after. Remember that astonishing period of forty-eight hours after Hess arrived, when no one knew what was happening. Churchill was at odds with his Ministers. Statements were prepared and rejected. Beaverbrook told the press to provide a smokescreen of rumour and speculation. I have a hunch that Churchill decided to accept the offer Hess had brought.'

There was a long moment of silence.

'All right,' said Jane eventually, 'what went wrong?'

Dick shook his head. He had no answer yet.

Jane leant forward on her elbows, thinking. 'It's horribly plausible. It accounts for so much. The treatment of Hess at Mytchett Place – the psychiatrists, the injections, the amnesia. Something extremely damaging to Britain had to be suppressed from his memory before the Nuremberg Trials.'

'You're not kidding!' said Dick. 'Can you imagine the reaction of our Russian allies if he gave evidence that Churchill had seriously considered joining the German invasion?'

Jane nodded. 'It wouldn't do much for present-day Anglo-Soviet relations. If there's anything in this, I'm not surprised MI5 are onto us.'

Dick got up to look out of the window.

'Is he down there?'

'The car is. I can't see him. He's probably on the roof with the SAS.'

Jane made an effort to laugh, but the presence of the Volvo was not amusing. They both felt the unease of being under surveillance.

Jane brooded on what she had just been invited to believe. It was shocking and repugnant, yet a thread of credibility ran through it. She searched for a break in the thread. 'I'm still not convinced that Hitler sent Hess over. Are you sure it wasn't just a quixotic adventure dreamed up by Hess to make his own impact on the war? That's the way everyone tells it.'

'Everyone?' Dick repeated sceptically. 'You mean Churchill and his Ministers in their various memoirs.'

'*And* the German press statements,' added Jane.

'Can't you see it was in their interests to cover up the truth? Neither the British nor the Germans wanted the Russians to know what was almost hatched between Hitler and Churchill.' He snatched a book from the shelf above him and started leafing through it. 'But the people close to Hitler knew. Listen to this, written in 1951, by Göring's biographer, Willi Frischauer: *Every single surviving member of Göring's entourage ... is convinced that Hitler not only hoped to make peace with the West, but to persuade the British Government to join in Germany's attack on Russia. Hitler's bewilderment in Berchtesgaden was due to the fear that his plot had failed.*'

Jane was silent, weighing what she had heard. She didn't mention it to Dick, but she had at the back of her mind a phrase from Albrecht Haushofer, after one of his meetings with Hess: *From the whole conversation I had the strong impression that it was not conducted without the prior knowledge of the Führer.* This assessment from the judicious, reflective man who had shared in the planning of the flight carried conviction. 'All right,' Jane declared. 'I'm prepared to go along with you almost all the way. I'm even prepared to believe that Churchill was in two minds about accepting Hitler's offer.'

'Good! We're going places.'

'To Cedric's, you mean?'

'Not yet.' He smiled sympathetically. 'I'm sorry, but we haven't buttoned it up. We still don't know what made Churchill turn the offer down.'

Jane gave a shrug. 'The War Cabinet, I suppose. They weren't all rabid anti-Bolsheviks.'

'They weren't all consulted,' said Dick tersely.

'They were eventually.'

'Only to a limited extent,' insisted Dick. 'I've seen a note in

Churchill's own handwriting in the Public Record Office saying Hess also made other statements which it was not in the public interest to disclose.'

'Barbarossa?'

Dick didn't answer. A useful idea had just occurred to him. 'I wonder if the PRO has a copy of Churchill's appointments diary. Then we can find out exactly who was in on the discussions.'

Jane shook her head. 'I have news for you. There was a diary, but it mysteriously disappeared, and hasn't turned up since.'

'Are you certain about that?'

'Positive. Sir John Colville mentions it in his memoirs. He ought to know.'

Dick hammered his fist on the table. 'You see? It's a cover-up, Jane.' He reached for another sheet of paper. 'We'll make our own bloody diary. We've got enough books and notes. Let's get it all down, everything we know about Churchill's actions and decisions from the time Hess landed.'

It took another hour and a half of double-checking, but the result was spectacular.

'Now we're ready for Cedric,' Dick declared.

They each had an armful of books when they went out to the Renault at 7.10 p.m. The Volvo was nowhere in the street. If they felt relieved, it was only temporary. Jane was watching as they drove away, and a green BMW started up and pulled out behind them. It stayed in obvious attendance all the way out of London and along the M4 to Henley. The driver was younger than grey-eyes. He sported a heavy dark moustache and was wearing a tan-coloured windcheater. Presumably MI5 was no different from any other organization when it came to duties at unsocial hours. The junior officers copped the night-shift.

They were at Cedric's inside the hour, drawing up in front of the converted cottages while the BMW was obliged to cruise slowly past, seeking a less obvious parking spot.

'If Cedric says anything, we've no idea who was in that car,' Jane murmured before they got out.

Cedric hailed them like old friends. Here in his weekend home, he was unrecognizable as the tyrant in the editor's

180

chair. He kissed Jane and took over the books she was carrying. There was coffee waiting inside.

He sat benignly in his armchair, smoking cigars and listening to Dick relating the visits to Salter-Smith in Brighton and Frank Perry in Richmond. When the question of Churchill's secret meetings with the Germans came up, Dick made some remark to the effect that it must sound like something out of a spy story. Cedric shook his head and amazed them both by saying, 'I believe every word of it.'

Jane's eyes widened. She exchanged a baffled look with Dick.

Cedric shifted in his chair, and it was almost possible to believe he was embarrassed over something. 'I owe you both an apology, because a call came in last week from Washington, and I didn't see its relevance at the time, so I didn't pass it on. You remember our man found a report in the National Archives about ex-President Herbert Hoover, who was taking an interest in the Hess case?'

Dick nodded. 'You mentioned it the other day on the Embankment.'

'Regrettably, I didn't tell you everything. Hoover claimed to be getting his information from reliable inside sources in London. This is the part that will interest you. He heard that Hess was the seventh German emissary of peace sent to England since the outbreak of war, and that the others had all come through Dublin and been picked up from there by a British plane.'

Jane clapped her hands in excitement. 'Fantastic! Frank Perry had it right.'

Cedric remarked penitently, 'I deserve a kick up the backside.'

'To hell with that,' said Dick. 'Is there anything else you haven't told us?'

'You know as much as I do now,' Cedric humbly assured them both. 'Probably more, by the expressions on your faces. Let's have it. What else have you dug up?'

'Plenty,' Dick crisply answered, 'but Jane will tell you later. There isn't a lot of time. How long will it take me to get to London Airport from here?'

'The airport?' Cedric blinked in surprise. 'It's not more than twenty-five miles. Where do you need to go?'

'Paris.'

'Paris? You mean tonight?'

When you had the ascendancy over Cedric, you didn't yield. Dick went on, 'I need to see Justin Stevens – the guy who put together that story on the Resistance for the colour magazine last year.'

'Justin Stevens. Dick, what is this. . . ?'

'I need his address.'

'I should have it in my desk.'

Jane crossed the room and picked up the phone. 'I'll make the flight reservation.'

33

Dick glanced in his mirror and confirmed that he was still being tailed. He was resigned to it. The young MI5 agent in the BMW ought to be grateful. A dash to Heathrow was better than sitting all night in a Buckinghamshire wood. Presumably he would pass the flight number to his superiors, and it would be up to them to decide whether it was worth providing another shadow across the Channel. So far, they couldn't fault Dick. He had consulted his editor, and now he was visiting a staffman in Paris. Unimpeachable conduct.

The turn-off to the airport came up fifteen minutes after he had joined the motorway. He would make that 11.10 p.m. flight with ease. Charles de Gaulle Airport by midnight. What could be more appropriate?

Back in Henley, Cedric had got out the brandy. He handed a goblet to Jane. 'If you're not proposing to fly off to a European city in the next half-hour, it would be an act of charity to enlighten your bewildered boss as to what the flaming hell is going on.'

Jane gave a relaxed smile. The strategy they had worked out together had succeeded so far. Dick was out of England, and he would make sure he was beyond recall so far as a D Notice was concerned. Cedric could have his explanation.

She eased herself deeper into the armchair and sipped the brandy. 'Well, the story we heard from Frank Perry has transformed everything and just about accounted for everything as well. It's such a help to have it corroborated.'

Cedric pulled a face. 'Don't rub it in – I'm still wearing sackcloth and ashes.'

Jane went on evenly, 'It was quite a bombshell to hear that Churchill was receiving deputations from Germany, but Dick and I both have a hunch that the story is more sensational than that. We believe Churchill was taking the overtures seriously.'

'That's not a bad hunch,' Cedric commented. 'In fact, I'd

183

say the evidence of six secret meetings makes it an odds-on bet.'

'But would you believe he decided to accept the offer – when it was made by Rudolf Hess?'

Cedric's eyes opened very wide and his skin turned noticeably more pink. 'Jesus! Let me think about this.'

Jane picked out a book from the pile they had brought with them. 'Listen to something Churchill himself wrote in his history of the Second World War. He's describing his second meeting with Stalin, in 1944. Stalin questioned him closely about Hess.'

'Stalin was very touchy on the question of Hess,' put in Cedric.

Jane read aloud, '*I had the feeling that he believed there had been some deep negotiation or plot for Germany and Britain to act together in the invasion of Russia which had miscarried. Remembering what a wise man he is, I was surprised to find him silly on this point.*'

'A nice Churchillian touch,' commented Cedric. 'As if such a thought had never crossed Winston's mind. Do you think Stalin had inside information? Anything MI5 knew was probably passed to Moscow by certain traitorous gentlemen who went through Cambridge together.'

'He got it from Lord Beaverbrook,' said Jane simply.

'Max?' Cedric sat forward in his chair.

'Beaverbrook visited Moscow in September 1941, as the head of an Anglo-American arms supply mission. He was the first minister to go there after the German invasion. Shortly before he went, he made a special visit to Mytchett Place to interview Hess. When he got to Moscow and Stalin put the inevitable question, Beaverbrook said quite candidly that Hess had flown to Britain expecting to persuade the Duke of Hamilton and his friends to depose Churchill and form a new government to make peace with Germany. Then the two countries would join forces and attack Russia.'

'Jesus Christ! Where did you get this account?'

'From Averil Harriman's book, *Special Envoy*. He was present at the meeting,' said Jane.

'Max was covering up like mad, I presume?'

Jane gave Cedric a knowing smile. 'It seems likely.'

'And Stalin wasn't taken in?'

'Well, he harped on about it at every opportunity. He said he couldn't understand why Britain didn't bring Hess to trial as a war criminal. In 1942, the Cabinet sent Moscow a report on the whole escapade, but it didn't stop Stalin from badgering Churchill about it when they met at Teheran in 1943 and Moscow in 1944.'

Cedric sized up Jane over his brandy-glass and curled his finger at her. 'Come on, you're holding out on me. What did Stalin know?'

She answered, picking her way with care, 'We're not certain yet, but let me give you an informed guess. In 1941, Hess flew to Britain on Hitler's orders to negotiate a peace with Churchill. The previous missions had prepared the way. Churchill had made sympathetic noises. The deal was to include a joint attack on Russia to destroy their mutual enemy, the Bolsheviks.'

'But what about the right-wing coup to unseat Churchill?'

'A bargaining-point,' said Jane dismissively. 'Threats were always in the background when Hitler negotiated. He knew he had to deal with Churchill in reality. As Stalin knew.'

'Ah, hence the scepticism in Moscow.'

'Yes. You see, Hitler, being smart, or devious, had covered his bets. He had made a counter-offer to Stalin. At this time, Germany and Russia were still on diplomatic terms. He suggested Russia should join Germany in defeating Britain and then carving up Europe, Asia and Africa between them.'

'Bugger me!' Cedric frowned, took a sip of brandy, scratched his head and produced a more considered response. 'Sounds to me as if you're spot on. Hitler *would* think of something like that.' He then had another thought. 'Where does America fit in?'

'Still officially neutral,' answered Jane. 'It's quite possible that Roosevelt knew what was happening and was waiting on the sidelines to see which of the deals would stick.'

Cedric lit a long cigar and drew on it strongly. 'This certainly explains why Hess is still in Spandau and kept under such close scrutiny. Not one of the Allies comes out with much credit. Except France.' He peered at Jane through the smoke. 'Isn't it time you told me why the hell Dick has flown off to France?'

185

'All right.' She held out her glass for more brandy. She was beginning to enjoy herself. The prospect of staying behind while Dick flew off to Paris had not pleased her much, even if she had seen the necessity of one of them being on hand for information from Don or Red. It might as well have been either of them, but she couldn't help feeling she was cast in the old, old role of the patient woman who stays at home and waits.

Somehow, she was going to get a slice of the action.

She started to tell Cedric what had happened. 'Dick and I agree with Stalin. We think some kind of deal was being done with Germany in that second week of May 1941, but we had to discover what put the stopper on it. Churchill's diary of appointments – as you might expect – is missing, so we tried to reconstruct one ourselves – not just for Churchill, but for Hitler as well. We wanted to know who they were seeing and what was happening in that all-important week.'

'The blitz, for one thing,' suggested Cedric. 'The night-bombing was at its worst.'

'Mm. And on 16 May, the night that Hess was moved to London, it miraculously came to an end.'

'I never realized that,' pondered Cedric.

Jane let that point rest, and moved on. 'The main thing apart from Hess that occupied everyone in London and Berlin that week was Syria. Do you know about Syria in 1941? It's terribly important.'

Cedric took out his cigar and said, 'In that case, my dear, I won't hedge. I know sweet fuck-all about Syria in 1941.'

'It was a French possession. To be exact, they held a mandate, and it was still administered by the defeated French government in Vichy. There were 30,000 French troops there, said to be loyal to Marshal Pétain.'

Cedric obligingly picked up the inference. 'Said to be?'

Jane nodded. 'The Free French had other ideas.'

'Ah, the alternative government. General de Gaulle,' said Cedric heavily. 'I *do* know a few things about him.'

'But not many people did in Britain. Churchill disliked him from the start. He wanted to know why this lanky, gloomy Brigadier had been brought to London, and he was told that no one else would come. Right from the start, Churchill regarded him as a thorn in the side. De Gaulle was ambitious and imperious. He wanted to reclaim the whole of the Empire for the Free French. Churchill wanted him replaced. In December 1940, there was a fiasco in West Africa when a combined Free French and British force tried to seize the port of Dakar from Vichy control. They were forced to withdraw.'

'I've got the message: de Gaulle was bad news as far as Churchill was concerned.'

'Right,' confirmed Jane. 'Let's concentrate on the Middle East. In the spring of 1941, trouble flared up for Britain in Iraq. There was a military coup, led by Rashid Ali, a pro-Nazi. He attacked one of the two British airfields in Iraq, laid siege to the British Embassy and appealed to Germany for arms supplies. The only way Germany could supply them was through Syria, using it as a staging-post. There was also a stack of French arms conveniently cached in Syria. So the Vichy French were invited to give their stamp of approval. This was agreed on 6 May. Admiral Darlan, their Foreign Minister, was brought to Berchtesgaden to meet the Führer on Sunday 11 May.'

'The day the Hess story broke?'

'Yes. But while this was going on, Rashid Ali had been beaten off by the British and had fled to Iran on 8 May, three days earlier.'

'Panic over, then.'

'Not entirely,' said Jane. 'German planes still started arriving in Syria. De Gaulle wanted to go in with a Free French force, but he would have been outnumbered five to one, and neither Middle East Command nor Churchill would sanction it.'

'Not after the Dakar defeat,' put in Cedric.

Jane gave a nod. 'It was unrealistic to go in without Allied support, and that raised all kinds of problems. For one thing, the Foreign Office were trying to keep a line open to Vichy.'

'And for another,' added Cedric, 'we were appallingly over-stretched already.'

'Yes, General Wavell, the Commander-in-Chief in the Middle East, made that crystal clear to London. He was desperately defending Egypt against Rommel after being beaten back in Libya. There was still fighting in Abyssinia.

Greece had just been lost, and Crete and Malta were under imminent threat. Wavell told London that he believed the Free French alone would be ineffective in Syria and he didn't want to be burdened with another front.'

'Not unreasonable'.

Jane paused. 'But what happened? He was ignored. On 20 May, he was ordered to prepare a force to invade Syria with the Free French. He asked to be relieved of his command.'

'He resigned? In the middle of a war?'

'He telegraphed to London to say that if the Chiefs of Staff preferred to rely on the advice of the Free French leaders, he didn't wish to carry on.'

'He blamed de Gualle? What happened?'

'He was pulled out of bed in the small hours and given two cables. The first was from Churchill. It ordered him to back the Free French in Syria regardless of anything. And the second came from de Gaulle. It said the same thing.

'Wavell came back into line and Syria was taken in six weeks. It wasn't the bloodless takeover de Gaulle had promised. Frenchmen fired on Frenchmen, and I believe over ten thousand lives were lost. But it brought de Gaulle out of the wilderness. He was a credible leader after that.'

'OK,' Cedric agreed, eager to move on. 'Let's come to the crunch. How do you think he fixed it?'

Jane was inwardly amused to see him on tenterhooks, but she resisted the urge to pay him back for the times he had kept the team in suspense that first weekend. 'Some time in the week after Hess arrived in Britain, de Gaulle found out the truth about Churchill and the peace plan and threatened to trumpet the whole story from the rooftops.'

'How did he find out, for God's sake?'

'Probably from Germany. Admiral Darlan was in Berlin to do that deal with the Nazis, and you can bet your life there were Free French agents monitoring everything that happened. They excelled at intelligence-gathering, and the Vichy French were as leaky as sieves.'

Cedric sat looking into his brandy, assimilating what Jane had said. 'So it was political blackmail. De Gaulle got his way by threatening to expose the peace plan before anyone could make it stick.' He sat back and stared at the ceiling, thinking hard. 'It answers all the questions I can think of. De Gaulle was one man who wouldn't have peace with Germany on any terms. And he has desperate enough to play a card like this. It must have been wholly justifiable from his point of view. But the problem is how to prove it. That's why young Garrick has hared off to France, I take it?'

Jane answered, 'He's hoping to get in touch with some of those resistance people Justin Stevens interviewed last year.'

Cedric heaved himself out of his chair. 'I'm ready for my bed. I can see agonizing decisions looming. I take it you'd like to have the room you slept in before? Everything you need should be there.'

Everything except Red, thought Jane.

At about the same time, Dick was lining up with the foreign passport-holders in Charles de Gaulle Airport. When it came to his turn, he showed his passport and was nodded through without a word. Then, out of Dick's line of vision, the immigration officer nodded to someone else, who followed Dick through customs and out to the taxi-rank.

189

34

Dick telephoned Justin Stevens from the airport, and they arranged to meet for breakfast at a crêperie in the Rue de Rome, a narrow shop with a tall wooden counter, behind which *madame* cooked with a stack of prepared crêpes, while the *patron* received the customers and dispensed drinks and a shy *jeune fille* managed the half-dozen small tables. There, with the breakfast rush finished, they had the place to themselves, except for one late arrival in a dark suit who sat on a stool at the counter and opened a newspaper. He didn't seem near enough to their corner position to overhear much.

Whoever had assigned Justin Stevens to Paris had known his man. He was a charming and fluent conversationalist, whose mobile, expressive face showed just that suggestion of the sardonic that finds favour with the French temperament. After Dick had updated him on Fleet Street and Stevens had declared how fortunate he was to be out of it, even if he sometimes suffered from the foreign correspondent's malady of 'peripheritis', they got on to more urgent matters. Dick explained that he was on a project involving Churchill and de Gaulle in the early years of the war. There was no reason to bring Hess into the explanation, so he didn't.

'Marvellous stuff to work with!' Stevens commented. 'I envy you enormously. Literally great characters, each with a sense of theatre the like of which we've rarely seen in statesmen. And the bickering and backbiting: terrific! De Gaulle was constantly calling Churchill on the phone to press the case of the Free French over this and that, and poor old Churchill, who liked his meals, couldn't even get through dinner at Chequers without interruptions.'

'De Gaulle probably ate later,' said Dick.

'Quite. Anyway, on one occasion, Winston was determined to get through his meal. The soup was hardly served when Sawyers, the valet, announced that the General was on the line. Churchill set his mouth in the bulldog grimace and refused to go to the phone. In a few minutes, Sawyers came back, his ears buzzing from the haranguing he had just been given, and pleaded with Churchill to relent. Out to the phone storms Churchill, and when he comes back the soup is cold. He sits hunched in his chair for some time. Then he says, "Bloody de Gaulle! He had the impertinence to tell me that the French regard him as the reincarnation of Joan of Arc." There's a long Churchillian pause, and then he adds, "I found it necessary to remind him that we had to burn the first!"'

Dick had heard the story already, but he chuckled convincingly before homing in on the real business of the morning. 'I'm hoping you can give me some background on the Syrian campaign. It was the turning-point for de Gaulle when Churchill agreed to back the invasion.'

'Syria? Yes, it set him up. Terrible shambles, of course. He admitted it later. A civil war, in effect. The Free French had something like ten light tanks and eight guns between them. They went to war with camels, horses, private vehicles, buses, anything. And the British contingent sang "We are Fred Karno's Army" as they moved in. Good thing the opposition was half-hearted.'

'What I'd really like to discover,' Dick persisted, 'is how de Gaulle persuaded Churchill to support the campaign. When you did your colour feature on the Resistance, did you come across anyone, or hear about anyone, who was with the General in London about that time?'

'You mean in Carlton Gardens?'

'Yes, if that's where he had his headquarters.'

'He was more often holding court in a suite at the Connaught, old boy. Portraits of Joan of Arc and Napoleon on the wall behind his desk. Better food, too.'

'I can imagine,' said Dick, trying to be patient with this affable man. 'The problem I have is tracing someone who was with him in London in May 1941, when the discussion with Churchill must have taken place.'

'That's not going to be possible,' Stevens told him. 'You see, de Gaulle wasn't in London then. He was in Brazzaville.'

'*Brazzaville?*'

'His power base. Most of French Equatorial Africa rallied to him in 1940 and he saw that it was properly administered.

He went there from London in March 1941, or thereabouts, and stayed until he moved to Cairo when the Syrian thing began.'

Dick was stunned, his visions of de Gaulle in secret conclave with Churchill, facing him with the truth about his dealings with the Germans and putting his demands in return for silence, were dashed. It couldn't possibly have happened like that. Maybe it hadn't happened at all.

'Bad news?' queried Stevens.

'Makes a large dent in my pet theory,' Dick admitted. 'I thought there were discussions in London.'

'There may have been,' Stevens pointed out. 'De Gaulle had his representatives in London.'

Dick shook his head.'The discussions I had in mind could only have taken place between the two leaders.'

'There must have been some sort of communication. Cables, I expect. De Gaulle was a great sender of cables.'

Dick nodded, reassembling his thoughts.

Stevens continued, more to himself than Dick, 'I was once given the name of a woman who was with de Gaulle as his cryptographer. Everything had to be in code. I wonder whether she was in Brazzaville with him.'

Dick was fully attentive again. 'How could we find out?'

'I could try a couple of calls to people who might know.'

'Would you?'

'It's rather a long shot.'

'It's all I've got now.'

'All right. We'll use the phone on the wall.'

'I'm afraid I don't have any small change.'

'It works on tokens. You buy them from the *patron*.'

After a couple of unproductive calls, Stevens located someone who could help. Yes, the woman had travelled everywhere with the de Gaulle entourage, so she was probably in Brazzaville in 1941. Her name was Madeleine Guillon, and she lived on the coast near St Malo.

'How far is that?'

'A good 350 kilometres. At least 220 miles.'

35

Dick had rented a Porsche 944 Lux for the journey to St Malo, which would probably send Cedric through the twelve levels of the office and into outer space when he got the bill for expenses, but he had asked for quick results and they would have been longer coming in an economy car. And if Dick were tailed, he stood a decent chance of shaking them off in the Porsche.

Madame Guillon, he learned at the post office in St Malo, actually lived several kilometres along the coast to the west, near Cap Fréhel, one of the great landmarks of the Emerald Coast. Weaving through narrow coast roads, and being forced to stop several times for oncoming traffic, he cursed himself for not having had the sense to backtrack and take the more established route from Dinan to Lamballe and then up to the coast. Yet it was still early afternoon, not yet 3.00 p.m. He was betraying signs of stress. He had been driving too long without rest.

He told himself to relax and take encouragement from the empty lanes behind him. Once or twice on the autoroute, he had stared in the rear-view mirror at other cars, but he was damn sure he was not being followed now.

So he could give all his attention to what was to come. The old lady might be difficult. She lived alone and had no telephone, suggesting she might be some kind of recluse. In the post office, they had asked if he knew her, and he thought he had detected a significant exchange of looks between the staff. A pity he had not been able to let her know he was coming.

The main thing he hoped was that she was mentally OK. And if so . . . He took a deep breath, not daring to guess what she might be able to tell him.

The house had been described to him as granite-built in the local pink stone, and standing alone on the cliff road south-west of the Cape. He soon spotted the only possible house, sited spectacularly above the red and black granite cliffs, at least 150 feet above the foam that was surging up intermittently between the reefs. He took the car as close as he could, and still had to climb some way on foot. As he mounted the last steps he was conscious of being watched from inside. He could imagine the feelings of an old lady on seeing a stranger approach the house.

She opened the door before he had his hand to the knocker, an exceptionally small, bright-eyed woman with white hair scraped back from her forehead in the French style. In her left hand, clutched to her chest, was a black, snuffling pug.

'*Bonjour, madame.*' Dick showed his press-card and explained that he was a British newsman researching the participation of the Free French in World War Two. He mentioned the name of the Resistance agent who had suggested he should speak to her, as she had been a personal assistant of de Gaulle.

She said in French, 'I was very unimportant. I don't see what use it is talking to me.'

'On the contrary, madame. I understand that you accompanied the General everywhere.'

'Yes, but I hardly ever had a conversation with him.' She flicked her eyes upwards to indicate the problem she would have had trying to parley with six feet four inches.

Dick smiled and so did she.

'But you had better come in, if you've come all the way from England.'

A press picture of de Gaulle in uniform addressing a crowd was hanging in the narrow hall. He was standing in front of the Tricolour, flanked by the Union Jack and the Stars and Stripes. Dick's memory for dates came in handy. 'The liberation, June 1944.'

'But, yes!' she peeped, delighted. 'His first speech in the square at Bayeux.'

'A moment of history.'

She took him into the front room and asked him to wait there while she made coffee, which he felt it would be ungracious to refuse. The pug sat in a chair by the window and growled softly as Dick inspected the pictures on the walls. Many were photos of places he didn't recognize, but there was one of the Sphinx.

'You were in Egypt, then?' he commented as she came in with the tray.

'Several times. When I look back, we seemed to be travelling all the time.'

'Would this be 1941?'

'I can't tell you. It was so long ago. I expect you take your coffee white.'

'Please. De Gaulle made several visits to Cairo in 1941.'

'You must be right, then.'

Dick persevered, trusting that something would trigger her memory. 'He was there first in the spring, in April. He had a plan for the Free French to enter Syria. There was a meeting with General Wavell, but it was unproductive, because Wavell couldn't offer any support. De Gaulle was angry, and returned to Brazzaville.'

'I remember Brazzaville,' said Madame Guillon. 'The picture on the left of the fireplace. That's Brazzaville.'

'Yes.'

'I'm not very helpful, am I? The diplomacy all went over my head.'

'Perhaps you remember when a message came from Churchill inviting the General to go back to Cairo?'

'No.'

'It was the turning-point of de Gaulle's career. He was given the go-ahead to work out a plan for the conquest of Syria with General Wavell.'

'It meant nothing to me.'

'It was the campaign against the Vichy French, madame.'

'I was a foolish young girl with other things on my mind,' she admitted. She moved to the window and stood looking out to sea. 'I'm sorry. It's a wasted journey for you. Before you go, why don't you walk up to Cap Fréhel itself? On a clear evening like this, you can see the Channel Islands.'

'You don't remember anything that might help me?'

'I'm sure if I did, you couldn't rely on it.'

A pendulum clock ticked like a metronome as Dick tried to decide whether to admit defeat.

Madame Guillon turned from the window and asked, 'Wouldn't your friend like some coffee as well?'

195

Dick frowned as the possibility arose that she was not only woolly-minded, but mad. 'My friend?'

'The gentleman down there by the car.'

'I came alone, madame.' He got up to have a look, but he could see no one in the area of the car.

'He was probably walking to the Cap. Some people think this is a short cut.' She put down her coffee and picked up the dog. 'We've been caught like that before, thinking visitors were coming, haven't we, Jojo? And now that we have a visitor, we have to send him away disappointed.'

He braced himself for a last attempt to unlock her memory. 'Your work involved encoding and decoding messages, I understand?'

'That's correct.'

'Important work.'

She shook her head and laughed. 'It was purely mechanical. I didn't have to think about what I was doing. These days a computer would do it in a fraction of the time.'

'Did you see de Gaulle's reaction when he received the messages after you decoded them?'

'No. I had to pass them to his adjutant in a sealed envelope.'

'And I suppose when the General had a message to put into code, it was handed to you in the same way?'

'Yes.'

'In his own handwriting?'

'Always.'

'Obviously you had no difficulty reading it.'

'Only once, when he wrote in English.'

'In English?'

'Yes. It was the only time I ever knew him write a message in anything but French.'

'Do you remember the occasion?' asked Dick, holding his breath and hoping that the fates would favour him this time. 'No.'

His sigh of desperation was probably heard in the Channel Islands.

Madame Guillon added casually, 'But I could turn it up for you.'

Dick stared at her blankly. 'What do you mean?'

'If you don't mind waiting. My box of messages is in the wardrobe upstairs.'

'You kept copies?'

'Oh, no. That would have been against regulations. I typed one copy of each message in French and it went back to his office with a copy of the coded message.' She smiled. 'I kept the originals, in his handwriting. I had them in my desk for ages, thinking someone would ask for them, but no one ever did and at the end of the war, when the time came to clear my desk, I decided to keep them as souvenirs. They're not worth anything, because he never signed them. I've often thought of throwing them out.'

'Madame, I would very much like to see them.'

'Then you'd better come upstairs. They're too heavy for me to carry at my age.'

Dick's mouth had gone dry and a pulse was beating in his temple as he followed the old lady up the bare wooden staircase. Was it too much to hope that his luck had changed, or was this going to be another kick in the teeth?

The bedroom had a crucifix, candlesticks and a print of a Raphael Madonna over the fireplace. The white counterpane on the brass-framed double bed was stretched so that not a crease was visible. Madame Guillon went to the only other piece of furniture, a massive Normandy wardrobe, unlocked it and pointed to a cardboard carton at the bottom.

'May I?' asked Dick.

'Please do. You can put it on the bed. It should be clean.'

He folded back the flaps. She had sorted the messages and put them in large brown envelopes, one for each period of three months, beginning in July 1940.

'Take them all out, and spread them on the bed,' she told him.

'There's only one batch that interests me now,' he said, pulling out the envelope marked *Avril-Juin 1941*. It was one of the bulkiest.

War historians and archivists would have blanched at the way Dick handled the precious documents in de Gaulle's own handwriting, licking his finger and leafing through them like a clerk with a ledger. But this was make or break time. She had arranged the papers in sequence, so it was a simple matter to turn up the crucial dates. Some of the writing was in pencil and had faded as the paper had aged, but it remained legible. De Gaulle had a clear, neat hand.

Dick scanned each one for the name of the recipient. There were several sent to Churchill in the first days of May, tartly drawing the attention of the Prime Minister to a Free French blockade of Djibouti, where British support was 'indispensable', but not, from the tone of the messages, forthcoming. The first message to Churchill that did not concern Djibouti was dated 7 May 1941, and when Dick read it, he spontaneously caught hold of Madame Guillon's hand.

'This is it!' he told her huskily. 'This is what I'm looking for.'

It was marked TOP SECRET. The terse wording ran: *Reliable source in France suggests Germany is in negotiation with you through Dublin. Kindly deny by return.*

De Gaulle *had* learned about the German peace missions flown in by Frank Perry. Three days before Hess arrived, this had landed on Churchill's desk in Downing Street. It could not have been ignored. Was a denial ever sent, and, if so, had it satisfied de Gaulle?

Anything Churchill had telegraphed must have been shredded before the end of the war. In an imperfect world, there was not going to be a little old lady somewhere on the south coast with a boxful of Churchill's messages, Dick reflected. He had to read between the messages.

Which brought him to the next: TOP SECRET. *To PM of GB & NI. 14 May 1941. Free France demands immediate rejection of Nazi peace terms and imprisonment of Hess. Failure to notify by midnight will be treated by Free France as collaboration and communicated to other interested governments.*

The clincher! The irrefutable evidence, in de Gaulle's own hand, that he had blown the whistle on the Hess mission. What else could *other interested governments* mean but Russia, threatened with a joint invasion by Germany and Britain?

Whilst Dick read and re-read the crucial words, Madame Guillon had picked up the rest of the batch and was looking for something.

'*Ah! Voila!*'

She handed Dick the message de Gaulle had drafted in English, the only message he ever wrote in anything but French: TOP SECRET. *To PM of GB & NI. 21 May 1941. 1. Thank you. 2. Catroux remains in Palestine. 3. I shall go to Cairo soon. 4. You will win the war.*

The date was informative. On 20 May, Churchill had ordered General Wavell in Cairo to prepare to move into Syria – the about-face that had stunned Middle East Command. Catroux was the Free French General who led the advance into Syria. This was obviously de Gaulle's pithy reply to what he had so long worked for, and now achieved: the agreement by Churchill to the Syrian adventure. And there could be no doubt any longer why Churchill had capitulated over Syria.

He had even come to heel over Djibouti. Dick read all the remaining messages to Churchill in the envelope, and it was evident that, from 20 May, Britain had enforced the blockade repeatedly urged by de Gaulle.

The story was there. Proof positive. An investigative journalist's dream come true.

Dick turned to his fairy godmother. 'Madame, it would help me enormously to photograph these messages for my newspaper. There would, of course, be a generous payment.'

'Take anything you wish,' Madame Guillon told him. 'They've been sitting at the bottom of my wardrobe for forty years, so I'm not likely to miss them. I shall still have plenty of others.'

'Thank you. I can't begin to say how grateful I am. I believe you're not on the phone. Where is the nearest public one?'

'In Plévenon, not more than two kilometres from here. Go down the lane and you'll see the sign.'

He thanked her again at the door, gripping both her hands. She would never understand the extent to which she had helped him, or the significance of her carton of messages, in rewriting the history of the Second World War.

He checked the time. A few minutes after 6.00 p.m. Still, unbelievably, Monday. Cedric would be at home in Henley, but Jane was going to be the first to hear. A transferred charge call from France would cause a flutter of excitement in Brook Green.

He raced so rapidly down the granite steps that suddenly the bulky envelope slipped from under his arm. He grabbed for it, cursing his clumsiness. Up there on the headland, the precious messages could have scattered literally to the winds and the waves.

He had not bothered to lock the Porsche. He opened the door, tossed the package onto the passenger seat and stooped to get in. Then he froze.

Something jammed against his ribs, and somebody said in English, 'Hold it, Mr Garrick.'

He didn't know the voice. He turned and looked into the eyes of a total stranger. Tired, narrow eyes in the face of a man in his forties who needed a shave. A forgettable face, compact and undistinguished. The clothes, too, fell into the category of nondescript – a check shirt and faded blue jeans.

'What do you want?'

'The package, Mr Garrick. Reach in and get it, would you? This is a gun in your side, in case you were not certain.'

'Who are you?'

The gun jerked hard into his ribs. 'Get it!'

There might have been something a Hollywood stuntman could have improvised to outwit the gunman, using the car door and some acrobatic leap, but it was not in Dick's repertoire, and he knew it. He believed in that gun, and he believed it would be used if he didn't obey. So he obeyed.

'How did you get onto me?' he asked, as he handed over the messages. 'I didn't see you following.'

'Got here first,' the gunman answered simply. 'Didn't need to follow. I knew where you were going. Had twenty minutes start on you.'

'How did you know?'

'Listened in. It's not the glass against the wall these days, you know. Things have moved on.'

'What are you, MI5?'

'Get into the car now, Mr Garrick. You're going home.'

Dick got into the Porsche. The gunman still covered him through the open window. 'OK,' Dick said. 'You've got the papers, but I've still got the story. I know what happened, and I'll bloody well make sure it gets into print!' He started up, revved and moved away at speed.

He would still go down to Plévenon and phone Jane. He had been robbed of the evidence, but they couldn't take away the knowledge he had. He would pass it on to Jane and Cedric, and they would get in touch with Red. It would all come down to Hess and how much he would say, but that was how they had planned it from the beginning. They had to shock the old man with the truth and let him tell the story.

The Porsche was moving fast, too fast for safety on the *corniche*, the narrow cliff road. Dick touched the brakes slightly. There was no response. He pressed the pedal harder, but the car, if anything, went faster, accelerating on the downward slope. The brakes were useless.

The bastard had tampered with the car.

He tried changing down. The gears were functioning, but there was a tight bend ahead and he was not going to get round. He knew he was not going to get round.

The muscles of his stomach flexed as the Porsche failed to respond. It was too much to ask of any car. It went into a screeching skid and broadsided off the road, smashed through a wooden barrier and careered over the cliff.

The car was falling, turning, diving through the air.

You're going home.

He thought of Jane and the message she would never receive. And Madame Guillon, who had not understood what it was all about. And Churchill and de Gaulle and Hitler, all dead. All silent.

The car plunged a hundred feet and hit the rocks.

Dick's spine was severed by the impact. He died instantly.

36

'Red.'

He felt a hand creep over the small of his back and come to rest on his left buttock. The fingers pressed gently into his flesh.

Tuesday morning. He opened his eyes to check the time from the clock on the bedside shelf. 6.55. He closed them again and did some arithmetic. Heidrun had to be at work by 8.30. She needed to leave by 8.00 to be sure of the bus. She would want twenty minutes in the bathroom and fifteen for breakfast. That still left a gaping half-hour. He stayed immobile and began to simulate the regular breathing of deep sleep.

The hand slid over his hip and assertively down towards his crotch. The fingers found some hair, teased it out and curled it around one of them like a ring.

'Red.'

He tensed, anticipating one of Heidrun's playful squeezes. Playful could be painful for the recipient.

'You *are* awake!'

'Not really.'

She pressed against his back. They had both slept naked, Red from habit, Heidrun because she had not been back to her apartment since Sunday.

She murmured in English, 'Turn over.'

'Too tired, love.'

'I am not wanting sex.'

'You really mean that?'

'I want you to hold me.'

He rolled towards her and put an arm around her. She clung to him, grasping his shoulders.

'Red, I'm scared of Kurt Valentin.'

'Scared of that jerk? He's rubbish. Forget him.'

'There are others. There will always be others.'

'Coming home to roost?'

'I don't understand. What does that mean?'

'Tell them to piss off, you have other fish to fry. It's a mixed metaphor, but they'll get the message.'

She gave a heavy sigh and lapsed into silence.

'I ought to get up,' she murmured after a while, but without much conviction.

'True,' said Red, smartly unwinding himself from the embrace. 'Is the table-tennis still on tonight?'

'The Moabit match? Yes,' she answered bleakly. 'I don't think we shall win without Cal. I'll have to play the doubles with Frank. He's rubbish.' She sat up and slid her legs off the bed, then stood up entirely and started her exercise routine, standing astride and rotating her hips, hands clasped behind her head. 'I wish I knew what is the matter with Cal. I'm sure if he really wanted, he could have changed the shifts to make sure he played tonight.'

'He told you,' Red reminded her, watching the work-out; it was a spectacle worth sitting up in bed for, even after two heavy nights. 'He has to fill in for some guy who is off sick.'

'I don't believe him. He told me once before that he could always get time off. He isn't being honest with me.'

'Maybe he's had enough table-tennis.'

Her answer to that was to turn her back on him and touch her toes.

Later, after Heidrun had left for work, Red gave the matter some undivided thought. There was something in what she had said. It was mean of Cal to let her down after he had promised to play the matches with her. The impression Red had got was that Cal was dependable, the sort of guy who kept his promises. Conclusion: either Cal had been ordered by the prison directors to stop mixing with the locals, or there was some conflict of loyalties, and Heidrun had lost out on this occasion. On balance, the second explanation seemed the likelier. Could it be anything to do with Hess?

The lone prisoner in Spandau was notoriously wary of the prison staff, but he seemed to have got on terms of some sort with Cal. And Cal's few utterances about Hess had conveyed a certain respect for the old man, even a sneaking admiration for his bouts of insubordination. He had said on Sunday that Hess had been unsettled by something he had read in the paper about an old building in Munich being destroyed by fire. Maybe Cal was helping Hess over an emotional upset, putting in extra time to keep him from getting too depressed.

Strange that a burnt-down building should bother Hess at all. It wasn't as if he had spent his childhood there; he had been raised in Egypt. Maybe there was a link with the founding of the Nazi movement in Munich, the beerhalls where Hitler had first sprayed spit and racism over anyone who would listen. Perhaps it was a beerhall that had just gone up in smoke. Most of last week's papers were still lying about the apartment. After a shave and a few bites of breakfast, Red gathered them up and searched for the report of the Munich fire. He couldn't find it. He took out a cigarette, put up his feet and told himself his job was reporting the news, not reading it.

Then he had his inspiration. Cal worked shifts. If he had fixed an extra evening on, it followed that he ought to have the morning off. What better time than now to look him up at home and get to know him better, for once without Heidrun in attendance?

He slung his jacket over his shoulder and took the next bus out to Spandau.

Cal had lodgings in the *Altstadt*, the 'old town', at the meeting-point of the rivers Havel and Spree. Red knew the name of the street, but he would need to ask for the number. Cal had lived several years there, so someone ought to be able to help.

His luck was in. Two-thirds of the way along Reformationsplatz, who should he meet but the man himself, dressed for once in a jacket and slacks, complete with grey and blue striped shirt and brown, hand-woven tie?

'Hi,' said Cal, without looking too delighted. 'How're you doing, pal?'

'Great! So you are off duty. I was coming this way to look you up. Thought we might have a coffee or something.'

Cal was already edging away. 'That would be nice, but I have an appointment this morning.'

'Obviously.'

Cal glanced down at his clothes and smiled self-consciously. 'Yeah.'

'Anyone I know?'

'Probably not.'

'Some other time, then?'

'Sure.'

Cal nodded and moved on rapidly. Red stood back, watching for a while, and then followed. He had tumbled to the strong possibility that Cal had not, after all, cried off from the table-tennis match to spend the evening with Hess, but to keep his appointment this morning. If Cal believed it was worth getting out of a tracksuit for, it had to be important.

Cal moved briskly through the old town towards the pedestrian walkway of the shopping complex, past the black fountain where the husbands chatted while their wives went round the supermarket shelves, and south to the bus station. He got straight onto a waiting bus, paid the driver and went upstairs. It didn't look like moving off right away, but Red increased his pace to be sure of getting on. Then he pulled up short.

Ahead of him, a mere ten yards or so ahead and about to climb on the bus, was Heidrun's *bête noire*, Kurt Valentin, accompanied by two other guys Red didn't recognize. They were all in suits. If they were going to the same place as Cal, Red thought, he wished he had brought a tie with him. It looked like being a dressy occasion.

When they were all safely upstairs, he entered the bus. He didn't join them. He felt more comfortable among the elderly and disabled.

It was now a matter of watching the exit-stairs at each stop. In the movies, they would all have had fast cars and raced along Spandauer Damm ignoring the traffic-lights. It was more sedate on a fifty-four bus, but it suited Red. His driving wasn't up to much.

They travelled three-quarters the length of Spandauer Damm before Cal's brown shoes and camel-coloured slacks appeared in view on the stairs. Red swayed out of sight behind an old man reading *Stern*. Right behind Cal came Valentin and his three friends, exchanging conversation like any businessmen, not in the least like shadows.

Red let them and a couple of other passengers get off

205

before he left his seat. Cal had already started along Königin Elisabeth Strasse, and the others were crossing to the other side, but they turned in the same direction when they got over.

Coincidence could now be ruled out. They were tailing Cal as surely as Red was. The guy on Valentin's left was the shortest of the three, but the best-dressed. His grey pinstripe was definitely tailored, probably by Selbach or one of those big-name outfitters on Kurfürstendamm. His dark hair was thinning at the crown, but he still had about fifteen years on Valentin.

Those two continued to talk, for the most part ignoring the third member of the party, who was a head taller than either of them, and broader in the shoulders. The back seam of his jacket looked to be under strain. It was the kind of cheap blue suit you buy in chain-stores without trying on the trousers. He was carrying a large, black briefcase.

The street was busy enough for Red to remain inconspicuous on the same side as Cal, some sixty yards behind. He would have treated the whole thing more lightheartedly if it were not for Heidrun's fear of Valentin. This morning she had talked despairingly of others, and it certainly looked as if Valentin hunted in a pack. Did they expect Cal to lead them to her?

Near the Kaiserdamm end, Cal turned left into a side-street. It caught everyone by surprise. Valentin and his companions immediately stopped talking and moved fast, dodging into the road to break out of the slow procession of pram-pushers and window-shoppers. Red, on the opposite side, had to trot to keep up with them.

Cal was not in sight. The street was part-residential, with entrances irregularly located between small shops and up staircases. There were several basement flats. He could have been in thirty or forty different places.

The man in the smart suit took over, sending Shoulders to check the shops on one side, Valentin those on the other. Red observed them from the corner of the street, standing by an open-front shop that traded in electronic parts.

The search was unproductive, so an agitated consultation took place on the pavement, heads turning repeatedly in case

Cal reappeared. Finally, Shoulders was posted to the far end of the street, and the two older men kept watch nearer to Red.

Ten or fifteen minutes went by. Everyone kept checking their watches. Red moved from the electronics shop to a new position beside the revolving stand of postcards next door.

He was taken completely by surprise when a door opened behind him and Cal came out, passing close enough almost to brush his shoulder, and moved off without apparently noticing him. Not wishing to be caught in the spotlight, Red dodged out of sight behind the postcards. The place Cal had emerged from was a private doorway between the electronics shop and the newsagents.

Across the street, Valentin was sent after Cal. The short man also signalled to Shoulders, who came running. Red, in two minds, plumped for his original intention and followed Cal and Valentin back into Königin Elisabeth Strasse. He had plenty of ground to make up, so he broke into a run. It committed him absolutely to following Cal, but he regretted not finding out who he had visited, and why the others had remained behind.

Valentin's silver hair was suddenly in view again, so Red slowed to a walk as they approached the traffic lights at Spandauer Damm. Increasingly, the depressing conviction pressed in on him that he had made the wrong decision. Even the incentive of the chase dwindled when Cal crossed Spandauer Damm and tamely joined the bus queue. Valentin dutifully stood a couple of places behind, and Red glided to the other side of the bus shelter and smoked his second cigarette of the morning. He felt a strong sense of anticlimax.

As the bus drew up at the stop and Cal prepared to board, with Valentin almost holding onto his shirt, Red decided to cut his losses and let them go. He was a newsman, bugger it, and a bus ride home wasn't much of a story. He was going to work.

A half-hour had gone by when he got back to the side-street. Valentin's companions were nowhere in sight, but plenty of others were. A crowd had gathered outside the place, the lights of two police cars were flashing and someone was using an intercom.

Red shouldered his way through and asked one of the crowd what had happened.

'Some woman murdered. The people in the electric shop heard screams and called the cops.'

Red broke through the cordon and headed for the open door that he had last seen Cal come out of.

'Hey, you!' One of the police grabbed his arm. 'What the hell . . .?

Without actually stopping, Red took out his press-card and passed it so rapidly across the policeman's line of vision that it might just as well have been a season ticket. Or a police ID. 'Take your hands off me, officer,' he ordered with authority.

The grip loosened, and he was through the door.

The place was stiff with uniforms. Red wished he owned a suit. Someone immediately asked him who he was.

'A vital witness. Is it a killing?'

'Herr Ulzheimer. A guy here says he is a witness.'

A movement among the uniforms gave Red a glimpse of a dead woman lolling in an armchair. Her face was badly cut about. A gory mess. Unrecognizable. From the look of her fine white hair, she must have been old.

Ulzheimer, a detective in plain clothes, shouted, 'Take him outside and hold him in the car until I'm ready. All of you flatfeet get outside. I have a job to do here, and you're not helping.'

'Any idea who she is?' Red asked the officer who showed him to the car.

'Her name is Edda Zenk. Unmarried. Lived alone. She was shot through the head. Before that she was pistol-whipped. God knows why. Harmless old lady with nothing worth stealing.'

'Maybe she knew something.'

'Just who are you?'

'I'll save it for Herr Ulzheimer, if you don't mind.'

By then there was another witness, a woman who worked in the electronics shop. Ulzheimer spoke to her before he got to Red. He questioned her closely and then handed her over to one of the uniformed men to make a statement.

He got in beside Red and studied him minutely. He took in

everything with his grey eyes and then said, 'Show me your hands.'

Red obeyed in silence. Ulzheimer wasn't the type to enjoy a quip about fortune-telling.

'Now turn them over . . . OK. Name?'

'Goodbody.'

'From?'

'England.'

'Identification?'

Red showed his press-card.

Ulzheimer sniffed. 'What have you got to tell me?'

Red was glad of the time he had been given to prepare for this. 'I may be able to help. I was passing earlier this morning. I noticed two men watching this place. There was a third one up the street. They were signalling to him.'

'Three men, huh? Describe them.'

Red provided accurate word-pictures of Valentin and his associates.

'Pretty good,' conceded Ulzheimer. 'How is it you took such a strong interest in them?'

'I'm press, aren't I? You learn to be a good observer. Part of the trade.'

'Where exactly were you . . . passing . . . when you noticed these suspicious characters?'

'Just about here. The two short guys were over the street approximately where the red Volkswagon is now. The other was up there.'

'And you?'

'I was here.'

'Passing by?'

'Well,' Red guardedly admitted, 'I spent some time looking at the shop-fronts.'

'The electronics shop?'

'And the postcards.'

'You interested in electronics, Mr Goodbody?'

'I was watching the men, wasn't I?'

'So that was why you lingered so long outside?'

'Yes, I told you.'

'OK, you saw them and you wondered what was going on, right?'

209

'Right.'

'In that case, why did you walk away? A good newsman doesn't walk away from a promising story.'

'One of them left. I decided to follow him.'

'Ah, which one?'

'The silver-haired one. I followed him up the street to Spandauer Damm, where he got on a fifty-four bus. I decided to come back and see if the others were still here.'

'And were they?'

'No.' Having regard to the not over-friendly narrowing of Ulzheimer's eyes, Red added, 'I offered myself as a witness, didn't I?'

'Yes, and I think you may be able to help us, Mr Goodbody. I want you to come down to the station and spend a little more time with me. You weren't planning anything else?'

37

Jane caught her breath and closed her eyes. A chill feeling spread over the surface of her body like a cold garment. 'How?'

Cedric's voice at the other end of the line was so subdued that it was barely audible. 'A car crash. Late yesterday afternoon.'

'Where? In France?'

'Somewhere on the north coast, near St Malo.'

'St Malo?'

'I've spoken to Justin Stevens in Paris. They managed to trace de Gaulle's cryptographer and Dick drove out there to see her. She lives right on the coast, on a steep headland some miles west of the town. He spent some time with her and then started back. He was using a powerful car. It seems he misjudged a turning on the cliff road. It was a hundred-foot drop.'

She made an anguished sound. She had a vivid mental picture of the scene.

'He must have died instantly. He didn't suffer.'

'Cedric, I can't believe this. Dick was a careful driver.'

'Yes. I can only presume it was a lapse of concentration. His mind running over the interview. And a car he wasn't used to . . . Jane why don't you pour yourself a stiff drink, and then get in a taxi and come over here to the office? We can talk things over.'

'Dick's dead. What is there to talk about?'

'My dear, we are a newspaper. I shall have to decide what we say about this.'

Embittered by the shock, she shouted down the phone, 'Is that all you can think about, how you report it? Don't you have any feelings at all, Cedric?'

After an interval, when she began to suppose he had put down the phone, he answered stiffly, 'Jane, it isn't easy to break appalling news like this to a close colleague.'

211

She let her breath out slowly, trying to be reasonable. 'I'm sorry. It's the shock, I suppose. All right. I'll come.' She hung up. She was shivering. She did exactly as Cedric had suggested, taking out the brandy and drinking it from a teacup.

Dick dead? She bit her lip and crossed her arms and paced the room, trying to come to terms with what she had just been told. The sense of loss was personal and profound. She had felt committed to Dick in a way that went beyond professional ties. She had been trying earnestly to know him and understand him. How could he have allowed this to happen? Of all the men she had known and worked with, he was by far the most stable. Lapses of concentration simply didn't happen to a guy like that. If this had happened to Red, she would have been devastated, but she would have understood. She could picture him racing a car down a cliff road, but not Dick. It wasn't in Dick's character. It wasn't remotely possible, not as Cedric had described it.

She couldn't blame Cedric, but she deeply resented his response to the tragedy. She had lost almost all respect for him over the past two weeks. He might be one of the better editors in Fleet Street, but what had that made him as a man? The whole of humanity, as Cedric perceived it, fell into three groups: newsmen, news subjects and readers. In death, Dick had become a news subject, and Cedric had to decide what angle to take on the story. It sickened Jane.

Going by recent experience, he wasn't calling her in for a consultation. He had made the decision already. He just wanted to make sure she didn't step out of line. In this frame of mind, she left the flat and took a taxi to the office. He was ready with the brandy when she arrived. To do him justice, he looked paler than usual.

'No, thanks. I had a large one before I came.'

'Sensible.'

'I can't believe this has happened. Have you heard any more about it?'

'A little. Stevens has driven out there. I gather the trip was abortive anyway. The cryptographer woman wasn't able to help Dick at all. She wasn't close to de Gaulle and she doesn't remember much.'

212

'Are you sure? Why was he distracted, then? What went wrong with his driving?'

'Your guess is as good as mine. The car was checked by a good mechanic before he rented it. The police experts will examine it, no doubt, but I gather it's a mangled heap now.'

Jane shivered.

'Are you sure you won't have that brandy?'

She shook her head. 'Have you called Red yet?'

'Been trying all morning, and can't raise him. I sent a cable asking him to call me urgently. Nothing.'

She managed a cynical comment. 'So what's new?'

Cedric grunted ill-humouredly and got out a cigar, the usual prelude to a statement from the editorial chair. 'There's another reason why I need to speak to him. I had a visitor last night. The security services have been alerted to your investigation.'

Jane sourly noted the *your*. 'I know. We had a tail put on us on Sunday. He followed us all the way out to Henley.'

Cedric looked shocked. 'You didn't tell me.'

'We didn't want to risk it. We had the impression that you were going cold on the story.'

He observed a Mandarin silence.

Jane justified herself by adding, 'Well, you *were*. You told us it was finished.'

'True,' conceded Cedric, 'and if I had stood firm, this would not have happened. I know you can't legislate for an accident like this, but . . .' He shook his head.

'What did the security people want?'

'An undertaking from me to drop the investigation.'

'Why?'

'They don't have to give a reason other than the interests of national security.'

'Is this a D Notice?'

'Not exactly,' said Cedric, 'but I was left in no doubt that we'd be in serious trouble if we didn't back down on this one.'

'So you did?'

Cedric drew on his cigar and exhaled. 'Yes.'

'Then Dick has died for nothing,' Jane exclaimed accusingly.

'Jane, that's unworthy and illogical and I don't believe you would say it under different circumstances,' Cedric responded with all the dignity he could command. 'I'm as shattered as you are at what happened to Dick, and I take some blame for it, but I refuse to commit my newspaper to some sentimental and utterly futile crusade to appease my conscience, or anyone else's.'

Jane, too, was implacably controlled in her response. 'You didn't use words like sentimental and utterly futile that first weekend at your cottage.'

'For heaven's sake, Jane! The story has changed out of all recognition.'

'What's different? Hess is still in Spandau. We still don't know why for certain, but we're getting close. We must be, if the secret service wants to spike the story. Is this what a so-called independent newspaper does: backs down when the editor's arm is twisted by MI5?'

Cedric said, like a judge delivering sentence, 'Jane, this may be painful for your idealism, but the answer to your question is yes. I'm telling you now that the investigation is over. There will be nothing published. The story is dead.'

She lowered her eyes and said nothing. This time there would be no timely telephone call from Red to salvage the project. She might never see or hear from Red again. She bit back her despair.

She had never felt so desolate. She was consumed by one idea, one need: she had to find some way of achieving it. She looked up at Cedric and said, 'If you can't contact Red, I'd better go to Berlin and find him. I can tell him what has happened.'

Cedric studied her for a long time, weighing the suggestion. No doubt, Jane decided as she faced him through the cigar-smoke, he considered it a brazen bid to get a freebie to Berlin. She was demanding a consolation prize. Yet she could also sense that he was genuinely alarmed not to have heard from Red. He had nightmare visions of sparking some international crisis over Hess. He had always feared Red's impetuosity. He had to be warned off as a matter of urgency. Was it enough to rely on a cable that had so far brought no response?

214

He reached his decision: 'How soon could you be ready?'

She opened her eyes just a fraction wider, but her heart pumped furiously. 'I'm ready now.'

38

At twenty-five minutes to closing time in the main city branch of one of the largest and oldest banks on the Bahnhofstrasse in Zurich, the KGB officer referred to as Julius entered the front door and stated his business to the offical on reception duty. He was admitted to a room known as the secure area and obliged to wait there while the identity he produced was checked. Left alone, monitored by television cameras, unable either to gain admission or leave, Julius waited some four minutes until a female clerk in a navy blue suit and pink blouse came from the inner sanctum and spoke his name. He clicked his heels, gave the suggestion of a formal bow and followed her into the banking hall. She led him across the bronze-coloured marble floor, past the tellers' positions and through an unmarked door.

Inside was a large room reserved for consultations between customers and bank executives. Julius was invited to sit in one of the brown leather armchairs ranged in a semi-circle on a deep golden Afghan carpet. Immediately, a door opposite him was unlocked and a slight, balding man in a grey worsted suit with a bow tie stepped forward and introduced himself as the sub-manager responsible for safe deposit facilities.

Julius presented a visiting-card and explained that he was the nephew of Fraulein Edda Zenk, a West German resident in Berlin, who in 1964 had arranged with the bank to deposit an item of value in one of its lockers. She now wished to retrieve her property, but she was in her seventies and unable to travel. She had nominated Julius as her representative and entrusted him with the key to the locker. The bank should have received a telephone call to this effect during the course of the afternoon.

The sub-manager confirmed that a lady had phoned from Berlin. He explained that the bank was obliged to insist on a properly authenticated letter of authority before it could authorise the opening of a locker by a customer's representative. Julius handed over a paper bearing a note in Edda Zenk's handwriting, naming him as her representative. He also produced the key. The sub-manager thanked him and asked him to wait while the signature on the note was authenticated.

Alone in the room, but overlooked by the revolving cameras mounted in the ceiling, Julius got up and examined a Corot landscape on the wall opposite until the sub-manager returned with a bank guard. The documents had been verified to the bank's satisfaction, and Julius was invited to come to the safe deposit room.

A different door was unlocked and he was led along a passage, through another locked door and down some steps to the vaults. There, a second guard unlocked a gleaming steel grille and relocked it behind them.

On one side were rows of hundreds of steel lockers, and on the other a set of cubicles where depositors could examine their possessions. The sub-manager walked up one of the aisles with Julius, checking the numbers until he found the right one. There were two locks. The sub-manager used the key held by the bank to open the first, and then withdrew discreetly, allowing Julius to open the locker with the key he possessed.

Inside was a cheap imitation leather suitcase with chrome fastenings that were beginning to peel. Julius lifted it out, surprised by its heaviness. He closed the locker door and carried the suitcase to a desk where the sub-manager was waiting to obtain his signature against the record of withdrawal. He refused the offer of a porter's assistance and carried the suitcase himself back through the system of doors and checks to the main hall.

He thanked the sub-manager, shook hands again, clicked heels and walked out through the exit door to where a chauffeur was waiting in a grey Mercedes. Julius got into the back seat with the suitcase beside him; the chauffeur closed the door and drove off sedately to the Soviet consulate.

39

The girl at the British Airways desk explained that there was a trade fair starting in Berlin at the weekend and most flights from Heathrow were fully booked. Jane spent two tense hours waiting for a standby and expecting all the time to hear her name called over the public address. If Cedric could find a reason for stopping her, he would. It only wanted a message from Red. So she had resolved to ignore any announcement; they would have to drag her screaming off the plane if necessary. She finally got a seat on a BA flight that was due to touch down at Berlin-Tegel at 7.20 p.m.

Some of the passengers may have suffered take-off jitters, but Jane closed her eyes and breathed evenly for the first time in many hours. Soon, she let her thoughts return to the circumstances of Dick's death. Disbelief and outrage were supplanted by more measured reactions as she forced herself to analyse the event as Dick himself would have done. In the light of what had happened in the last forty-eight hours, the chance that he had simply made a driving error was slight. The incident had happened late in the afternoon on a remote section of the French coast. Some time that evening, Cedric had been visited in London by one of the security service and ordered to drop the Hess investigation. Were the incidents unconnected, or was there secret service involvement in Dick's death? Had he, after all, learned something vital from the Frenchwoman he had visited? It would not be difficult to stage an 'accident' on a cliff road, perhaps forcing him off the edge with another vehicle. Nor was it any problem to frighten a lonely old woman into silence. Jane wasn't going to let it rest, and nor would Red, she was certain. They would go to St Malo and find out what had really happened. To hell with Cedric and his D Notice.

By the time she had gone through the airport formalities, found a taxi and travelled to the Haselhorst district where Red lodged, it was getting dark. She was put down beside a

218

grey tenement, one of the stark, ten-storey blocks erected in the emergency reconstruction programme of the late forties. Parts of the façade were chipped away and many of the windows were cracked. Two small boys were kicking an empty Coke can against a wall. Five more with cigarettes watched her from the interior of an abandoned Volkswagon.

The odour of stale urine hung around the entrance, but it had not discouraged a teenage couple in studded leather from choosing the foot of the stairs to explore each other's intimate parts. Nor were they inconvenienced by Jane switching on the light – a single bulb behind a metal grille – to study the list of floors and rooms.

She started up the stone stairs, wondering if the accommodation improved as you went higher. Red's flat was on the eighth. She prayed he would be at home. She was not sure what she would do if he wasn't. The small amount of money she had happened to have with her, and had changed into Deutschmarks at the airport, had all gone on the taxi. There were credit cards in her bag, but she didn't relish asking any of the locals where she could use them.

The air did improve appreciably somewhere above the third level, and there had been attempts to paint over the graffiti. She continued upwards. The eighth was not in bad shape compared with the rest. She looked for 808 and was heartened to find R. *Goodbody* printed on a sticky label over the doorbell.

She pressed and listened.

Pressed again.

Red was not at home.

Jane leaned against the door and moaned.She couldn't take another setback. Be rational, she tried to tell herself. You knew he was out, or he would have answered the cable. But he'll be back. If you pull yourself together and wait, he'll come, some time. He'll come. She squatted on the stone floor with her back against his door and closed her eyes. Welcome to Berlin.

When she opened them, someone had switched on a light. A female voice asked something in German that she didn't understand.

She looked up at a girl in a blue and white tracksuit with

short dark hair with silver highlights, who was staring down at her and saying something else that sounded more like an order. She was holding a sportsbag away from her, as if she meant to swing it at Jane to move her on.

Jane struggled to her feet. 'Please, do you speak English?'

A pair of green eyes scrutinised Jane. 'You're from England?'

'Yes.'

'What are you doing outside this door?'

'Waiting for the man who lives here.'

'Red?'

'Yes.'

Their eyes locked as they assessed each other, a positively feral confrontation. The German girl was neat-featured, with full, sensuous lips and plenty of natural colour in her cheeks. Her breasts were prominent without running to grossness. She could probably have pulled any man she wanted, though her shoulders were too wide and she hadn't much waist.

'Who are you?'

'Jane Calvert-Mead. And you?'

'Heidrun Kassner. What do you want?'

'I want to see Red.'

'Have you rung the bell?'

'Of course,' said Jane disdainfully. 'He isn't in.'

Heidrun wasn't taking that on trust. She pressed her thumb against the bellpush and kept it on for about ten seconds. When there was no response, she said sourly, 'He ought to be in.' She tossed her bag against the door and strolled to the end of the passage to look out of the window. There was a definite swagger to the movement. Everything in her manner wanted to assert that she shared the flat with Red, but Jane noted with satisfaction that she didn't possess a key of her own.

After an interval to ponder the implications of Jane's arrival, Heidrun sauntered back and asked, 'Do you work for a newspaper?'

'The same one as Red.'

'Ah.' She looked a shade less hostile. 'Something you want to tell him? If you would like to leave a message with me, I'm going to wait for him.'

'That's all right. So am I,' said Jane equably.

Heidrun gave Jane a long stare. 'It's getting late. You should be going home.' She made it sound like an order.

'My home is in England. I don't live in Berlin.'

'You mean you're staying somewhere?'

'Here.'

Heidrun tightened her mouth into a shape that was small and mean. She rested her hands on her hips and took a menacing step towards Jane. 'I think you made a mistake.'

Jane stood with her back to the door and shook her head. She kept her hands where they were, one at her side, the other fingering a button of her jacket.

Heidrun moved her eyes slowly and calculatingly over the length of Jane's body and then gave her a pitying look. She was about to say something else when the sound of footsteps came up the stairwell. They both turned to look. Heidrun let her arms drop.

It was Red. He saw them both as he reached the top stairs. 'Jesus Christ!' he said with a weary but amiable grin. 'I was planning to wash my hair tonight.' He approached the door and put a hand on each girl's shoulder, lightly kissing Jane first, then Heidrun. 'I've probably lost my key.' But he found it and opened the door. 'After you, ladies.'

Heidrun stooped to pick something off the doormat and hand it to Red. 'This looks like a telegram.'

'You can ignore it,' Jane informed him. 'It'll be from Cedric.'

They all went through to a small kitchen.

'Coffee, I expect,' said Red, opening a window. 'I'll have a beer myself. I've been drinking coffee all day that came in plastic cups and tasted like chocolate.' He filled a kettle and switched on. 'How long were you waiting? I guess we can cut the introductions.'

Heidrun changed tactics. She was going to play hostess. She opened a cupboard ostentatiously and took out two cups. 'Coffee for you, Jane?'

'Please.'

'We're being sociable, then,' Red observed. 'Does that mean we hammered Moabit?' He explained with a wink to Jane, 'Heidrun plays table-tennis in the Berlin league. Let's get the suspense over before we do anything else.'

'We lost,' said Heidrun thickly.

Red shook his head, and told Jane, 'Heidrun's regular partner couldn't play tonight. He's a prison warder.'

She gave him a glance that said she had made the connection. 'It must be difficult playing with someone else.' She moved closer to him and murmured in a low voice, 'Red, something dreadful has happened. I need to talk to you alone.'

He nodded. He said in German to Heidrun, as if he were making a suggestion of profound significance, 'Why don't you leave the coffee to me, love? It'll be ready when you've had your shower.'

A puzzled frown. Clearly the suggestion had wrong-footed Heidrun. She had probably taken a shower at the sports-hall. It may have crossed her mind that she was sweating again, and that could undermine a girl's confidence. But she obviously decided something else was intended. She accepted it, instead, as Red's personal invitation to claim priority as his house-guest. 'All right.' She flashed him a dazzling smile. 'Thank you, darling.'

So Jane got her opportunity to summarise all that had happened. She told it out of sequence, starting with Dick's death. Red shook his head in disbelief, as stunned as she had been. He put out his hand to hers and held it, and the contact said all that needed to be said. They were united in shock, grief and determination. Dick had died for something they had shared in and they were going to see it through.

Jane had to be brief. She outlined the facts that had come to light about Churchill's secret meetings with the German delegations and the probability that Hess was sent to finalise a peace deal linked with a joint attack on Russia. She pointed to the evidence that something had scuppered the deal in the few days after Hess's arrival, and she showed how she and Dick had noted what was simultaneously happening over Syria in London and Berlin. De Gaulle had miraculously got his way, and ever afterwards appeared to run rings round Churchill. So Dick had gone digging in France; and now Dick was dead.

'. . . and if you read your cable from Cedric,' she added, 'you'll see that the whole story is spiked. I was officially sent

222

to make sure you got the message. The security people were on to Cedric before the news about Dick came through.'

Red said, 'To hell with that. If Cedric wants out, we'll go freelance. There's no shortage of outlets for a story like this. It's international.'

'It's going to be dangerous.'

'It's dangerous already, love. We know too much.'

Jane had to agree. If Dick could be murdered, so could they, even if they dropped the investigation. She held out her hand to Red and he squeezed it. After a moment, she murmured, 'I think we just resigned from our job.'

He grinned. 'That's progress. I usually get the sack.' Keeping hold of her hand, he said, 'I'm bloody glad Cedric had the sense to send you.'

'I suggested it,' Jane told him simply.

Surprise showed briefly on his face, then something else that she didn't see for long because he moved towards her and kissed her. And that single kiss signified more than any of their lovemaking at Henley. She returned it rapturously. She knew she was crazy to commit herself to a man who shrugged off practically all the obligations a woman was supposed to insist upon. He was a rebel, a socal liability, the guest who was never invited back, a shabby dresser, a heavy drinker, a male chauvinist and a bed-hopper. The shower spattering noisily in the next room should have been an alarm bell. Jane heard it, saw everything that threatened, and still wanted no one else.

She didn't tell him. You didn't say that kind of thing to Red. She said instead, 'What are you going to do about the German girl?'

'Heidrun?' From the glance he made towards the bedroom door, he might have forgotten all about her. 'Leave it to me, love.'

'She's expecting you to get rid of me.'

'Bugger that,' said Red. 'She's a natural competitor. You know why she's here, don't you?'

Jane commented coolly, 'I take it she's the demanding fraulein who's been helping you with your inquiries.'

'You've got it in one,' he admitted, without a flicker of embarrassment. 'I'm going to get some straight answers from her in a moment. She's in deeper than I expected.'

223

It was a pass worthy of a matador, but Jane still smiled her scepticism.

'On the level, darling,' he insisted. 'I've had a heavy day, and she knows why.'

He poured the coffee into two cups and took a can of beer from the fridge. 'Something to eat?'

Jane shook her head.

'Tired, I expect,' he ventured.

'Not too tired to stay and listen.'

He nodded and went towards the bathroom, thought better of it, and called out, 'Coffee's ready.'

'I'm coming, darling,' answered Heidrun in a voice that was trying to be kittenish.

Jane looked towards Red, but their eyes didn't meet.

Heidrun appeared in a maroon-coloured bathrobe that must have belonged to Red, tied predictably loosely at the front to make an exhibition of her cleavage. She had her handbag with her and she planted it on the table and took out an eye-liner, toner and lipstick. She had given up playing *hausfrau*; she was the seductress now. It would be fascinating to see how Red would deal with it. 'Don't wait for me,' she told them as she propped a mirror against a milk-carton. 'I won't be a minute.'

'Do you have an interesting job?' Jane asked Heidrun. It was more than a cocktail party ploy, because she had noticed that the toner had a Laszlo label. She had once inquired about their products herself and learned that they were linked to a course of skin care she could not have afforded without a major reappraisal of her spending.

'She's a waitress,' Red answered for Heidrun. 'Serves the pastries and coffee in one of the Konditorei on Spandauer Damm.'

'Möhring,' said Heidrun. 'The best.'

'I'm sure,' Jane said tolerantly, thinking to herself that the tipping must be generous there. The handbag was white leather, and it bore the Lanvin logo in gold.

Red downed his beer and took another from the fridge. 'You haven't asked me why I was so late home,' Red complained to no one in particular.

Heidrun took out a tissue and blotted her lips. She was

224

strikingly pretty in feature, Jane had to concede. She really didn't need to let the bathrobe gape so – nor to be quite so blatantly suggestive when she replied to Red, 'Come on, then. Don't keep me waiting. You know I can't bear it.'

'I was pulled in by the police, wasn't I?' said Red.

Heidrun's mouth lost its pout and gaped. 'The police?'

'Those guys in green uniforms.'

'What for?'

'For murder.' After a gratifying gasp from both his guests, Red added, 'To be exact, for questioning about a murder.' He upended the beer-can and took a long swig. 'They held me for nearly nine hours. Rocks your confidence a bit when you take nine hours to prove your innocence.'

'What happened? Who was murdered?'

'Some old lady,' Red casually answered. 'I've told this so many times I'm beginning to forget how nasty it was. I'm walking up Königin Elizabeth Strasse this morning, when who do I see ahead of me but Cal Moody.'

Heidrun looked genuinely puzzled. 'Cal?'

Red turned to Jane and explained, 'We mentioned Cal not long ago. He's the warder from Spandau Jail who partners Heidrun at table-tennis. Well, I'm about to catch him up and say hello, when I notice three guys taking a good look at him from the other side of the street.' He threw a well-timed glance at Heidrun. 'One of them was your obnoxious friend Kurt Valentin.'

She widened her eyes and played nervously with the cord of the bathrobe.

Red explained in an aside to Jane, 'All I can tell you about Valentin is what I've heard from Heidrun: that he helps her with her tax-forms, and that she doesn't actually like him.' Then he resumed, 'I didn't know the other two, and, as it turned out, I'm glad I didn't ask to be introduced. I decided to watch from a distance.' Addressing himself mainly to Heidrun now, he gave an abridged account of the morning's events, leaving the impression that his own part in the story was a matter of sheer chance and casual interest. 'So I was picked up as a suspect just because I happened to choose the wrong spot to stand. They drove me off to police headquarters at Tempelhofer Damm and spent the morning firing questions at me. I kept Cal's name right out of it. Didn't want to land him in the shit. Well, he's a decent guy. Wouldn't say boo to an old lady, let alone beat her up and shoot her throught the head. The cops gave me a break and a sandwich and then they were back for descriptions. I had to make photo-fit pictures. Anyone ever tell you how difficult it is to piut one of those things together?'

'Did you identify Kurt Valentin?' Heidrun interrupted, suddenly much more pale under the make-up.

'I described him, but I didn't give his name,' Red informed her, watching her reactions. 'Well, that would have opened another can of worms, wouldn't it? You wouldn't want the fuzz questioning you, would you? It was obvious he didn't do the killing. So I just gave them descriptions of all three. I thought they would let me go after that, but they were getting more information all the time from the forensic boys at the scene of the crime.'

'Did they tell you anything?' Heidrun asked keenly. 'Did they find out why it happened?'

Red drew a line on the table with his finger, looking down thoughtfully. 'The police have a theory that she knew something her killers wanted to find out. They beat her up badly, the bastards. There was money in her handbag lying on the floor where she was found, but it wasn't taken. She was still wearing rings and a pearl necklace. There was no sign of the place being searched. They got what they wanted by beating her up, and then they shot her so that she couldn't talk.'

'Who was she?' asked Jane. 'Is there a line on her background?'

'Her name was Edda Zenk, a spinster of seventy-three, retired for thirteen years or more. Used to do secretarial work for a solicitor.'

'Did she always live in West Berlin?' asked Heidrun.

'She had no connections with the East, if that's what you're asking,' said Red. 'At one time she lived in Munich, but that's going back to the forties.'

'I don't understand this,' muttered Heidrun. But from the way she was frowning, it was evident that she was making a determined stab at it.

Red leaned across the table until his face was hardly a foot from hers. 'If you want to stay friends with me, Heidrun, you'd better start talking about Valentin. I've had a hard time protecting you. I'm in trouble over this. Just who is he?'

She pulled the edges of the bathrobe together protectively. 'I don't know much about him. If you want my opinion, he's a dirty old man who follows me around. He came into the shop a few times and tried to talk to me. Too much.'

'Chatted you up?'

'Yes. Then I kept meeting him in other places – on the way home from the sports-hall, in the restaurant there, on the beach. He likes to look at girls all the time. He buys porn magazines, and sometimes he makes suggestions to me. Stupid things, like will I let him buy me some sexy underwear. That's all I can tell you about him.'

'Come off it,' Red snapped at her, with a sudden show of anger. 'The other day you told me he did your tax.'

Heidrun swayed away from him. 'That wasn't true. I don't need an accountant and I couldn't afford one. I lied to you because I didn't want to tell you about him then. I didn't want trouble between you.'

'You're lying now.'

'No!' She raised a hand to shield her face, expecting Red to strike her.

'All this dirty old man stuff is horseshit,' he told her vehemently. 'He's in with a gang of murderers, sadistic, bloody killers, and you'd better get that into your head, Heidrun, because I want some straight answers from you about Kurt Valentin. Do you work for him?'

She reddened suddenly. 'What do you mean? I am not a street girl, if that is what you are saying.'

'Darling, if you were, it would be simple,' he said in a cold, quiet voice. 'This isn't about sex, it's about Cal Moody. You teamed up with Cal a couple of weeks ago. You got to know his routine, his hours of duty.'

'Only for the table-tennis matches,' protested Heidrun.

'Shut up. You've also been seeing Valentin. Today, Valentin and his friends were tracking Cal, remember? What a bloody coincidence! He visits Edda Zenk and she is dead the same hour.'

Heidrun said on a rising, hysterical note, 'I know nothing about this. I have never heard of this old lady.'

'But you told Valentin that Cal had changed shifts, didn't you?'

She lowered her eyes.

'Didn't you?' repeated Red.

She said in a low voice, 'He scares me. He is a violent man.'

'Now we're getting somewhere,' Red commented. 'That's why you came here, isn't it: to get away from him?'

'Yes.' She shifted in the chair and lifted the hem of the bathrobe to show the ankle bruised by Valentin's hands. 'He did that on Sunday.'

'Is Cal in danger?'

'I don't know, Red, I don't know anything,' she pleaded.

Red turned to Jane. 'The last I saw of him, Valentin was following him. I'm going to have to find out if he's OK.'

She frowned. 'How can you do that?'

'I'll call the prison. See if he's there. He should be on duty this evening.'

'Would they tell you if he is?'

'I can only try. I'll say it's some kind of emergency – one of his family on the line from America. If he isn't on duty, they ought to tell me.' He went out of the kitchen to the phone in the hall.

Heidrun wiped her eyes with the sleeve of the bathrobe, got up from the table without looking at Jane and went back to the bathroom.

In a few minutes, Red was back. 'He didn't report for work. They think he must be ill. He has no phone at his lodging. Jane, I'll have to go round there.'

'Tonight?'

'You can come if you want.'

'I will.'

Heidrun called from the bathroom, 'I want to come, too, Red.' She padded into the hall in bare feet, tugging the tracksuit-top over her head. 'Please, I want to make sure he's all right. Believe me, Red. Please believe me.'

Red stared at her for a moment, undecided. Jane could see the dilemma he was in. The question was whether Heidrun was more of a liability to take, or to leave behind, with the chance to phone Valentin and his friends. Her dislike of

228

Valentin appeared genuine enough, but her actions might be governed by her fear of him.

Red made up his mind. 'Get your shoes on, then, and be bloody quick about it.'

40

There was a time when the fastenings on a piece of luggage were a testimony to the craft of the locksmith, but mass-production methods ended all that. As anyone knows who has bought a suitcase in the last fifty years – even a smart, up-market, leather suitcase with a brand-name – it comes with two keys on a piece of wire, and can be opened almost as simply with the wire as with the keys.

After Julius had been driven into the Soviet Legation in Zurich, he carried the suitcase he had collected across the courtyard and through a side entrance. Using the back stairs, he moved inconspicuously upwards to the privacy of the bedroom he had been allocated. Having gone to so much trouble to obtain the suitcase, he felt he was entitled to a sight of the contents.

He locked the door and heaved the case onto the bed. The fastenings opened ridiculously easily with the aid of the pointed end of his tiepin. When he lifted the lid he saw why the case had weighed so heavily. It was stacked solidly with bundles of paper, tied with string and wedged so tightly that it was difficult to remove one without tearing it. He prised one out with the pocket-knife. It consisted of several hundred scraps of paper, end-sheets torn from books, pieces of news-paper, calendar date-sheets, toilet paper, labels soaked from bottles – in fact, almost every paper surface that human ingenuity could improvise in prison conditions. Each fragment was covered in minuscule handwriting and indexed with a serial number.

Julius harboured no illusions about Hess; he was an enemy of the Soviet people, and according to Soviet thinking was justly condemned to see out his days in Spandau. Any re-duction of the life sentence would be an insult to the twenty million Soviet citizens who died as a direct result of Nazism. Yet as Julius stared down at the bundles of paper, he could not fail to be impressed by the sense of purpose represented there.

He lifted out several more bundles, stacking them methodically on the bed so that he could replace them later exactly as he had found them. Underneath were more, every one tied with string by Edda Zenk when she had finished typing the script that had been delivered to the Munich publisher, Sigmund Beer, in 1964. Julius had not discovered how she had been assigned the task; he had needed only to establish that she was the typist and that the manuscript still existed in the Zurich bank vault.

The logic that had brought him this prize was pleasing to Julius. He was going to enjoy recounting it to his superiors. His man Valentin had learned through the girl Heidrun Kassner that Hess had been disturbed about a newspaper report of a fire in Munich. It was, of course, the fire that had destroyed Beer Verlag. Hess had become alarmed, believing, possibly, that the typescript of his book had been burned with the house, or even suspecting, if he were still capable of recognizing a KGB operation, that it was in Soviet hands. He had wanted to be reassured that the original manuscript was still safe in Switzerland. So he had asked the warder he trusted most, the American, Cal Moody, to visit Edda Zenk and check that all was well. This Moody had done, innocently leading the KGB to Fraulein Zenk, and so to Zurich, and the prize.

But it would not be wise to spend too long enjoying this private moment of self-congratulation. The suitcase had to be closed again and prepared for its removal to Moscow Centre. For this, a well-tried but efficient stratagem had been prepared. Downstairs in a locked room, an open coffin was waiting. Julius had instructions personally to place the suitcase in the coffin and screw down the lid. Word had already been passed to the Swiss that one of the Soviet mission had suffered a fatal heart attack. The coffin was to be conveyed to Zurich Airport under the cloak of diplomatic immunity and put aboard an Aeroflot aircraft. Julius would oversee every stage of the loading and unloading. His responsibility did not end until the cargo was delivered to the top man at Moscow Centre, KGB General Vanin.

He took care to replace the bundles exactly as he had found them. It took only a few seconds to re-engage the locks with his tie-pin. He unlocked the door of his bedroom, made sure the corridor was clear and then carried the suitcase down the back stairs and through a corridor that connected with the medical bay. He reached the room he wanted without meeting anyone.

He let himself inside and went straight to the open coffin standing on trestles in the centre and swung the suitcase into position. It lodged snugly in the satin-padded interior, where the shoulders of a corpse would normally lie. He reached for the hinged coffin-lid and froze as a voice behind him said, 'Not yet, Comrade Julius.'

Footsteps crossed the stone floor. Julius turned and looked into a face he had only ever seen before in one studio portrait photo that appeared from time to time in Party newspapers and magazines: a broad, high-boned face with deceptively primitive features, almost the features of an Eskimo – slit eyes, thick brows and flat, wide-nostrilled nose.

Julius swallowed, took a short, deep breath, and made a sort of bow. 'Comrade General.'

General Mikhail Vanin smiled and revealed a set of teeth the colour of a cornfield in Kazakhstan. He was clearly pleased to be recognized out of uniform. His blue suit had the sheen of an expensive Soviet-made cloth. 'Yes, I decided to make a change in the arrangements,' he announced with the air of a conjurer who has just materialised unexpectedly. 'I have saved you a trip to Moscow. When I have checked that the contents of the suitcase are in order, you may consider your assignment completed. Hand me that tool, will you?'

Julius picked a heavy-duty screwdriver off a chair beside the trestle. He felt sick at the thought that while he had sneaked his look at the Hess papers, the military head of the KGB was waiting for him downstairs. But General Vanin appeared not to suspect anything. He, too, was curious to see inside the suitcase, only his methods were more crude. He grasped the screwdriver like a dagger and thrust it downwards, ripping through the lid of the case and carving a long gash in the plastic material. Two more stabs, and he was able to tear most of the lid apart, like a lion eviscerating its prey. He drew out several bundles of Hess's papers, glanced at them, wrenched off the string and let the pieces scatter in the coffin and on the floor.

The savagery of the exercise came as a further shock to Julius. It was alien to everything he understood about the KGB. Its officers were trained to be efficient and dispassionate, ruthless but unemotional. Documents of any sort were treated with respect. Everything had a value of some sort to the service. Everything had to be indexed and filed and retained until it was required again. Yet General Vanin was attacking the Hess papers as if they were the Deputy Führer in person.

He was breathing rapidly as he addressed Julius again. 'Comrade, you have done well. This is the end of Herr Hess's literary enterprise. Do you like slivovitz? I have a bottle upstairs and I should like to drink with you.'

'Shall I pick the paper off the floor?' Julius offered.

'Leave it. Filthy garbage. It will all go in the shredder.'

'It's not going to Moscow after all?'

'Filth and lies are better destroyed where you find them, Comrade,' answered the General. 'I shall take care of it later.'

Three minutes after, they stood in the carpeted luxury of the boardroom on the first floor. 'We serve ourselves,' the General explained, 'because we have sensitive matters to discuss.' He filled two cut-glass goblets with the liqueur and handed one to Julius. It would have been a generous helping of wine, let alone slivovitz. 'To a successful operation, Comrade.'

Julius touched glasses and drank deeply of the plum-flavoured drink, grateful for its warming properties as he prepared to discuss 'sensitive matters' with General Vanin. He felt more comfortable here than downstairs beside the coffin.

'Sit down now, and give me your comprehensive account of the operation,' said the General, pointing to a velvet-upholstered, horseshoe-backed chair. It was the finest chair in the room.

Julius sat in it like a hero of the Soviet Union and told his story. His confidence grew as he recollected just how smoothly the whole operation had gone.

General Vanin looked well pleased. He came over to top up Julius's glass. 'So. Thanks to you, Comrade Julius, we have acquired the only two copies of the Hess memoir. We

233

have already destroyed the typescript, and now we shall deal with the manuscript itself. There will be no record that the book ever existed.'

Even to a man as case-hardened as Julius, such destruction seemed regrettable and crude. Emboldened by the slivovitz, he said with deference, 'If I may make an observation, Comrade General, would it not be profitable to retain the manuscript in Herr Hess's own handwriting, expunging any passages detrimental to the honour of the Soviet State?'

The General frowned. 'Profitable in which sense, Comrade?'

'Not as a money-making venture,' Julius answered in a suitably shocked voice. 'I meant profitable to the highest enterprises of the State. We have skilful craftsmen at our disposal who could edit certain sections of the manuscript. They would be undetectable by scholars.'

'Which sections did you have in mind?' enquired the General casually.

Julius was not so far gone as to step into that morass. 'Nothing I could name, Comrade General. I haven't examined the script in detail myself. I simply anticipate the poisonous lies one must expect from an enemy of the State.'

'Ah.'

'Don't you agree, Comrade General, that an edited version of the Hess book might be put to the services of the State?'

General Vanin shook his head. 'Too dangerous. Every scrap of paper must be shredded.'

Julius found himself wishing he had taken an opportunity to read the book in full. His thoughts went back to his meeting with Harald Beer, when the publisher had talked of the Russians going berserk when they read the book. When General Vanin had ripped the suitcase open, those words had seemed prophetic. The sensitive issue was the Polish soldiers liquidated in 1940, Julius recalled. He should have taken the trouble to read that chapter, if no others. But on reflection, perhaps he had been wise to remain ignorant.

'I shall top up your glass,' the General told him.

'No more for me, I think,' said Julius, putting his hand towards the goblet, but the General was already pouring.

'We must finish the bottle,' he said.

234

Julius nodded in acquiescence. The drink was too fruity for his taste, and his head felt muzzy; but who argued with the head of the KGB?

'Always finish everything,' explained the General, still managing to sound remarkably lucid. 'When I was a child, I didn't need to be trained to eat everything on my plate. I was hungry. I have always endeavoured to finish everything I start.'

'An excellent principle, Comrade General.'

'Yes. One small matter that I should not like to overlook in this highly satisfactory operation is the girl who supplied information about the warder,' the General confided.

'Fraulein Heidrun Kassner,' said Julius.

The General nodded. 'You didn't meet her yourself?'

'Comrade Valentin was her contact, Comrade General.'

'How much did she know about the operation?'

'Practically nothing,' Julius declared confidently. 'She was of no importance, except as a contact with the American warder. She can be paid and dismissed.'

'I think she should be induced to leave West Berlin now,' said the General.

'I will arrange it,' Julius affirmed.

'No,' said the General. 'You will not.' He smiled as if to soften the prohibition. 'It will not be possible for you to perform that service, Comrade. You have another duty.'

'What's that, Comrade General?'

There was a pause. General Vanin slipped his hand into his pocket and took out a white pillbox, which he passed to Julius. 'In there, Comrade, you will find a cyanide capsule. Your duty is to swallow it.' As Julius gaped in horror, the General raised his hand like a fighter acknowledging a low punch, but he didn't apologise. He went on, 'You will do it because you are a loyal servant of the State, a true hero of the Soviet Union. Your name will be honoured and your family, your aged mother and your unmarried sister in Leipzig, will be given a generous gratuity and an annuity for life.'

Julius swayed in the chair. The room was beginning to reel. As if it mattered any more, he was suddenly afraid that his bowels would loosen. 'Why?' he managed to ask. 'Why me?'

'Because the secrets at stake are more precious than any

235

one officer of the KGB, however valuable his services have been,' the General explained. 'You have become a security risk, Comrade Julius.'

'And if I refuse?' Julius shook his head. 'All right. I know the answer to that.' He sat staring into the middle distance. 'You could trust me,' he hazarded, then stopped and closed his eyes in resignation. After a moment, he opened them and asked, 'What about the others – Valentin and the hit-man? They knew almost as much as I.'

'They were taken care of in East Berlin this afternoon,' said the General.

'Taken care of . . .?'

'By a man with a gas-gun.'

Julius knew for certain that he had no alternative. 'This is what you meant by finishing what you started.'

'But I have offered *you* the means to finish it,' the General pointed out.

'What will happen afterwards, to my . . . body?'

'Your death will be diagnosed correctly as due to cardiac failure and I shall make arrangements for your remains to be returned to your family for a dignified disposal. Why don't you take the capsule now, Comrade? It is mercifully quick, as I am sure you know.'

'The coffin downstairs . . .'

'. . . is for you,' murmured the General tolerantly.

'Everything planned to the last detail,' said Julius, mustering a smile. Before he closed his mouth, he had forced the capsule between his lips and bitten it.

'Good man,' said the General, raising his goblet.

It is doubtful whether Julius heard the tribute. He had already collapsed, lolling over the arm of the chair, taking huge, stertorous breaths, which stopped before the General put down his glass.

236

41

Red had phoned for a taxi and it was waiting beside the derelict Volkswagon by the time he got downstairs with Heidrun and Jane. He sat beside the driver, leaving the women in uneasy proximity on the rear seat. The clock on the instrument panel showed 11.05 and the streets were quiet, except for a party of teenagers throwing beer-cans into the Havel from Juliusturm Bridge.

Cal's lodging in Old Spandau was over a small petrol station and repair garage, which probably kept the rent down in what an estate agent would have described as a much sought-after locality. Red settled the fare and they climbed the iron staircase at the back of the building and pressed the bell on Cal's door. No lights showed in the flat and there was no response. The venetian blinds on the nearest window were in the open position, but it was too dark to see inside.

It was a solid wooden door, not the sort that yields to a shoulder. 'Keep your hand on the bell, love,' Red told Jane. 'I'll be back in a tick.' He clattered downstairs and into the garage, where he had noticed someone still working. 'The tenant upstairs, the American, do you know him?' he asked, crouching beside the feet projecting from under the chassis of a Volvo.

'No.'

'Seen him today?'

'No.'

'See anyone else go up there?'

'No.'

'Thanks. I'll borrow this.' Red picked a spare inspection-lamp off the floor. Consistent at least in his indifference, the mechanic carried on with his work while Red returned upstairs.

He shone the lamp through the adjacent window, which turned out to be the kitchen. They could see a cut loaf, a coffee-mug and a magazine open on the table.

He handed the lamp to Jane and climbed over the iron railing onto the window-ledge. It projected enough to give him a foothold if he held on to the shutters at the sides. He wanted to reach a second, larger window, probably part of the living-room.

'Red, that's dangerous!'

'Just hand me the lamp when I say,' he told Jane as he edged towards the second shutter. 'OK.' Gripping the top of the shutter with his right hand, he took the lamp in his left and continued the manoeuvre.

He had to make an over-long stride to the second ledge, but with the help of the shutter he got there and shone the beam into the room.

He had half-expected what he saw, but he still felt a sudden pricking of the skin and the nausea rising in his stomach.

'Red, what is it?' Jane called out.

He didn't answer. Close to the window, stretched across the floor in the fawn-coloured jacket he had been wearing that morning, was Cal, his head angled against the base of an armchair in a position that would have told anyone he was dead, even without the blood that had seeped from the exit-wounds at the back of his skull.

Red swung the lamp hard at the sash-window and smashed a hole large enough to get his hand through and free the catch. He shoved the window upwards and climbed inside.

Cal had been shot twice in the face, one bullet passing through the left eye and the other through the cheekbone, close to his nose. It must have happened hours ago, because the blood on his skin had dried and rigor mortis had tightened his jaw and neck.

Red shook his head and said out loud, with crass inadequacy, but in genuine pity, 'You didn't deserve this, mate.' He thought back to his last sight of Cal, waiting for a bus back to Spandau – with Valentin close behind him.

Valentin. While the other two had murdered the old woman, Valentin must have followed Cal here and conned his way into the flat and gunned him down. Why? What had Cal done to be picked off by an assassination squad?

The girls were shouting and ringing the bell. Red knew he must shake off the paralysing sense of outrage. He had seen gun-deaths before, in battlefronts and once on a hijack he had covered, but this was the first time he had personal knowledge of the victim. He picked a newspaper off the armchair and spread it over Cal's mutilated face. He got up and switched on the light. Then he went to the front door and let them in. Jane peppered him with questions, but Heidrun tried to push past, so he grabbed her arm.

'Listen to me, will you? Cal is dead, shot through the head. It must have happened this morning.'

Silence for a moment.

'Who?' mouthed Jane without saying the word.

'Valentin.'

'How can you be certain?' asked Heidrun in her sing-song intonation, which suddenly sounded insufferably sanctimonious.

'He was with the others who killed the old lady. He was tailing Cal when I last saw them.' He took a tighter grip on Heidrun's arm and asked her in German, 'For the last time, what can you tell me about that guy?'

She glared back at him defiantly and traded scorn for distrust. 'Are you deaf, or something? I told you everything. I told you he was violent, but I didn't think such a thing as this was possible. Let me pass, please. I want to see him.'

She didn't want to see him at all. She just wanted to evade more questions. It showed in her face. Red shoved her roughly against the wall and closed in, bringing his face up to hers. He was barely able to control the anger he felt. 'Who's behind Valentin?'

She pressed her lips together until they whitened.

'Answer me, whore!'

She spat in his face, a frothy gob of spittle that stung his left eye.

He slapped her hard across the face and back-handed the other cheek on the return.

Behind him, Jane cried out in protest, speaking his name.

A bead of blood formed on Heidrun's lower lip and rolled down her chin. She bucked her knee hard into his groin, and the pain seared through his testicles. He shouted and swayed away. As she aimed another kick between his legs, he had the wit to grab her foot and twist it hard, jerking her off balance. She fell heavily.

Then Jane acted. She threw herself on Heidrun like a wrestler and got an arm-lock on her, tightening it until she screamed with pain. Red couldn't stand upright, but he crouched against the wall and gestured to Jane to ease the grip.

Heidrun moaned.

'I think she'll talk now,' said Jane.

Heidrun shook her head, but it was unconvincing. She sheered away in fear as Red came closer.

He told her, 'They beat Edda Zenk with a pistol. They cut up her face before they killed her. Those are the people you helped. Are you going to force me to do it their way?'

'No!' Terror showed in her eyes.

Jane said, 'Red, you don't have to hit her again.'

He grabbed a hank of Heidrun's hair. 'Who do they work for?'

She whispered, 'The East.'

'The KGB?'

'I don't know. It was never told to me.'

He tightened his grip. 'You're a fucking KGB agent.'

'Not an agent. I'm of no importance.'

'But you're on the payroll?'

'Once you start, it's forever.'

'You were planted on Cal?'

'Yes.'

'Because of his job in Spandau? They wanted to know if Hess told him anything?'

'Yes.' She added quickly, 'I learned nothing of any use.'

'He didn't fancy you.'

Stung into defiance again, she flung back, 'He didn't get much chance, did he?'

He kept his eyes on Heidrun's, though he guessed the effect of the rebuke on Jane. 'Valentin was your case officer, is that the word?'

'I suppose so.'

'You set Cal up, and they got what they wanted and murdered him.'

'Please let me go, Red.'

He nodded and moved away. He had learned enough. Jane, too, released her hold, allowing Heidrun to stand up.

Red said to Heidrun. 'You were going in to see Cal. Why don't you take a look at him? See what your friends did to him.' He let her go past him into the living-room and said in a hollow voice to Jane. 'That was pretty sick-making. I'm sorry.'

She shook her head in a way that signified understanding, if not acceptance. She felt shamed by the violence, her own as well as Red's, but that was unavoidable. The verbal abuse had been harder to take. She had known without being told that he had slept with Heidrun, but she had hated hearing it thrown back at him, like muck. Yes, she felt pretty sick.

She said flatly, 'Shouldn't we call the police?'

He summoned the faintest grin. 'My mates from headquarters?'

'Heidrun will have to talk to them,' Jane emphasised. 'If she tells them everything . . .'

'We'll be here all night answering questions,' commented Red. 'There's something more important to do.' And intuitively, with startling clarity, he envisaged a way to do it. He had always been governed by impulse, and often it had failed him; but this was irresistibly simple, brilliant and timely. Mad, quite mad, but right. If he never lived to do anything else, he was going to try this. He took hold of Jane's hand. 'We said we owed it to Dick to discover the truth about Hess. Do you still believe that?'

'Of course, but—'

He cut in excitedly, 'I reckon we owe it to Cal and Edda Zenk as well, don't you?'

She saw the point of that, but she was still at a loss to understand what Red intended. 'Well, yes, but now that Cal is dead, we've lost our line into Spandau. How will we ever get in touch with Hess?'

'I'll go in and talk to him,' Red answered with absolute seriousness.

She screwed up her face in mystification. 'What?'

'I'm going to bluff my way in there.'

'That's crazy, Red.'

'Maybe, but the crazy ideas sometimes work.'

'You can't walk into a prison.'

He smiled. 'I'm not going to walk in, darling. I'm going to

241

run. I'll put on Cal's tracksuit and cap and jog over there, just like he does. I know the routine, don't I?'

She was practically bereft of words. 'It isn't possible.'

Heidrun's discouragement was suddenly added to Jane's from the living-room doorway. 'Only a fool would try it, Red. They have orders to shoot.'

He answered, 'They don't shoot the bloody warders.'

'Even if you got inside, they'd arrest you before the gate was closed.'

'Who? The military? It's the Russian month for guard-duty. They bring in a new set of soldiers every time. Those boys don't know one warder from another.'

'Red, you haven't planned this. You haven't thought it through,' Jane tried to impress on him.

'He's mad,' said Heidrun.

'It wouldn't surprise me if the bloody Russians have a go at Hess after what's happened,' Red persisted. 'Somebody in Spandau needs to be told about the carnage out here. The old man is in real danger.'

'Who are you trying to convince?' asked Heidrun.

Red crooked his finger at her. 'Come here.'

She shrank back into the room.

'I said come here.'

She hesitated, fearful of more violence. 'I'm sorry, Red. I don't want you to get shot. That's why I said those things.'

He continued to beckon her with his finger and by degrees she came, until she stood just out of arm's reach in front of him.

He said, 'Take off your trainers.'

She obeyed.

'Now take out the laces and hand them to me.'

When that was done, he made her face the wall while he bound her wrists. 'You're too bloody dangerous to let loose, he told her. 'If I was one of your mob, I'd kill you, wouldn't I?' He led her into Cal's bedroom and, with help from Jane, finished the job of trussing her up, finally tying her to the bed itself with strips of sheet. She made no resistance, realising, probably, the truth of his remark.

That accomplished, he stripped to his underwear, took Cal's tracksuit from its hook on the bedroom door and changed into it. 'I need your help, love,' he told Jane. 'In the back pocket of my trousers is a small wallet with my press-card. Got it?'

She picked the trousers off the floor. 'Yes.'

'Somewhere in there is a scrap of paper with three phone numbers, right?'

'Is this it?'

'Great. The first number will get you the chief warder's room in Spandau Prison. There's a public phone in the U-Bahn Station at the end of Breite Strasse, where the taxi put us down, OK? Tell the guy on duty that you're speaking for Warder Calvin Moody. Cal had some aggro with a break-in at his flat and that's why he's reporting so late, but he's on his way, and should be with them in twenty minutes. Leave it at that. Nothing else. Can you do it, love?'

'Of course, but—'

'Then I want you to take my own clothes back to the flat. You'll get a taxi in the same place, no problem. The key's in the pocket and money as well.' He winked at her. 'You'll find a bottle of Johnnie Walker Red Label beside my bed. Have a good slug.'

She wasn't capable of smiling any more, even for Red.

He still had something else to ask. 'Also by the bed is an address book. Look up a guy called Willi Becker. He lives in the Chamissoplatz, in the Kreuzberg section of the city. If anything goes wrong, anyone gives you flak, anything, go to Willi. Don't phone. Go and see him. Tell him where I am, why, everything he wants to know. Willi is OK. He'll take care of you. Got all that?'

Jane whispered that she had. She tilted her head towards the bedroom. 'What about her?'

'Forget her. If you feel inclined, you can make another call in the morning and tip off the law.'

Jane clung to his arm as he tried on a pair of Cal's jogging shoes. She held back her tears, but only just. 'Red. It's too dangerous. It can't possibly work.'

'I almost believe you, love,' he admitted, 'but if I don't try, I can't live with myself – or anyone else.' He drew her to his chest and they held each other for a couple of seconds. They didn't kiss.

She tried to snatch him back as he pulled away. But he was too quick for her.

42

Jogging was a new activity for Red, never to be disclosed to the press colleagues who frequented his usual drinking haunts in the city centre. He had asserted many times over jars of beer that he would never make an exhibition of himself on the public highway so long as he was capable of the sort of exercise that could be enjoyed with a pretty girl in private. In a parody of the late Sir Winston Churchill, he would sum up his personal recipe for good health as 'jig-jig, not jog-jog'.

Yet now he was compelled to set aside his principles. To make a credible impersonation of Cal, he could hardly take a taxi to the nearest street corner and then jog up to the front gate of Spandau. He had to show some sweat for the mile or so between Old Spandau and the prison. He took it slowly, much more slowly than Cal's customary pace, not wanting to give himself away at the end by looking like a man finishing a marathon.

He would have died rather than admit it in the press club, but Red actually found the jogging beneficial. It gave him time to prepare mentally for the job he had set himself, literally to get his act together. In one of the pockets of the tracksuit top was Cal's pass, the ticket into Spandau. It bore a passport-sized photo of Cal. There wasn't much facial resemblance to Red. The best to be hoped was that when Red approached the prison entrance, the powerful down-beam from the arc-lamps would throw his face into shadow under the peaked cap. The two men were similar in build. Cal must surely have been well known in the prison as the warder who jogged to work, so the running-kit should call him strongly to mind. It ought to be possible to get through the gate.

Then the problems would really begin. Several of the books on Hess showed rudimentary plans of the interior of the prison. If Red got through the gate, he would find himself in the guard-house, which was a separate building, isolated from the main cell-block where Hess was under guard. He would have to satisfy the Russians of his identity before a second gate could be opened to admit him to the courtyard in front of the cell-block entrance. If he got that far, and past the guard on the cell-block door, he could not fail to be recognized as an impostor by the other warders, who might be Russian, French, American or British. He would need to persuade them that it was vital that he spoke to Hess. He would have to pass more guards armed with sub-machine guns to penetrate to the last cell at the extreme end of the block, where the old man was held. And more daunting than any of the physical obstructions was the prospect of meeting Hess himself.

Red wasn't new to the game of meeting famous people. Early in his career, he had learned the wisdom of the dictum that the best way to fail as a journalist is to be uncertain about anything whatsoever on this earth. You treated celebrities like you treated your friends, and most of them responded positively. They needed you as much as you needed them:

But Hess was like no one else. He was the loneliest man in the world, and, according to those who had known him in Spandau, one of the strangest. It was for the psychiatrists to speculate whether more than forty years in prison, twenty of them in solitary, had shaped his personality. Maybe he had always been suspicious by temperament, reluctant to confide and rigid in his personal decisions. This was the man who had been unwilling to bring his wife and son to Spandau on a visit until Christmas 1969, twenty-eight years and six months after he had seen them last; who had said that if he had his time over again he would still serve Hitler and still make the flight to Scotland, even with the prospect of the rest of his life in Spandau. A man who had often driven his fellow-prisoners to the point of exasperation. Iron-willed, secretive, caustic, cranky, yet, as Albert Speer once wrote, . . . *now, thanks to his consistency, he was regarded with a certain respect, even among his enemies.*

How could you succeed in extracting confidences from such a man when you arrived unexpectedly in his cell by night, the first pressman he had seen in nearly half a century?

Was it reasonable to expect a rational response from a man over ninety years old? Not for the first time, Red was going to have to make snap assessments. He couldn't plan the conversation – if he was lucky enough to get one. It would be improvisation all the way.

He could feel moisture in the air as he trotted along Wilhelmstrasse, three-quarters of his journey done. A light drizzle cooled his face and made aureoles around the streetlamps. There wasn't much traffic now. He reckoned it was close to midnight.

The school at Wilhelmstadt with its athletics track came up on his right and after that the red-bricked military barracks, the place where the British forces were based. Ahead, the street forked into Gatower Strasse. By the intersection was the Melanchthon Church, where he had kept watch on the prison entrance.

No loitering now, Goodbody, he told himself. Keep running right up to the gate.

The castellated outline of the directors' building loomed through the trees. The prison itself was set further back on the right, behind its electric fences and walls and watchtowers.

Red turned off Wilhelmstrasse onto the cobbled approach to the prison entrance. He faced the twenty-foot arch in its sham-medieval façade of twin turrets and crenellated battlements, the great blue doors, the warning notices, the lights mounted on the turrets and at the margins of the electric fence.

He trotted forward into the pool of light. Not the moment, he thought, to wonder whether Jane had managed to get through on the phone to the chief warder's office. Or whether she had even found a coin to fit the slot.

He came to a halt in front of the small door built into the main gates, through which he had seen Cal come and go a number of times. He hesitated. What happened now? Did he press the bell, hammer on the door, or wait?

There were sounds on the other side. The grille in the door was slid across and a pair of eyes scrutinised him. Obviously he was expected to say something.

He cleared his throat and said, 'Warder Moody, reporting

for duty.' He relied on his Cornish accent to pass for
American. He sometimes put on voices when he was telling
stories in pubs, but he didn't fancy trying them out on a
Russian with a sub-machine gun.

The grille was slammed shut again, and for several seconds, which he reckoned aged him by as many years, Red
waited.

Then, Sesame! They were unbolting it from the inside. The
door opened and he stepped in. It closed at once behind him.

The Soviet sentry was shorter than Red expected and not
much more than a boy, yet he looked capable of using the
gun. He spoke something in Russian. Repeated it.

Of course! Red fumbled in his top pocket for Cal's ID. He
meant to show it briefly and pocket it again, but the sentry
insisted on taking it from him. Fortunately, the light wasn't
too good on that side of the gate.

Unfortunately, the sentry indicated that Red should move
into the guardroom on the left, where there was
strip-lighting, and other Russian guards waited. He ambled
in, trying to make it seem like routine, and nodded to the
NCO behind the desk. The glare of the lights made him blink.
There was a German shepherd-dog lying on the matting at
the rear of the room. It pricked up its ears and took a long
look at Red. Something else he didn't understand was said
and a book was pushed towards him. There was a ballpoint
attached to it with string.

No panic. They wanted him to sign in.

But there was a problem: he didn't know how Cal signed
his name. He hadn't bothered to examine the signature on the
ID card. He had been wholly taken up with the photo that
didn't resemble him.

The ID had been handed to the NCO, who was holding it
face down as he waited for Red to sign.

Red held out his hand for the card and said casually, 'OK?'

The NCO kept hold of it and pointed to the book.

Red nodded. Maybe if he scrawled some kind of signature,
the card would be handed over without a comparison being
made. Somehow, he knew it wouldn't. So he had to try
another ploy.

'Did I sign out yesterday?' he said rhetorically, flicking

back to the previous page and looked for a signature that might be Cal's. 'I have a feeling I missed. No, I was wrong. Here it is.' And a million thanks to Cal, rest his soul, for having a simple, spiky signature that could be copied with confidence.

Red turned the page over, signed and put down the pen.

Immediately, the NCO shouted an order and three guns were trained on Red.

'Christ!' he said. 'What is this?'

Nobody answered. Someone came from behind and frisked him. Something had gone horribly wrong. The muzzle of a gun was jabbed into his back.

The NCO said in English, 'You are not Moody. Who are you?'

Red stared back at him and was made sickeningly sure that there was no possibility of bluffing the man. The widely-spaced, slate-grey eyes were not particularly intelligent, but they were utterly certain. They knew for a fact that they were looking at a phoney. Yet he had to go on with the act. 'Is this some kind of joke?' he asked. 'The Russian sense of humour?'

'What is your name?'

'It's on the card in your hand.'

'You are not Warder Moody.'

'Listen, buddy, I know who I am.'

The NCO spoke another command in Russian. Two guards grabbed Red's arms and jerked them upwards behind his back, forcing his face down onto the desk. His nose crunched against the wood as if he had run into a wall. It went numb momentarily, then spikes of pain drove through it.

The dog was barking excitedly.

The NCO made a grab for the cap Red was wearing and slung it aside. He took a grip on Red's hair and screwed his face to one side on the desk. The guards maintained the excruciating hold on his arms. Blood seeped hotly from his nose.

'Who are you?'

'I told you,' Red blurted out. 'Call the chief warder if you don't believe me.'

'You are not a warder. We have pictures of all the warders. What do you want in this prison?'

'To do my bloody job!' Red groaned.

248

Something else was said in Russian and the holds on his arms were relaxed. He straightened, still wincing with pain. 'Buggers!' he said. 'I'll report this to the bloody directors.'

The Russian was unimpressed. 'As you refuse to identify yourself correctly,' he said stiffly, 'we are obliged to search you. This way.' He beckoned.

Red hesitated. Unwisely, because another order was rasped out and he was grabbed and hustled across the guardroom by the two young soldiers who had held him. The dog snapped at his legs, disclosing, mercifully, that it was chained to the wall and just out of range.

They dragged him struggling through a door at the back into a cell not more than seven feet square. There, they used their boots on his shins, kicking his legs from under him. Helpless, he rolled into a foetal position in one corner, but they soon had him flat to the floor and face down. One guard kneeled on his spine, while the other dragged the clothes from his body. Inside half a minute, he was stripped naked, his clothes tossed outside. They allowed him to lean against the back wall. But the 'search' didn't end there, because one of the guards stood over Red with the stock of his sub-machine gun poised to brain him if he moved, while the other removed the sling from his gun and wound one end of it around his fist. The way they worked together had the makings of a well-drilled routine of sadism.

Red felt a trickle of something against his inner thigh. He looked down at an involuntary jet of his own urine. The Russians pointed and cackled with amusement. Then the voice of the NCO broke in, bellowing some order. He materialised behind them in the doorway. The guards backed off at once.

'Get up!'

Red obeyed, using the wall as an extra support. He might have been standing on stumps, because all feeling in his shins and feet had gone. He didn't care about the loss of dignity. He didn't care that much about the pain. He was overwhelmed by the sense of failure, and that really hurt. Two good guys had died, and this was the best he had been able to achieve.

The NCO appraised the work of his men, running a long

look over Red's suffering body. 'Now you had better tell me who you are,' he advised with heavy menace. 'What is your true name?'

Red simply shrugged.

'There is a procedure for dealing with intruders,' the Russian told him. 'We are permitted to shoot them. The orders are categorical. These are orders that apply to the guards of each of the occupying powers. I quote for your benefit, so that you fully understand. *A guard will fire his weapon against persons who have gained entrance into the courtyards by force or other illegal method.* You have gained entrance illegally.'

'According to you,' commented Red.

'We shall therefore take appropriate action. First, I shall inform the Soviet director. He may order me to interrogate you or he may simply give the order for you to be shot. Now do you wish to tell me your name?' He waited a second, and then said, 'Very well. Your underclothes will be returned to you and you will be locked in here until I receive my orders.'

Red looked away.

His tee-shirt and pants were slung into the cell and the door was slammed.

43

Jane had never felt so desolate as at that moment when she stood at the top of the iron stairs of Cal's flat after Red had run off into the night. She had a horrid conviction that she would never see him again, whatever the outcome of his foolhardy scheme to get into Spandau Prison. She was angry with herself for having tamely acquiesced in the plan – if it deserved to be described as such. She had known from the day she met him that Red was his own worst enemy, a creature of impulse, destined for trouble. It wasn't hard to see how vulnerable he was. Yet this evening she had let herself be dominated by the force of his character, when she *knew* it was insane to try what he proposed.

It was no good pleading that the pressures of the past twenty-four hours had got to her, that she was mentally and physically exhausted. The man she felt herself to be in love with was putting his freedom, maybe his life, at risk. She should have done anything to stop him. She could only despise herself now. If her instincts were right and she had lost Red, it was because she didn't deserve him.

She turned and went back into the flat, mindful of those things that Red had asked her to do. Maybe it was inconsistent to collaborate in what he was attempting, but she couldn't stop him now, so the best she could do was try and help. She was grateful for the chance to occupy herself. Thinking was too painful.

Heidrun was shouting from the bedroom. They ought to have gagged her. Jane wished she could block her out of her mind, but she had to go in there to collect Red's clothes off the floor where he had left them.

Heidrun was making a strange sound, a shrill moan, so high-pitched that it was barely audible. To Jane's ear, it was more blood-curdling than a full-throated scream. She approached the bed. She couldn't ignore the impulse to find out what was wrong; there was no harm in looking, because Heidrun was still securely pinioned.

251

Her face was flushed and contorted, her eyes shut tight.
Jane bent closer. 'What is it?' she asked. 'What's the matter
with you?'

Heidrun kept her eyes closed. 'The cramp. My right leg. I
can't bear it.' She made that eerie sound of distress again.

Once or twice in her life, Jane had suffered the excruciating
pain of cramp. She knew that it could be brought on by
restriction of the blood supply. Red had tied Heidrun's legs at
the ankles and just below the knees with strips of sheet. To
Jane's eye, the bonds certainly looked excessively tight
against the thin fabric of the tracksuit.

With Heidrun's cry blocking out every other consideration,
imploring relief from the agony, Jane took the humane decision. She loosened the knots at the knees. She would tie
them again, securely, but less tightly. Even if the knots no
longer held, Heidrun's arms and ankles would remain firmly
tied, and she would still be pinned to the bedstead by the
broad strips around her body.

She gently massaged the flesh above and below Heidrun's
knee. Heidrun groaned, but with less urgency, and gave a nod
of thanks. Jane refastened the knots as well as she could
without reactivating the constriction. Then she switched her
attention to picking up Red's clothes and putting them into a
sportsbag she had found on a chair beside the bed.

In a plaintive, little-girl voice that sounded grotesquely out
of character, Heidrun asked. 'Are you going to leave me
here?'

'Of course,' said Jane matter-of-factly. Her sympathy had
been used up. She transferred Red's keys and money to her
shoulder-bag. First she would make that phone call to
Spandau.

'I could be dead before I am found here,' Heidrun said with
more of her old aggression.

'Yes,' Jane agreed in a bored voice that conveyed what she
thought of such melodramatics. She took a last look around
the room. Then she picked up the bag, switched off the light
in the hall and left the flat without another word, closing the
door but leaving it unlocked. Someone would go in there and
find Heidrun the next day.

A strange city by night might have been intimidating to a

solitary girl in other circumstances, but not for Jane tonight. She stepped out purposefully through the shadowy streets, oblivious of herself, her mind entirely taken up by the danger Red was in. At Altstadt Spandau U-Bahn Station, she located the phone booth and dialled the number Red had given her.

It bleeped for a long time before a voice answered in German.

She asked, 'Please, do you understand English?'

'But of course.' He sounded French, and in those three words he managed to convey that he was intrigued to find himself speaking to a woman.

To be certain she had got the right number, Jane asked, 'Is that the chief warder?'

'The duty warder. What can I do for you at this time of night, my darling?'

The last thing she felt like was a risqué conversation, but at least he was friendly. She spoke the message Red had asked her to deliver. The Frenchman thanked her for the information and asked if she was a friend of Cal's. Just as Red had instructed, she said goodnight and put down the receiver. She leaned against the side of the booth and tried to breathe more evenly. She could have used a cigarette.

Red had promised there would be a taxi. There were none waiting at the rank,so she crossed the street to look for one on the busier highway of Am Juliusturm. Her mind was still running over the things Red had asked her to do. She had collected his clothes, made the call to the prison and now she had only to find her way back to the flat in Haselhorst.

Then she stopped in her tracks. There was something they had both overlooked: the inspection-lamp that Red had borrowed from the garage. It was still in Cal's flat. The man in the garage would be wondering what had happened to it. He might easily go up there. He would find Cal lying dead there; and Heidrun. The police would be called. Spandau would be alerted.

Jane stopped looking for a taxi. She knew what she had to do: retrace her journey through the streets to that place she had been so thankful to leave, into the room where Cal was lying dead. It was her duty to retrieve the lamp and return it to the garage. She crossed back to Breite Strasse.

253

To her relief, when she got back to the garage the man was still working under the car. She hurried around the rear of the building and up the stairs, opened the door and switched on the light.

Heidrun stood facing her, holding a carving-knife. The strips of sheet lay about the floor of the hall and in the kitchen doorway where she had cut them away. There was blood on one of her wrists. She must have squirmed free and dragged herself to the kitchen.

Jane took a step backwards towards the door. She didn't dare turn away. Her hand groped for the handle and found nothing. Light flashed on the knife-blade as Heidrun twisted it threateningly in front of her. She began to move forward.

'No!' said Jane, still feeling for the door handle. 'We didn't harm you.'

Heidrun sneered. 'We didn't harm you,' she echoed, mocking Jane's voice. 'The famous English sense of fair play. I don't give a fart for fair play. I'm going to cut you up.' She advanced on Jane with the knife extended. Then she thrust it towards her.

Jane still had the sportsbag in her left hand. She swung it at the knife as Heidrun lunged and felt it take the force of the blade. She tried to move aside, but there was no room in the narrow passage. She staggered, tripped and fell, striking her head on the door-handle she had failed to locate. Heidrun stepped over her, opened the door and was away down the staircase.

Jane watched the ceiling blur and spin. She was losing consciousness. She wanted to fight it, but she couldn't move a muscle.

How long she lay there, she had no idea at the time, although in retrospect it was probably not much over five minutes. She was aware only of a searing headache and limbs that felt encased in plaster. She dragged herself into a sitting position. In a moment, she was able to crawl through the door and get some air at the top of the staircase.

By degrees, the urge to get away from the place overcame the lethargy in her body. She hauled herself upright, went in and collected the bag. The carving-knife clattered on the hall floor, revealing a six-inch split in the sportsbag.

The rest of that night was confused. Later she decided that she must have suffered some concussion. She had a faint recollection of finding her way back to Breite Strasse. Whether it actually happened, she never discovered, but she retained a persistent image of Heidrun ahead of her in the street, leaving the telephone booth and hailing a taxi; of herself getting into the taxi behind and asking the driver to follow; of being driven at speed through lighted streets towards the city centre and beyond, to the wall, with its graffiti scrawls; of stopping somewhere because Heidrun had got out of her taxi; and of being told by the taxi-driver that it was no use trying to follow Heidrun because that was the checkpoint for German nationals, and she, as a foreigner, could not use it; and of the sense of helplessness and bitter, bitter failure.

44

Time was difficult to estimate in the darkness of the cell, and Red had no watch. Certainly two hours, and maybe as many as three, had passed before he heard the bolts being moved. He hauled himself stiffly off the concrete floor, knowing he was defenceless, but feeling marginally less so on his feet.

The light that streaked in from the guardroom was painful to his eyes. He was aware of a figure outlined in the doorway, then of something tossed in towards him, landing at his feet.

'Put on your clothes.'

'Why?' he asked in amazement. 'What's going to happen to me?'

'Just do what you're told. Quickly.'

He didn't argue. The cell had been like an ice-box.

The clothes were the ones he had arrived in – Cal's tracksuit and trainers – no longer of interest, apparently, to the Russian guards. Even the cap was there. He put them on gratefully, at a loss to understand what could have prompted such clemency.

The guard watched him from the doorway. 'Now put your hands on your head and step out here.'

He obeyed. Two guards moved close with their sub-machine guns levelled.

The same granite-featured Russian NCO was standing by the desk. He looked Red up and down as if it were a uniform-inspection. 'Are these the clothes you were wearing when you entered the prison illegally?'

Red gave a nod. 'Are you going to release me?'

There was a gleam of malice in the grey eyes, but no response.

'You want to question me?'

Still nothing.

So Red waited in silence, wary of antagonizing his captors with further questions. After about two minutes, the NCO picked up the phone, dialled a number and spoke in Russian.

His eyes didn't leave Red. He put down the receiver. 'You will come this way now.'

Red followed him across the red-tiled floor to a different door from the one he had come in by, leading, if his sense of direction could still be relied on, to the courtyard that separated the buildings at the entrance from the main cell-block. He was at a loss to understand why. This was exactly the way he would have taken if he had been able to bluff his way past the guards. He would have crossed the yard to the building where Cal worked, and Rudolf Hess was held.

And now they were allowing him to go there. One of the guards had opened the door. The open courtyard lay ahead. Across it, some forty yards away, the lighted windows of the main cell-block. The NCO stepped aside and gestured his prisoner through. It couldn't have been from politeness.

Only then was Red seized with the suspicion that he was about to take a death-walk. Some words came back to him, the orders so precisely recited by the NCO: *A guard will fire his weapon against persons who have gained entrance into the courtyards by force or other illegal method.* The Russians, meticulous in their observance of the regulations, were about to carry out his execution. They had given him back the clothes he had arrived in because they meant to shoot him. A corpse in false clothes riddled with bullets would convince the other powers that he was an impostor, shot in the act of penetrating the security system.

He had seen diagrams of the yard. He didn't have a chance. The sides were walled. He would be picked out by the searchlights and shot.

But not without a fight. As he reached the doorway, he wheeled round, reached for the top of the door-frame, gripping it with his fingers, and kicked with both feet at the chest of the guard behind him. The man staggered back. Red hurled himself forward to grab the sub-machine gun.

There was never much chance that he would succeed. As he fell on the guard, another gun crunched into his ribs and something smashed across his shoulders. He was pinned face-down on the floor with army-boots pressing on his arms and legs.

'Shoot me now, you bastards!' he yelled through the pain.

But no gun was placed to his head. There was just a bedlam of shouting in Russian, and it didn't seem to be directed at him. Recriminations, threats, fresh orders – Red didn't care. He waited angrily for the beating that would now precede his execution.

It didn't occur. Instead, he was lifted up by his arms and dragged backwards through the door and into the yard. Fully expecting to be dumped in the centre and left for the snipers on the watchtowers to pick off, he made no resistance, trying to conserve what strength he had left for a dash to one of the darker corners.

Again, he had miscalculated. The guards didn't leave him. They frogmarched him right across the yard to the main cell-block, up some steps to a door that he heard being unbolted, and straight inside. Then he was hauled up an iron spiral staircase, his heels scraping against the steps. Each of his trainers came off, but someone collected them and, with a mystifying show of consideration, slipped them back onto his feet at the top of the staircase. There, he was faced towards the front and led across the landing to a door marked in Russian, French and English, 'PRISON DIRECTOR'.

A meeting with the man in charge. Why?

The NCO came up the stairs last and looked Red up and down again, walking right around him and stopping once to rub some dustmarks off his shoulder. He said in a low voice, 'Colonel Klim, the prison director, has indicated that he wishes to interview you.'

'Why didn't you tell me over there, for God's sake?' Red asked. 'It would have saved some hassle all round, wouldn't it?'

The Russian went on as if Red hadn't spoken, 'Whatever he decides to do with you, he will require me to execute the order. I would like to make something clear to you before we go in. Any injuries you have sustained, any rough handling you have been given, was of your own making. You had to be restrained. The Colonel will not wish to hear about it. Do you understand me?'

'Transparently,' answered Red.

'Then we will go in.' He knocked and opened the door.

Colonel Klim, small, sallow, distinctly oriental in feature, was standing by the arched window trying to operate the blind. He was wearing a Soviet army raincoat over bottle-green pyjamas. He must have come specially from his quarters. His neat toes peeped out of leather sandals. He seemed to have been caught unprepared. Giving up his struggle with the blind, he glided behind the director's desk, a teak and metal status-symbol, massive enough to serve as a screen for a man of his size. He gave an order in Russian to the two guards who had entered the room with Red. They saluted and withdrew, leaving only the NCO in attendance.

Another order, and a chair was placed in the centre of the room for Red, a couple of yards back from the desk. All that was now visible of Colonel Klim was his face, framed by his hands so that even the collar of the pyjamas was obscured.

Formality restored, he said in correct English that sounded like lesson one of a language laboratory course, 'Good morning. My name is Colonel Klim. What is yours?'

'Calvin Moody,' answered Red, knowing it would not be believed, but with no alternative to offer.

Colonel Klim tilted his eyebrows and said with gentle sarcasm, 'How strange! We have a warder here with the same name, but he is nothing like you.'

Red made it clear with a sideward glance that he wasn't interested in a verbal chess game.

The Russian continued, 'To avoid misunderstanding, I will tell you that my position here is permanent. I have been the Soviet director of the prison since April 1982. I know the warders personally. Moody has a narrower face than yours. His hair is darker and certainly shorter. Feature for feature he is quite unlike you. What is your name?'

'Calvin Moody.'

Colonel Klim scowled. 'This is very unwise, young man. My sleep has been disturbed by this breach of prison regulations. My patience has a short limit. However, let us try another avenue of conversation. How did you enter the prison?'

'Through the front gate.'

The NCO interposed something rapidly and earnestly in Russian that Red guessed was a first attempt to paper over the breach of security.

259

Colonel Klim barked back a few syllables and then resumed to Red, 'It seems that the normal procedure at the gate was not observed. There should have been a warder on duty there. We were a man short tonight.'

'I know.'

'A telephone message was received that Moody was coming in late. Was that part of your scheme to enter the prison illegally?'

'That's a leading question,' commented Red.

'But you had better answer it,' Klim insisted.

'I didn't make a phone call.'

There was another exchange in Russian.

'It was a woman who called,' Klim informed Red. 'She spoke to the duty warder. He passed the message to the guardroom. That is why you were admitted. I presume that this woman is in league with you.'

And how! Red thought. It's the super-league if I ever get out of this place alive.

Colonel Klim asked, 'Is that assumption correct?'

'I don't know what you're on about,' Red answered with a baffled expression.

'Very well. Let's turn to something we can both agree on.' Klim picked Cal's pass off the desk and held it up by one corner. 'This appears to be genuine. It has Moody's photograph, not yours, and his signature, not the poor imitation you scribbled in the guardroom book. How did it come into your possession?'

Red was tempted to answer with the truth, just to see whether the fact of Cal's murder would make any impression on the Buddha-like repose of the face across the desk. But the truth was his defence, not to be surrendered. So long as he remained of interest to the Russians, kept them puzzled about his identity and his reason for being there, he stood a chance of survival.

When it was obvious that no answer was forthcoming, Klim said with a harder edge to his words, 'You stole it. You stole his clothes as well. You had better tell me the reason now. You tricked your way in here. Why? Are you politically motivated? Making some form of demonstration?'

'Like saving the whales?' Red flippantly suggested.

260

Colonel Klim snapped out some sentences in Russian and the NCO came from behind Red, grabbed his arms and strapped them together at the elbows and hard against the vertical struts of the chair-back. The pain was bearable, but not for long.

'How about the electrodes?' Red muttered. 'I thought you people had all the latest gear.'

'We are not torturers,' said Klim with a show of umbrage. 'This is a necessary safeguard while I speak to you in private.'

'Yes?' said Red sceptically. Then he heard the door close as the NCO withdrew. 'So what is there to say?' He braced his arms, and one of the struts snapped, bringing him some relief.

Colonel Klim got up and moved around the desk, tugging his raincoat across his chest. He stood facing Red, studying him, making up his mind. 'I will be frank with you. I know that Moody is dead. The information reached me earlier this evening.'

Aware that he was under the closest scrutiny, Red made no attempt to fake a reaction. He wanted to know where this was leading.

Klim continued like a judge summing up, 'You were able to trick your way in here because the prison staff have not yet been informed about Moody. But it was a crude attempt at impersonation which the guards detected easily. Occasionally, we have to deal with crazy people and publicity-seekers who make trouble at the prison gate. I would treat you as such a minor nuisance if you could persuade me that there is not some more sinister motive governing your actions.'

Red didn't respond. His tired brain was wrestling with the implications of what he had just learned. Klim had been informed about Cal's killing. *Earlier this evening*, he had said, implying that he had heard the news early enough to have put the guards on alert if he had chosen. So it could only have come from Cal's murderer, Valentin, or his employer, the KGB. Colonel Klim was either a KGB agent himself, or he was acting on their orders.

The realisation led to a significant shift in Red's tactics. His entry into Spandau had started so disastrously that up to now he had scarcely given a thought to anything but survival. He had fully expected to be shot. Now other possibilities were emerging. The Colonel knew things. He probably knew the reason why Edda Zenk and Cal had been murdered. It might be possible to draw it out of him by trading information.

'I knew Cal,' he volunteered. 'He was no villain. He didn't deserve to be shot in the head.'

Klim's brown eyes gleamed with satisfaction. 'Yes, it will come as a shock to everyone in Spandau. So you have been to his apartment?'

'I broke in,' admitted Red.

'And found him dead? Then, for some reason, you dressed up in his clothes and tried to enter Spandau. Why?'

'To get some answers.'

'From whom?'

'Anyone who knew anything.'

Klim looked disbelieving. 'I think you could be more precise than that.'

'How?' asked Red.

'I think you had ideas of meeting the man we call Number 7.'

'Rudolf Hess?'

Klim nodded. 'You believe he can tell you why Moody had to be shot.'

'Had to be?'

'But I doubt whether he would have helped you in the least, even if you had miraculously arrived in his cell. Number 7 is singularly uncommunicative. He would be suspicious of your motives. Do you deny that you intended to make contact with him?'

'Of course I deny it,' Red affirmed. And now he would stonewall again, because he had got as much from Colonel Klim as he was likely to give: the admission that Cal's killing had been carried out because it 'had to be'; and the strong suggestion that Hess would know the reason why, even if he refused to talk.

More questions followed and, as Red reverted to short answers, Klim showed increasing signs of annoyance. The questions began to be replaced by thinly-veiled threats. 'If you persist in this way, I shall have to bring in people who are experienced in questioning suspicious persons.'

262

'The police?'

'Not the police. They have no jurisdiction here.'

'The military police?'

The phone on Klim's desk bleeped. He picked it up and spoke his name. Then something was said that made the blood run from his face. He had been standing with one sandalled foot turned downwards, resting on the tip. He brought the heel down sharply and practically stood to attention. He clutched at the collar of his raincoat and drew it across his chest. His contributions to the conversation were minimal.

As soon as he was able to replace the phone, he picked it up again and dialled a two-digit number, presumably internal. This time he was doing most of the talking, evidently passing on urgent information. Red tried to understand some of it. The only certain thing he gleaned was a name, spoken and repeated with great emphasis, as if to make sure there were no misunderstanding: General Vanin.

Colonel Klim cradled the phone again, staring at Red as if he had no inkling how he had arrived there, and went across to the door and opened it. He shouted something to the NCO outside.

The guards came in and loosened Red's arms. They hustled him outside, past Klim, who stood distractedly at his door, rubbing his face with his hand. He said nothing.

They took Red down the stairs, this time allowing him to use his own feet. Down one level, they steered him into a once-whitewashed, now yellow-grimed and flaking corridor that stretched the length of the block, almost a hundred yards. Dim lights under old-fashioned conical shades showed open cell-doors from end to end on each side. If ventilation had been the intention, it was not a success. The place smelt musty and unused.

The NCO ordered a halt while he looked into a couple of cells. He selected the second on the right.

'You want me to go in there?' asked Red, as if there were any choice.

Nobody bothered to answer. As he went in, he asked, 'Who is General Vanin?'

The door slammed shut.

263

45

Spandau.

Its bleak reality closed in on Red. The cell had the stale smell of many years' disuse. The walls were coated with mould. This disregarded section of the prison had probably not been used in forty years.

The place was still furnished with its iron bedstead, wooden table and stool. Red stretched out on the steel mesh of the bed-frame and stared upwards. Either the moon was clear, or dawn had broken outside the small, arched window, because there was enough light to count the panes behind the bars. Eighteen, three of them cracked.

The last occupant would have been one of the outcasts of Hitler's Germany, detained here for 'processing', prior to execution, or transportation to a concentration camp. In 1947, it had seemed grimly appropriate to bring the men convicted at Nuremberg to this place where the victims of their system had suffered.

Seven Nazi leaders, ranging in age from forty to seventy-four, had been brought here, handcuffed to US soldiers. They were the so-called 'difficult' cases of the Nuremberg Trial. Twelve others had been sentenced to hang and three had been acquitted. Of the Spandau seven, three – Raeder, Funk and Hess – had been sentenced to life imprisonment. After eight years in Spandau, Admiral Raeder, ill and in his eightieth year, had been released; two years later, Walter Funk, 66, physically and mentally depleted by the years he had served, was allowed to walk out to freedom, 'with allowance for his age and ill-health'. That was in 1957. Spandau's other lifer was still waiting for clemency.

Red pictured Rudolf Hess lying in a cell on one of the lower levels, in the block he had once shared with the other six. They had all gone by 1966, having served their terms or been granted compassionate release. Hess alone was left to bear the burden of guilt for the Third Reich. Yet he alone of the seven had been found not guilty both of war crimes and crimes against humanity. He had received his life sentence for being guilty of conspiracy and – a curious irony – crimes against peace.

The impact of nearly half a century of confinement was beyond imagination. Red didn't fool himself into thinking that a few hours locked in Spandau would bring him any closer to understanding Hess and how he had endured his punishment. He could pity the man and wonder at his power of survival. He could touch the walls and lie on a prison bed and breathe the prison air, but he would be no nearer to comprehending the scale of the experience.

He was sure of one thing: if he was lucky enough to get out of the place alive, he wouldn't have much self-respect if the best he could produce would be a piece for the tabloids entitled 'My Night in a Spandau Cell'. His story wasn't going to be about Red Goodbody. He was certain that the secret of Spandau, the reason why Hess would never be released, was behind the killings of Cal and Edda Zenk. Someone – maybe Hess himself – had lit a fuse and the KGB were in a panic because the story was about to blow sky-high. Hess was certainly at risk. He deserved to be told. By some means, Red was going to reach him. And survive to tell the story.

Daybreak. Emphatically. The light grew stronger, picking out the details of the cell, the divisions between the bricks, the studs in the iron door, the square opening that served as a Judas-hole.

An hour or more passed. Sometimes he heard slight movements from the Soviet guard posted in the corridor. Once or twice there was the clatter of steps on the iron staircase. They went away.

Unexpectedly, because this time Red had heard no steps, the small sliding panel in the door was opened. '*Café noir?*'

'*Oui.*' He got up quickly and came close to the hole. In French, he asked if the owner of the voice was a warder.

'Yes. The chief warder. I speak English. You want something else?'

Red knew that this could be a Russian trick to get him to talk. He was guarded in his response. 'Do you know about me?'

'Of course.'

'But you don't know about Cal.'

After a pause, the voice said, 'I will come back with the coffee.' The panel closed.

Red paced the cell, trying to decide whether the French accent was genuine. To his ear, most Frenchmen speaking English sounded like con-artists. If this were really a warder, possibilities emerged – remote, improbable, but worth exploring in a no-win situation. If he could convey to the warders that their colleague Cal had been murdered and that Hess himself was in imminent danger from the KGB, they might be persuaded to help. They knew how Spandau operated. With their co-operation, and if they were willing to take exceptional risks, he might have a chance.

While he pondered the risks, his brain was busy, subconsciously turning over the significance of something he had noticed; and now it made the connection. He recalled a detail he had read in the press clippings back in England. Out of consideration to Hess, most of the warders had taken to wearing soft shoes, so as not to disturb his sleep. That was why the Frenchman had been able to approach the cell unheard. So he *was* a warder . . . wasn't he?

The risk had to be taken. Trust him.

The panel was slid open again. It came as a shock to hear another voice, American this time. 'Coffee, no sugar.'

He took it through the hatch and waited there expectantly. 'Thanks.'

'You're welcome.'

And with that, the panel closed.

'Fucking hell!' Red practically threw the stuff at the door. It had been a perfect opportunity for more communication, and it had gone begging. He had waited there, primed to speak. Christ, it was maddening! An American, Cal's buddy, and all he could find to say was a bloody platitude! Why hadn't the Frenchman reappeared when he had promised? Livid with rage and disappointment, Red sank on the bed with the paper cup of coffee in his fist. It was some time before he could bring himself to take a sip.

Then he felt something solid touch his teeth. He lifted it out of the cup and stared at it.

266

A small ballpoint pen.

The warders were not so dumb. They wanted him to write a message for them and pass it out. He felt through the pockets of the tracksuit for a scrap of paper. Nothing. Looked around the cell, under the table, under the bed. Plenty of dust, but no paper. He even tried taking a flake of paint from the wall, but it disintegrated in his hand.

Still in his other hand was the paper cup.

He shook his head and cursed himself for being so obtuse. He owed those guys an apology. For not only had they provided him with a writing implement and a surface; they had given him the means to return it undetected. There were two cups pressed together. He could write on the outer surface of one, using the whole of the space, and then enclose it tightly in the other. It would look like the one pristine cup they had appeared to hand him.

He wrote, compressing the size and content of the message: *Cal murdered by KGB. Also Edda Zenk, visited by Cal. Hess now in danger KGB Gen Vanin. I can explain. R. Goodbody, Brit. newsman.*

There was enough there to guarantee a bullet in the head if the cup was seen by the Russians, but he had to entrust his life to the warders. Not only that. He was banking on their outrage at Cal's death and their concern for Hess to shock them into helping him.

In a moment, the hatch opened.

'More coffee?'

'No thanks.'

He passed the empty cups through, and it was done. He wedged the pen into a corner on the underside of the table.

And waited.

Soon, he guessed, Colonel Klim would want him upstairs for more interrogation, possibly by General Vanin, whose name had provoked such alarm. If there was going to be action from the warders, it could not be long delayed. He wished to God he had stressed the emergency more.

He tensed. Words were being exchanged outside the cell door. He stood by the hatch, not knowing what to expect. Then he heard the bolts thrown across and the key turned. The door swung open slowly. The Soviet guard was there with his sub-machine gun. And so was a short, grey-haired man in gold-framed glasses and wearing the blue uniform of a prison official.

'You must come for the ablutions now,' he said in the heavily-accented voice Red recognized as the chief warder's. 'Put your hands on your head and follow me.'

No intimation of how the message had been received.

Red followed the instructions. He decided to leave the initiative to the Frenchman. There was nothing either of them could usefully do while the point of the gun was against his back. The bathroom was a short walk to the right down the corridor between walls coated in a pale green mould. An open doorway revealed a row of basins along one wall and eight lavatories without doors. Red went to one and relieved himself. Then he crossed the floor to the nearest basin and ran some water. He took off the tracksuit top and splashed water on his face and body.

As he bent over the basin again, he sneaked a glance behind him. The gun was still trained on him. Nothing was happening.

'Enough,' said the chief warder in a bored voice. 'Now we return to the cell.'

Red used the tracksuit to dab himself dry and put it on, looking with increasing desperation for some signal from the warder. Surely nothing could be done until the Russian was overpowered and disarmed. They needed the help of the American warder. Where the hell was he?

No clue was offered. 'Put your hands on your head.'

He was the least demonstrative Frenchman Red had ever encountered. Even when their eyes met briefly, he communicated nothing. The encouragement Red had derived from the pen and the paper cups was draining away like the water in the basin. He was beginning to suspect he had made a hideous error.

A prod in the back from the gun, and he found himself retracing his steps along the corridor.

What now? The opportunity to act was almost past. At the cell door, he paused and said, 'Thanks for the coffee.' Then, with slow emphasis, 'Is there a chance of anything else?'

The chief warder answered tonelessly, 'You want something to eat? I will try to arrange it.'

268

The Russian guard pressed the gun harder into Red's back. He had his own way of communicating, and there wasn't any ambiguity about it. Red sighed, stepped back into the cell and felt the rush of air as the door slammed behind him.

The missed opportunity rankled so much that it was a moment before he responded to the sight of something in the cell that had not been there before: a neat pile of clothes at the end of the bed – dark blue in colour, with silver buttons. A warder's uniform!

He lifted the jacket from the bed. Under it were a white shirt, black tie, trousers and black shoes. He clenched his fists and all but shouted in elation. He shouldn't have doubted the warders. This was brilliant, far more useful than anything he had dreamed up himself. The uniform was probably Cal's. He must have kept one at the prison to change into from his jogging gear. It was an excellent fit. The feel of the clothes gave Red a lift. There were still hair-raising problems to be faced, but he was in with some kind of chance.

Dressed up, he worked on his tousled hair with his fingers, trying to make it passably tidy. Then he waited in suspense, knowing that if he was summoned upstairs in the next few minutes, he was sunk. The sun had risen high enough for the first rays to streak through the barred windows. Red sat hunched on the edge of the bed, arms folded, staring at the stone floor.

Then he got up.

The bolts scraped and the key was turned. The door was pushed open slowly.

'Your breakfast.' The American warder entered with a tray bearing bread rolls and a bowl of cereal. He placed it on the table and made sure that the cell door was only slightly ajar. Outside, the chief warder was in conversation with the guard, occupying his attention.

The American ran a critical eye over Red's turn-out. 'OK,' he said in a subdued voice, speaking rapidly. 'You step out of here and bolt the door, leaving me inside. The guard has the key. Walk right past him like you do it every day. Turn right, head for the stairway and go down to the next level. The warders' room will be the first on your left. It's standing open. Got that?'

Red nodded.

'Hope you make it.' The American scooped the things off the tray and handed it to Red. 'You'd better carry this.'

Red didn't attempt to thank him. There wasn't anything adequate he could have said. It was an act of rare courage to sit locked in that cell and wait for the Russians to discover that they had been outsmarted.

With the empty tray under his arm, Red opened the cell door, stepped outside, closed it, slammed home the bolt, turned past the chief warder and the guard and strode down the corridor at the measured pace he imagined warders used, wishing that the rubber-soled shoes didn't give the impression of stealth, and trying to decide at which point it would be worth making a dash if he were challenged.

Before he reached the stairs, he heard the key turn in the cell door. There was a change in the volume and tempo of the conversation behind him. It was the chief warder taking leave of the guard.

Red took the stairs at a quicker rate and found himself in a green and white corridor that looked more used to habitation. He found the warders' room and went inside. No one was there. It was furnished as a sitting-room, with a row of lockers, a fridge and a sink. The chief warder followed Red in. He pulled the door to and gestured to him to take a seat at the table.

Like a consultant with an anxious patient, he took off his glasses to polish them and said in a measured, emollient tone, 'Now would you tell me precisely what happened to Cal Moody?'

Red stood gripping the chair-back. 'For Christ's sake, there isn't time. They're going to send for me and all hell's going to break loose.'

The chief warder said in his deadpan manner, 'I insist. I have responsibilities. If you want me and my colleagues to break the prison regulations, you must convince me it is necessary.'

Red's nerves were stretched to the limit, but he knew he couldn't do anything without the warders' active support. So he picked out the crucial events of the past twenty-four hours and related them succinctly, expecting any second to hear the

270

clatter of army boots along the corridor. 'Now do you believe me?' he asked earnestly when he was through.

The chief warder had listened impassively. 'It is asking a lot. I must be frank with you. I cannot understand why it is necessary for you to speak to the prisoner Hess.'

Red had guessed this would be the sticking point. 'Can't you see? He's in trouble. There's something he wants the world outside to know, some secret he has guarded for over forty years. He put his trust in Cal Moody and asked him to get in touch with this woman, Edda Zenk, and now the KGB have killed them both. They beat up Edda Zenk before they shot her, so you can bet that they found out the secret. Hess doesn't know this yet.'

'That is probably true.'

'You guys who have been close to the old man for years must have some regard for his well-being,' Red hazarded. 'Don't you think he ought to be told what happened?'

'*Ought to be?* No. In this matter, he has contravened the regulations.'

'Sod the regulations!' Red almost howled.

'But I was going to add,' the chief warder persisted staidly, 'that we may feel a human obligation to tell him.'

Red clenched his fist as if to trap that human obligation in his hand. 'Right! Only who would Hess trust, now that Cal is dead? Another warder?'

The question clearly made an impression, although the chief warder avoided answering it directly. 'Why should he trust a total stranger?'

Before Red could answer, the phone buzzed.

The chief warder picked it up. He listened, and then responded in Russian. He frowned and changed the receiver to the other ear. His composure snapped at last. He protested angrily to the caller, gesticulating with his free hand. The to and fro continued for about a minute, at the end of which the caller must have put down the phone while the chief warder was still in full flow, because he suddenly stopped in mid-sentence, listened, held the receiver six inches from his face, stared at it, said, '*Merde!*' and fairly thumped it down.

He picked it up again, cradling the mouthpiece as he explained to Red, 'Insufferable! Not only do the Russians flout

271

the regulations by allowing this General Vanin to enter the prison without the agreement of all the directors, now they tell me he is already here and has a matter to discuss with Hess. I am ordered to escort Hess to the interview room. I will not do it without the consent of the other directors.'

'Who is Vanin?' asked Red. 'The Soviet director spoke about him on the phone last night. He was practically shaking in his shoes.'

'I think he is KGB.' The chief warder impatiently rattled the contact-bar. 'They won't give me an outside line, blast them. I don't mind who I speak to – the Allied Commission, any one of the directors. I refuse to capitulate to these Russians with blood on their hands.'

'I've got to go in and talk to Hess now,' Red insisted.

'Do you know? – I think the bastards have pulled the switches on me.' The chief warder rattled the phone again, and then pushed it away from him. He was outraged to the point of revolt. 'OK,' he said tensely. 'We will try, but it will be difficult. I will have to take you past two guards. There is the usual one on the inner cell-block door and an extra man who was posted outside the cell this morning. There is also Shaporenko, the Russian warder, on duty in the block.'

Red took a deep breath. 'A warder? Christ, he'll know I'm a fake. Can you take care of him?'

'I cannot promise. Straighten your tie.'

Red followed him out, turning left, across the intersection of the main block and the wings. Ahead was the entrance to the cell-block where Hess had been held since 1947. No-one had ever entered there illegally. The Soviet guard on the door stiffened and scraped one of his boots on the stone floor.

'Ignore him,' muttered the chief warder. He walked up to the steel door, took out a bunch of keys attached to a chain and unlocked and unbolted it. They stepped past the guard and inside the inner cell-block.

It was not markedly different from the rest of Spandau, though the dark green and cream paint was fresher and the floor buffed as in the guardroom. Some relics from the nineteenth century, a set of ornamental iron brackets picked out in a white gloss, supported the twelve-foot ceiling. Modernity was represented by hot water pipes and radiators and a

272

fire-hose attached to the wall. There were two plain tables. Steel cell doors stretched ahead on either side.

Red's skin prickled. He had shed most of his fears. Now he felt a rush of exhilaration.

This, he thought, is where it has all been leading. Jane, darling, you said it was crazy, I couldn't walk into Spandau, but here I am, about to come face to face with old man Rudolf. If I get out – for God's sake, *when* I get out – you're going to have to admit that even if most of what I say is bullshit, one time, one never-to-be-forgotten time, it wasn't.

Keeping a yard behind the chief warder, partly to indicate respect and partly for reasons of cover, he started the thirty-metre walk to where the Soviet guard stood on duty at the far end of the corridor, beside an open door. To his right were the white-painted doors of cells once occupied by the seven war criminals. Hess, he knew, had been moved to the other side of the corridor in 1970, into a double cell knocked into one, which had formerly been used as a chapel.

They had not gone more than a few paces when someone in warder's uniform stepped out of a door midway along the block. The chief warder reacted quickly. 'Ah, Shaporenko.' He spoke in Russian, evidently giving some instruction.

Red knew it was impossible to stay obscured behind the small Frenchman, so when Shaporenko caught his eye, he nodded sociably. There was an awkward hiatus. The Russian stared back, frowning, then moved past them to carry out the order.

Now for the man on guard. They approached him casually. Like the other Soviet Army soldiers Red had met in Spandau, he was probably no older than twenty. He had both hands on his sub-machine gun, but his posture was relaxed. He must have been told that the men in blue uniforms were prison warders.

Then it all happened.

Shaporenko, his suspicion alerted, shouted something from the far end of the block. The chief warder wheeled around and shouted back. Red had no idea what was said, and he wasn't waiting for a translation. He attacked the guard. He shoved the muzzle of his gun upwards with such force that it caught the man on the chin, jolting his head back. In the same

273

movement, he swung his knee hard into the Russian's groin. He felt the impact of bone against bone. Anything between made no impression, except on the soldier, who creased and fell towards him like wet wallpaper that had failed to stick.

The man was conscious, but in no state to resist. Red tugged the gun away and trained it on Shaporenko, who raised his hands. 'Lock him in one of the empty cells,' he yelled to the chief warder, without taking his eyes off the Russian. 'Tell him I won't hesitate to shoot.'

The chief warder crossed to one of the cell doors and unbolted it.

Shaporenko made no trouble. He was thankful to be out of Red's line of fire. The door slammed on him.

'This one, too,' said Red, eyeing the guard, who was trying to sit up. His face was bleeding where the gun had struck it.

The chief warder opened a second cell and helped the soldier into it. He climbed onto the bed and was lying still when the door was shut.

'Thank God!' Red muttered.

Turning slightly, he was conscious of a figure almost at his elbow. White-haired, in a white singlet and dark trousers, a man was standing in the cell doorway in the act of putting on his glasses.

Rudolf Hess.

46

Jane sat alone with a mug of black coffee in an all-night café somewhere north of the city centre. She had asked the taxi-driver to find a place that was still open. On the floor at her feet was the sportsbag containing Red's clothes. The gash in the side was proof that she had not been dreaming.

Two shabbily-dressed, middle-aged men occupied other tables. They probably took Jane for another of the city's homeless. There was no point in returning to Haselhorst. The mental agony would be worse in Red's place, surrounded by his things, knowing she had failed him.

She despised herself. She had screwed everything up. She had to hold the mug with both hands to stop it from spilling, she was in such a state. Whatever illusions she had had about herself as a frontline journalist were shattered. At the first flurry of action, she had caved in. She had read about violence often enough and watched it on the screen, deeply moved by the suffering, but without ever understanding what it is like to be involved. The act of grappling with Heidrun, twisting her arm, helping Red to tie her to the bed, now filled her with revulsion. And the moment of terror when Heidrun had come at her with the knife would stay with her for ever.

But what was that to the violence coming to Red because of her stupidity? That bitch Heidrun had crossed the border to shop Red to the Russians.

'Oh, God. God help me!'

One of the shabby men stared across at her, and then back at his newspaper. He would probably not have given a glance if she had spoken in German. It was nothing remarkable to hear someone talking to God in an all-night café.

Jane had a vivid picture of Red risking his life to bluff his way to Hess, actually getting into the prison, only to be betrayed by a phone call from the KGB. What would they do to him?

She was going to vomit. She retched.

275

The café owner pointed to the door marked *Damen*. No one else looked up.

When she came back, one of the men had gone, and so had the bag with Red's clothes. She ran to the door and looked up the street. It was deserted.

'Bastard!'

But her head was more clear and her brain was functioning better. There was something else Red had told her to do. She ran over to the counter.

'Where is Der Chamissoplatz?'

'Chamissoplatz? That is Kreuzberg. Near Tempelhof, the airport. You know?'

'How far from here?'

'A taxi-ride. You want me to call one?'

'Please. And do you have a telephone directory?'

He was positively eager to help, no doubt wanting to be rid of her. He turned to the shelf behind him. 'What name?'

'Becker. Willi Becker.'

'Plenty of Beckers in Berlin.'

'But in Chamissoplatz?'

In twenty minutes, a taxi was setting her down in a spacious, poorly-illuminated square formed by a children's playground surrounded by trees. Five-storey blocks with darkened windows and arched entrances loomed up on each side. She looked for numbers, found the entrance she wanted and went upstairs. Willi Becker's name was on the door.

Jane pressed the bell, conscious that this was some ungodly hour of the morning and she spoke almost no German. She had to press it twice more before she heard the click of a light-switch inside. The door opened a fraction.

'*Ja?*'

'*Herr Becker? Sprechen Sie Englisch?* Please, Red told me to come.'

'Red?'

'Red Goodbody.'

'Ah . . . Red!' A spluttering cough turned into a laugh and he came out with a passable impression of Red. 'Now pull the other one, darling.'

Willi Becker opened the door to admit her. Short, dark, almost bald, in his forties if not older, he had only one good

276

eye. Where the other should have been was a depression overlaid with loose skin. He was wrapped in a brown duvet. She had expected him to be a pressman, but there was a bright yellow jacket hanging in the hall, the sort worn by people who work on the roads.

'You look all used up,' said Becker. 'Want to get some sleep?' Jane shook her head. 'I need help.'

'Give me two minutes, then.'

She walked into a cheaply-furnished room that smelt of tobacco. There was a framed photo in black and white over the fireplace of Becker and his bride, a slight, dark-haired girl in a sixties-style, calf-length dress. Jane could hear no voices from the room where Becker had gone to dress, and the place didn't give the impression of a woman's presence, so she assumed that the girl had died.

He came back in green cords and a black sweater. He had put in an artificial eye which didn't match the bloodshot look of the real one. Despite his unshaven face, creased from interrupted sleep, he still managed to look approachable, a sympathetic listener.

'So who are you and what sort of trouble are you in?'

Just as Red had suggested, she told him everything.

Occasionally Becker interrupted the narrative to say affectionately, almost in admiration, 'He's a bloody madman, you know.'

By the end, she knew he would do anything in his power to help, but the process of telling the story had brought home to her the realisation that there was little anyone could do now. Willi Becker was a reassuring listener, a comfort in adversity, but he was in no position to influence events inside the walls of Spandau Prison.

'This Heidrun Kassner. You're sure she is working for the Soviets?'

'Red is just as sure as I am.'

'And you are certain she has gone over?'

'I watched her go.'

Becker shook his head. 'Let's face it – Red is finished. Don't blame yourself. He was a crazy idiot. Cigarette?'

'But he said if I came to you . . .' Jane sobbed, and couldn't go on.

'I would try to help, huh? Because I'm a crazy idiot also?' He put a cigarette to his lips and reached for a lighter. 'I have to be crazy to go on smoking these things.' He lit up and exhaled. 'Would you pass me the phone? Let's see who else is out of his mind in this crazy schizoid city.'

47

He had the look of a man who has heard a disturbance on his doorstep and comes outside to see who is responsible. Frowning, peering through his plastic lenses, he took in the scene. His face and forearms, tanned from the hours he spent each day in the garden, were differentiated sharply from his lily-white upper arms and shoulders, lank where the muscle had wasted. He seemed conscious of the exposure, and crossed his arms. Age had given him a slight stoop, but had left him with a good head of soft, white hair. Few traces remained of the stiff-backed, brown-uniformed figure with the swastika arm-band pictured so often at Hitler's side or on the rostrum at party rallies.

Red scrutinised the face. Among the many strange theories about Hess was the elaborate one that this man was a fake, a lookalike substitute for the real Deputy Führer. Allowing that the old man had not yet put in his dentures, it was difficult to form an opinion, but it was possible to recognize an unusual characteristic of the man pictured in pre-war photographs: the width and angularity of his jawbone below the ears, tapering to a short, neat chin.

For Red, the features that fixed this aged man in carpet slippers beyond any doubt as the *Stellvertreter* were the eyes. Cavernous under still-dark, still-thick brows, they surveyed the scene without a flicker, penetrating and analytical. To be the object of their scrutiny, even briefly, was disturbing. Red was made to feel an unwelcome intruder into the humiliation of a man of high rank who had not entirely lost his pride. He resisted the impulse to back off.

Rudolf Hess didn't speak. He turned and shuffled back into his cell without a word. Presumably, he had taken stock, formed his judgement, and retired. In his long imprisonment, he had seen and experienced a variety of human behaviour – cruelties and kindnesses, loyalties and betrayals. He was obliged to take whatever was handed out, but not always in

279

silence. If the accounts were true, no one had protested as forcibly or as persistently as he about every aspect of the regime: food he regarded as poisonous, work in the garden growing tobacco 'for the slaves of nicotine', insensitivities from the warders and the other prisoners. Latterly, he had given up complaining. He had detached himself mentally, fatalistic, expecting nothing and accepting everything.

Unusually, Red hesitated. There was precious little time, but so much rested on getting this right.

The chief warder was at his side. 'You see what I mean? He has been here so long that he's become a brick wall himself.'

'He thinks I'm a warder. Could you tell him I'm not one of the warders?'

'Let him put his teeth in first.'

There was sense in that. Allow the old man some self-respect.

The chief warder glanced at the sub-machine gun and shook his head reproachfully. 'You shouldn't have attacked the guard. It means trouble.'

'I was in trouble already. He would have shot me, wouldn't he? Shaporenko would have buggered off and raised the bloody alarm.'

'It won't be long before the bloody alarm is raised, anyway,' the chief warder pointed out. 'I'm supposed to be taking Hess to the interview room. Russian generals don't like to be kept waiting.'

'Jesus, I'd forgotten the bloody general. Can we lock ourselves in?'

'No. The locks are on the outsides of the doors.'

'We've got the gun.'

'I cannot agree to use the gun.'

'Thanks. I needed some encouragement.' Red started unbuttoning the tunic. 'What's your name, squire?'

'Petitjean.'

'OK, I'm Red Goodbody. Will you go in now and tell Hess I'm not a warder, I'm a journalist from England with important news for him? Then I'll take over.'

'You want me to leave you alone with him?'

'Please. And keep watch at the cell-block door.'

'What if the Russians come?'

'Tell them I'm with Hess and I have a gun and I'll use it if anyone else sets foot in this block. Now, shall we see if he's at home?'

With a shrug and a sigh that said that in this situation it didn't much matter how they spent the small amount of time remaining, Petitjean entered Hess's cell, while Red, in shirt-sleeves and tieless, lurked just inside the doorway.

It was a brighter place than Red had imagined, with a high, white ceiling equipped with strip-lighting. The walls were painted cream and green, with a horizontal dividing-line precisely half-way up, in the time-honoured style of public institutions. A black composition floor gleamed with many applications of wax. The furniture consisted of a bed with adjustable back-rest, provided by the British Military Hospital after Hess had been treated for a duodenal ulcer there; a brown table with an electric hotplate, Nescafé and a copy of *Frankfurter Allgemeine*; a straight-backed wooden chair; and shelves containing plates, two enamel cups, hair-brushes, a row of books and a portable television set. From the underside of the shelves were suspended his greatcoat and jacket. There was one picture attached to the wall: a chart of the surface of the moon.

Hess was now in a check shirt that he had buttoned to the neck and grey denim trousers. He stood with his back to the door, laboriously folding a blanket on his bed.

In German, Petitjean announced Red in the way he had requested. Hess continued with his task, apparently oblivious.

'Is his hearing all right?' Red asked.

'Better than yours or mine,' muttered Petitjean, passing close to Red on his way out.

The moment had come. Alone with Hess, not quite face to face, but working on it.

'Herr Hess?'

Preoccupied, the old man squared off the blanket and started on another.

'I got in here by impersonating Warder Moody, the American. He is dead. Yesterday he was murdered by the KGB.'

There may have been a slight hesitation in the blanket-folding routine. It was hard to tell.

281

'I knew him,' Red affirmed. 'I won't claim he was a friend, because I wanted to use him to get in touch with you for my newspaper.'

Red paused, priming himself for the disclosure that had to make an impression. 'We have evidence about what happened in Britain in 1941, sensational evidence concerning Winston Churchill that has been suppressed all these years. We believe we know the true story of your peace mission and why it went wrong. Some things you may not even know yourself. I was counting on Cal Moody's help. Then I discovered that the Russians had tabs on him. Yesterday morning, three of their agents followed him to an address in the Charlottenburg district.'

Hess stopped folding the blanket. He didn't turn, or make any sound. He simply stopped what he was doing and stood staring at the blank wall.

'I saw what happened. Cal went inside, and later came out again. One of the agents followed him. The other two went into the house and murdered the woman who lived there.'

Hess turned and stared. The force of those strange eyes turned on Red was almost palpable. They were blue, pale blue, a discovery that made him aware that he had only ever looked at Hess before in black and white. They were disbelieving, unfriendly, angry, but at least they had reacted.

'Her name was Fraulein Edda Zenk.' Red paused. 'They beat her up before they shot her.'

Hess rested his hands on the bed, and lowered himself awkwardly to a sitting position, as if his legs had suddenly refused to function. It appeared for a moment that he might be in pain, even possibly in the first stage of a heart attack. He seemed to be fighting for breath.

Red moved towards him. 'Are you OK?'

Hess leaned forward and covered his face with his hands. He said in German, in a low voice breaking with emotion, 'She was an innocent woman.'

'You knew her, then?'

'I asked Mr Moody to make sure she was safe.'

'Safe from the Russians?'

He murmured some sort of confirmation.

'Why? Why was she in danger?'

A sigh.

'You knew if the Russians found her they would kill her. Is that it?'

Hess had retreated into silence.

Red tried the question again and still got nothing. He had to find some other lever. 'A Russian General has come to the prison. His name is Vanin. I think he is KGB. He didn't arrange it with the Allied Commission. He just picked up a phone and informed the Soviet director he was coming to question you. The chief warder is supposed to escort you to the interview room.'

'I will not go,' Hess flatly announced, sitting up straight as he spoke.

'Do you know what they want?'

No answer.

'But it must be connected with Edda Zenk?'

Hess looked away.

Desperation drove Red to say, 'For God's sake, Edda Zenk was pistol-whipped by the KGB. Whatever it is that you insist on keeping to yourself, the bloody Russians beat it out of that old lady before they killed her. They silenced her, they silenced Cal, and now they're coming for you. What happens if they kill you, too? What will you have achieved?'

Hess remained silent, but seemed less obdurate; he was visibly pondering what Red had told him.

Perhaps, Red thought, I'm asking the impossible. His thinking is so rigid after all those years in solitary that he's incapable of modifying it.

At last, Hess said, 'Why should I believe you?'

It was a fair question. His experiences as a prisoner of the British in the war years could not have filled him with confidence.

'Because I'm a newsman,' Red answered. 'I'm interested in reporting the truth, not suppressing it. I'm the only chance you have to tell the world what you know.' Even as he was speaking, he was conscious of how much he was asking Hess to take on trust. He wasn't carrying a notebook or a tape recorder. He didn't even have his press-card with him.

Hess sniffed and looked away.

But fortune is said to favour the brave. Red was standing

beside Hess's table and his eyes happened to light on the newspaper. He snatched it up. 'Is this today's? Have you read it?'

Hess shook his head, but fortunately in response only to the second question.

Red opened it and flicked through the sheets looking for the regional news. 'There!' he told Hess, jabbing his finger at a news item at the foot of one of the inside pages.

It was a small paragraph listed miscellaneously with others from around the German regions:

BERLIN WOMAN MURDERED

Edda Zenk, 73, a former secretary, was found shot in her Fredericiastrasse apartment in Charlottenburg, West Berlin, yesterday morning. The police have started a murder inquiry.

Hess put on his reading glasses to examine it. His hand crept up his shirt-front and pinched at a fold of the wrinkled skin around the base of his neck. He took a deep breath, and put the paper aside. 'So it is true,' he admitted. 'I will listen to what you have to say.'

Grateful for any concession, Red made an immediate switch to 1940. Tersely, picking out the salient facts, he took Hess through the discoveries Jane and Dick had made about the German peace missions that had come in through Dublin: the ferrying trips to Oxfordshire in Frank Perry's Anson; the Transport Command sergeant who had seen Churchill's car at each of the houses where he had to drive the Germans; Herbert Hoover's statement that six such peace missions had come in through Dublin, a revelation Lord Halifax had swiftly attempted to discredit.

Without pause, he turned to the subject of Hess's flight to Britain and the panic it had caused in high places: the chance interception of the phone call from the Duke of Hamilton to Sir Alexander Cadogan; the summons to Ditchley Park; the news blackout; the War Cabinet at each other's throats while statements were cobbled up and thrown out; the decision to give no explanation at all of the Deputy Führer's presence in Britain; Beaverbrook's talk of the need to 'strangle the infant' and his invitation to the press to invent wild stories accounting for the flight.

Hess was listening with close attention, leaning forward, supporting his elbows on his thighs. Once or twice, he gave the nod to a detail, as if he remembered having heard of it.

Red moved into a still more sensitive area: the four years Hess had spent in custody in Britain. 'Mytchett Place, do you remember? You spent the first year there with MI5 and a team of psychiatrists.'

He straightened up and Red thought he was about to make a response; but just as suddenly he folded his arms and looked away, as if something had distracted him.

'Stop me if I get it wrong, won't you?' Red put in, not expecting to be stopped, but wanting to be reassured that he was getting through. 'The official version is that they discovered you were mentally unstable, but there's evidence that MI5 made it their business to confuse you and undermine you psychologically. No one but you, Herr Hess, can really say how successful they were.'

It was obvious from the way Hess was staring at the ceiling that he wasn't proposing to throw any light on the matter.

Red felt increasingly uneasy as he went on, 'The way I see it, they wanted to play up the idea that you were mad. And you encouraged them by saying you had lost your memory and suspected they were trying to poison you. Maybe you *did* lose your memory.'

There wasn't a flicker of interest. Worse, there was no way of telling whether Hess had switched off mentally as a discouragement, or whether his mind was atrophied, unable to concentrate except in short intervals of lucidity.

'They didn't want you talking about the real reason for your flight to Britain,' Red persisted. 'The trial at Nuremberg was coming up.'

By good fortune, the mention of Nuremberg triggered a reaction. Hess locked eyes with Red and said with heavy irony, '*Trial?*'

It was as if he couldn't resist the impulse to take a sideswipe at the proceedings in 1946, and it was profoundly encouraging to Red – because although it was just the voicing of a single word, it was an intelligent response, not a mindless repetition.

'Your half-starved appearance at Nuremberg was a shock

285

to everyone who knew you. That's how everyone remembers you – looking mad, behaving oddly. But you had your reasons, didn't you?'

No reaction. He was abstractedly tracing the raised blue veins on the back of one of his hands.

Red talked on staunchly in the hope that something else would light a spark. 'Well, it suited someone who wanted you discredited. I'm thinking of Sir Winston Churchill.'

The hands stopped moving.

'You wouldn't have seen Churchill's history of the Second World War. He described you as a medical case, a neurotic.'

Hess lifted his face and there may have been a flicker of amusement under the dark eyebrows.

Red hammered the point home. 'He used the word "lunatic" to describe your flight.'

It provoked a response! The ghost of a smile from Hess, then: 'Did you say it was history that Churchill is supposed to have written?'

This was the opening Red had been battling for. 'What *is* the history, Herr Hess? Did Hitler send you to Britain to make a deal with Churchill?'

The mention of Hitler was unfortunate. It clearly disturbed him. His expression became vague and he muttered, 'These things happened so long ago.'

Red had been a reporter too long to let him off with that kind of evasion. 'But you remember them, because you have written about them.'

A sharp look from Hess. 'Written what?'

'Your published letters to your wife. You wrote that your mission failed because you miscalculated. You said Churchill no longer had the power to act freely or check the avalanche. What did you mean by that?'

A pause. Was it too much to hope that after all the years of silence he was ready to make a statement that would clarify the mystery of the flight?

Instead, he wanted to complain. 'Letters!' he said bitterly. 'What use are letters?'

At least he was talking now, so Red did his best to encourage it. 'You mean they are censored?'

Hess said with contempt, 'I am permitted to write and

receive one censored letter a week. This week, no letters at all.'

'Why? What happened?'

He ignored the question. 'Your people, the British, are still afraid of things I could say. A couple of years ago, my son, Wolf Rüdiger, came to visit me, with the usual audience sitting in. We are prohibited from discussing the past, the years of the Third Reich; or the present, the conditions in Spandau; or the future, my campaign to be released. So what is there to say? Wolf attempted to embrace me; the British reported it and made a formal complaint. You see?'

Red seized on this. 'They thought you might pass him a statement for the press. Herr Hess, you have the opportunity now! I'll see that whatever you say is published.'

'Not yet,' said Hess, with more force than anything he had spoken before. 'It must wait until I am released.' He added grimly, 'One way or another.'

'But you have to tell someone, for God's sake!'

'There is no need.'

'Why?' Red felt a shock wave run through him as he answered his own question. 'You already have! Cal Moody and Edda Zenk were murdered for it!'

Hess set his mouth in a rigid, implacable line.

'What is it – a statement on tape? A letter?' Red demanded. 'You can at least tell me that much. It's almost certainly been destroyed by now anyway.'

'No.'

But Red had detected a note of uncertainty in the denial and now he made use of it. 'Can you be sure? They'll follow it up. They'll find it. If the KGB don't find it, MI5 will. Can't you see you're on to a loser?'

It was a crucial moment in the battle of wills. Hess leaned towards Red as if about to pass on a confidence, and instead stood up stiffly and took a few steps across the cell. He muttered inaudibly in front of his chart of the moon, as if a crisis was upon him. Then he turned slowly and looked at Red in a different way, sizing him up. He sighed nervously and rubbed the back of his neck. He had come to a decision. 'Herr . . .'

'Goodbody.'

'Would you be willing to put your life at risk for this story?'

'I already have.'

'No. A bigger risk than you have taken already?'

There was no doubt what he meant. Cal and Edda Zenk had died for being taken into his confidence. Red nodded.

'Then I will tell you. Twenty years ago, I wrote my memoirs on scraps of paper and had them passed secretly to Fraulein Zenk, whom I knew and could trust. She was to type them and take a copy to Beer Verlag, the Munich publishers, with an instruction from me that the book should not appear until I was released, or until I died. It cleared up all these so-called mysteries.'

'The deal with Churchill?' Red could scarcely contain his excitement. A manuscript!

'More,' Hess answered cryptically. 'Last week a letter was addressed to me by the new chairman at Beer Verlag. He had found the typescript in the office safe, and inadvisedly he wrote to me about it. Do you know why I say inadvisedly?'

'It got you into trouble?'

'As I told you, my letters are now stopped. But it was far worse for Herr Beer. His publishing house was burned down and he died in the fire.'

Red's eyes widened. 'Another death! How did you hear about this?'

'I read it in my newspaper,' Hess answered prosaically. 'Not everything escapes my attention, Herr Goodbody.'

'You suspect the KGB?'

Hess clicked his tongue as if to dismiss the question as superfluous. 'Naturally, I became anxious about Fraulein Zenk. These people are extremely thorough. I knew they would go looking for the original manuscript, my scraps of paper.'

'The proof that the memoir was genuine.'

'They would try to trace the typist. To guard against such a possibility, I had instructed Fraulein Zenk to deposit the manuscript in a Swiss Bank. I thought it would be secure there, but I worried about her safety.' He allowed a rare glimpse of his personal situation. 'When people outside take risks on your behalf, your feeling of helplessness in prison is hard to endure. Stupidly, I asked Mr Moody to call on her, just to make sure she was all right. You know the consequence.' His eyes had moistened. He took out a handkerchief and wiped them.

Delicately steering him back to the matter of most interest, Red said, 'Presumably, the KGB took possession of your memoir before they murdered the publisher and set fire to his office. And they'll almost certainly have got the original out of the Swiss bank.'

'That can be taken as definite,' Hess bleakly agreed.

'They murdered three people to stop it being published. And now they want to question you.'

He treated the prospect lightly. 'Let them. I'm just a crazy old man, an embarrassment to everyone.'

Red was determined to pin him down. 'Come clean with me, Herr Hess. You want the world to know the truth. It was a brave idea to put it in a book, but it's failed, like the peace mission. What can you do now, except tell me the secrets you wrote in your book? My prospect of getting out of here alive isn't too rosy, but I'm still the best bet you have.'

Hess deliberated for longer than Red would have cared to estimate. Any moment there could be a shout from the chief warder that the Soviet guards were at the cell-block door.

He wagged a finger at Red. 'You *will* get out of here.'

'I'll do my damnedest.'

'There is writing paper on the shelf if you want it. And a pencil.'

'There isn't time. Just tell me about your dealings with the British.'

Hess took a breath. 'The Führer wished to make peace with England after the defeat of France. Will you believe that?'

'Of course. It would have suited him. He announced it in the Reichstag, didn't he?'

Hess gave Red an approving look. 'We made secret approaches to Churchill.'

That was it! Red felt goose-bumps rising on his skin. 'Through Dublin?'

'And other neutral cities. Churchill's public statements were antagonistic to Germany, but secretly a peace formula was under discussion for many weeks. It was taking too long. The Führer wanted to bring the talks to a positive conclusion.'

'Because of Barbarossa, the plan to invade Russia?'

A penetrating stare, which gradually became vacuous. At this, of all times, his concentration was going!

Red prodded the memory. 'Britain was to join with Germany in the invasion of Russia, is that right? To defeat the Bolsheviks, eh, Herr Hess? That must have had some appeal to Churchill.'

He snapped out of his reverie. 'Together we would have succeeded.'

'And carved up Europe, Asia and Africa between you?'

Hess shook his head slowly. 'That is a crude interpretation. The important thing was to neutralise the Bolshevik threat. Then there would have been no cold war, no iron curtain.'

'And no divided Germany,' said Red.

He was in full flow again. 'Unhappily, Churchill was dragging his heels – is that the English expression? For many months, I had been preparing to fly secretly to Britain to talk with Churchill, to demonstrate our serious wish for peace with Britain. You see?'

Red nodded.

'Then I received an alarming intelligence report. General de Gaulle, the leader of the French in exile, had learned from his agents about the secret peace talks and demanded of Churchill that he repudiate them.'

'De Gaulle!' echoed Red. It sounded like an expression of surprise, but was one of satisfaction, tempered by sadness, that Dick Garrick, who had died pursuing the theory of de Gaulle's involvement, must have been justified in his theory.

Hess was speaking fluently now, as if to give the lie to the stories that he was crazed or senile. 'You must understand that Churchill was first and foremost a politician. He could have sold the idea of peace to the British people. He intended to, I assure you. But he insisted that it had to be revealed to them at precisely the right moment, when it would not appear like a defeat.'

That had the authentic Churchillian note. The test of leadership was whether the people followed you, and no one had mastered it better than he.

Hess continued, 'But to de Gaulle it was an outrage, the worst of all crimes – collaboration. He threatened to break the news prematurely. So you see, Churchill was no longer in control. A terrible blow to our hopes.'

'When did this happen?'

'Early in May.'

Red frowned. 'But you still went ahead with the flight?'

'And almost succeeded.' He drew himself up straight and gave a fleeting impression of the spare-time flier who had piloted that Messerschmitt further than the Luftwaffe had believed possible. 'You see, I had good information that there were members of the titled class and right-wing politicians who favoured a peace deal. The deal with Churchill was aborted, but these were powerful men, Mr Goodbody. So powerful that they could have overthrown Churchill and ignored de Gaulle. I flew to Britain to make contact with them and rally support. As you explained, by sheer chance Churchill was informed too soon for my plan to succeed.' He turned away. 'And that is why I have been held in prison for forty-three years.'

'You blame the British?'

'Powerful, privileged men.'

'Most of them must be dead by now.'

He flapped his hand dismissively. 'But their reputations have to be protected. Do I have to tell you how the British establishment operates?'

'Their names, Herr Hess?'

'You will learn them.'

From the corridor, Petitjean called out, 'Someone is coming! I can hear them coming!'

Hess stiffened. 'What is happening?'

'We've got to be quick. You talked about a risk you wanted me to take.'

He blinked and looked bewildered.

'Come on!' Red urged him. 'What is it that you want me to do? Is there someone to contact?'

The focus sharpened again. 'My adjutant of the old days.'

With a facility that would have done credit to Dick Garrick, Red said at once, 'Pintsch?'

'No. He is dead, I think. The younger man, Leischner.

Lives in Rominter Allee ... or something like that.' He looked distractedly around him, then slipped a gold ring from his finger. 'Put this on. Give it to Leischner. He put out his hand and grasped Red's arm in a fierce grip. 'You bear the trust of an entire generation.'

Hess's eyes, fervently fixed on Red, said much more. The *Stellvertreter* was fulfilling his last duty to the Reich he had helped to found. In his own mind, he was uncompromised, unbought, loyal to the end. It was the triumph of the will.

Red despised the system Hess was determined to vindicate. But he respected the man himself for his resolution and his personal courage.

'If I get out, I'll do what I can,' Red told him.

The pale eyes glittered. The old man turned away and sat on his bed.

48

Red snatched up the gun.

Petitjean shouted, 'It's the guard. You can hear their boots.'

Red joined him at the cell-block door and listened. 'Can we stop them opening this door?'

'Impossible.'

'Is there any other way out?'

'Only the elevator down to the prison garden where he takes his exercise.'

'Where's that?'

'You get into it from the far end of the cell-block. The access is through the cell opposite his. We keep it locked.'

'Have you got the key?'

'Yes, but it would be certain death. There is a watchtower with a full view of the garden, and the garden is sealed off by a three-metre wall.'

'Would you give me the key, chief?'

'They will all have been instructed to shoot.'

'The key.'

Petitjean took the bunch from his pocket and unfastened one. He was shaking his head. 'If there was a possibility, I would tell you to take it, but this is suicidal.'

'Delay them as long as you can. You can tell them I'm with Hess.' Red ran back to Hess's cell and unbolted it.

The old man was still sitting on the bed. He looked up, frowning.

'I'm borrowing this, OK?' Red told him, picking the overcoat off the hook below the bookshelves.

Hess gestured with a movement of his shoulders that he had no objection. He showed that he had an immediate understanding of what Red was about to attempt. 'My old hat is in the pocket.'

'Great.'

'These days I walk slowly, and look at the ground.'

'Thanks.'

'On the left side of the garden at this end are some bushes growing against the wall. That is the way I would choose. The wall actually forms the side of some disused workshops, one storey high.'

'If I get out—'

'I'll hear about it,' said Hess with a nod. He got up and picked a brown paper bag from the lowest shelf. 'Put this in your pocket.'

'What's in it?'

'Breadcrumbs. For the birds.'

The overcoat was faintly military in style and reached to just above Red's ankles. He took the hat from the pocket and tried it on. It was a soft, grey pillbox-type cap that effectively covered his hair. He closed the door on Hess and crossed the corridor. There was shouting from the other end.

He unlocked the cell door opposite and let himself in, closing the door behind him. The lift stood open, so he stepped in, pulled the gate shut and pressed the button.

Nothing happened.

It occurred to him that they could have cut off the power supply. He stepped out again, spotted a switch on the wall, flicked it down, and heard a reassuring hum from the lift mechanism.

Inside again, and it responded at once.

He was conveyed down to ground level, wondering whether an armed guard awaited him. He had decided against bringing the sub-machine gun with him.

When the lift stopped, he paused a moment to compose himself, turning around to face the side from which he would make his exit. He took a long breath and slowly opened the gate.

No one was waiting outside. Directly ahead, positioned at the centre of the high garden wall some sixty yards away, was a flat-roofed concrete watchtower with a clear line of fire.

With his eyes down and his hands thrust deep into the pockets, Red started his impersonation of Rudolf Hess at exercise, shuffling towards the path around which the world's loneliest man had plodded since 1947. He tried to picture the grey figure in the film sequence that Cedric had shown the team during that now-remote weekend at Henley.

He joined the main path and turned right, in the anti-clockwise direction he had seen Hess take in the film. A 210-metre circuit. It took him towards the tallest tree in Spandau, an eighty-foot poplar that Dönitz had planted as a sapling soon after the seven prisoners had arrived there.

Mastering the impulse to hurry the routine, he stopped to scatter a few crumbs to some sparrows. He kept his eyes down, certain that he was being observed from the watchtower, knowing that the path would take him to within yards of its base. Then he resumed his slow progress. If something in his movement were to cause suspicion in the tower, his hope was that the Soviet guard up there would be in two minds about using his gun. To any young soldier on guard, the risk of mistakenly killing the world's most famous prisoner would be a nightmarish prospect.

So Red's slow steps took him into the shadow of the twenty-foot high red-brick wall that surrounded the prison, past overgrown, weed-infested flower-beds that had once been kept in immaculate order by Hitler's architect, Albert Speer, and breathlessly beneath the watchtower. A few yards on, the path veered left. Red raised his eyes enough to get his first look at the bushes Hess had mentioned. To reach them, he would have to leave the path and cross twenty-five yards of open grass. However he attempted it, that guard would know at once that something irregular was happening.

He decided to stay in the character of Hess and wander across the grass, scattering breadcrumbs. A dash for the bushes would have been easier on the nerves, but suicidal. Hunched and with his back to the watchtower, he tottered off the path.

Almost immediately, there was a shout from the tower, some warning in Russian that he pretended not to hear. He continued his meandering walk towards the cover of the bushes, still scattering handfuls of crumbs.

Another shout, this time through a loud-hailer.

Fifteen yards covered. Ten to go.

He bent lower and moved in a straighter line.

Five more.

He sprinted.

A burst of gunfire. But he was already in the bushes and had dived to the right, out of sight against the wall that formed the side of the workshop.

An alarm blared through the prison.

He took a foothold on the nearest bush, grasped the top of the wall and hauled himself up, to roll across the low-angled roof as the gunfire spattered around him. He had come in range of a second watchtower.

Flat to the roof, he spotted a skylight. He crawled towards it and got his fingers under the edge. A piece of tarpaulin came off in his hand, but the wooden cover wouldn't shift. He tugged at it frantically. It wouldn't budge. They must have made it secure with nails.

Another burst from the watchtower machine gun. He abandoned the skylight and slithered down the roof until his feet hit the guttering. He felt a stab of pain in the calf of his left leg.

He had been hit.

It was hopeless. He slid down and lay along the length of the gutter a moment, then gripped it and swung by his hands. Just below was a window into the workshop. Anything to escape the gunfire. He kicked hard at the glass, shattered it and swung himself inwards, feet first. The jagged glass at the edges of the frame ripped into Hess's overcoat, but miraculously Red got inside without further injury.

For a few seconds he lay immobile, fighting the pain in his leg. Then he forced himself to crawl away from the window. Gripping his leg above the knee with both hands, he tried to stand. He staggered a few steps and fell across a workbench. He wasn't going to get much further, however he tried.

The alarms screeched all over Spandau. He heard army boots on the gravel outside, orders shouted in Russian. The acute pain in his leg had subsided a little and was being supplanted by a more generalised ache. If it were only a flesh-wound . . . But he knew he was kidding himself. He was trapped. He could only wait and see if they wanted to take him alive.

A crash, as someone shattered another window. At the far

end of the workshop, they were battering their way through a locked door.

Red heaved himself into a sitting position and raised his hands in surrender. The door burst open and two soldiers moved in with guns levelled. The man at the window also had him covered.

He didn't move a muscle as they advanced on him. They shoved him face down on the bench, ripped off the overcoat and searched him for arms. One of them noticed the blood on his trouser-leg. They rolled it back to look at the wound.

More soldiers came in. Red thought he heard the voice of the NCO from the guardroom. He was using a two-way radio.

Someone else arrived and applied a bandage to Red's wound. As if to correct any impression that they meant to treat him gently, two men then handcuffed him, grabbed him by the armpits and dragged him off the bench and out of the workshop. He tried to get a footing, but the pain was too severe.

He was hauled across a yard and into the main block, up one of the iron staircases and through a couple of rooms, his perceptions blurred by the agony in his leg. Dimly, he became aware of a door he recognized. The guards knocked first, and took him in. He was facing Colonel Klim, the Soviet Director. A chair was found and Red slumped into it.

'Sit up!' ordered Klim.

He raised his head.

'You have committed many breaches of prison regulations. You have conspired with prison warders to attack a Soviet guard and a Soviet warder. You have gained illegal entry to the inner cell-block and spoken with prisoner Number 7. These offences will be reported to the military authorities. In my capacity as director, I shall now invite Soviet General Vanin to take you into his custody for interrogation.'

'Vanin?' mumbled Red. 'That bastard from the KGB?'

He was immediately struck from behind, a vicious punch against his cheekbone that tore the soft flesh under his eye and sent blood coursing down his face. His hair was grabbed and wrenched back.

He found himself looking upside down into a pale face

dominated by bulging eyes, yellow and bloodshot at the edges. He avoided looking into them. Instead, he found himself watching a blob of saliva slowly form between slightly open, fleshy lips. He was helpless as it dropped between his eyes in a dribbling string of spittle, and slid across his face. It smelt of vodka.

Klim said, 'General Vanin speaks no English, but he can make himself understood.'

'Sod off.'

There was an exchange in Russian. Someone opened a door behind him and a lighter set of footsteps crossed the room. A woman?

'Sit up,' ordered Klim. 'The lady wants a look at your ugly face.'

Blood and spit were smearing Red's vision, but he could see enough. It couldn't have been worse. Heidrun Kassner was standing in front of him. They had brought her in to identify him. Dimly, his brain told him that she shouldn't have been there. He had left her trussed up at Cal Moody's apartment. Jane had been with her.

God, what had happened to Jane?

Heidrun's eyes were directed downwards as if she preferred not to look at Red. Something was said in Russian. She raised her face briefly. Their eyes met. Hers were indifferent.

Heidrun nodded and told the Russians, 'Goodbody.'

'My name or your opinion?' said Red.

Someone struck his head from behind.

'Cow!' said Red inadequately.

With that, he was dragged off the chair and bundled out of the office. On the way, he had his first full glimpse of Vanin and it was in no way encouraging. The General was not in uniform, but wore a blue three-piece suit. Overweight and in his forties, with reddish hair that he probably tinted, he had the bloated look of an ex-boxer who has hit the vodka and neglected his fitness.

The descent was agonizing. That left leg was throbbing from thigh to ankle and, handcuffed as Red was, he was prevented from using his arms to steady himself. At each step, the pain was like a chisel being turned in the wound. As they started down the second flight, an order was given and the

298

guards supported his thighs and carried him the rest of the way. They hurried him along a corridor and out through the gates of the main prison block.

A brown Lada limousine with diplomatic plates was waiting in the yard. The chauffeur got out and opened the rear door. Red was lifted in, while one of the guards kept him covered with his gun through the open door.

After about three minutes, General Vanin emerged from the building with Heidrun. Vanin got into the back seat beside Red. He drew a small, silver automatic from inside his jacket, pressed it into Red's ribs and spoke something in Russian.

Heidrun was getting into the seat beside the driver. She said, 'He is telling you to lie on the floor.'

'I don't mind lying for the KGB,' said Red, shifting forward to obey the order. 'Where are we going?'

'I'm not allowed to say. They want to interrogate you.'

Red crouched on the space between the seats. Vanin gave an order and the car glided away, saluted by the guards.

They drove slowly across the cobbled yard to the first set of gates. The NCO came out to check. Noticing Red's blood-streaked face, he started to smirk; then, at a sharp word from Vanin, came smartly to the salute and gave the order for both sets of double gates to be unbolted. The Lada edged out of Spandau Prison and turned left on Wilhelmstrasse, towards the city and the Wall.

49

At the edge of the Südpark in the Wilhelmstadt section of Spandau is a highrise block of flats with a clear view across Gatower Strasse to the Allied Prison. At a window on the twenty-fourth floor, Jane was standing with a pair of Zeiss binoculars focused on the main gate. It was 5.35 a.m. At her side, in a nightdress and curlers, was the *hausfrau*, a stout, cheerful person in her fifties, whose name she had not discovered. Things had happened too swiftly for social exchanges.

Willi Becker had brought her here from his flat in Kreuzberg, driving one-eyed through the almost deserted city streets at speeds that had scared her, though she had tried not to show it.

He had already alerted the people in the flat by phone, so the woman's husband, a tall, bearded man called Alfred, had been dressed when they arrived. After a few words in German, both men had gone down by the lift to the car.

'You are afraid?' the woman asked Jane in halting English that sounded as if she had been putting it together for some time.

Without lowering the glasses, Jane answered, 'Yes, but not for myself. For someone else.'

'Your lover?'

For all her anxieties, Jane managed a faint smile. 'Yes. My lover.'

'Red?'

'Yes. You know him?'

'Of course. Willi and my Alfred.'

'I see.'

'Cold War, *ja*?'

'Yes?' responded Jane, not quite following.

'*Die Fluchthelfer?*'

She had heard the word, but where?

'*Die Mauer*? Berlin Wall, *ja*? Willi, Alfred, Red help many peoples. Over, under.'

Belatedly, it dawned on Jane, and she was angry with herself for being so obtuse. The shocks of the past twelve hours had dulled her brain. These were the people Red had written about in that series of articles she had read and admired: the escape-helpers, the daring or reckless men and women who secretly schemed the crossings of fugitives from the East. Over the beer on Saturday night in that weekend at Cedric's, he had told story after story about them. The woman appeared to be saying Red had been one of them; and it was not too incredible, thinking back. His writing and his stories had burned with the passion and vigour of personal experience. And now the *Fluchthelfer* were scheming to help him.

The knowledge warmed Jane like a brandy. The odds against rescuing Red were still enormous, but thank God the attempt would be made by an experienced team.

Twenty minutes went by.

Then Jane told the woman, 'Something is happening down there.'

There was movement at the prison entrance. A Soviet soldier came out of the small door in the blue double gates and moved forward under the arc-lamps, his gun levelled. He was followed by another.

'Two guards,' Jane reported. 'They seem to be checking that no one is outside.'

'I tell Willi.' Her companion picked up the two-way radio the men had left her and spoke into it.

Down below, they were opening the gates and a brown saloon car was visible under the turreted entrance. Jane trained the binoculars on the registration-plate as the light caught it and spoke the number aloud, adding, 'A dark brown saloon, very large.' Before the message was passed to Willi Becker, she had shifted her sights upwards to the windscreen. The car glided forward across the cobbles. For a moment, the faces inside were illuminated: a chauffeur in a dark uniform, not military; beside him, a girl in a close-fitting blue and white tracksuit-top – a pale, staring face, framed by short, dark hair. Heidrun.

'Oh, God! They *must* have got Red.'

'Red?' said the German woman. 'You see him?'

301

'No. Wait!' Jane watched the car accelerate and swing across the carriageway. 'One man in the back, not Red, I'm certain. Tell them Heidrun Kassner is in the car, but I can't see Red.'

Waiting in a narrow street between two blocks of flats off Wilhelmstrasse in his VW Golf, Willi Becker took the message and made his decision.

He made radio contact with the third section of his team, giving them the description and registration number. 'A Lada, I guess. Don't miss it.' To Alfred, seated beside him, he commented. 'You can bet they've got Red in there somewhere. They wouldn't make two trips.' He turned the ignition and moved forward to the intersection to wait for the brown saloon.

The early morning traffic. was already starting to build. When the Lada cruised past, Becker swung the Volkswagon smoothly on to Wilhelmstrasse behind it. They travelled in the fast lane for about a kilometre, Becker driving one-handed and speaking instructions into his handset. Then the traffic slowed. Unusually for this time of day, there was a hold-up ahead, a short way before the junction with Pichelsdorfer Strasse. The cars were actually stationary and three men in bright yellow safety-jackets were moving forward, stooping to speak to the drivers.

The Lada drew up behind a petrol tanker.

Becker brought the VW to a smooth halt, and said calmly, 'Guns.'

Alfred had two loaded sub-machine guns ready on his lap. He passed one to Becker.

They waited for one of the yellow-jacketed men to approach the Lada. As the chauffeur wound down his window, the other men in safety-jackets moved fast to the rear of the car. One of them looked through the rear window and raised his arm in a signal to Becker.

'Now!' said Becker, thrusting open the door of the Golf.

In the same split-second, a shot was fired from inside the Lada. The man who had made the first approach keeled back and crashed over the bonnet of another vehicle.

The Lada's engine roared as the chauffeur swung the wheel and bumped the big car over the raised strip of grass that formed the central reservation. A container lorry in the slow lane of the opposite carriageway was forced to veer on to the cycle-way with a shriek of tyres. The Lada completed its U-turn and raced away from the ambush.

Becker crouched on the grass and fired a volley of shots. One of them must have pierced a front tyre, because fifty metres down the street the Lada careered into the fast lane, almost jumping the reservation again.

'Come on!'

Becker was back in the Golf with Alfred, over the grass, into the fast lane and in pursuit. Ahead, the Lada was under some kind of control, but clearly too handicapped to burn off the VW.

'They're trying to make it back to the prison,' Becker told Alfred.

The prison wasn't far ahead. They were already past the red-brick barrack-blocks and approaching the trees that partly screened the entrance. The limping Lada slewed off Wilhelmstrasse on to the cobbles.

As the Golf skidded to a stop a few metres away, Becker saw that the doors of the Lada were open and the passengers were already heading for the blue prison gates. Two men and a girl. One of the men was trying to resist.

'It's Red,' Becker shouted as he snatched his gun and leapt from the car.

A shot screamed past him and smashed into the side of the Golf. The Russian chauffeur was behind the Lada, trying to give cover. Alfred peppered the brown saloon with gunfire and the chauffeur fell.

Becker raced forward a few paces and then had to take cover behind the Lada. The KGB officer who had been in the back was brandishing a silver automatic.

They had reached the prison gates. Heidrun was shouting into the grille. Suddenly Red broke loose and threw himself against the KGB man. They both fell. The gun clattered across the cobbles.

Heidrun started forward to recover it. Becker pulled the trigger and picked her off. Her body thudded against the prison gates as the bullets ripped into her flesh.

The KGB man struggled upright and was hit by the same volley. His hands clawed at the prison door.

Becker sprinted forward and grabbed Red. There was shouting from inside the prison gate. With Alfred's help, he hauled Red across the cobbles and thrust him into the back of the Golf.

Soviet guards streamed out of the prison gate and stepped over the bleeding bodies to fire at the accelerating Golf as the *Fluchthelfer* made their getaway.

'So you're back in Berlin?' Becker remarked conversationally to Red.

50

The following afternoon, Red and Jane took a taxi to Rominter Allee to see Hess's adjutant, Leischner. Red was using a walking-stick. The doctor who had removed the bullet and dressed his leg had promised him that the muscle-fibre would not take long to heal. The soreness in both legs from the kicking the guards had given him had left him needing the stick anyway. He also had a cracked rib and a cut eye that had required stitching.

The shooting incident outside the prison was headlined in most of the morning papers. General Vanin and Heidrun, erroneously described as an un-named Soviet diplomat and his German interpreter, were dead. The chauffeur was in intensive care. There were close-up pictures of bullet holes in the prison gates. No one appeared to know the purpose of the shooting, and the Russians were making no statement. There was heavy speculation about the group responsible. Some papers plumped for neo-Nazis, while others guessed at Soviet dissidents based in the West.

Red told Jane, 'We've got to make sure when we write this thing up that people like Dick and Cal are given the credit they deserve.'

'And Edda Zenk,' added Jane.

'Right. And that guy of Willi's who was shot in the ambush.'

'So many,' Jane said, shaking her head. She was silent for a moment and then told him gravely, 'And you're still terribly at risk. Red, they won't give up.'

'The KGB?'

'And the others.'

'Our lot?'

'The lot who murdered Dick. MI5, SIS or some other group we've never even heard of. Dick didn't crash accidentally. They were tailing us in England and they followed him to France.'

305

Red agreed. 'He found something. We know from Hess that de Gaulle was a key to the secret.'

'But why did Dick have to be *killed*? Just to preserve the fiction that Churchill and the British establishment wouldn't have any truck with Hitler?'

'Not only that, love. There's another fiction that every British government since the war has connived at.'

Jane nodded, sighing. 'You mean that the Russians are the only ones who want to keep him in Spandau.'

'It's the proverbial can of worms,' said Red. 'Everyone wants to keep the lid on – our lot, the Russians, the diplomats and the secret service.'

'Which is just the point I was making!' Jane said in desperation. 'You're on their hit-list.'

'Not for long, love. Once we're in print, nobody will care a monkey's about Red Goodbody.'

'So why aren't you in a safe place with a typewriter?'

'I promised the old man.'

'Isn't it just inviting more trouble?'

'I told him if I got out, I'd deliver it.' He turned Hess's ring thoughtfully on his finger. 'What a jerk! Who else but me would get an exclusive with the most famous prisoner in the world and come out with nothing on tape? Not so much as a signed statement. Just a bloody ring.'

She summoned a smile. 'Why don't you give it a rub and see what happens?'

'I'm trying to keep a low profile.'

His self-reproach was really meant, so Jane reminded him, 'You got the facts on Churchill's dealings with Hitler. That's the biggest story you or I will ever handle.'

'*Most* of the facts. I wish I'd got the names of the right-wing rebels who plotted to overthrow Churchill.' He grinned. 'I've known easier interviews.'

'Will there be any repercussions for Hess?'

'He'll stand a better chance of getting out when the story has broken.'

'I mean in the short term.'

Red shook his head. 'Reading between the lines, everyone is covering up like hell in Spandau, pretending nothing happened. He'll play along. He's wise to the game.'

The taxi drew up at the U-Bahn station. They settled the fare and started slowly along Rominter Allee. Red put his free hand around Jane's shoulder.

Hauptmann Leischner was expecting them, although Red hadn't mentioned Hess's gold ring when he phoned. The purpose of the visit was ostensibly to pass on a convivial message from an old comrade in arms. So they were admitted to an old-fashioned living-room with oak furniture, family portraits and a collection of ornamental beer-mugs. They sat side by side on a leather sofa. A black shepherd-dog pricked its ears and watched them from its basket.

Leischner must have been around sixty-five, but he looked spry enough for ten years less, with thick silver hair and blue eyes that gave nothing away when Red filled him in on the background to the visit. He was civil, reserved and alert. Even the news that Red had penetrated Spandau's security system and talked to Hess appeared not to impress him unduly.

There was no reason to prolong the suspense, so Red slipped the ring off his finger and handed it to Leischner. 'He asked me to give you this.'

The blue eyes narrowed. Leischner took the ring and examined it closely. He went to the window to get more light on it. 'So everything you have told me is true,' he said, after an interval. 'In that case . . .' He snapped his fingers. 'Lumpi!'

The dog rose from its basket and trotted towards him. For a frightening moment, Jane thought it was being turned on them. She saw Red's hand feel for his stick. But at a signal from its master, Lumpi lowered itself and settled on the carpet.

Leischner crossed the room and stooped to move the dog-basket aside. Then he rolled back one corner of the carpet and its underlay. He took a penknife from his pocket, opened it and eased the blade between two of the floorboards. A section of board came up. He put his hand into the cavity and took out what looked like a steel deed-box. He blew off some dust and carried it across the room to Red.

'My orders are to hand this over in exchange for the ring.'

Red glanced at Jane, shrugged and held the box on his knees.

'There is also the key, of course.' Leischner snapped his

307

fingers again and Lumpi came to heel. The key had to be removed from a small metal container on the dog's collar. Leischner handed it over.

Red unlocked the box and took out a brown manilla folder, from which he withdrew a sheaf of paper typed through carbon. The top sheet was headed:

MEMOIRS, 1894–1941
Rudolf Hess

Lost for words and shaking his head, Red leafed through the flimsy sheets of double-spaced typing. A script of over three hundred pages. Finally, he managed to say, 'I thought every copy of this had been destroyed.'

'There has to be a copy for the author,' Leischner pointed out with an unshakeable German respect for procedure. 'Obviously it was not possible for him to keep it in Spandau, so when Fraulein Zenk finished the typing, she delivered it into my care. I was instructed to keep it hidden until and unless he sent an unimpeachable signal from the prison. He obviously reposes the greatest trust in you.'

Jane turned and looked at Red with a flush of pride.

Nothing else was said.

Lightning Source UK Ltd.
Milton Keynes UK
UKOW02f1519020317

295719UK00002B/40/P

9 781847 517098